The Moneyman

THE
MONEYMAN

Judith Liederman

HOUGHTON MIFFLIN COMPANY
BOSTON

Library of Congress Cataloging in Publication Data
Liederman, Judith.
    The moneyman.

    I. Title.
PZ4.L7254Mo [PS3562.I452]   813'.5'4   78-14511
ISBN 0-395-27099-5

Printed in the United States of America
V 10 9 8 7 6 5 4 3 2

To my husband, Donald,
for his encouragement and understanding

It is the constant fault and inseparably evil quality of ambition that it never looks behind it.

Seneca

Gold's father is dirt, yet it regards itself as noble.

Yiddish proverb

Part I

The Sword and the Stone

(1)

ON A WARM EVENING in June 1923, Aaron Abel walked from his house to see a very special girl. He had only met her a few weeks earlier, but for three years he had dreamed about her, from the first moments he had seen her passing through the impersonal corridors of Brooklyn's Eastern District High School. She had become his obsession. Such sentiments made him uneasy; he was a breezy sort of boy, not much given to yearning. His style was sudden — energetic — nervous. It was evident in his athletic stride, in the electrically charged body that was lean and slight except for his shoulders and upper arms, which seemed to draw all the power away from his spare hips and legs. Aaron was not tall, five feet eight perhaps, a fact which irritated him and encouraged him to exercise ferociously at the gym in the hope of making the most of what he had to work with.

When he had graduated from high school in 1920 he was almost nineteen. Eve Levinson was only in her second year, but already a celebrity — head girl of Arista, the school's honor society, president of the Drama Club, and expected to be the next school president. He had tried bumping into her on the rare occasions he saw her changing classes, grinning at her in the halls, posturing and making admiring comments out loud, but she was oblivious, chatting with her friends and not noticing, or pretending not to, he wasn't sure which. He couldn't understand her indifference, he considered himself attractive, the most dapper dresser in the school, and a basketball star of sorts. Darting in and out among the feet of the huge players, he made an excellent guard. He knew of at least half a dozen girls who were hopelessly in love with him, but they were mostly large-featured, sallow-skinned girls, Italian or Jewish, the kind of girl he had always known.

Considering himself fortunate, he bounced along the busy streets with his elastic step. He waved jauntily to Johnny Donatello, the greengrocer at the corner of U Street. He liked Johnny — his Italian neighbors — their wares, like their personalities, spilling color into the streets.

He knew that no one ever got invited to Eve's house, except maybe his friend, Al Carton, and then only rarely. It hadn't been easy to wangle the introduction from Al — or this date. But he had done it through ingenuity and a touch of that good old razzle-dazzle, he thought with satisfaction, just like everything else he had made up his mind to do.

All around him Williamsburg droned, a beehive of activity. The black-coated Hassidim stood in clusters, absorbed in their usual polemics, waving their arms, their stiff beards bobbing up and down as they talked and gesticulated, like huge, frenzied blackbirds. Shapeless housewives rushed toward home carrying bulging bags from which occasionally a black-feathered chicken leg poked up ominously. Pushcarts carrying bright fruits and vegetables contrasted sharply with a background of colorless gray-brown houses that lined the streets in tedious unison. The old clothes man's plaintive cry of "I cash cloes, I cash cloes" was punctuated by the mournful sound of a foghorn from nearby Sheepshead Bay, and in the distance the organ grinder's metallic tune made a melancholy concert in counterpoint.

He found himself on Eve's street, South Ninth Street. He looked around as if expecting a whole new world, but if not for the fact that the gutters were even more dung-caked, and clothes hung out to dry from the tiny spaces between the rows (suggesting an absence of *any* back yard at all), he might have confused it with his own street or any other in the brownstone jungle that was Williamsburg.

Pressing the bell, he waited. It didn't seem to ring. He tried the door knob, the door was open. He walked in, closing it noisily behind him, as if to give warning of his intrusion. The hallway was black, as black as his own; the little square of stained glass above the door, smudged and greasy, did little to ameliorate the darkness. He walked a couple of steps more and found a small room that was, he supposed, the parlor. A round cut-glass lamp, a shabby copy of the Tiffany variety, cast a greasy light on the round table. Its shade was fringed, as was the long, slightly soiled cloth beneath it. The aura was of a gypsy tearoom. He was suddenly overcome with a rush of tenderness for Eve.

The Levinsons seemed to be clutching onto the last shreds of gentility, desperately, and the result was somehow pitiable, so much more so than his own family's forthright statement of genteel poverty. His eye was drawn to a china cupboard in the far corner that looked solid, expensive, and oddly out of place here. It held a few treasures seemingly seized at random from another life. He shifted from foot to foot, afraid to sit down.

He was considering calling up the stairs, when he heard voices growing louder. They were shrill, angry, the accents slightly foreign. The staircase was not steep and the upstairs doors were visible from the little parlor. He steadied his jangled nerves by playing a guessing game about which member of the family was behind each door and what they might be doing at this moment. Which was the magic cubicle that contained Eve?

The noises coming from the left door told him that that must be the room Eve's mother shared with the stepfather, or whatever he was. Rumor had it that she had met him while singing in one of those broken-down Rumanian cafes that proliferated amongst Second Avenue's Jewish population. He had been married then, probably still was, no one seemed to know for certain, and had four small children floating around somewhere. But after all, these were showfolk, a different breed entirely. A Bohemian background was different from an ordinary immigrant one. He thought of how his parents, his sisters, would frown on his lately acquired liberalism, his tolerance and sophistication.

Suddenly a door opened and closed, and Eve appeared at the head of the stairs. Her face was flushed, contrasting dramatically with the usual creamy ivory of her skin. She had small features — a delicate nose, her pointed lips, so fashionable then, gave her by chance, not design, the look of the current flapper — though somehow less contrived. If he hadn't known she was Jewish, he would have figured her for a *shiksa*, he thought, with a sudden indrawing of breath — to him she seemed chimeric, unattainable . . .

She came quickly down the stairs, bestowing on Aaron a radiant smile, and taking his hand intimately, she sat down at the round table. Between them on the table was a crystal ball on a teakwood stand. For one moment Aaron was sure that he had guessed her mother's current profession, but Eve, as if herself mind reading, remarked that it was one of her mother's treasures. "Bubble glass made in Austria. I think it's beautiful," she said, with an intensity that caused Aaron to look up quickly. He tried to look impressed, but he wanted only to concentrate on the face before him, uninterrupted by minutiae. Her delicate white fingers caressed the glass ball between them restlessly. Her hands seemed small and helpless. Aaron wanted to snatch them up and kiss them hungrily.

He remembered how enticing she had looked at her graduation exercise, as she posed on the stage as the Goddess Hebe, with three other girls representing the Muses. They all wore gossamer wisps of pastel chiffon draped sinuously, she in a pale green that matched her eyes and dramatized her rich chestnut hair. He couldn't take his eyes from her full breasts, emphasized by the diaphanous material that caressed them. He tried to keep his eyes averted from them now. He had tried to disguise the unsteadiness in his voice as he commented huskily to Al Carton, "She's even more beautiful than I remembered her." He wanted to sound respectful of Al's proprietary rights but he didn't believe in them, otherwise he wouldn't have insisted that he take him along to meet her. After all, he had seen her first, and had often confided to Al his secret feelings. From the beginning he had babbled about Eve so much that Al had fallen secretly in love with her himself without realizing it, without ever having seen her, except through Aaron's eyes. But ironically it was Al, the least forward of the two, who had finally met her first, in a sort of staged accident at the public library.

He recognized her instantly from Aaron's glowing descriptions. Desperation had provided him with ingenuity and he found a flattering opening . . . "I would have known that face anywhere, couldn't have missed it. I've seen it in a thousand dreams." He took her to Albie's for a soda, a hangout of sorts. They talked endlessly, she in her deep-throated, nervous, deliciously theatrical manner, and he red-faced and eager — just listening and looking around — hoping against hope to be seen with her.

Al fell in love with her, as good and in love as it was possible to be. It was his special kind of love: worshipful, fanciful, untarnished, thoroughly, completely romantic. He saw in her a kindred spirit — she with her head buried in her books, her myopic eyes dreaming over Tennyson or Sappho.

In those months that Al was seeing her, keeping his secret precious, he knew that she didn't exactly return his feelings, but he was satisfied that she loved him in a way . . . She had grown to rely on his friendship, on him. He was solid, dependable — values she had learned to appreciate with a passion since the death of her father and her subsequent gypsy existence. Possessed of infinite patience, he put up with her moods, mercurial as a Russian ballerina's, and her theatrics; he accepted it as an integral part of her singularity.

But in the end, the guilt was too much for his gentle nature to sustain. He had to tell Aaron, whose outrage abated only slightly when Al promised an introduction . . . With a sinking heart, Al had introduced them at the graduation . . . he had borrowed another man's dream and now he didn't want to give it back.

Fearful that she might not accept a date with him, Aaron had devised all manner of schemes to see her again — pyramided a thousand plans — tried forcing an invitation to her graduation party from Al, who was the host, and wrote her a curious note, even employing bribery:

Dear Eve,

I met you the other night with Al. I guess you remember me.

I just bought the most gorgeous pen and pencil set, solid silver, for your graduation party, and I'd like to come up to Al's Saturday night and present it to you personally. Please tell Al it's okay with you.

Yours truly,
Aaron Abel

He had started dropping the "son" from the end of his name lately, but now suffered sudden doubts that she might not connect Abelson with Abel, or worse still, that she might not remember him at all. Of course there was no silver pen set, but he thought it sounded impressive and flattering.

And as it turned out, he had to work that Saturday night of the party. There were two bar mitzvahs and a wedding at Webster's Hall. So, in spite of his machinations, he never made the party or even bothered to telephone. Eve dismissed him as an erratic nut, yet she found herself agreeing eagerly to this date tonight.

Now Aaron noticed that she appraised him at a glance. His dapper clothing was the height of fashion, perhaps just a shade too fashionable, hanging gently on his graceful, nervous frame. On his delicate feet there smiled a pair of ivory spats, like teeth against the jet-black leather of the shoe.

His blue eyes were alert and guarded, his light brown hair crisp and wavy, adding a note of sincerity to an otherwise sardonic face. The strong, prominent nose, the full lips, the chin cleft in two equal halves, also gave to his appearance a strong and sensuous quality that did not go unnoticed by women. He had counted on this, prayed that Eve was no exception.

He began with a sense of panic to probe his mind for material that would make suitable conversation, but he could think of nothing startling or impressive. He wondered whether he should tell her about his brother, Bennie. After all, he was becoming quite a famous character in the neighborhood. He was always material for lively conversation, with his hulking, powerful good looks, his rough friends, and his dark, mysterious business contacts, but Aaron rejected this as a dubious topic. He wasn't quite sure *how* to talk to her. He found himself suddenly tongue-tied before this exalted creature.

"Would you like to go out for a walk?" she asked with sudden and unexpected urgency, all the while glancing upward at the landing where voices were becoming louder and more menacing.

"Well, I thought maybe we could just sit here and talk a while first, kind of get to know one another. You know, I've known Al for years." Al was his entrée, his step in the right direction, he figured. "We went to school together. He works for me over at Webster's Hall. I own the concession there; been making a lot of money on checking hats and coats. I sort of invented the business." Then, ducking his head, feigning diffidence, "I used to be a checkroom boy myself, worked nights all through high school. That's how I made the money to buy the concession."

He scanned her face quickly to see what impression this had made, but as she only smiled politely, he went on quickly.

"Of course, I only do that at nights. During the day I go to N.Y.U., ya know. I really want to be a lawyer."

But she only said "How nice. I'll be going to Hunter College this fall. I'm very pleased about it."

"Yeah, I know," Aaron said, injecting into his voice a note of respect amounting to awe. "You won a scholarship, didn't you? I've read all about you in the school paper. I still get it sent to my house. You're a pretty famous girl, you know," he hurried on nervously. "I wasn't much of a student myself. Too busy chasing the almighty buck."

"Well, you seem to have caught it," she interjected dryly.

"Oh yeah," he laughed, not quite sure of how to take the remark. Was she mocking him? "But listen, I made the paper, too, in my last year. Did you happen to read what they said about me?" Without waiting for her to answer, he launched into a limerick.

In Spanish and in English,
He isn't overbright.

But when it comes to basketball,
Abelson's all right.

He laughed sheepishly. She found herself laughing, too — but the laugh seemed to die as quickly as it came.

"Well, very frankly, I don't know if I'll be able to accept the scholarship, much as I want to."

"What do you mean?"

"Oh, I don't know . . . well, my sister, she's very ill, you know — severely asthmatic — and there are, well, money problems, as you can well imagine."

Suddenly confidential, she said, "You see, Aaron, she's so good, she suffers so quietly. She doesn't want to bother anyone. I believe only the good die young," she mused wistfully.

Aaron was deeply impressed by this emotional outpouring and overwhelmed by Eve's literary and theatrical delivery.

She kept glancing nervously upstairs, but the upstairs was obscured in noncommittal blackness. He heard someone coughing, probably her sister, he thought, and then suddenly a startled, angry cry, then another, and a piteous bellow, like the unearthly sounds of a slaughterhouse. Eve reddened, then paled. Now the screaming was interspersed with sobbing. "My God," Aaron said, and reflexively ran toward the stairs.

"Don't," Eve begged, "please don't!" She pulled at his jacket with a sudden strength that caught him off guard.

"What do you mean, don't? I can't just sit here and let her be murdered! Is that your mother?" There came another scream in answer. Just then a door flew open and a heavy woman burst forth and began stumbling down the short stairway at a terrified pace, almost knocking Aaron down as she ran into the room, searching desperately for sanctuary. But a large man was already close behind her, yelling in some foreign tongue that didn't sound to Aaron like Yiddish. In a split second he caught her arm and forced her onto the sofa, where he fell upon her mercilessly, punching and beating her indiscriminately, while she screamed in that slaughterhouse bellow he'd heard before. Aaron stood frozen, momentarily hypnotized by the rapid pummeling and the indentations it created in the soft, fleshy upper arms and flabby breasts. The rest he caught in flashes like the movies of the day, slow motion — quickly — Eve's back, the sudden slackening of shoulders, a buckling of the diaphragm, as if she too had received a blow to the solar plexus — Eve pale and pulling at the man's long undershirt that seemed to be all he wore. Now and then Aaron caught sight of his large genitals. They hung down loose and heavy, and shook violently with his exertions. Without any physical consciousness of what he was doing, Aaron threw Eve out of the way and began pulling at the hulk of the man, who now almost completely concealed the woman burrowing deeper and deeper into the sofa for its inadequate protection. Aaron seemed unable to stem the maniacal flood of the man's fists. Then suddenly he turned and riveted Aaron with a pair of bloodshot eyes — He smelled of garlic and poverty —

Aaron felt his knees go wobbly, but he pulled him firmly from the round, quivering mass on the sofa. "For God's sake, leave her alone. Can't you see you're killing her?" he shouted. "I'll call the cops if you don't stop this minute!"

The man looked at him, stunned. "Who the hell are you?"

Out of reflex, Aaron hit him with a powerful uppercut to the jaw that sent him sprawling and semiconscious. Then he bolted from the room. He blanched, he felt sick to his stomach. He'd always had a delicate stomach, ever since he was a child. His mother always said that violence made him ill. She was right, he thought wildly to himself now. She was always right. He wanted to get out of there, out of the house. After all, he was only a stranger. He didn't belong here. He didn't even know these people. He was overcome with embarrassment to be so suddenly caught up in the intimacy of their lives. His own parents rarely spoke to one another, but when they did, it was quiet, gentle, with respect. He could not remember a harsh word between them.

He lurched out of the house blindly. He felt suddenly weak and angry, exploited. He had dreamed about this evening for so long, it had been so perfect in his dreams . . . The last place he expected to find sordidness was at Eve's house. It was all around him in Williams-

burg, everywhere he looked, it had grown up with him in the tene-
ments of the Lower East Side, in the checkrooms where he worked
at Webster's Hall in the Village, but here . . .

He didn't hear what Eve was saying behind him; all at once he
was running, his heart pounding, his breath coming in gasps. The
screams seemed to follow him down the street. The neighbors had
opened their windows, were looking out toward Eve's house, shaking their heads, mumbling in Yiddish and English.

She caught up to him. "Where are you going?" For a moment
he could not look at her; he just stared blindly in front of him.

"I don't know, call the police, maybe, or an ambulance . . . something. I don't know," he mumbled breathlessly.

"Don't, no, please, don't do that. It'll be all right now, you'll see.
It always is after a bit."

He looked up at her incredulously. Now he knew why she never
brought anyone home. "Is — is it over?" he stammered.

She nodded. "He's passed out in the bedroom. Please come back
inside with me. I don't want to go in there alone."

"Sure, okay," he answered readily, but he wasn't at all sure he
wanted to.

As they entered the house, they saw that her mother was still huddled in a fetal position on the sofa, sobbing and swollen, her arms
red from the heavy shoulders to the elbows. Aaron stifled a wild, uncontrollable urge to laugh. "Are you all right?" he asked foolishly.

"Mama, Mama." Eve guided her to a sitting position. "I'll get
some ice," Eve said quickly, as if seeking a way to get out of the room.
Aaron sat there with her mother, miserable, not knowing what to
say.

"I'm Aaron Abel, a friend of Eve's. Are you in any pain?" Eve
heard him the short distance away in the kitchen. Sick to her stomach with humiliation, she vomited into the kitchen sink. Aaron heard
the retching and raised his voice to block it out. When she finally
returned, he rose abruptly as if he had been eagerly awaiting his
cue to exit. He looked at neither mother nor daughter, mumbled
something unintelligible, and headed for the door, the same open

door through which he had entered so suddenly, a half-hour or so earlier, with his dreamy expectations.

*

Eve tried to talk to her mother, but she felt the anger rising hot in her throat like the vomit. "Mama, why do you let him do this to you?"

"He was drinking," she said quietly, as if to excuse him.

"He's always drinking. Why doesn't he try working for a change?"

"Only wine, it's only wine that he drinks," she said absently.

Eve looked away quickly. She hated her mother like this, cowed and compliant. She knew her mother's other side, her Rumanian gypsy temper, and preferred her that way.

Suddenly conscious of Eve, she said, "Where is he now? Where did your young man go? Oh my God, did I chase him away? Oh my poor Eve, what have I done to you, my poor baby!"

"He's gone home. It seemed best. I was in no mood to go out anyway."

She felt a sense of remorse after she said it. Her mother had sustained so much already. So much humiliation, disappointment, poverty since Eve's father had died — and then Lubowitz, this last desperate, lonely mistake.

She tried to blot out the image of her father, the one that kept wavering up to the periphery of her brain, his pale, sensitive face floating on the black water . . . delicate blue-veined lids stretched over his sad eyes like parchment. A chilly edict — death by drowning — everything washed clean — The London town house with its elegant parlor of red plush, a staff of uniformed serving maids whose bottoms the master pinched, the warm, admiring circle of her parents' friends ("arty" Lisa, her mother, had called them with amused tolerance). Overall, the slender, handsome shadow of Papa in his faintly fragrant detachment. Sometimes he teamed up with Mama, who had a powerful voice, but always *he* was the star, on two continents — English and Yiddish vaudeville — singing, dancing, satire; it had said so on the cover of the programs he always brought her — Eve — his favorite, his *sheine meidel.*

Eve remembered suddenly her mother's anguish as she talked to her friend Sonia.

"I begged him not to go. Everyone knew it would be dangerous. We were warned, but no, he would go, stubborn, selfish — she cries out . . . Sonia is muffled heavily in furs and theatrical make-up. "Maquillage," *she calls it. She has built herself a reputation of sorts on the fact that she is the discarded mistress of King Carol of Rumania, the predecessor of the eminently more successful Madam Lupescu. She carries her jewels wrapped in a handkerchief in her voluminous handbag, all that remains of her worldly goods, her vestiges of former glory. Eve wonders why she never removes her cossack-style hat or her heavy fur scarf. Eve feels uncomfortable. She slips away unnoticed into the next room, but she cannot seem to shut their voices out.*

Sonia says in a placating but unconvincing whine, "But, Lisa, darling, you know he had to go. He was booked into the Palladium. You couldn't expect him to pass that up."

"Palladium, my behind, it was that little whore he was chasing. Did he think I didn't know? I always knew. Oh, actors, actors, all rotten to the core," *she lamented.*

"Sh-sh, Lisa, darling. No — don't say that. The children will hear. Eve is only in the next room." Sonia sounds agitated. Eve imagines the beads of sweat melting through the maquillage *on Sonia's crumpling face. Sonia doesn't argue with her mother's accusation. She doesn't say anything. Why doesn't she deny it? Why doesn't she defend her father? She remembers him as he was that day he sailed — handsome, slender, esthetic, smelling of some foreign cologne. Like all showpeople, he is wildly superstitious and unhappy with his cabin, Number 13, on the* Lusitania, *but it is the last one available and he must take it or not go at all.*

"Eve, darling, I'm so sorry," her mother's voice brought her back to the present. "He seemed like such a nice boy." Eve wondered why her mother referred to Aaron in the past tense. "So handsome, wonderful blue eyes." She put her head in her hands. She began to cry softly.

"My poor Eve, my poor Eve," and then as if she felt some general explanation was expected, she murmured half-aloud, "I was so tired, Evie, so tired. Four children, no money, I thought he'd take care of us." Another memory, distant, but suddenly in sharp focus now, ruffles through her brain while her mother moans and talks. *Eve recalls herself, a rosy-cheeked girl of thirteen, pubescent, round eyes soft with wonder. She is watching her mother singing. It is the Gitana Café on Second Avenue, across the street from the Yiddish Theater, where Jacob Adler is the current matinee idol. After Mama finishes delivering her song in her robust contralto, slightly nasal, she begins to move around in a saucy pirouette, banging a tambourine over her head, jingling, jangling, tum-de-dum-tum. She is surprisingly light on her feet for such a heavy woman. The four-piece band whines in the background with a detached shrillness, the air in the room seems heavy and smells of face powder and perspiration. Suddenly, the lights come up bright and hot, Mama bangs the tambourine once more high over her head to denote the finish! Eve can see beads of sweat jeweling the soft dark down above her lip. Suddenly the floor is a shower of coins glinting like the paillettes on Mama's generous bosom. Some of them hit Mama in the face, but she is oblivious as she stoops and grovels, dodges and weaves, amidst hoots and catcalls. The child trembles in her seat and sinks farther back into the corner, wanting desperately to be invisible. A glazed look has spread over Mama's face. Now she reaches too far downstage with her half-filled tambourine, and falls forward, sprawling in all directions like the coins. Her skirt hikes up, displaying her generous rump. Eve jumps suddenly from her hiding place. She begins tugging at her mother, her cheeks a flaming red. "Mama, Mama, are you all right?" She helps her to her feet and pulls at her damp hand. They must get out of there. People were laughing, laughing at her, at Mama. "Mama, we have to go — hurry, hurry."*

"Eve, go away," she says, as if swatting flies. "Go away. What

are you doing?" She is breathless and in pain from the fall. "Help
me, help me to pick up the money — over there." *Her eyes darting
wildly, she pushes Eve to the left, then to the right, but not really
seeing her.*

"No, please, Mama, please let's go." *She doesn't hear, scurrying
and darting, her long skirt swishing the white dust from the floor.
Eve obediently bends her head and studies the coins, eager to hide
her face. She sees that they are only pennies. Tears of shame fall on
the floor, turning the dust into muddy droplets.*

Childhood memories are painful, misleading. She is too often
flooded with them against her will; she forces herself back to the
present moment, but it is the same sort of pain — "Oh leave him,
Mama, leave him. We don't need him." Eve leaned forward, shaking her mother's arm, unmindful of the bruises there, the loose flesh
indented at the touch. Her mother turned toward her, her dark
eyes wide and helpless, deep with tears . . .

"I can't, Evie. I can't. I'm pregnant," she mumbled into her
bosom.

ARON BOUNDED UP the steep stone steps of his house, two at a
time, but his gait did not at all reflect his mood. He was still
shrouded in a melancholia that grew more intense by the minute.
The walk home from Eve's house had been a nightmare for him. A
sense of having been exploited mingled with acute disappointment.
The evening haunted him. No matter how hard he tried, he couldn't
put it out of his mind for even a moment. His naturally suspicious
nature threw him into agonies of doubt. Eve's tense face and

hysterical manner kept coming back. A feeling of encroaching responsibility hung like a yoke around his neck. He wanted to rid himself of the sensation, and yet he felt at home with it. Although he was the youngest of seven children, he was already the unspoken head of the family, the breadwinner.

He slammed the door closed behind him and entered the dark hallway of the house he shared with his aged parents, his oldest brother, and two of his sisters. He had to adjust to the sudden onslaught of odors and stifling heat. The rancid smell of mold, decay, and stale chicken soup assailed his nostrils, but he barely noticed it, he had become inured to it through the years.

His unmarried sister, Rachel, was sweeping earnestly in a corner near the kitchen. She had overturned a jar of sourballs and was trying to sweep them backwards onto the dustpan, but they kept rolling off. She was large and heavyset like most of the Abelson family except Aaron, and she kept bending down over her bulk, breathless and sweating from exertion and the heat.

"Them balls, they roll," she mumbled half-aloud, frustrated.

If Aaron's oldest brother, Bennie, had been present, they would both have roared with laughter, but now Aaron barely heard her and sat down heavily at the small round table that served as the nerve center for the three-story house. It stood in the middle of the tiny parlor, which was separated by a pair of glass-paned doors from a stuffy bedroom on one side and a wedge of a kitchen on the other. Rachel slept on a sofalike contraption in the center room, her parents in the bedroom. Aaron had long ago pitched a tent in the muddy back yard. He wanted the fresh air, he'd said, and his privacy, but secretly he dreaded the winters. The two upper floors, exact replicas of the linear apartment beneath, were occupied by his married sister, Leah, and her family, and (on the top floor) his oldest brother, Bennie, his wife, Neva, and their son. The others had long before married and moved away.

As if by a secret signal, his mother shuffled out of the tiny kitchen with a plateful of chicken soup sloshing recklessly in the dish, for all that she squinted into it intently with her half-blinded eyes. Her long skirt rustled softly when she walked, like dead leaves in the wind. She placed the bowl lovingly before him, like a sacred chalice.

"Nu, Avrom? Eat is goot," she said in her broken English.

"Yes, Mama," he said, absently patting her hand. Her skin felt dry and dusty, she smelled faintly of camphor. For an immigrant's son, he had a delicate appetite and immaculate tastes, but he ate the soup, dutifully avoiding with a spoon the black pinfeathers that floated here and there like some exotic herb.

His mother hung over him, straining and squinting her eyes to catch his reaction.

Although he was used to this ritual, tonight it irritated him. He answered by rote, "You know I love your soup, Mama." This seemed to satisfy her. The others ate as little of her cooking as possible. They made coarse jokes about "her mistaking pepper for pinfeathers," or "throwing the sponge into the soup instead of the chicken."

He heard the familiar powerful thump of his brother Ben on the rickety stairs. Ben punched the door open and entered the room with a resounding boom. "What the hell are you doin' here? I thought you was going out with that fancy dame from your school. What she do, send ya home early?" He bellowed at his own cleverness, then added as an afterthought, "Jeeze, I thought at least she'd keep you after school." This brought on a fresh belly laugh from him.

"Yeah, yeah," said Aaron noncommittally.

"Whaddya mean, ain't ya gonna tell us what happened?" His brother hunched over the table confidentially. "For chrissakes, I'm ya brother, ain't I?"

"Big Bennie," as he was called around the neighborhood — "six foot and built like a bull," Aaron would brag to whoever would listen, unable to keep the envy out of his voice. But the envy was only for his physical strength; he secretly considered this brother brainless. Benjamin, the eldest, was at least twelve years Aaron's senior. Nobody was exactly sure of their ages in the Abelson family, and birthdates long ago had become a tangled web of mystery.

Bennie was a bouncer at a nearby bar and grill. He ran around

with some of the toughest boys in the neighborhood, an assortment
of Jews and Italians. He had earned a somewhat precarious reputation for himself as a friend of both the union and management, and
whenever a strike broke out on the nearby docks or elsewhere, he
was immediately called in, his big bulk visible here and there in the
midst of seething crowds of men.

"So it don't look like you're gonna get to first base with her,
huh, kid?"

"Jeeze, Ben, is that all you can think about? I just met her, and
anyway, that's not what I was after, not with her anyway."

Ben let out a guffaw of disbelief. He was not an unattractive
man. Large and vital-looking, with a bull neck, he had crinkly blue
eyes, golden brown hair, and a smile that bathed his whole large
face, but there was a wary expression, something of the *gonif* in his
eyes. He bounced up and down on the balls of his feet as he talked,
restless, preoccupied, eyes darting everywhere.

"Well, I gotta go. It's almost nine, time for work." And then, as
if suddenly forgetting his job for the moment, he came back and
said to Aaron, "Listen, kid, they giving you any trouble down at
the place?"

"Who?"

"Who?" he echoed his brother's words incredulously. "Why
dem goddamn thieves, of course, they'll steal the eye outa ya head
if you don't watch 'em like hawks."

"Who are you talking about, the kids who work for me? Naw,
most of 'em are good kids. They're okay." But Aaron looked up,
suspicion slowly creeping into his eyes, his expression becoming
crafty like his brother's.

"It ain't just the kids," Bennie said. "It's them others that come
in off of the streets, them hoodlums smell cash lying around, ya
remember like last time." Bennie was always looking for a good
fight. "It's like lemon juice on an empty stomach, it cleans the
blood," he would say.

Rachel walked back into the room from the kitchen. "They're
all the same, them little bastards. They don't want to let you live.
They don't want anyone else should make a living."

"Jeeze, will ya listen to the *cooch*, the big businesslady," Bennie said with a raucous laugh. *Cooch* was a nickname Bennie had coined ("bedbug" in Yiddish) and somehow it had stuck, almost as if after the initial joke no one knew or cared what it's meaning was. It was just a nickname, breezy, raunchy, irreverent, like the family itself.

Rachel had worked in Aaron's checkroom, too. He had given her the ladies' checkroom concession and the washrooms. There were heavy tips to be made there and he told her she could keep the money for herself. Otherwise he'd have to hire someone and pay them a salary.

He was making enough to support himself and his parents now, and this way Rachel could feel independent. The money made her feel strong and brave. She and her mother clung together like frightened peasants at a city fair. They never really adjusted to life in the new country. Poor thing, he thought, she's worked in sweatshops and factories here since she was ten and now she's Mama's martyred nurse for the rest of her days. But in fact she preferred it to the unknown terrors of marriage and, as she often said, "Doing them dirty things that men make you do."

There had been prospects, and for that she was grateful. At least she was saved the humiliating services of a *shadchen*, not to mention the expense to her father. There was Jake the butcher, Herschel the curtain man, they had both proposed and she had considered accepting Jake. He wasn't bad, but he had made the mistake of buying her a diamond engagement ring "on time." This in itself she considered an act of the most outrageous extravagance. But while walking with her in the street he took the ring from his pocket to dazzle her by the light of a shop window and dropped the tiny object down a subway grate. And that was the end! She couldn't seem to erase from her mind the picture of his beefy contortions as he tried in vain to fish up the sparkling dot that eluded his hysterical probing. When a curious crowd began to gather, laughing and jostling, she simply turned on her heel, and walked out of Jake's life forever. Such a *shlemiel* — just made her feel foolish — if possible more foolish than usual, and who needed him anyway!

No, now that she was making her own money, thanks to her beloved baby brother, she didn't give a damn about getting a man.

"They only rob you anyways, and you got to wait on 'em hand and foot," she would say. "Better I should wait on my brother."

"Well, listen, kid," Bennie said, his hand on the doorknob, "if you have any trouble down there . . . I'll come around and take care of 'em. Remember them two hoodlums who held ya up after the crap game behind the checkroom last year, huh? Betcha you was never bothered again by any of 'em. It gets around, ya know."

Aaron thought of the two of them dangling from their collars like puppets in Bennie's hands and stifled a smile. Two punk kids who'd come off the street to slink around the dance that was in progress in the main room. They came to get their coats early and somehow involved the other two checkroom kids in a game of craps. In the dull, static hours that ensued between the check-in and check-out flurry, Aaron joined the game, too. The two boys had been losing heavily and must have known there was plenty of cash lying around behind the counter in that gray tin box. One of them suddenly pulled out a revolver while the other one went for the cash box, but what they hadn't counted on was Bennie being out front as he usually was on weekend nights. He had a small percentage of the checkroom, and this was his contribution. He simply picked them up and threw them out the back door, but not before he had cracked their heads together — like rag dolls, their bodies swaying dizzily in the white light of the street lamp . . . Oh, Jesus, Aaron thought, how he hated it, he hated the violence, the dirt you had to wallow in. But he loved the money.

He learned about people, and violence, and greed early in those years at Webster's Hall. He learned to handle it, to cope, he didn't have to learn to compete, it was built in, God-given. From the time he was fifteen and was hired as a delivery boy there, until now, his nights were filled with Student Union Balls, Art Students League Balls, Beaux Arts Balls, Fag Balls, and Drag Balls. There in the Village, the famous drank with the infamous — poets turned radical, radicals turned poet, artists who painted politicians, politicians who painted the town. Famous actors passed out under tables in black

tie, celebrated playwrights urinated in their tuxedos, and homo-
sexuals, like wraiths, floated nude or in drag, in and out of its seedily
hallowed halls. They all wound up, sooner or later, at Webster's,
their coats hanging docilely in Aaron's checkroom. That is, when
they wore coats. Some more reckless (and cashless), like Maxwell
Bodenheim, went coatless and in rumpled shirtsleeves. He was a
regular, busily replenishing Maxwell with bootlegged spirits or, better still, by publicly nibbling on the exposed breast of his current
mistress, a buxom brunette to whom it was whispered his scandalous
novel *Replenishing Jessica* was a tribute. Scott Fitzgerald was seen
often in similar condition, though sartorially more acceptable.

But Aaron was too busy to concentrate on these legends. That
was outside his province. Inside the checkroom, he scrupulously
collected a five-dollar bill anytime a drunk lost his coat ticket or
forced him to wait all night until every coat was claimed. When
the hapless drunk hit the fresh air, his head reeling, Bennie's hired
thugs picked his pockets and Ben and Aaron split the profits. Al
pretended to know nothing about the rolling of drunks, but of
course he knew and despised it, as he did the checkroom work.
Aaron hated violence, ugh, it made him sick to think about it, so he
usually didn't; but after all, a guy had to make a buck, didn't he?

He really didn't need all this, he could always be a lawyer, but
money kept flirting with him, and he grew weak at its touch, weak
in his resolves, weak in the knees. He became giddy. It was like
falling in love, in love for the first time. God, how he loved it, the
cash. This business was all cash, no waiting — no hoping — just
cash in the hand. He didn't care much about buying things, most
things were a waste of money when you got right down to it. No,
just having the cash meant peace of mind, satisfaction, a ticket out
of obscurity. Except maybe for clothes, he didn't yearn much to
own anything.

He loved to buy himself beautiful clothes, "cake-eater duds," Al
would say disdainfully. But he didn't care what anyone said. He
carried clothes well, he knew it, he could see it in the admiring
glances of the girls. When he'd get a couple of more concessions,
make some real money, he'd buy the creamy coats and velvety

fedoras that the rich customers parked in his checkrooms. Sometimes he'd stroke the sleeves unconsciously, getting an almost sensual thrill from the softness under his fingers. The pungent perfume of the ladies' furs made his senses reel. It wasn't that he felt frustrated, far from it. There was no doubt in his mind that someday he would have it all. It's just that he was impatient, nervous, just marking time here.

Bennie slammed the door loudly as he left. Somehow, tonight, his night off, the one night he'd set aside for this special event, Aaron felt he deserved some peace and quiet — but it was impossible in this house. His tent, in the muddy excuse for a garden, was a feeble attempt at privacy, but it was too Spartan, even for him. Of course, that was one of the more positive aspects, he rationalized; at least he wasn't too comfortable here, he wouldn't sink into the house on Harrison Avenue like the others . . .

For a brief moment, Aaron put his head into his hands and thought, I've got to get out of here. They're killing me. They're suffocating me, Mama especially, and Rachel too. They're bringing me down, down to where they've brought Papa. Poor Papa with his immigrant dreams . . . where are they now? He's no better off than before. In Vilna, Papa was a tailor. Papa is still a tailor, a pants presser. Except maybe now they own this house, and that's only because I worked nights after school to help pay for it. True, Bennie chipped in some too, but after all, what is it? Just another tenement with a rotting back yard.

The eternal monotony of living in this overcrowded enclave, of life viewed through the wrong end of the telescope, was beating him down. Suddenly, Aaron longed to be joined to something, someone other than his family and his own suffocating ambition.

His father came home from the synagogue. He entered the narrow doorway and seemed to fill it up as he filled up the empty spaces in Aaron's life. His father, Joseph, was tall and leonine, his shaggy red-gold beard now silver-frosted, he was almost biblical in his bearing, like his namesake. "Aaron, my son, how are you?" he spoke in Yiddish, though it was not usual for him. But he had just come from the *shul* and it was as if he wanted to reaffirm his identity, his Jewishness, here in his home with the green wooden clock, brought from the old country, and the brand-new, cathedral-shaped radio Aaron had just bought them.

With the exception of the two eldest, all of the children had been born in America. They were modernized American children, products of the new world, *goyisher Yidden*. Joseph accepted this, was even proud of the fact. He was particularly proud of Aaron, this youngest of his, this afterthought, squeezed from the last drop of his fading passion. Aaron, the survivor of twin boys (the other dead at two), seemed to have been left a legacy of double energy that exploded into fireworks as if in celebration of his good fortune at being free, unduplicated. One of a kind, he was never meant to share the limelight. This one was different, his parents said it all the time, within earshot of the others.

Aaron had fought hard for that. Besides being the youngest, he was the smallest in this family of giants, but he had clawed his way up from the bottom of the litter to top place in his parents' hearts, the little breadwinner, Mama's favorite. The others resented this overbearing runt in their midst, but did not dare to make it known. Better to keep the door open, never know when little brother with his big ambitions may come in handy. So they all fawned on him, and Aaron ate it up.

"Why don't you come to *shul* with me anymore, my son, not even on Fridays?"

"Oh, Papa, you know I work most nights."

"But not tonight. I see you're here."

Aaron missed the camaraderie that he had shared with his father in his boyhood. The smallest of the four boys, he used to walk next to him each Saturday on the way to the synagogue. He would sit close to him on the narrow, hard bench, his lean buttocks aching from the long hours of rising and sitting. In an effort to fight sleep, he would study the long, snow-white fringes on his father's prayer shawl as they waved back and forth in rhythm with the ancient prayers. Sometimes it made him imagine the snow-blown village of Vilna on the Polish border, where his parents were born. He'd heard about the bone-bitter cold . . . No. No more *shul*, he was finished with that. The older boys had given it up long ago. Papa never asked them anymore.

"Yes, I took the evening off. I got some kids working there. I had a date with a girl."

"So, for a girl you'll take off from work, but not to go to *shul* with your father. What girl?"

"You wouldn't know her, Papa. Just a girl I know from high school."

"I know I wouldn't know *her*, but maybe her family?"

"Oh no, never," Aaron said, smiling a little now.

"You'd be surprised, Aaron, at the things I know," his father said obliquely, nodding his head.

But Aaron wasn't surprised. He had always felt that his father was omniscient.

He had an urge to tell him everything, confide the whole evening. Maybe he did know something about the Levinson family, but just then his mother came into the room, and he looked at these two old people and thought how odd it was, they had been old as long as he could remember — He could never think of them as anything but old. He had a sad, sweet feeling for his mother, a combination of love and pity and undefined guilt. He wished that he could take her out and buy her something, a hat, a new shawl. Something to replace the floor-length colorless cotton skirt she always wore. He'd like to show off the world to her, but he knew she would never leave the house, she would continue to shuffle through the narrow confines of her life dreaming behind her sightless eyes, her secret dreams.

"So, Aaron, you got home from work early tonight?" his mother asked.

"No, Mama, I didn't work tonight. I . . ." And somehow he trailed off — as if a sort of sixth sense prevented him from another wearisome explanation.

"So what did you do? You wasn't here for supper and it is Friday night!"

Aaron felt the gentle rebuke; for some reason it bothered him more than usual.

"Esther, leave him be. He had some private business, personal. He's a man, not a boy."

"What does that mean?"

"That means it's none of our business." Joseph bit into a lump of sugar emphatically and sipped his hot tea, its steam creating a vapor before his eyes that made them for the moment unreadable to Aaron.

Aaron caressed the seltzer bottle on the table, turning it every which way.

"Aaron is a boy, twenty-two only, he shouldn't be wasting time with girls."

"Ach, Mama, what crazy talk, he's a man and anyway, who said anything about girls!"

Why are they discussing me as if I weren't here, or as if I were still a child, he thought. They were speaking in rapid Yiddish, that dark, secret language that he imagined was now being used to exclude him. They knew he was barely fluent in it.

"I heard you talking to Benjie; who is the girl?" Esther asked.

"Her name is Eve, Mama, Eve Levinson."

"What's wrong with Sara Gottleib's daughter, a nice plain girl? You'd never have any trouble with her, hard-working too."

"Mama, what are you talking about? You don't even know who or what you are talking about."

"Avrom," she said, cajoling now, using the Hebrew of his name as if better to stroke him. "Whoever she is, for what do you need her? You shouldn't go away from here, you're the youngest, the baby, you . . ."

"Stop, stop," he was shouting now. "Who said anything about leaving, about anything . . . I just met a girl. I spent a couple of hours at her house. They weren't even particularly pleasant hours, and right away you've got me married. I don't even know if I'll ever see her again. I don't know anything. How come you all know so much, huh?"

His mother mumbled something. Aaron didn't wait to catch it. He was suddenly very tired of today, tonight especially. He longed for tomorrow, a fresh new day. He would go over to the Knights

of Columbus. That should be a good concession to buy. They
would sell it cheap. They didn't know what they were doing over
there or what they had. Nobody really understood this business. It
was new. At least his approach was new. Anyway, he was only
marking time with it, making much-needed money that he'd use for
his law career. If Al could be a lawyer, so could he — only he'd
be a better one, everybody told him so.

He slammed the back door and walked quietly to his tent. He
had paid $1.98 for it at a sporting-goods firm in Flatbush. He con-
sidered it a good investment.

He lay down with his hand behind his head. The faintly fishy
smell that blew in from nearby Sheepshead Bay reminded him of
the Sundays he'd spent with Al on his brother Bennie's rowboat.
They'd take turns rowing around the bay, inhaling the salty air, the
tempting smell of fried fish and potatoes coming from the large
restaurants on stilts that circled the docks. Half-asleep from standing on his feet all night behind the checkroom, no sound other than
the gentle flapping of the oars, he'd feel drugged, hypnotized by the
deep, down-dragged holes, the great thirsty, sucking gulps each
time the oar dipped the water. Here they could trade yesterday's
faded hopes for tomorrow's illusions. But Aaron had little time for
illusion or patience. He was too busy turning it into reality, hard
and cold like the nickels and dimes he squeezed out of a hat each
night, like a magician. Al Carton had patience, endless patience
. . . How different they were . . . He brooded about this for a
moment; he hated cutting him out with Eve, and yet the thought
excited him . . .

Aaron and Al had become friendly in high school. Al was really
Aaron's *only* friend. He was as hard-working and ambitious as
Aaron, but a softer, toned-down edition; he did not regard money
or its power with as much awe and reverence. A kind of friendly
rivalry, a lively competition, had sprung up between them. A brilliant student, Al was attending City College, an honor of sorts, and
was planning a law career. He was poor, but he had an air of class
and refinement, a knack for sorting out the subtle from the crass,
and he secretly considered Aaron crass. He liked him anyway, even

admired his outward brashness, his razzle-dazzle. He was self-conscious about his scant five feet seven inches, and, like Aaron, competed ferociously in every other way to compensate for it. Al, too, worked nights and weekends, but it was half-hearted and he was underpaid. They were odd jobs garnered here and there, a grocer's assistant, a weekend cashier. He openly considered the jobs demeaning and resented their intrusion on his study time. When Aaron asked him to come to work for him, he had at first refused, considering the checkroom just another menial job, and the idea of working for Aaron, who was already in a position of authority, left him with a sense of defeat. But after some prodding he agreed, not at all averse to taking home a fixed salary each week, no matter how paltry. Anyway, it might be interesting working with him. Aaron was unpredictable, and he hoped that somehow he would let a little fresh air into his life.

Aaron remembered clearly the conversation one Sunday on the boat.

"Ya see, Al, when I approach 'em, they think I'm nuts because nobody ever made a buck on the checkrooms. It's just a service, a necessity, something they've got to put up with. Usually the kids keep the tips, they don't get any salary. But that's just where they go wrong — the real money's in tips. I'd rather pay the kids a salary; oh, nothing very big (after all they only work five or six hours a night), and keep the tips. Customers don't know this, and they ain't gonna know it, not if I can help it."

All the while Al's eyes never left Aaron's mobile face, digesting the information. It fascinated him, but somehow repelled him, too.

"They feel sorry for the kids, figure they're working for tips, and they always give them something. If the guy's had a few drinks, he'll give more, a dollar, maybe more. The kids are happy because they feel more secure with a salary, something they can count on each week, you get it." Al got it; the concept wasn't hard to grasp, but he had to admit it involved a certain slyness.

"How do you make certain the kids turn in all their tips, that they don't steal?"

"Well, there's bound to be some of that. I'll make allowances for that, but right now with only one place, and even with two, I just watch 'em like a hawk and when I'm out front checking or down at another place, you'll watch them for me, or my brother Bennie. Anyway, I count the coats and I know what to expect at minimum from each coat and hat. I've got the washroom concession, too, and I'm going to put a matron in the toilets at the Knights of Columbus on weekends." His cheeks were pink with excitement; he imagined himself a glorious bamboozler. "Anyway, we'll make a barrel there," he said, poking Al fraternally.

"What do you mean, 'we'? The salary you pay isn't exactly a fortune."

"Listen to him, he hasn't even started yet and already he's complaining. How do you know I won't cut you in for a piece? You know if I trust a guy, that's all; it's not easy for me to find a guy I can trust, and I trust you."

Al, with his gentle ideals, his fresh, flushed face, his whole air of openness and innocence, was stung by the intensity of Aaron's needs, by the whole harsh concept of making money by *ruse*.

But Al continued working for Aaron, nursing his own enormous hopes and dreams, not the least of which was Eve Levinson.

Aaron was tired, but as usual he could not sleep. He looked up at the chinks of stars through the tiny opening in the apex of his tent. He stared hard at them until their dazzle began to blur, as if by sheer force he could bring them down and touch them, light up his life with their brilliance.

THREE DAYS LATER, on a Monday, Aaron found himself walking rapidly across the Brooklyn Bridge heading for Greenwich Village. He figured that it would take him almost an hour from his door to the Knights of Columbus, but he loved the exercise. He hadn't had much time for his usual workouts at the gym lately and he felt logy. He enjoyed the walk over the Bridge, particularly when he had something pressing on his mind. It seemed to fill him with a momentary strength, an inner peace that was otherwise alien to him.

He felt dwarfed by the giant harp, rendered as toylike as the tiny tugs below, but here surrounded by the gossamer beauty of the Brooklyn Bridge, with its endless contradictions of toggles and bolts that seemed to rivet him permanently to this miraculous city, he felt at ease, his own importance temporarily diminished. The luxury of solitude and space was heady excitement to him, coming from the choking confines of a Williamsburg tenement. The bridge was in a certain sense his lifeline, his conduit out of obscurity.

He'd have to sort out his responsibilities. He knew that, but he didn't exactly know where to begin. What were his options, his priorities? Could he afford to take on any more dependents? He searched his mind, probing painfully to try to find his motives for thinking about Eve Levinson in this way. She wasn't his responsibility, not yet anyway, but it seemed to him that love demanded rescue. He must rescue his beloved from danger, but he sensed somehow the danger to himself, and became confused. She was so helpless, fighting so hard to keep her pride, that air of elegance, fighting to keep that crazy family together, to keep her sister alive, and fighting to fulfill some of those glorious predictions for her future. Not with that brutal stepfather, that smelly son of a bitch. He'd just hold her head under water until she drowned. Al had told him that they were usually one step ahead of the last landlord, hadn't paid their rent there in months. Lubowitz was supposed to be an electrician of sorts, but he broke more than he mended. Sometimes the unlucky client never got to see his toaster or iron again unless they could find the pawnshop he had taken it to.

It was funny, he thought, she's the oldest in her family, so the whole responsibility seems to be resting on her, but I'm the youngest in mine . . .

He put Eve out of his mind now. He told himself that he was just dramatizing. After all, Bennie was probably right. All I really want to do is lay her, and here I am making a big *tsimmes* out of it. Oh, she puts on those high and mighty airs, but she's ready. Somehow he sensed she was ready for him.

He had to save some money for law school. He knew he could be a good lawyer if he could only concentrate on studying, but whenever he looked at a book his mind began to wander, to dart furiously here and there, anywhere away from the material in hand. Often during high school he'd fall sound asleep in class. Lately the same thing was beginning to happen at N.Y.U. He needed money for equity. Supposing, for example, the Knights of Columbus demanded an immediate payment. He just didn't have it. Jesus, he only had one concession right now and he was really milking it, he thought. True, it was good for about two hundred fifty dollars a night, maybe more, but Rachel got some of that and Ben came in for his cut too.

Now his brother Ben, *he* was making good money, not just as a bouncer in the bars, but more often and more sizable, it was the kickbacks and side schmeers he earned as go-between in the labor disputes. Aaron remembered some years ago standing with him down at the stinking Wallabout Market near Sheepshead Bay in the middle of a truckers' hauling strike. At this huge wholesale marketplace, produce from all over the country was dumped and unloaded for distribution throughout the eastern seaboard. Aaron remembered the pavements caked with rotting lettuce, bits of every possible spillage and sewage imaginable. Overall the vinegary smell of urine, a slimy, macabre salad underfoot, steaming and rotting under the July sun . . . Bennie was talking earnestly, mollifying a big heavyset Italian, a lot of arms were flying. Aaron heard his brother say, "Now listen, leave it to me, pal. I'll help you get your number, but the demands you're making are, *pazzo*, crazy, but I think I can help you anyways. I'll ask for twenty percent more and leave room for negotiation."

"Ah, they ain't gonna pay it. I don't even think they can afford that much, Bennie."

"Screw them, let them raise the prices. Your boys gotta get more. They work like pigs, don't they?"

"Yeah, sure." The Italian was obviously impressed with Bennie's sincerity, his interest.

Aaron didn't have to overhear Ben's conversation later with the management. He knew his brother well enough. He'd go to them and say: "Don't give in to them bastards. Give 'em a finger, they'll take an arm. They'll bleed you dry if you let 'em. I'll get you some scabs in the meantime. I got a lot of good guys, take your pick. I got Jews, Poles, guineas."

And he did. He had an international melting pot of ruffians and characters gleaned from everywhere and nowhere, and the amazing thing about it was that he was like a traffic cop; he always knew when to say stop to one side and give a go-ahead to the other, and both sides liked and trusted this rough-voiced, hard-drinking man. He was more like a big Irishman or a Swede. You'd never figure him for a Jew, Aaron thought, for the son of Joseph Abelson. Anyway, he didn't behave the way a son should, Aaron thought. He's making plenty of money, but he banks every cent he can get his hands on. Funny, he sticks every penny in the bank and his sister Rachel is scared to death of banks. She stashes her money away in boxes or bags in the closets, packed tightly in mothballs, where she keeps the sponge cake for occasions.

At the foot of the bridge he picked his way carefully through a tangle of horse-drawn vehicles, pushcarts, and automobiles. That was another thing — he had to have a car of his own. But he wouldn't be satisfied with a jalopy, some black, shapeless lump of metal. He was waiting for a sleek, shining chariot, a rich dark green maybe, plenty of chrome, long fenders. He'd buy a Cord maybe, it wasn't impossible, not if he handled things right, kept a cool head.

*

"How much do you make on your checkroom on an average per month?" he asked Artie Gallagher, president of the Knights. "Nothing worth speaking about," he answered in a heavy brogue. Already Aaron could feel the blood begin to beat in his temples.

"That's what I figured," he said quickly.

"Yeah, it's a pain in the neck. I have to have it as a convenience for members and guests. Most of the time my son or one of the committee watches the coats and hats, but it's a mighty pain in the ass, I'll tell you," he mumbled sourly, then, suddenly wary, he said, "Why? Why do you want to know?" He didn't know Aaron, or why he had called requesting an appointment.

"Well, I might be able to relieve you of that pain in the ass, *and* pay you for the privilege."

"Whaddya mean," he peered at Aaron through bleary eyes, calculating him narrowly.

"Well, I own the checkroom concession over at Webster's Hall. I run it for them, see, and they're glad to get rid of the responsibility. Ya need insurance for people's coats or the stuff they leave in the pockets, ya know," Aaron said.

"Yeah, so?"

"Well, I'll be willing to make you the same deal. Tell me what it would be worth to you and I'll rent it from the Knights for a year, then we'll go from there."

"You're crazy," Gallagher said. "Whaddya renting, a stall for people's hats 'n coats? They don't hardly even tip here. They figure it's a private club and it's enough if they pay their lousy twenty-five dollars a year in dues."

"I know, I know," Aaron said, seeming to commiserate but undaunted. "So what do you care if I want to throw my money away."

"Oh yeah, you got so much money, you can just throw it away?" He looked at Aaron appraisingly, as if sizing up his net worth in one glance.

Aaron was glad he wore his best suit and his gray fedora.

"What kind of money are we talking about here?" Gallagher asked, suddenly all business.

"Well, I'd be buying potential, wouldn't I, because there's not much precedent for this. You said yourself the checkroom takes in no income worth talking about, so anything I'd pay would be gravy and you'd get rid of the headache." Gallagher thought a moment but no more. It wasn't necessary. It made sense, good sense.

"So what's the offer?" he said.

"Two hundred and fifty dollars," Aaron said quickly. That was all he could get his hands on at the moment and not touch his nest egg in the bank.

"Five hundred dollars," Gallagher shot back.

Aaron was prepared for this.

"Three hundred dollars, I tell you. That's the best I can do."

The old man agreed but looked confused. He added as an afterthought, "Of course I'll have to have the okay from the others."

"Listen," said Aaron, giving him a convivial punch on the shoulder, "if you're smart, you'll take the three hundred dollars and put it in your pocket. Just tell 'em that you got 'em off the hook with the checkroom, some dumb slob came along and wanted to take it off your hands. You'll be a bigshot and three hundred dollars richer."

Gallagher licked his lips and gave a wary glance around him. He held his hand out.

"I'll give you two hundred and fifty dollars now and the other fifty out of my first profits. But I want it in writing that I got it for a year."

First Gallagher looked impressed — then he sized Aaron up once again, carefully, with his bloodshot eyes —

"What did you say your name was now?"

"Abel, Aaron Abel," he answered, unabashed.

"Uh huh — that's a Jew name ain't it?"

Aaron could feel the skin on the back of his neck begin to crawl, "a Jew name," when they were ignorant that's how it invariably came out. He shoved his fists deep into his jacket pockets, as if to imprison them there. He remembered now that the Knights of Columbus was restricted, a membership whose charter strictly forbade any Jewish invasion — well, what matter, he did not wish to socialize with them, merely to take their money — with relish.

Aaron was delighted with the deal. He had been afraid that Gallagher would insist on a percentage of the take but it was obvious that the old man didn't understand at all.

He made five thousand dollars from his three hundred dollars in that first year. This became the format of all of the deals he was to make, varying in degree of sophistication, depending on the proposition, the size of the hall, or projection of volume and, of course, the ability of the landlord to "outfox" him, a favorite expression of his. As his concessions grew, it happened of course, but only rarely. Aaron was used to getting what he wanted.

4

IN THE FIRST YEAR of an uneasy courtship, Aaron proposed recklessly, then suffered an enormous amount of reservation, and Eve accepted, with an even greater reluctance. She had resisted him for as long as she could, out of an intuitive sense of self-preservation, and then she surrendered with abandon, passionately, hysterically almost. It seemed the easiest, most beguiling choice at the time. She had to get away from home, such as it was. Since the rude invasion of Lubowitz, it didn't seem like home anymore, and Mama didn't even seem like Mama anymore. Her mother's passion for this big, lusty man with the golden teeth and powerful arms embarrassed her, embarrassed them all. How could she tolerate a man like that after Papa, so fine, so sensitive, so delicate in his black silk frock coat.

Aaron could be very persuasive when he wanted to be. She wasn't really quite sure exactly what it was he had proposed. Somehow she got the cloudy impression that marriage was the ultimate destination. The trouble was there were too many stops along the way, and by the second year the original proposal had been ground down to a series of evasive promises that somehow never seemed to materialize. They fought constantly, each sensing in the other their ultimate destruction.

Eve's feelings were ambivalent almost from the beginning. She seemed attracted and repelled by this brash, forward boy. His crackling self-assurance lent him an aura of strength that she wanted to be fooled by.

But oh, the endless inquisitions — endless. He had the knack of humiliating her, bringing her down. After all, she was poor and she was a woman, that made her suspect to begin with — What sort of girl was this? Was she as pure, as angelic as her face proclaimed? Impossible — with a face like that. He mistrusted beauty as he did any luxury, any bonus that was handed to you without a fight. So Aaron checked and double-checked, he picked clean the bones of neighborhood gossip; it was growing harder for him to sleep at night.

A man, forty years old, they said, used to wait for her after school, walk her home, some said *drove* her home in a "nice car," an eighteen-year-old girl, beautiful, poor, smart — an older man, unattractive, bent, they said, even with a strange rolling gait —

He went with her to the office of a famous eye doctor (she was severely myopic). Paranoically, he quizzed her about a portrait that hung on the wall in the waiting room and bore a strange resemblance to her. (She had in fact been the model for the painting, and for a handsome fee.)

He forced her into a weary catechism of reasons and excuses for these rumors — he practiced tricks and dark deceptions, even to disguising his voice on the telephone to catch her in some defection from virtue. If she would dare to accept a date with anyone else, this was to him, and to his family, a sign of her complete instability and abandon. It was impossible for him to sleep at night.

Aaron often wondered exactly why his parents were so opposed to this girl, and why his sisters seemed to hate her so. When he tried to discuss Eve with his mother, she was reluctant to talk about her, as if the very discussion would lend substance to her, would dignify the relationship, as if she feared putting her "kosher" stamp of approval on it. That they resented her lofty airs, her classical education, he never doubted for a moment. All this set her apart hopelessly, especially from his sisters. And she was beautiful! None of the women in his family was beautiful, hardly attractive even. Of course, that accounted for their hostility, he reasoned. The women felt awkward in her presence, bulky and masculine, and Eve probably patronized them slightly and made them feel oafish.

His sister Leah, who lived upstairs with her husband and small son, was certainly no ally of Eve's. At thirty-six, sly, officious and plain, she resented bitterly that her four brothers had all the looks in the family. She had tried to compensate by studying diligently in high school, then went on to a business school (with Aaron's financial assistance). She prided herself on holding down a good bookkeeping job when she met Lon Berkman, an educated man, twelve years her senior — and gentile. She had married him in despair after a short and uneventful courtship rather than follow in her spinster sister's footsteps. That the family disapproved of Leah's marriage to that "lazy goy upstairs" was an open secret.

The problem was that Aaron hated going to her house on South Ninth Street, ever since that first time. He never knew when he'd walk into the midst of some humiliating scene. He was not very good at handling scenes; he preferred to avoid them altogether. He had become adept at escaping any and all sorts of unpleasantness. He hated having to duck Lubowitz. "If I see him I'll punch him through the wall," he'd said once in an excess of sympathy for Eve. He hated making polite conversation with her mother, of whom he secretly disapproved.

Most of all he dreaded the sad, eviscerating visits with her sister,

Fredda, watching her in her little bed gasping for air like a fish out of water, her face turning from gray to various shades of blue with the enormity of her efforts. He and Eve would sit for long hours, imprisoned in her tiny airless room that had become more like a cell (her mother would allow no crack of air into the room for fear it might bring with it a speck of dust, a sudden chill). Aaron would try vainly not to stare at the thin white arms, blue-punctured with the needle marks of her various medications — her stigmata. Sweet-faced, hollow-eyed because of the dark circles beneath, she reminded him of the pictures of the saints he had seen in his history books. At times he was overcome, and found himself choking with the heat, the held-back tears, and he would bolt from the room to recover.

Fredda was more like Eve than the others, was in fact a darker edition of her older sister, and with the same intense intellect. She was brilliant, wise beyond her years, with the profound sensitivity of the doomed. Their symbiosis was almost mystical.

On a stifling June afternoon the family made a sweet sixteen party for her in her room. She loved the company; it was a welcome respite from the long hours of loneliness. Lisa, Eve's mother, baked her celebrated chocolate walnut cake for the occasion. Eve had been sitting there all afternoon when Aaron came in, and the sick girl's face lit up with joy and she clapped her hands and cracked jokes. She seemed to love him, really love him, as she loved anybody remotely connected with Eve. Aaron began to lose the rhythm of his own breathing as he watched her contortions, struggling for breath in the unbearably hot little room, already overcrowded by three. Why did she have to be so full of love for everything and everyone — for life? Her bravery made it harder for him to bear, harder for Eve, he thought. Why pretend that the world had been such a joyous place for her? After all, what did she ever have? No father that she could remember, poverty, insecurity, not even the common, ordinary luxury of drawing a breath in peace. If only she would cry out once in protest — a little of that familiar Judaic self-pity, "Why me? I am so young . . . ! I want to live!" But she never did, perhaps from fear of adding to the existing struggle of their lives, the already overburdened household. Once when he passed her room he thought he heard her crying softly, but he did not go in or tell Eve about it.

She joked casually with Aaron on this day, almost offhandedly, irreverently calling him "Abelson," in mock style of her sisters' teasing manner with him. So they all crowded into the little room, her brother Jules, twelve, the youngest sister, Pauline, nine, promising to be beautiful but with eyes like burning green marbles. Lubowitz poked his head in once, but no one paid much attention and he didn't dare to share the occasion, as he must have realized his presence might cause Fredda a renewed fit of coughing and gasping. He was there to service Mama, and beyond that — well, there wasn't much beyond that — they wanted to have as little to do with him as possible. The only thing he was getting out of this, Aaron figured, was support, and Mama's *Lusitania* money had almost run out; he wondered idly if Lubowitz would go with it.

Eve complained that Aaron's only loyalties were to his family. He could not bring himself to displease his mother or even his sisters. It seemed to him a sort of holy alliance that he could not defame, almost like spitting on the Torah. He never asked himself why he did not feel about Eve in the same way, but there was a cruelness in him that dismissed or ameliorated his responsibility to her because he had been helping to support her and her family lately.

Often she would remind him of her own half-forgotten glories, in an effort to hold onto a shred of her fierce pride. "We had a big home of our own, too, in London, and seven, yes seven, servants to wait on us when Papa was alive. I know you don't believe it."

Aaron was unimpressed, as always when she talked about her other life. He believed only what he saw, now, in the present, tangible evidence. He had no patience with the past, other people's pasts anyway, although his own fascinated him, if only as a base of comparison to measure his accomplishments, to chart his successes.

Oh, there had been good times, too, of course. Like the time some months ago when they had walked the boardwalk in Coney Island, he in his straw boater, she in her favorite sailor dress, as if protesting her innocence, his arm around her waist protectively. They sucked on lemon ices. She watched fascinated as the little Italian vendor sprayed the giant snowballs with yellow from his mobile palette. They ate nougat bars and jelly apples. How she loved nougats! (Her sweet tooth was childlike.) The stickiness of them hurt his teeth, but he would always associate that candy with her; he thought of them as rather foreign, elegant.

He had won two beautiful dolls at the shooting range that day. He prided himself on being an excellent shot. Eve clutched the two brightly painted, tawdrily dressed dolls, smoothing the coarse taffeta of their ruffles again and again. Her face took on an odd little smirk when Aaron told her casually that he would like to give one of them to his mother. She would put it on her big, lumpy bed. She would appreciate it, he said almost apologetically. "Why don't you give it to her when we get home?"

"I don't think she'll like that very much. She will only look at me suspiciously as if I'm trying to put something over on her, and mumble under her breath in Yiddish so that I can't understand. No, no thanks, she would want it to come from you, not me."

"Oh, Eve, you're exaggerating, like you exaggerate everything, all this making a mountain out of a molehill. She's an ignorant, foreign woman, what do you want from her? She doesn't understand the new ways, your ways."

"Anyway, she pretends not to. What's so new about a boy and a girl being in love, being together; what's hard to understand about that? She managed to understand it for five of her other children. But you, the baby, no — the breadwinner — with you it's different."

"Sweetheart, let's not fight, we're having such a nice afternoon." Aaron kissed her warmly on the cheek. When he was close to her he felt his nameless irritations disappear. Her histrionics melted into the soft whiteness of her flesh, the rough edges of their relationship smoothed themselves out in the creamy depths of her breasts. They drove home in his car, "the old tub," that afternoon in a blinding rain storm.

"The old tub," as Eve affectionately called it, was "a second-hand convertible" Ford with a jaunty little rumble seat, in dark green. He had bought it outright; it wasn't very expensive and he could afford it now. It was a necessity, he told himself, he needed it to travel between his two concessions. His sister Leah muttered her resentment at the outlay of "such a large amount of cash that could be put to better use." His sister Rachel muttered *meshugge* under her breath. But Eve was delighted. It seemed to her the most magical toy in the world. So the rain didn't really disturb Eve, and although they were drenched and she worried about her only good dress, they laughed a lot, too, and Aaron wished that his parents could see her now. Alone with him she was so different, so much more informal. He didn't really care if she did act, well, different, strange sometimes; that was precisely what he liked about her. Shrugging his shoulders, his father had said with a sigh, half aloud, as if thinking to himself in Yiddish, "I don't understand that girl — one minute she's laughing, the next she's crying. What kind of a life can you have with such a girl?" But Aaron suspected that out of all the family, his father was the only one who did understand her, and he and Eve were friends. It was Aaron who did not, could not, understand, even begin to comprehend the intricacies, the subtleties of her darkly romantic nature. He understood vaguely that she must refine every aspect of life, of daily living, before she could digest it, while he swallowed it in one gulp and found it delicious!

It was in character that she would find his urgent physical demands humiliating, demeaning. She wanted only courtship — romance, but Aaron was too busy for these refinements. He was busy with school, which was not easy for him, as it was for her, with his all-enveloping family, with his business. It was putting him through school, supporting his family, and now and then sustaining Eve's family so that she could remain at college rather than go out to work.

He guessed that she felt beholden to him — he made himself out as a benefactor of sorts, but he took pride in doing that with everyone in his life. She's in love with me, he thought. Sometimes she goes to extremes to deny the fact, signs letters "Your friend, Eve Levinson," but he knew that she loved him — passionately. In fact she romanticized him out of all proportion. She had summoned all her dreams together and invested them in Aaron, in an Aaron *she* had invented, and when he stepped out of the character she had fashioned for him, she became alarmed.

PRIDE OF OWNERSHIP had been almost more than he could bear — his first car, two concessions, and Eve. But still, he wasn't completely satisfied with himself, he didn't really possess her. Oh, they had petted and fooled around but after all, this *was* 1924, the girls were bobbing their hair, drinking in speakeasies, smoking, making love in the back seats of automobiles — but this was for other girls, not for Eve Levinson.

Privacy was an outrageous luxury for them. Her house was impossible, his out of the question under ordinary circumstances. The new car, "the old tub," became his last hope, his chariot to heaven. He knew her well enough to guess that the last place in the world that she had imagined her ultimate surrender, would have dreamed of her loss of innocence, would be in the front seat of a cramped convertible, but he had convinced himself that it had just worked out that way, unplanned.

It was well after midnight of a murky January night. They were parked in an abandoned lot near Sheepshead Bay, in the middle of a sea of old tires. The combined smell of salt water, fish, and burnt rubber was anything but inspiring. Aaron kissed her mouth and throat. He unbuttoned her blouse and kissed her breasts. Eve tried lamely to take his hands away from her skirt, where his slender fingers were struggling with the clasp.

"Let's go into the back seat," he murmured.

"Aaron, no," she said emphatically, but she strained toward him, her arms around his neck, her blouse open, revealing her heavy white breasts, garish for the moment, illuminated by a sudden shaft of moonlight. If she agreed to go into the back seat, he knew that her guilt would be unbearable, but if he let her pretend that she was taken unwillingly, she might manage to face herself and him afterwards. As much as he wanted her at this moment, he did not want to alienate her, have her turn on him later, feel exploited. No, he would never get her in the back seat, that would destroy the spontaneity. She would not become an accessory, he was sure of that. She arched away from him, frightened, tense. He forced her knees apart, he thought how cold the wheel felt on his bare buttocks, he felt it dig into his firm flesh, a fresh cold shock with each movement. She seemed to him disjointed, somehow like a puppet, her head sometimes wobbling out the window or down onto her chest, one kneecap jiggled perilously against the hand brake. Aaron had been so nervous, excited, it was over almost before it began; but he knew that for her it hadn't been over soon enough, that she felt soiled, humiliated, demeaned. Eve cried softly all the way home. Aaron felt first a thief, then a conqueror.

The whole experience was a painful reminder that they really had no privacy. They could certainly not get it in the respective confusions they called home. With the mounting tensions at the Levinson's, it was becoming increasingly difficult for Eve to study. They were living from hand to mouth; her mother was unable to work at all now. Even the few singing engagements she used to get from time to time in a café were better than nothing, but that was impossible now. A heavy woman naturally, she was enormous since the birth of the new baby, and had to stay home to care for him. (Eve thought the over-large boy baby, her half brother, grotesque, repulsive.) The occasional iron or toaster that Lubowitz fixed was barely enough to feed seven mouths. So they survived on credit based on the *Lusitania* claim, expected when each child reached his majority, an endless wait for all but Eve.

For the past two years Aaron had been making as much as three hundred and fifty dollars a week some weeks, and even considering the few salaries he paid — and always the nugget of savings for equity, which was to be money for future concessions — he could well afford to rent a place for Eve not far from his own house. It seemed the obvious solution. "A cozy little love nest all our own," Aaron had said in his best musical comedy style, a style he adopted playfully when feeling sheepish. "And you can do your homework in peace here."

"And you can do *your* homework in peace here, too," she answered ruefully.

"Aw, Evie, what's wrong? You didn't want to be in that house with your mother and Lubowitz anyway. They're not going to be able to stay there much longer, they can't pay the rent, and I can't just keep on paying it either. You've got to have a place to call home." She looked around the sparsely furnished room; it was surprisingly large for a Williamsburg rooming house, but that was about all she could say for it.

"What do *you* call home? Sixteen Harrison Avenue, I suppose?" Without waiting for his answer, she ran on nervously, "Well, I don't call this home, not when you're living somewhere else." She couldn't keep the resentment out of her voice. She felt like an outsider, excluded from what she facetiously called the "Club 16." She knew how his family felt about her. Aaron hardly talked about it, but he rarely brought her there anymore, either.

She was strangely uncomfortable with the arrangement, imagining by turns the landlady's disapproval of Aaron's visits and the embarrassment if *his* family found out that he was keeping her, however humble the keep. Her own mother simply looked away discreetly, unruffled by what was common practice in Europe amongst her circle. Mama was sophisticated — and she was practical too. He talked constantly about their future together, but nothing seemed to crystallize. He held marriage out to her as a plum of sorts, a prize for good behavior. But it was a vicious circle; his actions caused her constant pain and she reacted negatively, so there were constant arguments.

She disliked asking him directly about getting married, because she considered it to be groveling, and humiliating. She wasn't even sure that she wanted to marry him. She doubted that he could make her happy, he was so immersed in getting and spending, so involved in his ambitions, his family, and his gym. He had already built for himself a little life that seemed to be growing bigger and farther away from her all the time. She felt left out, lonely, only an appendage. He had once told her that he doubted if *anyone* could make her happy. Maybe Al, he had said ironically. He was better suited to her esthetic needs. He really seemed to understand her, and he had more time. More than anything, Eve wanted time, quiet time, but with Aaron it was seldom quiet, and he never had any time. It was only on rare occasions that he would spend the night with her. Usually he'd leave her at one or two in the morning and walk around the corner to his house.

"Why can't you stay a little longer, hold me in your arms until morning?"

But he would always end up leaving her with excuses about her landlady, clean shirts, or a business appointment early the next morning. She felt used up, unsatisfied. Most above all, she knew and resented that he didn't want his mother or sisters to know of the arrangement — a twenty-three-year-old man, self-supporting and supporting his parents as well, and he had to sneak around — "Ridiculous," she said.

So although she lived close by, she had inundated him with letters lately. He felt swallowed up, drowning in seas of words and paper, white paper, pastels, cream vellum, love letters, hate letters, letters of recrimination, of analysis. He couldn't swim out from under to answer them. He was too conscious of his own shameful inability to express himself on paper, his halting childish style, his uphill scrawl. She respected the letter as an art form in itself. She was "a master of letter writing," he had written her once, how could he hope to cope with her letters, analyzing, criticizing, romanticizing, sometimes just poetizing? Too often they described his shortcomings or his failures, poems about love, bittersweet little couplets she'd composed of a lonely spring evening when he would be working at one of his concessions or doing his law homework or studying for a test, sometimes just poems from her own vast anthology of favorites. Often he couldn't understand the letters, he couldn't read the unfamiliar words, words seldom used in his world, like *copious* ("copious tears"); *endeavor* (after running to the dictionary, he thought irritably, why couldn't she have just said "try"?); *banish, amity* (as in "I have sought to burst the bonds of amity" — did she mean by

that she wished to leave him?); *frivolities, emanating* (as, in lines
that he found particularly cutting, "a certain note of self and egotism
always emanating from you, it stamps its mark indelibly on you.
This has been the undoing of our friendship; think it over, and you
will see." He did not see).

Her letters, the poems that often accompanied them, haunted him
even now. He recited them in his head and spouted them unbidden
at a moment's notice, so much were they on the periphery of his
brain, the forefront of his mind, nudging out reason, ambition, even
thoughts of money. He had never forgotten the poem she had sent
him soon after that "first time we were lovers." "The following
lines have typified our state," she wrote.

> *She loved me, nay, she never did,*
> *She only played at loving,*
> *Her heart was quite too small and light*
> *For ought but mild reproving.*
>
> *I knew it even from the first,*
> *Ere she grew cold and ashen,*
> *For when I kissed I felt we missed*
> *The nobler part of passion.*
>
> *There were no bonds of common cares,*
> *No dreams, no kind devotions,*
> *And in her heart there was no part*
> *For wild and deep emotions.*

A sermon of sorts, he supposed (she had crossed out the "her,"
made it "his"). He knew that the words served her point. He
wanted to cry out that it was unfair, that it was not true, his emotions
were wild and deep as his emotions could go, considering that they
were rigidly bounded by convention pressed upon him by immigrant
mores, old-world ethics. And that while the noble part of passion
was most certainly *her* contribution, the ignobler parts of passion
had their merits, too. But no, he had robbed her innocence, robbed
her girlhood; she had said it a hundred times in a hundred different

ways. In place of joy, of satisfaction, their relationship was burying him in guilt. But Aaron seemed to welcome guilt, as a dying man welcomes death.

*

The nobler part of passion had little or nothing to do with the courtship and marriage of Ben and Neva Abel.

At this time, they had been married about five years. Their son, Marvin, was four and a half. The facts, if the truth were to be told, went something like this.

They had been "keeping company" for years, and Neva finally had succeeded in getting Bennie to set a wedding date only three months away. It had all started quite ingenuously really, quite properly. Bennie, from his generous source of undisclosed cash, had bought her a large round diamond, a "hot headlight" was how their brother Herschel the cop described it. Neva was thrilled wearing it everywhere, even to work in the garment center where she was a member in good standing of the I.L.G.W.U. It was an established fact among her coworkers that she was marrying a big shot of sorts — exactly what sort nobody seemed to know for sure, not even Neva. During the day she sewed *schmatas* for a living, by night she "lived." She would sit all night at the Magic Rail bar and grill where Bennie "bounced," flashing her ring and laughing with friends whom she would invite to keep her company through the long vigil. When Bennie quit, it was nearly dawn. They would go home to his house or hers and make love — sometimes on the roof, when weather permitted, but usually in the hallway. Pressing her against the crumbling walls he would push the bulk of himself breathlessly up into the soft folds of her body. Ben was virile and she was lusty, but, being "dead on her feet," she resented having to stand up during intercourse.

He was proud of the beautiful ring he had given her so magnanimously and often patted himself on the back, saying to her, to everyone, "See, I'm an honorable guy, I don't take anything for nothing." So Neva continued to sit at the all-night bar with the sensuous ultraviolet lighting and wait for Bennie, and then drag herself dead tired the next morning on the subway to Seventh Avenue and Forty-sixth Street to Reza Modes.

It grew difficult to find people to sit with her and pay for their own drinks. Bennie didn't spring for anyone's drinks except Neva's and he didn't encourage that either. He said nobody drank in his family but himself, and he could drink a quart a night and never get drunk, just redder — and more virile.

One night a big, good-looking stranger came over to Neva (who was by now reduced to sitting alone at a small table). It was not surprising; she was dark and pretty with eyes like black daisies and hair as rich as midnight. Bennie was working out front this night. His brother the cop, who usually hung around the place on his night beat, saw them leave by the back exit and lost no time informing Bennie. Herschel thrived on sexual falls from grace. Bennie looked confused then suspicious and commanded that he follow her. He couldn't find them anywhere, they seemed to have vanished, maybe the guy had a car — he didn't know what to think. So he went to her house and found they were not there. He waited in the unheated vestibule for over an hour, during which time nobody came in or went out. Should he be relieved or disappointed? He was in complete sympathy with the opinion of women held by men in his family. He didn't know exactly what to tell his brother — that is, not until a taxi inched up slowly to the curb.

When no one alighted, he impatiently rushed over and opened the door. In the uncanny light from the street lamp he caught a flash of white buttocks, enveloped firmly by Neva's plump white thighs as the couple moved together in the last gasps of delicious tumescence. Herschel pulled the man, with his freshly bedewed penis, onto the floor and dragged Neva screaming and kicking hysterically inside the tiny vestibule, her dress still hiked up in places, her face flushed with indignation and the memory of pleasure.

After that, when Bennie decided to forgive her, he told her she would have to wait for marriage now — five years on good behavior. After that he insisted on having intercourse regularly standing up in the narrow vestibule of his house, after all it wasn't as though she were such a great lady, not now since her fall from grace.

Neva saw herself growing old and barren and progressively broke during the course of this penance called an "engagement." So she got pregnant — with Marvin — somewhere between the third and fourth year of the five-year sentence, and they were married.

Aaron had told Eve the whole story, not without some relish she thought. Eve, like most romantics, identified with the underdog, and the women soon became friends.

Moonlight in my garden,
  Shadows on my wall,
And somewhere out in the nothingness
  A nighthawk's raucous call.

Shadows in my garden,
  Firelight in my room,
While through my curtained window creeps
  A mist of strange perfume.

Memories in my garden,
  A hurt within my heart,
That keeps me and a youthful dream
  Two thousand miles apart.

AARON LOOKED at the envelope with the Florida postmark, and read these lines with a sinking feeling of nostalgia, exactly the sentiment they were meant to convey both by the poet and the "sender," he guessed. He walked over to the little upright piano, following her advice hypnotically. "Try this on your piano," she had written. Ancient yellow keys, one blacked out like a dead tooth, it was so sadly out of tune that even the major notes sounded minor. He began tinkering with the keys at random until he found a little offbeat melody that seemed to fit the unsigned poem.

This secondhand piano he'd found somewhere down on the Lower East Side for fifty dollars, a small luxury he'd bought himself even before the new car, a fantastic toy on which to bang out the popular songs of the day, and he was able to do it, too, quickly, effortlessly. He had only to hear a song once or twice and with the accompaniment of a few monotonous base chords he would pick out the melody. *Sweet Rosie O'Grady*, or it was "Mary, Mary, long before the fashions changed" — he loved it when his sister-in-law Ida, his brother Max's wife, played these tunes. Max owned a hardware store in Borough Park. She played piano at a sheet music store in downtown Brooklyn, and when they came over for Friday night supper, Aaron would sing the words with glee and do a tentative little shuffle or two. He mimicked what he saw in vaudeville on those rare occasions that he treated himself, and sometimes Eve, to a show at the Palace or the Roxy on Broadway.

Why was he able to be so decisive about everything else in his life and so flabby about Eve, their relationship? Yes, she was right — "so without character." He had grown used to being deluged with letters when she was here, practically around the corner from him in Williamsburg. But considering the bitterness of their parting, he was really surprised to receive the poem today, and the ardent letter written on the train to Florida.

How unpredictable she was — The more she seemed unable to reach into his soul and touch him, the more she seemed to feel compelled to communicate to him her every nuance of feeling. Face to face, it had been hopeless. No one, not even she, could succeed in involving Aaron in any degree of intimacy; it was a thing alien to his nature, he was able to go so far, and then no farther.

So he only half expected to hear from her from Tampa, where she had gone to stay with her mother, sadly and in defeat. They had gone there for Freddie's asthma — always hoping — and they were running from an avalanche of unpaid bills. The original plan had been for Eve to remain behind in order to finish a brilliant sophomore year at college and because she didn't want to leave Aaron — but after what *happened* he could hardly blame her for leaving him. He glanced again at the sad little poem in his hand. There were tears in his eyes as he began to read:

Dearest,

I must bother you and write again. I can't keep my attention fixed on my book; my thoughts always revert to you, Aaron, my dearest. How will I pass the dreary days away from you? For you the cares and interests of business will dispel all lingering thoughts of me, but I will only think of you, and the two of us, how happy we might have been if others had not interfered. Do you know, dear, I believe that if you had really made it clear to your mother that I meant something to you, she would not have set up such stout opposition to me; but, of course, your tongue couldn't say what your heart didn't dictate. Enough of this moralizing. It won't get me anywhere; I suppose you are lost to me forever, but my pride, humble and little now, how it smarts to see beyond my worst predictions, that through your mother's efforts I am bound southward, riding farther and farther away from you. Somewhere there's no doubt a law that mothers must be ruthless despots.

He was not sure he understood that line.

Don't be angry at me, love, this is only a mild reproach for a grievance which I will always remember — the injury your mother has done me. Your father told me to stay; he believed you cared for me; he said you wouldn't let me go but would redeem the ticket; but you, on the contrary, didn't for one moment press me to stay, you seemed glad I was going — this burden would fall from your neck, where, dearest, I would want my arms always to be. Dearest, in spite of everything, I speak now with a belief that you loved me, but I am not at all certain. At any rate, you were faithful and shared what love you had with no one else. Aaron, dear, I did the same, only my love was purer and nobler; I cannot blame you — you are a man.

Please answer my letters right away, even if it's a line, that is, if you still want to keep in touch with me. Oh, there was so much I wanted to say, that must be left unsaid. Please don't show my letter to anyone. I unlock my heart to no one but you.

Faithfully,
Eve

P.S. Gee, I practically wasted five dollars — four for underwear, seventy-five cents for candy. At any rate, now I have enough underclothes.

Love and kisses,
Eve

Her innocence touched him, confused him — chaotic confusion crowding his heart and mind, interfering with his work, his resolves. It was all there in her letters, so neatly dated and properly indented, in her round, even handwriting, as if her hands were up in front of her face to fend off the blows, shielding herself, protecting herself from him. Maybe he really didn't understand his own motives. Why hadn't he insisted on their marrying as soon as she told him her stunning news, instead of just sitting there with that look of amazement? Reluctantly she had told him, cornered by her lack of options. They sat parked in "the old tub" and talked in whispers without knowing why they were whispering. He saw himself sitting there with such a stupid look on his face, as if it had been some kind of crazy miracle, the Immaculate Conception or something. He saw that brief, ashamed, hopeful moment when she seemed confused — uncertain even. He read her expressive face then. Maybe she *had* made a mistake, it said. Could she have been so naïve, so innocent as to think that what they did together could beget a child? Maybe there was — well — something more, other things you did that he hadn't told her about, protected her from, and then she must have realized that his look of amazement was only a ploy, a gathering of his defenses, because she began to cry. The tears flooded her dress, shook her body, and still he didn't say anything. He wasn't ready, wasn't sure, he had to be sure, after all, this was his only life wasn't it? And he'd planned it all so cleverly. He needed almost every cent he was earning to invest in his business now, he must be free for a while longer, unencumbered. An offbeat stroke of luck had directed him to concessions, he had a chance to be somebody, it was now or never, he'd have to be strong; if Eve loved him, she'd understand. If he was suddenly tied down with a wife and child, besides his parents, well . . . it might all go sour, the whole dream shattered. Crazy doubts plagued him — Eve was beautiful, much sought after — how could he be sure the child was even his? — He grew weak from the treachery of his own thinking —

As always when he could not make an emotional decision, he had brought it to 16 Harrison Avenue. He knew now that that had been a mistake.

*

Terrified and on the edge of hysteria, Eve had had no choice but to follow his instructions. He went with her to a crazy old doctor somewhere in Coney Island, around the corner from the Tunnel of Love — but a thousand miles away. She remembered that the doctor wore his suspenders over a rumpled shirt, and his false teeth clacked together noisily when he talked. She was hypnotized by the enamel basin freckled with flies, terrified by the battery of instruments that appeared to her rusty and archaic. She longed to be anesthetized even before she undressed.

With her family away in Florida, she felt the shock of her aloneness.

Mama had her own problems to contend with. She, Eve, was to have been their strength and their redeemer, and now this. She hated Aaron, wished that she had never met him, her first instincts had been right. She was almost glad this had happened, now she would forget him, be finished with him once and for all. He had given her a glimpse of what life would have been with him, a brief flash, a preview of his selfishness and arrogance.

The ugly scene kept flooding back to her — the table with its faded oilcloth covering, none too clean — the stirrups — ugh — stirrups were for riding a *horse*. For weeks after the operation she barricaded herself in her little room, refusing to see or talk to anyone, especially Aaron. Sick and alone, with only the landlady to bring up her meals, she suffered the greatest agonies of shame because of the heavily bloodstained sheets, and late at night, white and trembling with cold, she dragged herself down the hall to the bathroom, hoping against hope that no one was around. She tried in vain to wash them in the tub, on her knees. She explained obsessively to Mrs. Ryan that she had "a most severe bronchitis, which had practically been pneumonia." She wrote the same thing to her family. It would, she hoped, explain her pallor, her weakness and loss of weight, when they saw her. Her little sister, as always unmindful of her own illness, wrote to Aaron a remarkably probing letter for one so young, questioning her sister's condition, but received no reply from him.

The farther away from Aaron, his family, and the rest of her disappointments, the better Eve liked it. Tampa looked to Eve now like a golden Eden, even if it did mean putting up with Lubowitz once again, and the baby brother.

In the oppressive heat of August, her itinerant family decided to move from Florida to California; a Tampa doctor had promised them that the climate of South California would definitely help Fredda. They stopped off in Brooklyn between trips — staying with friends of Mama's. Eve intended *not* to call Aaron — but she telephoned him almost immediately. She did not know why exactly — it was a compulsion — perhaps it was his ardent letters promising marriage again. She wanted to believe in him — she was strangely, painfully drawn to him. They resumed their fragile relationship for a month or so but it was only an interlude slightly more discordant than the rest, and this time the separation seemed permanent. She longed for the sanctuary of California. Aaron, in a fit of dashed hopes and frustrated passion, made her promise not to write, threatening that if for any reason she did, he would tear up the letters unopened. She assured him he need not worry; she had no intention of contacting him ever again.

Her mother, who had left with the children some weeks before, wrote and told her that she had a good friend in Los Angeles whose son was a successful movie producer. She had no doubt that she could get her a job in the movies, or at the very least she could teach voice and elocution to the stars who were preparing for the advent of talkies. Eve sensed that Mama and Freddie needed her, emotionally *and* financially, and suddenly she needed them, too.

For a long time she had thought of Aaron as an available Eden, but a flawed one. Just as there are natural disasters, there are those of the spirit. The assault of this man on her psyche had proved such a disaster, she must prevent its happening again at all costs — run from it. A sense of dread lingered behind her dreams. Compulsively, she wrote a few letters in the beginning. Her early letters begged to be answered, and then suddenly they didn't . . . there was silence.

After she had left for California, Aaron instructed his sister Leah to intercept any letters that might come for him from Eve, to tear them up on sight; he didn't want to be tempted to read them, to soften his resolve. Leah would be the perfect conspirator for his self-preservation. He knew she'd enforce it rigidly and enjoy doing it.

*

In California, Eve began work as an extra, walking the dusty miles from their little rented cottage in Glendale to the studio, a cheese sandwich in her handbag, or sometimes a slab of chocolate between two slices of pasty white bread; she couldn't afford lunch at the commissary with the other girls.

Always on guard against exploitation by men, she felt victimized — by her circumstances, her poverty, her sex. Her beauty, she believed, was a curse misread by men to divert her from her goals, which were "serious and intellectual rather than frivolous." Her friend, the young director, told her, "With a face and tits like that, Eve, you can't expect to come out here and make it big by going home alone every night and studying." But she refused to believe that her success or failure rested on her sexuality. In a surprisingly short time she was slated for stardom — playing opposite the cowboy star Hoot Gibson.

Back in New York, Aaron worked hard nights. Without the influence of Eve, his interest in college began to wane, until it flickered and died. He'd had no contact with her in some months, and his usually buoyant mood was now subdued. He was even finding it difficult to concentrate on business. There seemed nothing much to look forward to. Fighting and making up had become so much a part of his life, had created drama for him, without which his life seemed empty now. There was no mirror to reflect his dazzle, no one to admire his clothes. His business successes had become hollow victories. He would send for her, she would come. But where to write? He didn't know where. He was seized with a sudden panic that they might no longer be at the old California address. Well, perhaps a letter would be forwarded. Then it began to dawn on him slowly that she might have learned to live without him. He felt eviscerated, as if his whole carefully constructed world had suddenly crumpled like a Japanese lantern.

He thought about California. It seemed a foreign place to him. Exotica. He imagined long patches of desert waste, Indian territory. But it was only Glendale. Aaron knew only what he saw on the silent screen, what he read in the newspapers about Hollywood, its scandals, its elastic morals — he wondered if it had changed Eve. His suspicions drove him crazy now. He had her old address somewhere, he'd take a chance writing there.

Downstairs he took paper and pen from the drawer where he had been keeping it for this purpose only. He did not write letters, not if he could help it, but he had hidden this packet of stationery in a drawer in the ancient rickety table that served now as a lamp holder, hiding it away from himself and the temptation to write to her, to ask her to come back as he had done so many times before. He hoped that he wouldn't make too many grammatical errors. He decided that the open, honest method would be his best bet, she always found that irresistible. Yes, he'd lay all his cards on the table. His hand trembled as he reached for the pen.

> *Dearest Eve,*
>
> I'm sorry for not having answered your letters for so long, but I did it on purpose for reasons you can guess. I have so many things to say to you now, and it is difficult for me to write them down, you know how poor I am at expressing my feelings on paper, so please be tolerant of my lowly efforts.

I want to say first how much I miss you, how lonely and bare my life has been since you have gone, how even lonelier it seemed without having your beautiful letters to look forward to, a stupid attempt on my part to be strong where I am really so weak. Maybe the separation has been all for the good, because since I saw you last, I've been able to get on my feet a bit and to start making some real progress toward my future, I believe. Of course, I've had to quit school, there is no use kidding myself, I just couldn't concentrate. I was too damn tired from working nights, but what the hell, you can't have everything though I would feel that I did if I had you. Well, like I said, you can't have everything, I mean, a real go-getter and an intellectual professor-type, too.

Can you ever forgive me for not writing? Even now, I don't know whether or not you'll receive this letter, because you may have moved and, to tell the truth, I didn't see the letters you wrote, I didn't want to, but that's all water under the bridge now, I've smartened up, you'll see. I'll be different, I can be all the things you want me to be. I know that with you beside me I can be somebody. I know one day I will be able to give you everything. Right now, I can only ask you to return to me and my love for you, because at present, I have very little else to offer you. So, would you consider coming back to be my wife?

> *Humbly, and with high hopes,*
> *I am your adoring,*
> *Aaron*

Two days after mailing the letter, he was overcome with panic that she would not receive it, and then he remembered Rose Zoltan, a close friend of Eve's. Rose's address in Los Angeles was somewhere in his disordered pile of notes and scribbled phone numbers, he was sure. He had met her a number of times, when she was staying with the Levinsons in Williamsburg. He knew that she would be in touch with Eve and he sensed that she was fond of him, even approved of him. He decided to wire Eve at Rose's house.

DID YOU RECEIVE MY LETTER STOP PLEASE COME BACK AS SOON AS POSSIBLE STOP SO THAT WE CAN GET MARRIED STOP LOVE, YOUR AARON

And then he deleted the word "your" because it cost him an extra nickel. Walking back from the Western Union office, he tingled with an electric, current of apprehension. Whichever way it would go, his stomach knotted with fear. At that moment, he wasn't exactly sure what he wanted her answer to be. He only knew that he had to end this sensation of suspended animation. When he received no answer after two weeks, he began to worry, and in desperation sent a second wire. His second wire crossed with her letter. In her round, even hand, slanting downhill somewhat, it began:

> November 5, 1926
>
> *Dear Aaron,*
>   Today was a very exciting day for me. I received two wires from you. One I found on visiting Mrs. Zoltan's daughter. Actually, I've been staying with her for a while, but she went to Frisco, and I went back to my mother's. So the mail addressed to her was either sent back to New York (*if* it had a return address) or else was sent to the dead-letter office. I suppose that was the case with your letter, which I did not receive, and which was apparently not returned to you.

His heart sank, he had put his all into that letter, he was really quite proud of it. He was sure it would have done the trick. He read on, hoping she would get to the point, but it rambled infuriatingly for a few more sentences. As always, her verbosity further aggravated his natural impatience.

> The first telegram did not reach me at my address, but was also sent to Rose's where it lay for five days until I paid her this visit here today and found it.
>   But I suppose you'd like me to give you an answer to your wires. Well, I'm doing entirely too well here in the way of friends, money, and the movies to think of leaving Los Angeles. I'm beginning to breathe once more after my nightmare with you. In fact, it was a lucky day for me when I left New York. I'm earning my own money and taking arguments from no one. I'm enjoying home life.

That was a mysterious comment, Aaron thought.

> What would I have with you in a little room, working and clean-
> ing? If you *should* marry me, which you know you wouldn't.
> You brought me from Florida on that pretense once before, but
> that was when I thought I loved you very much. I don't know
> anymore whether I love you or not. I know I haven't missed
> you a bit, I'll be frank. What happened suddenly? I received
> no letters from you here, and now you talk again of marriage
> after so long. You know we just settled our *Lusitania* claim. I
> am no longer destitute. Could that have anything to do with
> your renewed ardor?

Her sarcasm cut him to ribbons, he was amazed at the bitterness she
bore him.

> I notice too, that mail for you must be addressed in care of Jeanie
> Newman — so that Leah and the family won't know anything, I
> presume. Well, I'd be a fool to take it from your family all over
> again. A secret marriage, I suppose, if any at all — no thanks. I
> found my happiness here — movies, excitement, actors and ac-
> tresses, gorgeous costumes and effects, in short, the dazzle and
> glitter of professional life. I'm only sorry I wasted so much time.
> I've met some wonderful men, gentlemen all of them, with beau-
> tiful cars, and all real sports who can't do enough for me.

This didn't sound like the girl he knew. Hollywood must have
changed her already, for the worse, he thought. He read on, not
really believing what he was reading.

> However, even if things weren't so pleasant, if I were struggling
> (and money matters are still a problem for me) I doubt whether
> I would want to return to a man who had mistreated, abused, and
> cheated me, and Aaron, you did.
>
> November might have been a very important month for us,
> can't you guess why? I'm glad it was otherwise.
>
> > *With kindest wishes for your*
> > *health and prosperity,*
> > *Eve*

In his eagerness to receive her reply, he had given the address of a
mutual friend, Jeanie Newman, rather than risk trusting his sister or
anyone else in the house, but he had made a tactical error, he realized
now. He was virtually dumbfounded by her letter, her hurts and
angers had always seemed out of proportion to him. His peasant
heritage had provided a thick, shock-resistant coating to his own
emotions; hers were like uninsulated electric wires. He examined
and re-examined the facts concerning the accusation about her in-
heritance. The damn thing was, that he *did* know about the *Lusitania*
money. He had heard from her family lawyer (old Mr. Applebaum)
in New York, who was looking for Eve to tell her the news. But he
was not conscious of any ulterior motives, he couldn't even think of
why he would ever need the astronomical sum of ten thousand dollars. How unfairly suspicious she was, he thought. Perhaps she really
didn't believe that his business was prospering.

Some three weeks after receiving this letter, he found a telegram
waiting under the front door. It said simply:

FREDDIE DIED YESTERDAY I CAN'T BELIEVE IT STOP WILL
ARRIVE TWO PM TOMORROW GRAND CENTRAL STATION
STOP LOVE, YOUR EVE

THEY WERE MARRIED inauspiciously on a hard, bright day in
early January. As they emerged from the old rabbi's house, she
shielded her eyes against the sudden onslaught of sun and the tears
that were brimming there. She could not seem to rid her nostrils of
the rancid smell of that dark house, the pervasive odor of cat dung.

It clung to her nostrils like an acrid reminder of the little ceremony that had just taken place within. Only Aaron's father had come, although the Abelson house was only down the street, and even *he* had seemed uncomfortable.

The old rabbi who married them was also the local butcher, kashering the meat and circumcising the babies, his faltering eyesight giving rise to tremors of maternal terror. He had rigged up a makeshift *chuppa* in the parlor. For spring and summer weddings, he took it out to the scrubby back yard. When Aaron stamped on the glass according to ancient custom, Eve stared fixedly at the bits of broken glass beneath his feet. Like fragments of my life, she thought fleetingly — a thousand frozen tears. She was hurt and angry that no one had come to the ceremony but Joseph. It was sad enough that on her wedding day no one of her own family could be present, but Aaron's family — to ostracize her this way, and why? What had she really done? They had promised to walk with Joseph to the house and "drop in on Mama"; she would want to say *mazel tov*, he said. Eve knew he had had the grace to lie.

As they approached the house, it seemed to draw away from her, its decaying facade, stubborn, silent, suspicious. She saw as if in a dream the stone face of her own childhood home in that gentle London suburb, the name in stained glass above the entry, a small flourish of the showmanship her father was famous for among his friends, the Evefrejulina Villa: He had named it for his four children, Eve, Fredda, Jules, and Pauline . . . Ah, her father's romantic nature — but the great luxury of being cherished belonged to another life, one that was without confusion, scandal, sordidness. She wondered sadly if the little plaque was still there, her tiny bit of immortality.

When they walked into the Abelson parlor, she was struck by its emptiness, no one around, not even the usual confusion. She felt imprisoned here in this place. Now, sitting in the big stained armchair, she studied the white doilies on the chair arms, placed there in vain to hide the worn-out patches beneath, but puckered ludicrously by exposed tufts of filling. She had an urge to laugh — or cry. She looked around absently, making mental notes, trying vainly to ignore the heaviness of the Russian peasant atmosphere. She resented the ugliness of this room. She stared at the large, shapeless sideboard — it seemed to her a pine coffin painted a dull black. And the candlesticks irritated her too, heavy, made of some sort of metal that was durable, unimaginative. They were all just things bought or handed down by people uninterested in esthetics, impatient with beauty, people who were absorbed only with practical necessity. How unlike me these people are, how unlike me Aaron is, she thought sadly and felt a terror of isolation. But she was married now, for better or for worse, for love, for companionship. She need never be alone again. Here was this handsome, arrogant, resourceful man to protect her from the elements, from poverty, and the confusion of her past — so why was she trembling? She dropped her eyes to her wedding ring, a tawdry stranger on her third finger, left hand. Its brass yellow color offended her. Aaron had bought it hurriedly at the 5 and 10¢ store that morning. God, she thought, he could have afforded to buy a real one. What would it have cost, twenty dollars? He just didn't think of it, too busy to think of it, and even if he had given her the twenty dollars to buy it, she probably would have given the money to her mother to buy food. She thought of food, and realized that she was weak with hunger, she hadn't eaten all day. She longed for her mother's delicious cooking and her mouth watered, though she had stopped enjoying meals at home a long time ago. She couldn't bear to watch Lubowitz eat. (The children never referred to him by anything other than his last name, or "he" or "him"; if they spoke to him directly, they never called him anything at all.) She tried in vain not to see the elaborate mechanics of his eating, the "knife swallowing act," she called it, the blinding fireworks of cutlery flashing furiously. He maneuvered his fork like a spear, clutching it low at the neck, and shoveled the food onto it with the help of a knife, turning it in his left hand, precariously, to his mouth — all this deftly, without spilling a drop. There was no peace at that table anymore, not with that pig there, the constant shaking of the condiments, the squirting of the seltzer and slivovitz, all the intense intricacies he created for his sensual pleasures, made her ill, the food stuck in her throat.

"Mama," Aaron called in a falsely cheerful voice. "Where are you?" He went into the kitchen first, then emerged quickly and said that she must be in the bedroom where his father had gone the moment they entered. Eve heard mutterings, then raised voices. Still no one came out. Aaron and Joseph came back, Aaron tried to look relaxed. "She's just fixing herself up a bit for you. After all, this is an occasion." When a long, sad fifteen minutes had passed and still Esther had not emerged, Joseph once again went into the bedroom.

Eve stood up and said to Aaron with rising hysteria, "Maybe she doesn't know! You were afraid to tell her, is that it, is that it?"

He did not directly answer — instead he pressed her to stay. "No, Eve, please, not yet. She's just getting something ready, maybe a surprise for you."

"In the bedroom? And by the way, where are your sisters?"

"I don't know," Aaron answered dully.

"Well, I'm leaving. I didn't want to come here in the first place."

Just then Esther emerged with her husband. She kissed Aaron, murmured something unintelligible to him, and came over to Eve. Eve jumped up at once, out of politeness and nerves, and to be ready if an embrace were forthcoming, but there was none, only a tentative handshake and a mumbled *mazel tov*. Her mother-in-law slowly made her way into the kitchen and buried herself in her pots there.

Rachel came in with Leah, looking sheepish, both acting as if they knew nothing. Eve thought to herself, They're not even civilized enough to pretend.

"Well, Rachel, aren't you going to congratulate us, we were just married. Papa was there," Aaron said almost defensively.

"Oh, yeah? Well, I hope you'll be very happy," Rachel said in an offhand manner. Leah was silent after she had said hello to Eve, her hooded eyes revealing nothing as she went into the kitchen to talk to her mother. Rachel brought in a piece of cake wrapped in a small Turkish towel exuding a strong odor of mothballs, and began to unwrap it on the table. She cut into it carefully, as if it were some rare delicacy, and offered around the tiny pieces in celebration. Eve took a small bite of the dusty, camphor-reeking cake, and her throat closed over it. She remembered how they kept the sponge cake wrapped in mothballs — "Keeps it fresh," her mother-in-law had said. She wanted to gag, but tried hard instead to swallow it. A glass of wine would have helped — but none was offered. She would have settled for the sweet, sticky kind they served on Friday nights. "Esther," the old man called loudly, his voice husky with tension, "where is the wine?"

Neva, Ben's wife, came in on her way upstairs, her arms full of groceries. She looked frazzled, but red-cheeked and pretty, with her wide, generous mouth and teeth like summer corn — large, even kernels, faintly yellow. Eve was relieved. She always felt a little more comfortable with Neva and Bennie than the others. Neva was six months pregnant with her second child. Eve looked at Neva's swollen belly and then at her own flat, innocent-looking stomach and felt somehow depleted; but she always felt unsexed in the presence of Neva's insistent sensuality.

"Hey, congratulations," Neva said. "So you did it? Well, that's swell, really swell." She went over to Eve and kissed her shyly. Eve was thankful for the attention, however slight. "What's going on here? No celebration, I can see that! Where's everyone?" She went on, not waiting or even expecting an answer. "Well, Papa! No wine, nothing prepared here for them? Disgusting," she said. She passed into the kitchen where the women were huddled. Eve heard a furtive, mumbled conversation in Yiddish and then Neva emerged, forcing a bright smile. She said quietly, "Come on upstairs with me, you two, let's have a little celebration. Ben is home, he doesn't go to work till much later. We'll have some wine to wash down the mothball cake," she said loudly, and laughed.

It was funny how much she sounded like her husband, Bennie, Eve thought. Bawdy, irreverent — is that what must happen in marriage, a couple knit together like a healed wound, mannerisms almost indiscernible from each other? Aaron gave her a sign to go on ahead with Neva, he would join them soon. Eve looked disappointed, but she picked up one of the bulging packages and followed her new sister-in-law up the stairs gratefully, the spicy smell of cat dung strong in her nostrils.

They were seated at the table alone; Ben was sleeping in the bedroom.

Neva said, "Not much of a wedding day for you, is it? Well,

don't worry, kid, neither was mine. Weddings are usually over-rated, anyway." Digging into one of the brown paper bags, she came up with a can of beer. "Here, let's us drink to it anyway," Neva said, and pushed a can toward her.

Eve declined with embarrassment. She was ashamed to tell her that beer made her ill, that she considered it a truck driver's drink. "But Leah and Rachel, did you see how hostile they were? They wouldn't even talk to me, and his mother was worse, even worse."

"Don't pay any attention to those two witches," Neva continued. "They're just jealous. You got their baby brother, and they're afraid you might take their meal ticket away."

Marvin, her four-year-old son, came into the room, a dark, tousle-headed, sulky little boy. "Can I have three cents for some ices, Ma?" he asked. Neva got up and gave him the three cents from a broken china cup on the sideboard and sat down again, heavily.

Eve didn't say anything for a minute. Then she said, "What I don't understand is why he shivers so for them. Why does he al-ways knuckle under to his mother like that, take *their* part? He's different with her, he shows her more tenderness than he ever does with me."

"Well, he's a bit of a mama's boy still, all them women doin' for him, slobbering over him all the time. You know how it is, they kind of spoiled him."

"But he's supposed to love me, why do you suppose he never takes my part, always chooses them. Where is he now, on our wedding day? He's down there with *them!*" And I'm hiding out up here, she thought, but refrained from saying it.

"He feels sorry for the old lady," Neva said. "Listen, he's seen her working like a horse all her life. The old man don't pay much atten-tion to her; they let her haul a ten-pound sack of potatoes up to the attic every month. You think she'd wait till one of the men was back, but not her, she wouldn't ask them. She believes that women are put on this earth to wait on men hand and foot, and that's what she does. She's spoiled all the boys, you know that, and those girls — those two *klutzes* down there — they hate her guts 'cause she never gave them the right time! Everything was for the sons." She brushed a strand of black hair from her forehead, tilted the can sharply to extract the last drop, and continued in her soft, lackadaisical way. "Especially your Aaron. She dotes on him and makes no bones about it, either. Now the old man, he's a little softer than her, it was him that fought for Leah when she married that dope downstairs; if it had been up to Esther, she wouldn't have let either one in the house, not for anything."

"Maybe Leah'dve been better off," Eve said.

"Well, this way at least she's got a roof over her head and three meals; she can always go downstairs and freeload off of them. I don't know what that girl would have done otherwise." She pronounced girl "goil." Her shibboleths annoyed Eve, made her wince, although she appreciated Neva's openness.

"Why? She works, doesn't she?"

"Yeah, but only 'cause she has to. If not, there wouldn't be enough for everything and to take care of the kid. Why, she treats him like he's a king, nothin's too good for that kid."

"She surely hates me, that's all I know," Eve said, without anger, matter-of-factly.

"Ah, forget her. She hates everybody." Then, as if summing up, she said, "Ya gotta get outa this goddamn place, get yourself a cute little place somewhere else. Maybe Flatbush or somethin'. Wish to hell *I* could," she mumbled, as if thinking aloud. "But it'll never happen, no never. If Bennie's got money in this dump, I'll live and die here, I know that."

SHORTLY AFTER their marriage Eve and Aaron did rent a small apartment in Flatbush. It was unpretentious and inexpensive; Aaron was still saving for equity. And for posterity too, Eve thought, but she was happier and more contented than she had been in years. She was still confused at times by Aaron. She found it difficult to understand a love that could be shared so inequitably with ambition, but she was able to sublimate her longings somewhat by throwing herself wholly and completely into her studies now. She was excited about returning to college. She had only taken a leave of absence. Financial problems, she had told them — the understatement of a lifetime. So she was overjoyed at the prospect of returning to an academic environment, the only one where she felt truly at home. There, among admiring peers, she could foster her illusions of gentility, which she could not do at home alone while Aaron worked nights, and not even when she was in his arms. But one of the benefits of marriage, she told herself, was the great luxury of not owing petty sums left and right, of not agonizing over the $5.95 for a pair of shoes, or having to make a decision between a pair of much-needed bedroom slippers and a longed-for box of chocolates. Then the most glorious bonus of all — once in a while, once in a great while, there might be a five-dollar bill siphoned off somewhere, craftily, guiltily, but *there* nonetheless, crisp and green as spring, to send to Mama. At least she *hoped* Mama would get it. She had the terrible sinking feeling that even if Mama opened the letter first she would only turn it over to "him."

For two years she was completely happy. There was even a certain pride in being the only Mrs. in the school. She graduated from Hunter College in 1927, cum laude, with special honors in Latin and Greek — and two months pregnant.

She thought about the baby in waves of excitement that washed over her, making her just a little giddy. Her first child — she hoped it would be a boy. Aaron wanted a son. She would name it after her father, Eliah, though somehow that name just didn't fit with Abel. Eliah Abel — ugh! No lilt, no iambic pentameter.

Everywhere that Aaron went on his nightly rounds they were dancing the fox trot to the new sounds of jazz and the sweeter sounds of swing. The lovely ballads of a young New Yorker named George Gershwin filled the air and flooded the airwaves. Aaron found himself whistling the catchy melodies everywhere, almost compulsively, sometimes even at four o'clock in the morning while undressing. Eve would see him in the half-light of dawn, standing in his suspenders in front of her hard-won bureau, emptying his pockets with a jangling clatter and whistling softly to himself, "Someone to Watch over Me." Other times he'd croon these songs to her intensely, as he hunched up his shoulders and whirled her around in his arms in imitation of the latest dance. He was light on his feet and loved to dance, but it was getting difficult to lead her now because of her increasing bulk. "Button up your overcoat," he sang to her, laughing as he tried in vain to close her coat or jacket.

In the eighth month of her pregnancy, Aaron's father, Joseph, died of a massive stroke. He was seventy-six, had never been sick a day in his life, all the family said proudly. It had happened on an evening like all the other evenings before it, sitting at the table in the parlor where he had sat for thirty years, with his glass of steaming tea, and his tired dreams, the *Jewish Daily Forward* unraveled at his feet. The snow blotted out the grinding sounds of the chained wheels as the ambulance took the body away. He had died as he had lived, proudly as *Joseph Abelson*, always refusing to delete the "son" from his name. Now only Rachel remained an Abelson.

The baby girl, Jenna, born a month later in December, was named for Joseph. The year 1927 had burned itself out early and died somewhere in August with the Sacco and Vanzetti murders, so that December seemed already the new year. While the new life somehow filled the gap left by the old, their joy had been tempered. Besides, it wasn't a son, and Aaron was disappointed; he would have called him Joseph. For Eve, the shock of losing her "only friend at court," as she called Papa, had probably brought on the premature delivery, and for the first weeks of life the tiny baby slept in a drawer of the dresser until the crib arrived.

A few years later, over Aaron's usual objections to any price increase, they moved to a larger apartment with a second bedroom, in the Heights, a more fashionable section of Brooklyn. Clinton and Joralemon Street was barely a block from the melancholy harbor, with its brackish odors and rotting quays, and a block up the street from the apartment house where a Filipino butler had murdered his boss with a machete. Eve was sold on the romance of the neighborhood — she loved it! Pierpont Street, Montague Street — scion's names, names to reckon with. Some of the original families still lived there in dignified seclusion behind the imposing, green-garnished brownstone facades.

Each Friday night guilt propelled Aaron back to the house on Harrison Avenue to light the *Shabbes* candles, to break the *challeh* his mother baked especially for him, and carefully skim from the soup the pinfeathers that were becoming more plentiful each year as her eyesight grew dimmer. His mother petted and fondled him as if he were a lover, gazing adoringly into his eyes, kissing his hands. On these evenings he went alone. Eve would not accompany him. She couldn't sit there and watch that. Besides, she knew she wasn't welcome — her mother-in-law wanted to be alone with her son. Once in a while she did meet her sister-in-law, Neva, downtown for shopping. They'd have lunch at the A and S Department Store. They had been pregnant at the same time, Eve with her first child, Neva with her third, another boy, and they had given birth within weeks of one another.

Aaron was unaware that guilt had become a generating force in his life. He felt guilty about his choice of wife — it had offended his mother; about his devotion to his mother — it offended his wife. He didn't spend enough time with his wife and children, he should have finished law school, shouldn't be making big money while everyone else was losing theirs. In fact, as he made his rounds, skimming the glamour spots of New York, looking for new business, he became sharply aware of the contradictions of his time, the clear black and white realities. While chanteuses sang in the cocktail lounges of the rich, the apple sellers were singing their monotonous chants outside on the street, and sleek debutantes were tea dancing at the Ambassador, while the less fortunate were shuffling to a different tune on the bread lines. Even the very business that had drawn him in, tipping, that twilight zone of payment, was heavily associated with guilt. He realized that people really tipped only out of social pressures, out of fear of disapproval. Nevertheless, the concessions were a business ideally suited to his natural impatience; no waiting long months for payment or chasing around to collect receivables. The sole commodity was money, silver, flowing over the counter every night like white wine, just cash and carry home.

Summers passed. Business slacked off for Aaron in the summers, no coats and hats. Another winter passed, the time going quickly for Eve in the gentle pursuits of new motherhood and the persistent hum of the radio, a constant and benign companion. She was adjusting to the pace of the decade more gracefully than she had to the twenties that had just roared by, leaving her feeling somehow depleted. Another winter passed, and in 1931 another baby was born, this time a boy. Eve named him for her father, Eliah, but fancified it a bit by combining it with her own and called him Evan. It had a nice sound with Abel, she thought, and reminded her of a favorite young Shakespearean actor, Maurice Evans. For a time life seemed sweetly fulfilled, though always a little uncertain, like the skip of a heartbeat.

Yes, she was beginning to feel that she could handle her life, at least for the present. The children filled her with a sense of accomplishment and a feeling of personal worth that none of her past school successes had been able to furnish, though it was her nature to feel that whatever she had, there was always something missing from her life, something or someone around her who sounded a minor chord of imperfection.

A new conservatism became apparent, even in the fashions of the day. There was a humble, sincere, reticent quality about the

early thirties. Many women were still wearing their hair short, in
soft and gentle waves, but Eve's was long, and she wore it madonna-
style, caught at the neck in a knot, secured by dozens of tiny hair-
pins. The dresses were easy-waisted, often mauves, grays, or in-
offensive small prints, worn at a discreet length. Even the men
wore their hair neatly side-parted, softly natural, not slicked down
with Vaseline, in the Valentino style so popular only a few years
before. Their suits, soft and narrow, in dun colors, with vests, lent a
look of sincerity to the struggling businessman, almost as if to cancel
out the coruscating memories of the recent overindulgences. The
whole low-keyed atmosphere seemed a sort of collective penance,
tentative, nebulous, in tune with the depression.

Aaron held on for dear life to the money he was making. Almost
anything Eve got came as a result of ferocious haggling. Anything
that he considered an unnecessary luxury, such as furniture or an
extra bedroom for a second child, took months of bitter campaign-
ing on Eve's part. His parents' *shtetel* in Vilna that he never saw, his
own childhood memories of the Lower East Side, the last five years
of the country's disappointed dreams, haunted him, so that he felt
shaped by defeat and terrified of failure. Eventually Eve had to
lay out the money for the furnishings from her *Lusitania* nest egg.
Perversely, he returned it to her almost immediately.

The climate of brotherhood was in the air. So many were in
the same sinking boat, and the fraternal tempo of the times spelled
itself out in what seemed like one large game of political anagrams,
the alphabetical jumble of FDR's reconstruction projects — C.C.C.,
N.R.A., W.P.A., P.W.A. Until the big nightclub boom began
around 1935, fraternal orders, like the Elks' Club, were among the
most popular centers of social life.

Later on when Aaron looked back, he liked to say that it had
been rough sledding in those years, but Eve said he had been lucky
right from the start, had always been lucky, and she had brought
him some of that luck in the form of the ten thousand dollars he'd
needed to make a start.

Sometimes they entertained at home at the little apartment on
Clinton Street, mostly Eve's friends, whom Aaron considered

scholarly and pedantic. They were often teachers, when employed, sometimes considered radical, for those times anyway. There were even one or two avowed anarchists who talked incessantly about subjects that were Greek to Aaron, as he liked to say. Some of them even spouted quotations in that ancient, lofty language.

One evening Eve had invited a small, select group to a Dickens party in honor of the writer's birthday. The apartment looked cozy; a roaring fire crackled in the usually neglected fireplace, in a punch bowl of eggnog dusted with nutmeg there floated clouds of whipped cream. She planned readings from her favorite *Dombey and Son* and had written a clever little quiz game on the author's works. Eve talked about nothing else for days in advance. She was almost her old self again, enthusiastic, gay, vivacious, bursting with ideas, the way Aaron remembered her from their high-school courtship days. They had invited four couples, among them the Colebergs, who were Ethical Culturists and never let you forget it for a moment. Eve was fond of the husband. He taught humanities at De Witt Clinton High School in the Bronx. Aaron's view was that "he was pink and she was mousy." As the evening wore on, they were all getting silly on champagne, except for Aaron, who felt left out — he "didn't touch the stuff." They were laughing a lot about politics, the times, making jokes about the depression, the Roosevelts.

"Eleanor could have started the whole depression by herself with those hats she wears," Eve said. The Colebergs roared.

Somewhere in the middle of the evening Jennie got out of her crib and began mingling with the guests. Everybody was laughing and talking so intensely they hardly noticed. In a final bid for attention she began crawling around the floor, near the guests' feet.

Archie Coleberg wore white cotton socks, slack at the ankles and sagging down into his scuffed brown shoes. In her four year old's piping voice Jennie said, "Your socks are falling down. Why are they white? My daddy never wears white socks. You must be poor."

Aaron gulped, laughed nervously, and uncrossed his legs, which revealed well-gartered black silk hose. Coleberg rose up in fury, saying, "I don't blame the child, she's only repeating what she hears at home, what she's heard from her parents. I suppose that in your secret hearts you consider me a Communist. The trouble with you is that you are too busy getting and spending to recognize a true idealist when you meet one."

Coleberg took his wife firmly by the arm (her complexion had turned the color of weak tea) and headed for the door, leaving Aaron murmuring defensively, "After all she's just a baby." Eve, however, was unable to leave it at that, and a bitter fight ensued. She said loudly that if they were that sort of friends she was glad to be rid of them. The party broke up in a flurry of embarrassment and confusion. It had been the first real party Eve had had in years, since she was married, in fact. With a husband who worked nights, her social life was dwindling. She had little time for her old enthusiasms. She told herself that the children were all she really needed.

She stooped down and grabbed up the child, jollying her wildly in her arms, gliding and swaying, holding the tiny hand aloft in the manner of social dancing, her teeth clenched with the intensity of the moment, her eyes spilling over tears into the honey dampness of her baby's hair. At first Jennie giggled with joy, but then she began to cry with terror.

PAULINE LEVINSON regarded herself in the three-way mirror in Eve's bedroom and, all things considered, she was quite satisfied that she had captured the flapper look almost to perfection. She made one last slumberous face, rather like Garbo, she thought, though she had much more the look and style of Clara Bow. At seventeen, Eve's only remaining sister was beautiful and sullen. Her heavily mascaraed green eyes looked out on a world that already seemed to have lost its luster. Her lips were carefully painted cupid's bows, to which she kept savagely applying lipstick, tirelessly through the day with a satisfied, sensuous absorption, licking her lips and peering lovingly into her mirror. She relied heavily on her mirror because, unlike her sister, she hadn't grown up in a circle of admiring eyes. Pauline had grown up in the confusion that surrounded her after her father's death, so she glanced at her reflection every chance she could, and she swallowed compliments like bonbons, unable to satisfy her craving for more. She faintly remembered that Papa had looked at her sometimes approvingly, but she wasn't really sure. She only seemed to remember him with his hand cupped around her sister Eve's cherubic face. Sometimes, even now, she thought she caught the faint scent of his cologne, English Lyme. The very name tantalized her like the odor, elusive, elegant, and faintly foreign.

Her small body was more exaggerated than her sister's, more obvious, perhaps because of her choice of clothing, though her nonexistent finances didn't allow her much leverage and usually she wore Eve's leftovers, which she would redecorate to her own taste, a taste somewhat more flamboyant than her sister's.

She sauntered into the living room and plumped herself down on the sofa that doubled as her bed. She began picking the red polish off her fingernails, Passion Pomegranate, from Woolworth's.

"You know this sofa's awful hard for sleeping," Pauline said, fidgeting restlessly.

"If there was room, I'd put a bed in the children's room for you, but there isn't an extra inch of space in there," Eve replied.

"I don't want to sleep in with the kids, I'm just no good for a nursemaid."

"Well, what are you good for besides getting yourself into trouble?" Eve answered irritably. She had never really cared for this sister no matter how much she tried. It made her feel guilty and her guilt angered her. But she couldn't seem to generate any sibling warmth or real affection, the way she had felt about "dear

Freddie." Eve had never really recovered from the shock of her invalid sister's death. She had loved her so, had experienced such a sense of loss, a hollowness in her life that nothing could ameliorate, not even the children, though they had helped. She blamed her mother unconsciously and considered it an unnecessary tragedy, born out of ignorance and possibly even neglect.

"Anyway, you've got to get up early because you're going to school. You're going to finish high school if it's the last thing you do; otherwise you can go back to Mama and 'him.'"

"I'd die first." Pauline looked at her sister out of the corners of her almond-shaped eyes to calculate the effect of her words. Usually she could count on her sister's sympathy where Lubowitz was concerned.

She had been staying with Eve and Aaron almost three months now, ever since she had run away from home, such as it was, in California. She had been miserable there with them, terrified of Lubowitz's black rages. Since Freddie had died, her mother seemed wrapped up in the baby, and Pauline was left to drift erratically between school and work. One week her mother would tell her she must go to school, the next she'd complain to her that there was nothing to eat — she'd have to get a job. So she had run away. She wasn't really sure where she was going, but she knew Eve well enough to know that she'd never turn her away. She had mixed feelings about Eve even now, Daddy's darling, everyone's favorite; she envied her sister's present life, and yet, she didn't. She felt that there was something more out there for her besides taking care of a man and kids. She thought that her sister probably felt the same way, but that she was trapped, and after all of that fancy education, her dreams of Hollywood and the movies. Pauline didn't know exactly what it was she wanted, she hadn't Eve's background, that hunger to learn — "to burst joy's grape against the palate fine." Pauline's involvement was largely with herself. What good had all that fine education done for Eve, she rationalized. She had wound up like every other woman — with a sink and an ironing board and a couple of screaming kids. Of course, Eve wasn't poor anymore, Pauline was certain of that. Aaron, no matter how parsimonious he was in some ways, always exuded an air of luxury; he sported his success as he did his latest car, a long green Cord convertible. But she couldn't see what Eve was getting out of Aaron's growing success and his money. It seemed to be just a lot of time with the children and long, lonely nights.

As for herself, the only money of her own that she ever owned outright was two hundred and fifty dollars, her half of the second-prize money she'd won in the dance marathon a year ago in Glendale. It had been worth the fourteen-day ordeal and later the scene with her stepfather when she refused to hand over the money or to "share it with the family," as he had so quaintly put it. She had kept it on her at all times, carefully folded and rubber-banded and tucked between her breasts, giving her already full bosom an added dimension. Even at night, she slept with it in her brassiere.

She had to admit that in one way she had enjoyed the marathon; for those fourteen days she had felt as though she belonged somewhere. Dick Daylin, her partner, had been so supportive and cheerful throughout it all, the whole ordeal. She even made friends with some of the other girls. Once they staggered over the threshold of the ballroom into the cool, sterile atmosphere of the locker room, the fierce competition ceased and they became allies, conspiratorial chummy.

"Looky, looky, looky, watch those feet fly. These kids are really great, dancing their hearts out," the night announcer's voice would slip through the megaphone, mellow and slightly nasal. No, she'd never forget it. When she went to bed and closed her eyes, sometimes she still saw the giant mirrored ball gyrating on its stem like a garish art deco world in miniature.

She wondered idly what had happened to Dick Daylin. He was a sweet boy. She had liked him a little — of course that was before the marathon.

They had begun by dipping and weaving and doing all manner of dazzling steps to beguile the judges, Pauline's tiny spiked heels looking strangely like Minnie Mouse shoes, cartoon feet. She tried in vain to catch her reflection in the overhead mosaic-mirrored ball, but it was fractioned into a million tiny prisms of Pauline and Dick, none large enough for her to admire. Later, their dancing became less ambitious, and after six days, she was satisfied just to be standing on her feet (or more often, Dick's) and be dragged around the floor like Raggedy Ann, the naturally pained expression in her eyes exaggerated. By this time, she loathed Dick, prayed with what was left of her senses that she would never have to see his pasty blonde face again. She couldn't understand how she ever had thought it attractive. It looked to her like one of those English sticky buns she remembered from her childhood. The thought of having to split the prize money with him was keeping her going on sheer hysteria alone. She had counted on first prize, had mentally spent the money a hundred times before she ever set foot in the giant dance palace. She saw herself on buses and trains — out of there, away from *them*, wearing gorgeous clothes, sitting in nightclubs and dimly lit cafés, smoking with a gold cigarette holder, wearing a hat with a little jet veil over her mascaraed eyes — dancing to Paul Whiteman's orchestra.

10

WITH A FALSE CALM, Aaron stood on the winding staircase in the Elks' Club on Pierpont Street. He regarded the ornate ormolu railing with its elk's head finials dispassionately. His mind was racing faster than his heart. He was having second thoughts about the closed bid he had submitted in writing some hours before for the concessions at this prestigious fraternal order. Some ten or so other concessionaires still lingered on, pacing restlessly on the floor above or, like Aaron, lining the staircase in anticipation. After talking with some of the others, he realized that his bid had been well below the average, and his heart sank. He could have offered more and it would have been a worthwhile investment to have the Elks' concessions but it was 1931 and he had seen what could happen to fortunes, especially if there was no nest egg put aside. He didn't believe in the stock market. It wasn't tangible enough for him. He had gotten used to an immediate exchange of money, ready cash in his hand, crisp and reassuring, or soiled and wilted, but reassuring nevertheless. You've got to spend money to make money, he knew that by heart. How could he have been so foolish about the bid? At this moment he hated himself and his frightened, immigrant-bred insecurities. He felt a sudden surge of anger at his father with his little tailor shop, his shabby struggles; the petty thinking had rubbed off.

Joe Ardsley, managing director of the Brooklyn Heights branch of the Elks' Club, emerged from one of the upstairs rooms with the announcement that the concession had been awarded to Jim Mc-Hugh, and disappeared again. Aaron looked quickly to see if Mc-Hugh was anywhere around — he knew him by sight only — but he wasn't there, hadn't even bothered to wait. He couldn't have sent anyone, as all bids had to be presented in person. He must have been pretty damned sure of his number. Maybe he was tipped off, Aaron thought. But McHugh was small potatoes, a two-bit-candy butcher with a few little concessions scattered here and there, nothing that amounted to anything — candy counters in two nearby theaters, a few hatchecks in Brooklyn.

Aaron dug in his pocket and pulled out his gold pen. He carefully jotted down two telephone numbers on a small pad, his home and the checkroom at Webster's Hall. He closed it in the palm of his hand. The others had left, mumbling their disappointment, complaining quietly.

He remained on the stairs alone now. Ardsley had to come down sooner or later, unless there was some sort of back staircase that he had missed, Aaron thought with a sickening thud. A door closed with a click and Ardsley, tall and slim, was on the landing. He ran down the steps, loose-kneed, relaxed, until he came abreast of

Aaron, who, getting right in step with him like a dancer, continued the descent.

"How much did it go for?" Aaron asked casually.

"Ten thousand," he answered.

Without even the lightest indrawing of breath, Aaron said, "Well, listen, if for any reason it doesn't go through, or McHugh backs out, I'll meet his bid. Just call me. I can be reached at one or the other of these numbers."

Joe Ardsley took it from his hand, didn't glance at it, and with a brief thank you, said, "Good-bye, Abel."

Aaron was pleased that he knew his name, but he doubted that there was much hope. He wanted it badly, so badly he could taste it, and now he could pay for it. He could use Eve's money from the *Lusitania*. She still had the ten thousand sitting in the bank doing nothing. He could triple it within a year if he had the Elks' concession, and pay her back with interest.

He stepped outside and walked briskly toward his car. The day seemed washed in the candid blue of the sky on this ordinary Tuesday. In the distance he could see pieces of the jagged Manhattan skyline, still innocent of the bronze and glass clutter that was yet to come.

Three days later, on a Saturday evening, Aaron, dressed only in suspenders and a freshly ironed shirt, walked restlessly from the living room to the bedroom and back again, all the while talking to Eve between the incessant intrusion of the telephone. Its persistent ring seemed to follow her like a pulsing red light, frazzling her nerves. Weekend evenings were particularly long and lonely for Eve. Aaron spent most of Saturday and Sunday in his robe, on the phone, and when the evening came he began the ritual of careful shaving, pomading, and dressing. Buttoning his spats had become almost a symbolic gesture, a signal that their time together, no matter how short, was at an end. Once he was dressed, the gap between them seemed to widen.

They had been arguing about Pauline again — her future. Most of their time together was either spent in arguing or reconciling. In fact, Aaron could not easily summon to his mind a quiet time between them in years. Once again the phone rang sharply. Aaron absorbed the downward look of disapproval on Eve's face, but, as always, welcomed the familiar ring, not only because of the excitement of expectation, but because it was a convenient avenue of escape.

It was Joe Ardsley. Aaron's heart was beating in his ears, but he kept his voice smooth . . . "Yes, Joe, how are you?" Joe got right to the point.

"Look, Abel, did you mean what you said the other day, about matching the bid?"

"Yeah, sure," Aaron said.

"Well then, you've got it," Ardsley said matter-of-factly, "ten Gs."

"Fine, great, "Aaron said incredulously. "But what happened to McHugh?"

"He didn't want to spring for building the coatracks, thought that was included in the deal, he *said*."

Jeeze, what a cheap bum, Aaron thought to himself. Didn't he figure he could have paid for that from the first month's take? These guys were small potatoes, they just didn't understand the potential, that's why they'd never make it big in this business.

"How's Monday for you, Abel?"

"Okay."

"Well then, see you in my office at 10:30 in the morning," and before Aaron could breathe his thanks, Ardsley had hung up.

He was chuckling as he went in to find Eve. He was wreathed in smiles as he whirled her around in his arms, a habit he indulged in moments of elation.

"Evie, Baby, we're gonna be rich, wait and see. Your ten thousand dollars is going to make me a millionaire — then I'll be able to buy you everything, everything you've always wanted. Hey, you know that fancy store you like, that one with the violet-colored boxes and the purple ladies on 'em. Well, you'll buy all your clothes there, what do you think about that?"

At first she did not answer; then she said, "I never promised you that money. It's my only little independence."

Aaron looked at her askance, he wondered if she were joking. "But this is it, my big chance, the one I've always talked about. You'll get it back, with interest, you'll see." She was seized by a sudden panic. With the money in his hands she could no longer hold herself separate from him. A sense of impending doom enveloped her. She was his prisoner.

《 11 》

J ENNIE RODE HER TRICYCLE round and round the tiny living room in concentric circles. She kept singing the same two bars of music, "Wintergreen for President." Her father had been whistling it ever since he and Eve had seen the hit Broadway musical *Of Thee I Sing*. The five atonal notes, sung over and over again, were getting louder and louder, as if to drown out the ugly noise of her parents' arguing. Not that the children were unused to the raised, angry voices of their parents — only this time it seemed different, louder than usual.

"That's typical of you, everything behind my back. You're so damned sneaky," Eve said bitterly.

"What could I do? Pauline came to me, she begged me."

"What you could have done was to have discussed it with me, but you never include me in anything, even when it directly involves me — never!"

"Eve, she was afraid to go to you."

"But she wasn't afraid to come to me when she needed me, was she? She was only afraid she couldn't have her own way. So behind my back you plot with my own sister to rob her of an education, and at seventeen to stick her in the checkrooms with all the whores and tramps!"

"Jeeze, you make me sound like some kind of a white slaver or something. Oh, for Christ's sake, Eve, wake up — she's no lily, and she's certainly no student. She was cutting school most of the time when you *thought* she was there; besides, she needs the money."

"What does she need money for? We give her everything she needs."

"Yeah, I know, but you don't let her forget it, and she has to feel more independent. She doesn't like you telling her what to do."

"Of course she doesn't, because she's headstrong and rebellious, and — for God's sake, Aaron, I promised Mama I'd look after her . . ."

"Well, that's more than your mother did! Anyway, you've got your own family to worry about now. There's me and the kids, remember?"

"You! That's a laugh. When are you ever here? Anyway, she's got more of a chance with me than with Mama, you'll admit that much, won't you? What with a small child on her hands at *her* age, and on top of everything, no money coming in."

Aaron didn't like being reminded about the humiliating reality of her family. Eve continued doggedly, "That lazy son of a bitch won't or can't keep any kind of a job."

"I thought he fixes things," Aaron mumbled.

"Yeah, first he breaks them, then he tries to fix them, but don't count on it," she said bitterly. "Oh God, the whole thing is a mess, it's so degrading, there's no peace for me anywhere." She was crying a little now. But a moment later she returned to the subject with fresh vigor. "So what is she going to do with the extra money?"

"What extra money?" Aaron asked. "There won't be anything left over after she pays her share of the room rent, food, clothes. She's got to look good in this kind of a job." Aaron had to be careful not to assail Eve's generosity, no matter how misguided, and he had to force himself not to tell her that Pauline needed some clothes of her own. Eve was white with fury now.

"What do you mean, rent, food, clothes? Where is she going?"

"Eve," Aaron said placatingly, "didn't you just throw her out last week? This is the third time in a month you've thrown her out. You won't let her stay unless she finishes school, and that looks hopeless. Anyway, she can't stay with us indefinitely, she's been here almost nine months and she doesn't want to stay any longer."

"What are you, her self-appointed spokesman or something?" Eve asked, her anger rising again. "What's wrong with her finishing school? She's only seventeen. I don't need my sister tainted by the checkrooms. Because you figure she'll work cheap, because she's beautiful and broke — and stupid — you exploit her. Oh it's a good deal for you all right — "

"Jesus," Aaron laughed uncomfortably. "There you go, making me sound like a white slaver again."

"Well?" said Eve indignantly.

"There are thousands of girls looking for jobs today," he murmured defensively. "Oh, you know she doesn't get along with you, she just aggravates you."

"That's because you're always there manipulating behind the scenes — You planned this whole thing behind my back. You've got it all figured out already, where she's going to work, and where she's going to live." She pulled at the skin on her face now and began to wring her hands.

"Well, I could use a girl out at the Elks' Club in White Plains, and it's nicer for her out there than working in the city joints. The girls room in a boarding house nearby. Maybe I can fix her up with a roommate, another kid who works for me."

"I'm not interested in your fixing her up with those tramps, thank you."

Pauline came through the door, banging it noisily as she entered. "What's going on here? I could hear you two all the way down the hall. Why all the shouting?"

"Why?" Eve was furious and out of control. "Because you're a rebellious, ungrateful, disobedient little brat. I told you that you were going to school to graduate. That's what Mama wants, and that's what I want. Pauline," she said in a softer voice now, "we only want to help you make a life for yourself."

"I don't give a damn what you want," she said.

"Well, if you don't give a damn about me, the only family you've got left, you can get the hell out of here and don't come back. I wash my hands of you."

"You washed your hands of everybody a long time ago," Pauline said bitterly.

"I did, did I? Who the hell do you think has been supporting you and Jules, yes, *and* Mama these last few years?"

"Your husband, Aaron," she screamed, "that's who!"

"Yeah, thanks to my money that I gave him from the *Lusitania*."

"Well, nobody'll have to support me any longer, 'cause I'm going to work. I'm getting out of here."

"Who'd give you a job? Only Aaron, and that's because he's a sneak." Eve ran over as if to grab her. Aaron intercepted and managed to pull the two sisters apart. "Wintergreen for President," Jennie shrilled loudly, riding her bike in frenzied circles like a puppy chasing its tail. No one seemed to notice.

"Keep that sister of mine the hell out of here. I don't want to see that pouty face anywhere near me ever again," Eve said. She began throwing Pauline's dresses and possessions on the floor haphazardly. "Who took you in when that rotten Lubowitz threw you out, who cooked your meals, made you a home alongside of my own children? Here, even this," she picked up a discarded dress, "even the clothes on your back . . ."

Pauline snatched at the dress that Eve was shaking at her. "I'm just not cut out like you, Eve. I don't care about school. I hate it. That school is dirty and run-down and loaded with niggers!"

"Maybe we can get you into a different district school. Let me try, let's see," Eve said, desperate in defeat.

"Oh, you never give up! Why don't you mind your own damn business! What do you care if I want to work for a living? I don't want all of life to pass me by, like it's doing to you."

"You think that if you don't sink low, wallow in filth, in garbage, that you're not living, huh?"

"Well, listen, you're just as bad," Pauline answered, "because you're living off that dirty money, those 'ill-gotten gains,' as you would say, and living pretty good, I might add. That doesn't bother you, does it?"

In a somewhat quieter voice Eve said, "I have two children, have I got a choice? But *you* have, you don't need to get involved with him. Nothing good ever comes of getting involved with him." She seemed to have forgotten that Aaron was there — maybe she didn't care.

He began to laugh jerkily, nervously at first, then hysterically, his whole body was shaking, out of control. His face grew red, but he could not stop the spasms.

"You know you're something," he said, between gasps of laughter. "You're really something. How did I get to be the villain here? What the hell did I do? I just offered your sister a job after she asked me for one. I'm working like a dog, day and night; I don't have time to sleep," and then he dissolved into a fresh fit of laughter, saliva dribbling down the front of his shirt, but he couldn't seem to stop. Eve ignored him.

Pauline was not to be consoled. "That's the last time you'll throw me out! She thinks she can throw me out every Monday and Tuesday!" She was mumbling, as if to keep herself at a pitch.

Eve, trembling visibly, went into the bedroom and slammed the door. She turned the key and locked herself in.

"Christ," Aaron said, barely recovering himself. "She does that all the time, doesn't mean a thing, but it's goddamn annoying," still spluttering a last few drops of saliva. "Yeah, damned annoying." He was talking to himself now, and giggling in spurts, his eyes wet with tears.

Pauline really had no one to go to but Aaron for help. She hadn't exactly planned to leave Eve. No, she had planned to continue, if it was possible, to live with Eve and Aaron, and do exactly what she had been doing before, secretly. Nothing during the day, or sleeping as late as she could safely get away with, and moonlighting nights for Aaron, filling in as a checkroom or cigarette girl wherever or whenever he needed her. The only trouble was that she was achingly tired during the day from standing on her feet all night, and it was becoming increasingly difficult to fool Eve about school. She had told her that she was on the later shift at school, which meant she didn't have to be there until after lunch, but even so, when Eve began catching her coming home nights almost as late as Aaron, and noticed the absence of homework or school talk or friends, she called the school and found that Pauline had not been there in months. Well, the hell with that, Pauline thought. I'm not going to that kids' school anymore. I've had enough of it — I'm educated enough to know that being bored to death in the dirty, urine-smelling halls of Uutric High, in the tail end of Brooklyn, being pawed by smart-ass kids and leered at by niggers isn't going to change my life any. No, that's something I'll just have to do all by myself. She thought, I'm glad that bitch threw me out. She made the decision for me, in a way.

*

Pauline heaved her suitcase up on the bed of the small, bare room in the White Plains boarding house, paid for in advance by Abel Enterprises. She patted her hair nervously in the mirror. She thought she looked peaked, nervous, strained; but that was crazy — she was doing what she wanted now. That was all that counted; she was happy, a free spirit for the first time in her life. Free from Eve, from Mama, Lubowitz, the bitter memory of her dear sister, and then on top of everything, the humiliation of a bastard baby brother. No, it was asking too much.

She opened the closet to hang up the bits and pieces she had salvaged, and was overcome with the cloying scent of cheap perfume. The pitiful inadequacy of her own wardrobe struck her now as she gazed in awe at the enormous profusion of colors and styles, jammed tightly together. A rush of envy for this other girl, whoever she was, washed over her and rendered her suddenly helpless, immobile. She sat down on the little white chenille-covered bed and stared around her in confusion.

She must have dozed off. The next thing she knew it was five o'clock and the door was being opened noisily with a key.

"My God," the girl said on entering, "who're you?"

"I'm Pauline Levinson, your roommate, I guess."

"Oh, swell, nobody told me anything," the girl said in a hard voice. "My name's Martha, Martha Voccek."

"That's funny, didn't Aaron, er — I mean, Mr. Abel, tell you I was coming . . . ?"

"No, I just said he didn't. It's okay, kid," she said magnanimously.

They sized each other up quickly. Pauline thought: She's smooth-looking, maybe sixteen or seventeen, tall, slim, blondish, with those wide, Slavic cheekbones, good figure, good skin. She looks like a tough cookie, she thought; I wouldn't want to get on her bad side. They exchanged a few of the usual questions and answers, and then Martha said to Pauline, sarcastically, but with interest:

"You seem to know Aaron Abel pretty well. How come?" her voice was flat.

Pauline was about to tell her the facts, but then decided it would be better if they just came out on their own, after she had made some friends here, had gotten in the swing of it. "I've been working for him off and on for a while."

"Off and on who?" Martha said coarsely. Pauline tried to smile, but it didn't take.

Disappointment with the new job came to Pauline early. There was very little "swing" of any kind in White Plains. Just long, endless nights on aching feet, putting on and taking off heavy coats for male customers, while their wives fussed with fur coats she would never own. There were fat women, thin women, drab, tired women — the suburban housewives' big night out. Occasionally a glittering couple dropped in on the way home after a big night of theater and clubbing, dancing the new slinky fox trot in Manhattan. But these were rare sophisticates, and they were few and far between at the Elks' Club in White Plains.

Pauline couldn't help but notice how her roommate, Martha, flirted and exchanged rough jokes with the male customers. She isn't beautiful, Pauline thought, not even as pretty as I am, but there's something about her, a certain, well, sex appeal, I guess. That was it, and she had a good body, not particularly feminine or kittenish, but tall and long-legged and handsome. Her presence made a definite and pronounced statement that made the other girl recede into gray obscurity in comparison. Maybe it was her flashing dimpled smile, although her manner usually vascillated between arrogance and downright hostility.

Pauline was not pleased with this friendship thrust upon her, though friendship was not really the word for what Martha offered. It was more like a sardonic tolerance which Pauline resented. Particularly since she knew that this girl had only a sixth-grade education, and she, Pauline, was, after all, the boss's sister-in-law. She might as well have been back with Eve looking over her shoulder, breathing the hot air of disapproval down her neck. Pauline, with her fierce longing for an autonomy she did not know what to do with, found only that it brought with it vast blank spaces in her life that she did not know how to fill. She felt herself superior to her roommate, and the more superior she felt the more imperious Martha Voccek became. They talked together only occasionally, Martha always guarded in her confidences, silent and secretive, even with the other girls. Like night-blooming jasmine, she burst suddenly into life at night when men were present. Then she would become gay and effervescent, smiling often, pointedly displaying her remarkable dimples.

(12)

I N THE MIDST of the raging depression, Aaron was making more money than he'd ever seen in his young lifetime. Now he wore his gray fedora at a rakish angle, the brim snapped low over his sharp blue eyes, the ever-present spats a matching pearly gray. At nights he carried a gun, a delicate silver pistol about the size of a small woman's hand. It was a necessity, he told Eve, he had to carry a gun for protection. But he felt guilty; violence was for the *goy*, not for the son of a pious tailor.

Each morning between five and six, he collected cash from the concessions and brought it home, the nickels, dimes, and quarters neatly stacked and wrapped and marked according to denomination. Sometimes Al Carton came home with him to carry and count. He was now Aaron's general manager, working long nights until the early hours of the morning, sleeping only a scant few hours until he had to be in the law office where he clerked, at nine in the morning.

Somewhere about this time Aaron began calling everyone "crooked." Being suspicious by nature, he loved this new expression. He was surrounded by crooks, it seemed. His sister Leah who worked as his bookkeeper was crooked, well, maybe crafty would be a fairer description; his brother Bennie was crooked, well, that was true too; even his brother Herschel, the cop, was crooked ("Whoever heard of a Jewish cop, and with the name of 'Herschel' yet!" Harry's wife, Ida, said); and Joe Ardsley of the Elks' Club was a crook; only Eve wasn't crooked, and maybe Al Carton. Aaron had to admit to himself, grudgingly, that he was impressed with Al's honesty, a trait that he rarely attributed to anyone except Eve. But he felt they both exuded a faint holier-than-thou aura, and, surrounded by the purity of these two ingenuous people, he felt strangely uncomfortable, somehow culpable.

Al had remained close to them both, much to his own surprise. He had undergone a brief period of hatred for Aaron, right after the sudden surprise wedding, but that seemed like years ago now, although it was only four. He had thought that he'd have to quit his job, would be unable to tolerate Aaron's cockiness, but he had been wrong about that. He envied him Eve, true, but that was all; otherwise he pitied him a little. In Eve's presence he was still uneasy, as if she were a stranger to him now, someone he must get to know all over again.

Aaron knew the concessions were only an interim measure for Al, that he wasn't cut out for the work and didn't really have the knack for it, the spirit. He had the neat, rational mind of a lawyer, not the reckless daring of the gambler. Until now the business had been a kind of one-man operation and even Aaron, who was jealous of delegating authority, realized that he had to form an organization of sorts if he was going to build this business into the crazy patchwork of public pleasures he envisioned. Up until now, he figured, he'd taken the right steps haphazardly, accidentally, like everything else he did — it had all been unplanned, without specific design, it fell into place as if by sheer force of will. First the speakeasies, then this little coup, the Elks' Club — there he *had* a plan, and it ought to double his estimated profits.

In most places, a young colored boy would be stationed out in front of the checkroom to receive coats and hats. He would roll the coat up in a ball and stuff it unlovingly into a cubby hole, topped by the man's hat. Many a customer was seen to wince at the rude handling of his garments and they too often tipped accordingly, with much hostility and very little generosity. Yet Aaron's agreement with all the places was the same: A tip was a gratuity. They could not be made to pay for the service if they didn't want to, nor could the amount of the tip be regulated, but Aaron thought they could be encouraged, urged, even.

He brought an innovation to the heart-scratched and graffiti-worn counters of the Elks' Club coatroom. He placed a tiny sign above the checkroom that read: 25¢ FOR A HANGER. After observing the rough-and-tumble fate of the coat whose owner refused, most customers *insisted* upon hangers; so a quarter became the norm now, not just a gleam in the concessionaire's eye. Joe Ardsley never even noticed the sign until some six months after it was posted. He insisted upon its immediate removal, but Aaron was unruffled now, the precedent had been established, and that crook Joe Ardsley, who didn't want anyone else to make a living, could go screw himself. And to further encourage customers, he continued with the policy he had adopted at the speakeasies, beautiful girls in low-cut dresses.

Ah, the "speaks." They had been a crazy, heady experience. Aaron remembered clearly the sign that hung on the wall near the entrance to the Club 34. It had been placed there by the management:

DO NOT GET TOO FRIENDLY WITH THE WAITER. HIS NAME IS NEITHER CHARLIE NOR GEORGE. REMEMBER THE OLD ADAGE ABOUT FAMILIARITY BREEDING CONTEMPT.

DO NOT ASK TO PLAY THE DRUMS. THE DRUM HEADS ARE NOT AS TOUGH AS MANY ANOTHER HEAD. BESIDES, IT HAS A TENDENCY TO DISTURB THE RHYTHM.

MAKE NO REQUESTS OF THE LEADER OF THE ORCHESTRA FOR THE SONGS OF VINTAGE 1890. CROONING "SWEET ADELINE" WAS ALL RIGHT FOR YOUR GRANDDAD, BUT TIMES, ALAS, HAVE CHANGED.

PINCHING THE CIGARETTE GIRL'S CHEEK OR ASKING HER TO DANCE WITH YOU IS DECIDEDLY OUT OF ORDER. SHE IS THERE FOR THE SOLE PURPOSE OF DISPENSING CIGARS AND CIGARETTES WITH A SMILE THAT WILL BRING PROFITS TO THE CONCESSIONAIRE.

EXAMINE YOUR BILL WHEN THE WAITER PRESENTS IT. REMEMBER EVEN THEY ARE HUMAN BEINGS AND ARE LIABLE TO ERR — INTENTIONALLY OR OTHERWISE.

PLEASE DO NOT OFFER TO ESCORT THE CLOAKROOM GIRL HOME. HER HUSBAND, WHO IS AN EX-PRIZE FIGHTER, IS THERE FOR THAT PURPOSE.

He remembered how he had gotten into the speaks that year, how he had cajoled his brother Bennie into talking to one of the many

union officials who "owed him," as Bennie put it. This particular
one was a close friend of Nick the Greek, who was himself part of a
huge syndicate that numbered a string of speakeasies among their
vast enterprises. Bennie reluctantly arranged for Aaron to phone
Nick, but not until he made Aaron promise to give him a kickback,
or finder's fee, if the deal went through. Aaron was incensed, "My
own brother, for chrissakes!" he said, but he knew inwardly he
would have done exactly the same thing if the tables were turned;
after all, business was business.

Nick Scapapolous was pleasant enough to Aaron on the telephone,
but noncommittal. He said, "Tell ya the truth, Abel, I don't really
know much about these things, but I'll have somebody call ya back
who does."

"Well, okay, but remember I'd pay them for it in advance.
They're better off concentrating on the big stuff, the booze and the
rest of it all . . ."

But Nick cut in on him sharply. They didn't like being told how
to run their business, or to have the terms dictated to them by a
greenhorn punk. "Well, like I said, I'll have someone call ya," and
he hung up quickly. Aaron didn't like the idea of waiting for a call
and wished that he had asked for the guy's number; he had absolutely
no ability to wait.

A couple of weeks later, Eve answered the telephone to a man who
called himself Zaretti. She handed Aaron the phone distractedly.
She was generally disinterested in his business calls; they were simply
petty annoyances to her and she disdained the caliber of men her
husband consorted with. Actually, Joe Zaretti was only a hoodlum,
a punk hireling who fronted for some of the big boys, whom Aaron
never got to meet.

*

The split was half-and-half, and that was something he wasn't
used to, and the other thing that bothered him was those big monkeys
telling him how to get more tips out of the suckers.

"Use beautiful girls," Zaretti told him. "Ya know, with big tits.
Put 'em in costumes, ya know, like the chorus girls. Lots of legs

showing, that'll get 'em every time. None of them college boys in our joints, you understand? If you need girls, I'll send some around, ya can look 'em over," he added solicitously. Aaron figured maybe this was out of his league. Beautiful girls would demand big salaries. He had paid the boys next to nothing. But the idea on the whole had a certain appeal, he had to admit. It had style and he liked style.

As it turned out, he wasn't able to make much money in the speakeasies. The clientele was limited and small, the Mob had to get half of the profits, and he was forced to contribute his share of payoffs, kickbacks, the graft and schmeers to local policemen and union officials. He learned a lot about business from them, though, and the art of packaging, and there was no doubt that checkroom girls could make more tips than college boys. He'd seen the drunks leering down the girls' décolletages, slipping dollar bills between their breasts. Checking hats and coats had suddenly taken on a patina that it never had before, and he was able to contribute a little of his own style to his work. He had the flair for it.

His feelings for these crooks — monkeys, as he called them — were ambivalent, seesawing dizzily between fear and fantasy, dread and admiration. He frequently told himself that he had no choice. After all, there was a deep depression blanketing the world. He must do what he must do, make a living to support his family, his aged mother. It wasn't as if he had planned it that way, it had just happened, evolved out of a crying need. He had planned to be a lawyer, but could he help it if his own ingenuity and a little luck had intervened, had forced his destiny? What difference, as long as he met his obligations, shouldered his responsibilities? Within a year he had worked his way slowly out of the speakeasies.

He was falling in love with success, and at the same time he was fascinated by failure. The apple sellers on the street corners excited him, so that he could rarely pass one without stopping for an interview, while the vendor told his peculiar tale of woe in between hawking his wares. The stories were basically similar — how the mighty had fallen — and each time they seemed to enjoy Aaron's attention, didn't consider it patronizing. Aaron never questioned their stories, but he was painfully conscious of the fragility of success,

taking for granted that any moment he might suffer a severe financial relapse into the obscurity whence he came. So he kept himself
perpetually whipped into a froth of ambition. He openly considered
his brothers failures, all except Bennie, whom he viewed as an ig-
noramus — with luck.

Aaron experienced a growing awareness of his own self-imposed
isolation. The business was growing away from him, and ubiquitous
though he was, he was not able to keep as careful a check on income
as he would have liked. He began to panic inwardly. He knew he
needed someone, as much as he hated to admit it, to help run the
checkrooms and handle the girls, but the word was already around
that he was tough, tight, and hard to work for. Anyway, he thought
in his circuitous way, there's nobody who understands this sort of
thing, and he strongly doubted that he had the time or patience to
train them.

Aaron never had really needed anyone, at least that's what Eve
said, almost as if the frequent saying of it might negate the fact, but
she was wrong. He needed Jason Miller. Jason had been a lanky boy
of nineteen when he came to work for Aaron in 1929, straight out of
high school, green, unsullied, malleable.

He had been sent to Abel Enterprises (as Aaron now began to
call his little group of concessions) under the auspices of his Aunt
Neva, her sister Rita's only child. They both adored him. He had
the dark good looks of his aunt and the quiet manners of a gentleman.
He was eager to learn, and eager to please. Jason was born poor and
dreamed rich. He had heard the tales of his rich uncle, the romance
of "the business," and he was already in love with the job before he
even met Aaron, before he'd ever set foot inside a checkroom. Aaron
wasn't overly impressed with him at first. Jason didn't say much,
but somehow people felt he knew a lot. His poise radiated an aura of
confidence, was a perfect foil for the hectic excitement that surrounded Aaron like an electric halo. Confuse and conquer had become Aaron's personal strategy in all things, unconscious perhaps,
but nonetheless pervasive.

By 1933 Aaron was itching to get into the big nightclub boom that
followed the repeal of Prohibition. He wasn't exactly sure how he

would go about it, but he felt he had done a good job at the speak-easies and had established a certain relationship, however tenuous, with the Big Boys in the business, the Boys that Prohibition had made bigger and richer every year. He had no doubt that they would come in handy now. Maybe the Boys wanted to run all the concessions, together with the nightclubs, maybe not — He wasn't sure just yet, but he felt, like the new music that was sweeping the country, that he could somehow swing it.

In 1933 Aaron rented the house on Albemarle Road shortly after Eve had given birth to her third child, Reid. She was curiously unprepared for this renewed onslaught of motherhood. Three children in five years (this and the second were unwanted pregnancies, the result of unwanted coupling). She resented it. She had in fact gone for an abortion in the beginning of the third month, but the sordid details made her shudder in terror, and bitter memories of that other time engulfed her, so that at the very last minute she took her feet out of the stirrups ("a humiliating medieval device," she said, "in a class with chastity belts, invented by misogynists, meant to keep women forever in their place — on their backs") and heaved herself from the old butcher block table, feeling like a lamb fleeing the slaughter. And so, Aaron acquired a second son — by default. Two sons, he thought with pride, and he was satisfied.

The two-story house stood on a lovely tree-lined street of private homes in an old residential section of Flatbush. The discreet ping-ping of the adjacent tennis courts, an alien sound to their untutored ears, reminded them that this was a Gentile neighborhood, and only the exigencies of the depression had lifted the restrictions.

Eve's mother had returned from California several years before, in fact just after Pauline had left them to seek fame and fortune, or "infamy and misfortune," as Eve would say. So Mama Lisa was back in Williamsburg with Lubowitz and the "baby," as she insisted on calling the now nine-year-old, hundred-and-thirty-pound Albie. Their presence sent red-hot waves of irritation coursing through Eve's delicate blue veins. Lubowitz stayed at home most of the time, now laid up with some crippling malady or another caused by his latest curious occupation.

Lubowitz was litigious; he was not above throwing himself under car wheels, or falling down the stairs of municipal buildings. Whiplash became his prevailing chronic condition and his steady retirement allowed him to look after Albie, not without some degree of tenderness. So Mama Lisa spent most of her time down at the brick colonial house, scurrying around on her little bird legs, quietly ministering to her grandchildren and cooking with a passion that was thought to have burned out long ago in other more colorful arenas.

Oddly enough, years later when they were to look back on the house on Albemarle, it wasn't the gracious old house or even the new baby that they remembered, but only Bermuda — "the Bermuda Incident" as it became known in family archives.

Aaron was anxious to get away, he had never taken a vacation in his life. He had heard about vacations and thought they were some sort of glittering break from the workaday world that rich people took and usually returned from complaining about. The picture that he had formulated in his mind had been borrowed from all the shipboard movies of the day — Ginger Rogers and Fred Astaire, art deco interiors, white-washed decks, white tie and tails, Eve by his side, elegantly gowned, sipping champagne. Yes, a cruise, that was it.

Eve had always said Bermuda was the place to go for a rest. The British really knew how to pamper you, they were gracious and elegant hosts; to cruise on the Cunard White Star Line had been her dream — back to mother England — in some small way.

Aaron felt the compelling rhythm of acquistion. He had acquired this beautiful, albeit impossible, woman, he had sold his Cord convertible for his first Cadillac, which now squatted complacently in the garage. They had a charming English nanny for the children. He and Eve had recently taken a short trip together, their first, to the Chicago World's Fair, where Aaron went to see about acquiring some important concessions. He returned victorious, with contracts at the Blackstone Hotel and the Chez Paree Club. The more he got, the easier they seemed to get; as his holdings grew, his reputation grew. Owners had more faith in him, they began to know whom they were dealing with, true to Aaron's doctrine that nothing succeeds like success.

Eve had been shopping and packing for months. Clothes hung in profusion all over the house. A brand new rawhide steamer trunk stood for weeks in the bedroom, yawning open, waiting to be filled, but filling it was no easy matter because Eve's insecurities, combined with Aaron's money idiosyncrasies, rendered her nearly impotent. If she sent something home C.O.D., Aaron usually returned it with the excuse that he had no cash at the moment, or needed all he had — Eve had no checking account of her own, and the only department store at which she had a charge account was Bergdorf Goodman, solely a woman's luxury shop. Even if she never bought a thing there, just having the account made her feel luxurious.

On the morning of the sailing, the trunks were finally sent down to the ship. As the afternoon wore on, everyone bustled around officiously, Grandma Lisa, Esther, the children's nurse from the north country of England. Aaron hung onto the telephone until the last minute, then busied himself with closing suitcases. Only Eve seemed to be suffering from a strange lassitude, and instead of organizing her massive disarray, she was closeted with the baby all day.

Aaron had invited numerous associates and employees down to the boat for a chic five o'clock sailing. It would be festive that way — a champagne party in the cabin. He hated the sour stuff, but what the hell. Eve loved it. There would be mounds of caviar — those horrible little black fish eggs he despised, too. Eve had ordered it in advance.

Between phone calls, Aaron sat with Jennie and Evan snapping coins up his sleeve. "Now you see it, now you don't," Aaron said in his best sideshow barker style. The children shrieked with delight each time a coin disappeared up his sleeve. "Let's see you do it with a half a dollar," Jennie said.

"Hey, I like your style, Jen, nothing small about you." He was successful in getting it up his cuff, but the weight pulled it right down again and the children jumped up and down triumphant.

At three in the afternoon, Eve emerged from the nursery looking worn, as if she had been fighting a battle. In a flat voice she announced, "The baby is sick, he has a temperature of a hundred and three. His throat is on fire. I've called the doctor but he's out of town on Sundays."

"Well there must be a doctor covering for him," Aaron said, his voice muffled with apprehension.

"Yes, but so far he hasn't called back. If you could stay off the phone for a few minutes — "

"Eve, we haven't got much time. Will you please get ready so I can close your bags now?"

"Will you please give me a couple of hundred dollars in cash to leave for the house while we're gone? What with the baby sick and all, I feel like a rat deserting a sinking ship."

"You don't have to feel that way. Your mother's here, Esther's here, you've got charge accounts in every store in the neighborhood."

"Aaron, don't argue, there isn't time. I don't want to go away and leave three children, a sick baby, and not a penny in cash for emergencies."

"What emergencies? There are accounts in every store, I told you."

"Well I want it. It's not unreasonable to ask. If it gives me peace of mind, why not do it?"

"Daddy, give Mommy the money, so that you can go, or you'll miss the boat," six-year-old Jennie stood around shifting restlessly from foot to foot. Aaron ignored the child's outburst.

"Sh-sh, what's going on here? Such a racket!" Lisa said as she entered the room.

"Why aren't you getting ready, Eve?" her mother said. "It's late already."

"Because I'm not going, Mama, that's why. I'm not going anywhere with that cheap, selfish bastard."

The announcement was anticlimactic. Aaron had sensed it coming, he had felt it in his marrow for days now. It had very slowly dawned on him that he might never have a normal life with this girl, and then he thought disjointedly — she wasn't really a girl, had never been a girl, laughing and carefree like other girls he had known.

"I can't just go blithely off and leave the baby with a temperature of a hundred and three, no doctor, no money in the house —"

"I've left enough for everything, it's just an excuse — Why are you doing this to me, Eve? What — what will I tell my friends?" Aaron demanded.

"Go out of the room," Lisa murmured to Aaron. "Let me talk to her."

Aaron lunged out of the room red-faced and quivering. Lisa looked at her daughter. "Eve, darling, you're making something out of nothing. So the baby's got a cold, so? I'm here, aren't I? Go. Go with your husband. It's better, he needs you now more than the baby does."

"Oh Mama, don't hand me that. How can you say that? He never needed anyone, he's just worrying about Jason Miller and those other checkroom bums down at the boat and what they'll think. Maybe they'll laugh behind his back."

Aaron came back looking defeated, his naturally furrowed forehead puckered in myriad pleats. He was prepared to beg. She turned on him immediately. "Why don't you tell them that you'd rather leave me home than leave one hundred dollars for emergencies?"

"There are accounts in every store, I told you."

"But if I want an extra hundred dollars on hand for an emergency, you'd rather fight me to the death and leave without me."

"Please Eve, most of our stuff is already down at the boat, our clothes will go and we won't." Aaron seemed on the verge of tears, coloring and blanching in alternating blotches. Eve had a closed look about her, glazed, like baked-on enamel. "But Eve, there are fifteen people already down at the boat, all the people I work with. Please don't do this to me."

"I don't give a damn about those people — those vulgarians of yours. Who are they anyway? They don't mean a thing to me — and they mean too damn much to you. Go yourself. I can't leave the baby, you won't leave any cash for emergencies, for anything!" She was wringing her hands, her voice rose to a shriek, and white bubbles of foam began to form in the corners of her mouth.

Jennie began to cry and pulled at Mama Lisa's dress. "Grandma, please give Mommy the money so she will go. Can *you* give it to her, Grandma?"

"All right, I'll leave the goddam money, but I don't have much and I need all the cash I've got on me." He was thinking to himself that Mama would only take the hundred dollars to Lubowitz anyway. *Another* hundred dollars to line the pockets of that miserable son of a bitch.

Eve shrieked, "It's too late now, you've spoiled the whole trip for me. You go yourself."

Aaron said nothing but gathered his belongings, which were lined up at the door with some of Eve's things, and walked slowly to the baby's room. As he did so, he passed nurse Esther in the hall pleading with Eve in whispers, assuring her that there was "nothing to worry about. Babies' temperatures are alarmingly high, it means nothing."

Aaron looked at the baby, fussing fitfully in the crib. He looked very red and smelled slightly sour, he thought. He felt no emotion, only a faint irritation. He walked out again without a word, brought his few pieces of hand luggage to the front porch, and hailed a cab.

*

When Aaron found himself back in the graceful living room of Albemarle Road some ten days later, he was as surprised as his wife and mother-in-law. He really hadn't expected to return, he had whipped himself up on the whole nine-day voyage, and together with the frothing seas and his own delicate stomach, his misery had been superseded only by his sense of outrage. He wanted to frighten her, perhaps teach her a good lesson — with her high-handed ways — but he really had no place else to go and no time to look for anything. The ill-spent vacation resulted only in a return to an avalanche of compiled business problems. And then there were the children. He really had missed the children, and in an odd, ambivalent way he had missed Eve too. He was at base a traditional man, inclined to habit, and the very thought of divorce was both financially and emotionally untenable — it reeked of failure, a word that had no place in his limited vocabulary.

Diffident and strangely chastened, he came back that day determined to put the whole fiasco out of his mind and begin anew.

(13)

THE TRIUMPH DEMOCRATIC CLUB squatted complacently somewhere between the *gemütlichkeit* of Luchow's Restaurant on Fourteenth Street and Second Avenue, and the early boundaries of Little Italy. Joe Banti sat in the office of the club president, Gino De Santori, tilted his chair on its thin legs, and pushed his fedora back slightly with his fingertips, all in one easy gesture. He was the big man in the 26th District, and the recognized leader of the club, though his office on the top floor was considerably smaller than the president's, and considerably drearier. But he didn't give a damn about that; right now he was sitting on top of the world. He had just helped De Santori get himself elected to the state supreme court, and now he was Judge De Santori, and all of Little Italy spoke of him in hushed tones, reverently. The favor seekers and sycophants pled their various causes in tones equally mellifluous. But not Joe Banti or any of the other boys — they were different. Joe stared at the large crucifix that faced him from behind Gino's desk, noticed its heavy accumulation of dust, wondered briefly if that would be considered a sacrilege, and said nothing. He had been sitting there for a full quarter of an hour and hadn't said much, just teetered back and forth on the rickety chair legs. There was nothing unusual in that. He often sat around Gino's office, just talking, keeping him company, while the judge went in and out, made and received phone calls.

Sometimes he talked about his home in Sicily, his sainted mother, his wife who was too fat now, his mistress who was too blonde now, and sometimes he talked about his latest business enterprise. Gino secretly thought he talked too much and was too hot-tempered, wasn't polished enough, that he was bad for his image, especially now that he had acceded to the bench — but the boys were satisfied with him, so what the hell. After all, it was Banti who was largely responsible for getting him elected.

"So listen," Banti said, "the boys want to get into the clubs. It figures, they got the know-how from the speaks, and all that loose cash lying around, they want to sink it into something hot, and they feel there's a fortune to be made in nightclubs . . ."

"Yeah, well there's nothing wrong with that," De Santori said absently, riffling through some papers on his desk. He was tall and slender with distinguished Latin good looks and a prominent nose. He had the appearance of a delicate hawk.

"Yeah, so Luchese, Luciano, and Three-Fingers Brown just bought that old dump of a theater up at Fiftieth and Seventh Avenue. They want to turn it into some gorgeous spot, I think a French motif or somethin'. Clubs are doin' great, you know, in spite of the times . . ."

"Yeah, yeah, I know, the suckers never stop coming. They probably figure if they booze it up enough, they'll forget what they haven't got left to remember."

"Yeah," Joe said, waving Gino's little touches of homily aside, "so the boys need a liquor license."

"Well, I'll work it out I guess, I always do. Who's fronting it?"

There was a pause, "Er — I think Stern. Yeah, that's it, Stern."

"Not Yerme Stern?"

"Yeah, Yerme, that's it, one of the Jewboys — so what's wrong with Stern?" Joe Banti asked, frowning in that idiosyncratic way he had.

"I didn't say anything was wrong with Stern. It just might be easier to get the license for somebody who wasn't as close to Siegel or Cohen as he is."

"Yeah, well, that's what we got you for, Judge," and he said

"Judge" very slowly and juicily. "To make things easier for us."

"What do *you* expect to get out of it, Joe?"

"Me? Oh, nothing much. Maybe the concessions, that's all, coat-room, cigarettes, stuff like that, small potatoes," he sniffed as if to lend further unimportance to his words.

There was a momentary silence while the judge continued to shuffle papers around officiously. Then he said, "Hear there's big dough in that end if you know what you're doing, and boy, have you ever got to know what you're doing!" He sat back in his big chair, swiveled it around once, and seemed to be talking up to the peeling and flaking ceiling, untouched for years by painters, rather than have the office look too affluent to the tradespeople and union representatives that daily choked its narrow corridors.

"Yeah, you gotta watch those broads like a hawk," he continued, "otherwise they'll steal the eye outa your head. What do *you* know about the business?"

"What's to know?" Banti said uncomfortably. The judge didn't answer, he just kept staring at the ceiling, his hands clasped behind his head, his hawklike nose a majestic downward protuberance in his intense face.

When Banti left, Gino De Santori picked up the phone and dialed a number quickly. He was pleased that Joe Zaretti himself answered. "Weren't you friendly with a concessionaire, name of Azel or Abel or something, at the Club 34 . . . ? Yeah, I thought so. What's he doing these days, huh? Yeah, I hear he's doing good . . . it's a small thing, but why don't you come down here sometime tomorrow, I'd like to talk to you."

*

Exactly two weeks later, having made him wait just long enough to pique his interest but not so long as to lose it altogether, Joe Banti granted Aaron an appointment to discuss the concessions at the soon-to-be-opened Casino de Paris. Aaron did not comment to Jason on the chaotic condition of the building as they approached it. He had grown used to seeing these clubs spring into magnificence almost overnight.

In 1935, Jason Miller had been working for Aaron six years, and although it went against Aaron's grain to admit it, the younger man had a real feeling for the concession business. He handled the goons and the girls as if they were made of glass, made them feel as though they were all members of café society.

"You're no different than the customers," he'd tell the checkroom and cigarette girls, "only difference is your costumes, and most of them out there couldn't wear what you *haven't* got on."

But in general, Jason was cool and strictly business. He was a sophisticated, strangely serene twenty-four-year old, with something of the look and style of a taller, dreamier Bogart, at least that's what the checkroom girls said.

Aaron had formed the habit of taking Jason with him when he went to make or investigate a new deal. He said it was a good way for him to learn. Secretly, he liked the companionship, and Jason's quiet, steady idolatry made him feel secure. As they walked into the defunct theater on Fiftieth and Seventh Avenue, he was surprised at the progress being made on renovation — workmen everywhere, overall the pervasive raw odor of wet plaster and wood.

Aaron looked snappy as always in his "cake-eater duds," ever conscious to use the hep expressions that were now considered by the more sophisticated to be relics of the jazz age. But old ways die slowly, and his reluctance to let go, to relinquish anything or anyone he had acquired was becoming an obsession with him.

They made a handsome duo, these two men, Aaron, delicate, dapper, shorter by more than a head, in spite of the ever-present fedora; Jason, sleek and tall, as always hatless, his rich, dark hair generously pomaded, inclining a little as if not to overshadow the older man, the boss. He was dressed conservatively. He usually wore silver-gray sharkskin or navy, as if to counterbalance Aaron's flamboyance, to lend comfort, confidence, to the whole enterprise. They had just started buying their clothes at Kolmer Marcus. It was famous among the Broadway crowd for sartorial splendor — custom-made sharkskins and worsteds that hung from the back and shoulders in arrogant nonchalance. Shopping there had become a great event in their lives. Everything was an event then.

They walked into the makeshift office, and, from the white haze of sawdust and plaster, Joe Banti materialized like a genie from a bottle. "Well, well, I'm Banti. Which one of you is Abel?" he said, directing a hand tentatively between the two men. After the introductions, Aaron said, in his best vaudeville style, "Hey, looks like you've got your own W.P.A. project here." "Yeah," Banti laughed, "sorry I can't offer you a more comfortable seat," he said, indicating some paint-flecked, khaki folding chairs, "but you'll just have to take my word that it is going to be one hell of a place when we're finished here." They bantered a little about Roosevelt, the New Deal, the repeal of Prohibition. They sat in a sort of self-conscious semicircle, Jason trying in vain to tuck his long, unruly legs beneath the seat.

Banti then launched into a glowing description of what the interior décor would be like. He told them that every inch of mosaic mirror and crystal chandelier would come from France, that all glassware would be baccarat, that the china would be Limoges, that the drapery fabrics would be hand-woven in France. But Aaron was unaffected by interior design, never having experienced it. In fact, the only thing at all that he knew about it, had ever heard about it, were Eve's complaints that they lacked it, and her frequent threats to hire a decorator who might direct her heavy, overstuffed, lumpish Tudor pieces into some semblance of organization. Aaron meant to sound ingenuous, friendly, so he said, "What I know about decorating, you could put in a thimble." Banti continued his narrative as to size, capacity, and expected volume of the club.

"Yerme has engaged Billy Rose to sort of run the joint for us — Guess you've heard of him." At the mention of the name Billy Rose, Aaron's body tightened visibly. In a sense he'd be working for Rose, he thought; how come he hadn't heard about it? He usually heard about these things through the powerful Broadway grapevine . . . Jesus, that guy's reputation was murder, a wild man, he thought . . . Banti went on, as if reading his mind, "He's a great showman, but a tough little bastard," he shook his head and smiled ruefully. "Well now, suppose we get down to business. You're a concessionaire, Abel, and I understand you're doing very well. Where are some of your places?" Aaron listed the small sprinkling as if they were only a sampling of many, but he did so in an oddly self-effacing manner, figuring humility was the safest role when working with these monkeys, but never, never cringing, or they might think he was a greenhorn, a pushover. He couldn't decide whether to mention the burlesque houses or not. He was doing great there, with the candy counters and programs. He got some of his best bits from the vaudeville skits. He knew almost the whole Smith and Dale routine by heart, and did a soft-shoe at the drop of a hat. He sang in his strong, gravelly voice wisps of the latest songs picked up from the runways. No, he wouldn't mention it — not right now.

During the entire exchange Jason didn't say a word, but he didn't remove his liquid, dark eyes from Banti's face for one minute. Banti dropped his eyes and shifted uncomfortably.

"Well, so far you've told me mostly about the Elks' Clubs and catering halls, but what's your experience with an upholstered cellar like we got here?" he asked.

"Well, I thought Joe Zaretti told you. I used to have a couple of speaks." Aaron seemed momentarily confused; he didn't like being interviewed like an applicant for a job. "Anyway, it's all the same, ain't it?" He lapsed into the jargon of his boyhood, out of the long-dead dust of Delancey Street.

"Well, I guess you know that I have the concessions here already, that's definite." There was a silence, Jason and Aaron exchanging glances. Then Jason began buttoning his jacket slowly, his eyes still glued to Banti's face, his expression unchanging. "Well, then, what are we doing here?" he said. He straightened his tie and prepared to stand.

"Whoa there — hold your horses," Banti said. "Where are you going? Hey, he's a high-spirited kid, ain't he," he said to Aaron, as if Jason were not there. Aaron chuckled paternally and fidgeted on the small chair as he always did when he had to sit in any one place too long. Stretching out his legs, he said, still chuckling, "Sit down, Jason, we haven't heard what the man has to say yet. Let's hear his proposition, if he has one." Aaron loved these histrionics; Jason and he worked together like an adagio team, looping and curving, meshing into each other's nuances at just the right moments; their timing was exquisite, perfect. He was fascinated by the mumbo jumbo that went into making a deal, especially with these people. He wondered absently whether they picked up their style and mannerisms from the movies, or was it the other way around. He must remember to ask this question of his friend, Sy Barche, who was a district attorney now, another Eastern District boy who made good, he thought irrelevantly.

"Well, as I said," Banti continued, "the concessions in this joint are mine. I admit I don't know a hell of a lot about this business, and I'm really too busy to learn it, or to stand around and watch the kids for that matter. But it should throw off a good few bucks and I don't want to lose out altogether, so how about we go partners, you can buy half interest from me."

It wasn't exactly what Aaron had in mind; he was hesitant about partnerships, especially with any of the Mob, though Banti seemed like a nice enough guy. Still, it was no secret that three of the toughest guys in the rackets were behind this place, and most of the other big clubs in town, for that matter — but what could he do? — these were the breaks. If he was going to make the big time in this business he'd have to play ball with them. He was forced to admit that they were a necessary evil, they had the connections, a certain slick facility for the nightclub business, and since Prohibition, they had the real money. There was no doubt they wielded the power in this town.

"Well, of course, generally I don't go in for partnership deals, but what kind of money are we talking about here?" he asked innocently, though he had long ago estimated his profit, based on volume here, for the year.

"Five thousand," Banti said with no hesitation.

Aaron and Jason exchanged glances; that was just about half of what they had figured. They hadn't counted on a partnership, and then there was an extra thousand for Zaretti. He had told Aaron he would only get five hundred dollars out of that, a sort of finder's fee, he called it, for putting in a word for Aaron. The other five hundred dollars was for "a friend," he said. All and all, six thousand wasn't cheap, and there were risks involved. He was considering bargaining with him for a thousand dollars, five hundred dollars anyway, to cover Zaretti's cut, but he knew better than to chisel Banti now.

Aaron had planned to take it at any price up to ten thousand dollars. It would be worth it for the experience alone; it would be a steppingstone to other places, here in New York, Chicago, who knew where or what.

"Joe," Aaron said with a genuine warmth, "I like you, I'd like working with you. You've got a deal."

But Banti's look was guarded, and he said, "Well, you won't actually be working with me, Abel. You know Charlie Vallone?"

"Heard the name around town, a lawyer, isn't he?"

"Yeah, yeah. Well, er, you see, he's a good friend of mine, and he, er, he needs something to do with himself; he's on a one-year suspension from practicing law. Well, in any case, he'll protect my interests here."

Aaron had heard something about it, the usual thing, mouthpiece for the Mob, throws a case, bribes a witness, fixes a judge. None of his business, didn't bother him, what did he care if his partner was Joe Banti, Charlie Vallone, or Lucky Luciano himself, as long as he did his work and minded his own business. So Aaron became partners with Charlie Vallone when the Casino de Paris opened its heavily gold-embossed doors in the spring of 1935.

"I'll be here a good deal of the time myself, and when I'm not, my right-hand man here, Miller, will keep things going smooth as silk," Aaron said. Banti turned and stared at Jason for the first time during the entire exchange.

"You look like a kid," he said. "How long you been in the business?"

"Ten years or so," Jason lied smoothly.

"Uh huh, don't talk much, do you, kid?"

"I talk when I have to."

"He's a pretty cool cookie you got there," Banti said, smiling the tolerant, experienced smile of the older man for the younger.

They shook hands all around, and Aaron walked out with Jason. His head down like a charging bull, his shoulders hunched forward, he walked quickly to his car, a long, green Cadillac parked across the street. He hoped Banti was watching, he was dizzily proud of this latest acquisition.

"It's going to be okay," Jason said. "It's going to be great. Congratulations, boss," he said banteringly, punching Aaron warmly on the shoulder. "Guess I'll go out to the Elks' Club in White Plains now; there's a membership dinner-dance out there tonight."

"Yeah, I may see you out there later."

Inside the car, Aaron flipped on the radio distractedly. "Now Wheaties presents Jack Armstrong, the All-American Boy!" As the radio announcer shouted the magic words, a male chorus swung into the Hudson High fight song, "Raise the Flag for Hudson High, Boys." He couldn't believe it was five o'clock already; the sun was beginning to dip in the sweet, clear dusk of a February sky, promising a sudden spring. At five o'clock his children would be hunched up close to the radio in the living room, its conical face looking smug, somehow closed. He felt a sudden downward pull of emptiness as he thought of the faces of his children, towheads, with blue eyes, all rosy and shiny after their baths, squeezing their foreheads into wrinkles of concentration trying to absorb the heroism of "Jack Armstrong," or to understand the acrid satire of "Little Orphan Annie."

He had a sudden longing to be with them; could he stop home before he went out to White Plains, just for a moment? But then, he thought of Eve, how angry she'd be when he'd have to turn right around and leave. *It's just teasing the children that way*, she'd say. *It's better not to come back at all.* She had that way of negating things, of taking the wind out of his sails. *Okay, if you must do it, hurry up and get it over with.* He thought of that often. Most nights when he came home now she'd be asleep, or pretending — he didn't know. He was so tired, he really didn't care. No, he'd stop at some of the places here, then out to White Plains. He turned left on Broadway, driving slowly downtown, only semi-conscious of the tameness of this street at five o'clock, like the calm before the storm. In another few hours it would explode into lights, crazy-colored lights, diamond-flecked pavements, like a whore it would be dressed and painted for the night. Bemused, he was still thinking of the children, of how sweet they smelled after their baths, how little he got to see of them. Where had the last years gone . . . he was thirty-four years old already; it was all going so quickly, his youth, their childhood, the whole crazy-quilt dream. If only it were like a movie, he could sit there and see it all over again from the beginning, see the part he'd missed. He watched a fancy silver foreign car streak ahead of him authoritatively, weaving in and out of traffic recklessly. That was the way the rich drove their cars, he supposed, uninvolved with the rest of the world. He stopped for a light and watched the vendor on a corner in Times Square winding up his little mechanical tin men. They jumped around helter-skelter, bobbing up and down in a frenzied dance, falling down, being rudely put on their feet, and continuing right where they had left off. They fascinated him. He had bought the children at least a half dozen in the last year, but they had grown tired of them. He jumped out of the car on impulse — he just had to buy one more. The kids would get a kick out of it; the others were all broken.

14

THE SUMMER OF '35 was the last summer they were to spend all together as a family. Jennie sensed it, she could feel the time running out like the sand between her toes.

She loved that last long, lazy summer at Manhattan Beach. Aaron had the bandstand concessions there, the locker rooms, popcorn, peanuts, and hot knishes. She loved the feeling of the warm sandy hillocks beneath her feet (never mind that they were peppered liberally with soda bottle tops and other summer debris) while she and her brother Evan ate the steaming, spicy, potato and onion knishes, and the Rudy Vallee Band played irresistibly sweet tunes. Jennie spent most of that summer around the bandstand, leaning on the railing, staring transfixed at the handsome young male vocalist whom Mr. Vallee introduced as Mr. Tony Martin to the audience crowding around him in bathing suits. Sometimes a beautiful blonde lady came up to the microphone and sang with him, or alone, in a husky, exciting voice — Jennie thought she was the prettiest girl she had ever seen in her life, she looked just like a movie star. Her name was Miss Alice Faye. She wondered if they were in love.

"God, I wish I could grow up already," she said in frustration to Evan who was gazing upward into the lofty heavens of the bandshell.

"You probably will," Evan said with no apparent interest. Jennie gave him an exasperated look — little brothers, ugh. There was really no one to talk to about all this, this music and couples dancing close in their bathing suits, and, well, just everything —

Whenever her father was around he was rushing all over the main beach breathlessly on business, or taking a swim, or sparring on the beach with different strong-looking types in bathing trunks. Her mother didn't like the beach and rarely came with them, just to bring them or pick them up — their bungalow was only a few steps from the sand. She carried a copy of *Anthony Adverse* under her arm and always wore a pastel dress and kept her shoes on, and usually had on a big sun hat to protect her "delicate white skin." Jennie wasn't sure whether she preferred *that* to seeing her mother up on the bandstand in a bathing suit like the other adults — she decided that she did.

Most of the summer Jennie couldn't bear to look in the mirror for fear of seeing there a fat-cheeked, chubby little girl with dishwater blonde pigtails and absolutely no cheekbones. She told herself that Miss Alice Faye had a round face too, but somehow that didn't satisfy her, and anyway *she* (Jennie) couldn't sing a note, even in school she'd been embarrassed because she couldn't sing on key, or even off. For years to come whenever she'd hear "Red Sails in the Sunset," she'd think of that summer at Manhattan Beach and Rudy Vallee and his megaphone, and his two beautiful vocalists —

*

The end of August sizzled crisp around the edges of September and Jennie's parents seemed to her to draw closer, united in sadness. Aaron's brother Max's oldest son had died four days before his Bar Mitzvah, a brain tumor. The family whispered that it was all because he had slipped and cracked his head on the bottom of Bennie's rowboat the summer before — that was nonsense and Aaron knew it, but he understood the necessity to lay blame somewhere, to seek explanation for the fact that such a crazy, unjust thing had happened.

Jennie had eight cousins on her father's side, all boys — she always felt very feminine when they were around. She hadn't gotten to know any of them very well. Eve didn't push for much socializing with Aaron's ever-widening family circle, but she knew Davy — he had made interesting sand sculptures with her near the bandstand early in the summer, when he came to visit with his folks. Jennie thought that he was awfully *frail*-looking for an "older boy" and he had a strange sort of scary haircut.

It was decided that none of the younger children would go to the funeral, only Uncle Bennie's boys, twelve and fourteen, were old enough.

Max and Ida were too sick to make any *shivah* arrangements, they just wanted to be alone with their grief and their two remaining sons. Most of the others went to Grandma Esther's at Harrison Avenue. But after the funeral they came back to Aaron's house on Albemarle Road, Bennie and Neva with their two boys, who looked knowing and wise now that they'd been to the cemetery. Uncle Bennie just sat in a corner mutely and Neva beside him shaking the tears from her long black lashes, like summer rain. No one spoke much.

It was the first time Jennie saw her mother in black. The first time she saw her father cry — and the last time she saw her mother take his hand gently to her cheek and hold it there for a long, sad moment.

(15)

THE CASINO DE PARIS opened with all the promised flourish and fanfare, and it was almost impossible to pick up a newspaper nowadays without reading about it in Earl Wilson's or Walter Winchell's column. Just on the sale of cigarettes and favors alone, Aaron and his partners were taking in about two hundred dollars a night, and when the fall season opened with a blustery October, he knew that the checkroom would do even better than anticipated.

Charlie Vallone seemed satisfied, very satisfied, in fact he and Aaron had become good friends. Aaron liked his smooth manner, his background. Anyone who could generate the patience to graduate from college, and with a law degree yet, couldn't be all bad, he figured. He admired Al Carton for much the same reasons, and his other friend from good old Eastern District, Sy Barche. "There was a guy for you," he'd say, much to the irritation of Banti and Vallone, "top of his class now, only thirty-five and already assistant district attorney for Kings County." Sy was prosecuting the rackets and the racketeers, cracking down on the numbers mercilessly, the bookies, the Mob. He'd built an early reputation on prosecuting the bootleggers but now he blossomed out like flowering hibiscus into all the avenues of organized crime. Not that Aaron made a point about bragging about this high-school friendship; it was just better that he didn't exactly let them forget it, better not to have his partners become too complacent, figure him for a sap. He felt instinctively that they would tolerate no competition from an amateur.

But Banti was the real power behind the throne here, and Aaron knew it. He hadn't seen much of Joe Banti since the opening, but Vallone wasn't great on figures, so Joe hovered in the background, keeping the books and checking on the checkers. But Charlie Vallone was very good with the three-dimensional kind of figures — the girls. Aaron spoke to him, in a light, bantering way at first, about keeping his hands off the checkroom and cigarette girls. Vallone was — as were so many of these boys, Aaron thought — an exemplary family man, but that was when he was with the family. Once away from them, it was another story altogether.

Charlie had a certain polish and dark Italianate good looks, which, together with the fact that he was an educated man (if temporarily fallen from grace), only served to make him more attractive to the girls — a rake, a dilettante.

That many or most of the girls were beautiful was just a business fact to Aaron. He kept his eyes averted from them, they were merely the tools of his trade. He neither accepted or rejected them, he merely tolerated them. Just dumb *shiksas* with little or no education. Aaron considered them generally loose, immoral, one rung lower than the showgirls on his carefully graded social scale — just flamboyant props like the painted and feathered dolls that were pinned along the walls of the skeet-shooting booths at Coney Island. No, if he was going to expend any of his carefully garnered energies on a woman, it would probably be with his own wife, that is, if he ever got home at night. He had to admit that in spite of the constant tension between them, he still found her infinitely desirable. Eve had become completely detached about sex, even hostile. Perhaps since all the pregnancies, he told himself, three children in rapid succession. Her figure had grown fuller, her interests parochial, her life revolved around the children. His presence was little more than an irritant to her, her romantic illusions were transferred now from him to the children.

Well anyway, so far, so good. He'd stick to business and Jason Miller could handle the girls for him. He had no time or patience for all the placating and sudsing that went into soothing their damaged egos, and Charlie Vallone wasn't making it any easier. At least Jason was businesslike with the broads, and they in turn thought they detected a core of sympathy in those luminous, deep-fringed eyes of his. They loved him, these hard-eyed flirtatious girls who acted silly whenever he came around. He could whip them into a frenzy of production with his quiet voice and secret smile, in a way that the itchy and impatient Aaron could never do. Aaron knew it, and kept his relationship with the girls strictly impersonal, but he resented it a little, too. It would annoy him when even Eve, whose disdain for the checkrooms and anyone remotely connected with them he knew well, would say grudgingly, "I must admit Jace's always been a perfect gentleman with me." She liked his deferring to her, his obvious or pretended awe of her superiority. When she said this, Aaron smiled knowingly, and once he said, chuckling, "He's full of shit." But the fact was nobody knew for sure with Jason, and they didn't really want to know. Jason's importance, as far as Aaron was concerned anyway, was that he looked after the girls and kept a careful eye out for stealing.

Stealing was the blight that plagued his life and interfered with his dreams of glory. He lived in terror of the girls playing "one for you and two for me." He reckoned with the loss of "one for you and one for me." Even with that, he was able to make a tidy profit, but beyond it they could finish him off, wipe him out. That's why screening the girls carefully was so important. Even then, how could anyone know for sure? The temptation of handling so much cash all night was more than most could resist. (For this reason he had dresses especially designed without pockets.) Poor girls from small towns, off the farms, from coal mining families, a quarter every now and then just slipped between the breasts could augment their salaries considerably, enable them to send a few bucks home, support a boyfriend out of work — well, it was his job, Aaron's, to see that this didn't happen, not too often anyway. So Jason went around from place to place watching the girls, keeping a careful eye on the averages, knowing roughly what to expect from each night's take. If a girl came in much below for a few nights in succession, there was cause for suspicion. If it continued, she was fired. Soon there were other checkers employed, but then Jason and Big Ben had to check the checkers, and it was getting complicated.

Jason was fond of the girls collectively; individually he really didn't know one from the other, except for his remarkable memory for names. He'd hire a new girl, write down her name, and when she started work, look at it once before he went over to the place, and then never forget it.

*

The club looked denuded without its nighttime tinsel, like a beautiful woman without her make-up. Aaron and Joe were there setting up the checkroom one late afternoon, counting the brightly colored check stubs while a porter swept, dusted, and carefully polished the little brass dishes that served as the cash receptacles. Aaron noticed that Banti was quieter, as if lost in thought, sorting out something. His face looked very white and tense, his black hair seemed slicked down even more than usual, his pursed lips seemed almost blue, Aaron thought he looked a little like a vampire. He maintained a stony silence. Unable to contain his impatience, Aaron blurted out, "Hey, what's eating you, Banti? You look like somebody just murdered your old lady." Banti remained silent but looked up sourly now. Aaron talked on nervously, "No kidding, is something bothering you? Why not talk about it?"

"What's to talk about? I'm missing fifteen hundred dollars, that's all, there's fifteen hundred simoleons short on the books," he said, his eyes dilating.

"So," said Aaron, still unruffled, "what are you trying to say?"

"I ain't trying, kid, I'm asking you now for the first and last time, did you pocket the dough?

"Did I — " Aaron stopped, stuttered, seemed unable to go on. As if he'd risk his life for fifteen hundred bucks, was this guy kidding? He'd have to be kidding to think that he, Aaron Abel, would tangle with the Mafia (only to himself did he allow the luxury of this forbidden name) for fifteen hundred lousy dollars. Why, money-crazy, success-crazy as he was, he was smart enough to see that the experience he was getting here in his first really big New York nightspot was worth ten times fifteen hundred smackers! But he was also sharp enough to be scared, wary anyway. In a hoarse whisper he asked, "Do you think I stole the dough?"

"I ain't accusing you, just asking," he answered, feigning a subtlety he didn't possess.

"Well the answer is decidedly and definitely NO. I don't mess around with small potatoes like fifteen hundred dollars. You must be joking or something. What do you take me for, a two-bit penny-ante panhandler?" Aaron was indignant, but Banti remained unimpressed. He was used to these vehement denials, born out of terror. Aaron was furious now. "Why you lousy punk," Aaron said, his eyes bloodshot with uncontrollable rage. He moved toward Banti, but luckily Banti was looking at the floor. When he was agitated he'd look up or down or sideways, his head cocked sharply, anywhere but at his antagonist, so he didn't see Aaron move toward him ominously. This delay, this infinitesimal, momentary pause, gave Aaron the time in which to pull his thoughts together, to come up with some reasonable explanation or at least an arrangement. He sat back quietly now in his chair and began probing his brain for an explanation — who, what, why . . . ? But no one, no one handled the money after Charlie and he made the final count together . . . he was dumbfounded . . . It had to be Vallone, or maybe Banti and Vallone in cahoots, but for fifteen hundred dollars? That was crazy, that would be chicken feed to them . . .

"Now hold your horses there, Abel," Banti said coolly, still looking down at the floor. "I only asked, I didn't accuse. After all, I've been working with you for almost a half a year now. I know you for a pretty smart guy, too smart to get yourself killed for fifteen hundred bucks when you're making more than that here in a week. So-o-o-o-o . . ." he said, dragging out his "so" in a slow-motion whistle that caused Aaron to wince with annoyance, "we just gotta mark time and see what happens, check it out, ya know." He was talking suddenly folksy, almost like Will Rogers. Aaron was torn between laughing and crying. The ride he'd taken with his friend Sy Barche a few weeks before came suddenly into his mind in sharp focus, causing a band of moisture under his collar and above his upper lip in tiny hot prickles —

They had inched along the crumbling banks of the Gowanus Canal, the night sky was a sulphuric yellow mist and the air was heavy with the smell of rotten eggs. They had started out in the late afternoon in order to take advantage of the remaining light. They were not too sure where they were going; it had taken longer than they figured and they had gotten lost a few times. Now the unexpected grim weather had caused an early nightfall, just to make things harder all around.

Aaron leaned back against the gray plush interior of the Cadillac limousine and wondered silently how he had gotten himself into this joy ride and why? What did Barche really have in the back of his mind when he called him on the phone and asked him to ride out with him to the ragged ends of Brooklyn to identify a body. Was this supposed to be an object lesson of some sort, or was Sy trying to warn a friend, a *landsman*, of what these characters were capable of? Aaron put that out of his mind as ridiculous — what could that possibly have to do with him anyway. He figured, coming closer to the truth, that the guy was lonely, he simply wanted some company on these melancholy trips he had to make, sometimes as often as once a week. The black limousine with DA-4 marked clearly on the back license plate, snaked its way through the poorly lit, yellow-fogged streets and canals of Canarsie. The driver, in a black peaked cap and regular business suit, sat next to a burly Irish cop, whose presence for some reason only succeeded in making Aaron more uncomfortable. The driver turned around and asked Barche, "Left or right now, boss, which way do we turn?" The young D.A. looked perplexed. He squinted tensely out of the window at nothing in particular that Aaron could see, yet Aaron grew uneasy. He crossed and uncrossed his legs a few times, shifted around, trying to ease the tension and soreness in his meatless buttocks. They had been driving for over an hour already. "Well, the call said to turn left at the end of the canal, but there seems to be a continuation of it once again . . ." Suddenly the driver pulled up short with a screech of brakes, perilously close to the murky canal. The blurry yellow street lights were growing scarcer and scarcer.

"Dick, do you think this is about right?" Barche leaned forward intently.

"Well this would put us just about where you marked the X on the map you drew. There are some things that look like houses over there."

Barche had prepared a map from the description of the area given to him over the phone during the tip-off call that had come into his office the day before.

"Could be somewhere around here," he said uncertainly. But there was a series of houses with alleys that looked exactly alike for almost as far as the eye could see.

"Okay, we'll get out here and walk until we find it," Barche said. Aaron hurried along beside his friend, following the policeman through the slimy alleyway between the seemingly derelict houses. Usually the G-men were put onto leads like this, but this particular tip-off had been phoned right into the D.A.'s office. It was well known that Barche's platform had been racket busting and he had kept his promises. He was presently hot on the trail of the warring gangs.

"Nothing there." They walked silently up the street a few blocks behind the policeman, their car inching up alongside. Suddenly, Barche stopped and lowered his flashlight. "Looks like bloodstains," he said knowledgeably. The officer nodded in agreement. They began to follow the red-brown splotches now, their heads lowered like bloodhounds, until they found themselves in another back alley, distinguishable from the others only by the now unmistakable stains that seemed to have been daubed indiscriminately by a mad artist. On the ground there lay in the dubious light what Aaron thought at first must be a pile of dirty rags. The body was lying face down in a pool of dried blood. There were three or four bullet holes in the back. The policeman rolled the corpse over, and the grotesquely bloated face, the tongue clenched between swollen lips, made Aaron think for one crazy moment that this was after all only a mask that some sick kids had fixed up for a horrible Halloween joke.

"How long do you figure, Macadoo?" Barche asked the officer in a coolly professional voice.

"Oh, Jeeze, maybe three or four days, I dunno." Aaron felt sick, he wanted desperately not to vomit, but that delicate, queasy stomach of his was rolling around suggestively.

"Well, it's gangland, all right," he told Aaron confidently. Aaron tried to look concerned, but all he could think about was getting away from here. He had an urge to bolt, to run to the certain safety of the waiting Cadillac, its warm plush interior. He felt safe in a Cadillac, it was home to him nowadays, the only kind of car he drove. He was thinking up and away from the smelly corpse, the rotten-egg smells of the canal. But just then Barche turned to Aaron and said, "Come on, let's get into the car fast, gotta get to the nearest phone. Okay, Macadoo, you wait with the body," and he streaked off toward the car.

While they drove, Barche talked excitedly, explaining what Aaron considered the obvious. "You see, he must have been shot on the street from a moving car, then dragged into that alley."

But Aaron wasn't really listening, instead he was thinking what an ignominious ending, going out as undignified and bloodied as you came in. Life was so precious to him he would've gone to any lengths to preserve it. It had been good to him so far, going almost the way he had dreamed it. Well almost. It had been an uphill climb practically from the beginning with Eve, but all things considered, it had gone pretty well so far and he didn't want to do anything to jinx it.

"This is one hell of a business, a hell of a life," he murmured, visibly shaken.

"Hmm — wait until you make the dough," Sy said, sagely. "Then it really gets tough, kid!"

Aaron didn't much like his friend, and a contemporary at that, patronizing him — talking down to him that way. Why he could buy and sell him already, D.A. or no D.A. — unless of course Sy went crooked, and Aaron figured with *him* that was unlikely.

(16)

E WAS FORCED to wait ten long agonizing days to hear from
Joe Banti again. He caught himself looking over his shoulder every minute, frightened during those lonely twilight hours
when he drove home with his stacks of change, sometimes with
Jason Miller. The scant five hours that he normally slept were now
fitful; he was glad that he had a gun. He had no choice, there was
nothing he could do but follow the dictum that his questionable
partner had laid down, "We'll just have to wait and see." And then
one evening when Aaron was at the De Paris, he saw Joe walking
toward the checkroom; he was with Vallone. Aaron wasn't sure
whether this was a good sign or not but he felt secure in the attorney's friendship. He kind of liked the guy in spite of himself, even
trusted him. He wouldn't easily forget that night, not only because
of the peculiar resolution of the fifteen-hundred-dollar issue, but
because Eve was there, too, which was a thing unusual in itself and
only contributed to his jumpiness all evening. He was conscious of
a nagging at the back of his brain that told him to get back to the
table on the balcony where she was seated alone, waiting for him.
Eve didn't like to be kept waiting.

"Where are you going now?" Eve had said, as he jumped up from
the table the moment he seated her.

"I've got some business to do. I should only be a minute or two,
just order a drink or something," he said absently.

"Aaron, I don't want to sit here alone all night. You always do
that and people stare at me as if I'm a freak, people always stare at
a woman alone, can't you give me just this one night?"

"Are you nuts or something?" he said, his pupils dilating in
anger. "I got to work for a living, don't I?"

"But this was to be our night out, I thought. My mistake was letting you take me to a place where you have the concessions."

"We saw a nice show tonight, didn't we? So you sit alone for a few minutes . . ."

"But I didn't have to be alone. Mama could have come with me, kept me company; she would have enjoyed a place like this."

"Eve, for Christ's sake she hasn't even got a decent dress to wear. I got to make a certain impression for my business . . ." he trailed off in confusion when he saw the look of unbridled fury on her face. Oh Christ, he thought, what a night I picked to bring Eve here, and then to start her off like this. His mind raced ahead to Banti. "I'll be back in a minute." He hurried away, fearful that she would raise her voice in an uncontrollable rage, create a scene here; he'd be the laughing stock all up and down Broadway. He was particularly sensitive since the Bermuda fiasco, never knew what she'd do next. Big shot Aaron Abel can't handle his own wife. Well, it was true, he couldn't — he rarely invited her to come to the clubs where he worked at nights, he had to be free to wheel and deal, unencumbered, his movements agile as a cat's, and he couldn't risk scenes, not in these places. It was becoming difficult to find excuses like "She had to stay with the children." They had that English nurse now, lately her mother was always around. He idly examined his distaste for his mother-in-law as he walked across the room toward the checkroom. Yes — distaste was a better word than dislike. He disapproved of her perhaps but didn't really dislike her. After all she was a *berrieh*, he'd have to admit, surprisingly fast on those little bird legs of hers that had to support the heavy, breasty upper body, like a capon. A superb cook, in fact her cooking had become the last remnant of theatrics with which she could still capture and bedazzle an audience. She did lend an air of security to his home, eased somewhat the frenetic atmosphere created by the combination of Eve and himself. But even there, that was balanced off negatively, because Eve was constantly spatting with her mother, nibbling away at her about this or that, "that man," as she called Lubowitz, "that kid," referring to the half brother only a few years older than Jennie. Maybe it was just because she was fat. He hated fat people. Ugh, how he hated fat, such layers of fat. His sisters were fat, his boyhood neighbors were fat. He had the Jewish boy's fear of reversion to the ghetto — the passion to assimilate. Any deviations from what he considered the norm were embarrassing, obscene to him. No wonder she couldn't buy a dress! Eve gave her money for clothes all the time, he knew it, but she'd only give it to that bastard she lived with, or to buy things for their boy. He wondered if Eve would look like that eventually.

Eve didn't care for night life. She said so often. She thought it fatuous. She didn't drink or smoke, or dance the latest dances, but she read the ads daily from the nightclubs and cafés. They sounded glossy, risqué, a subworld in which her husband moved mysteriously and from which she felt excluded. So sometimes, just sometimes, she wanted to see what it was all about, what Aaron's other life looked like, a chance to see for herself instead of being always on the outside looking in. "Pressing my nose against the glass of other people's lives," she had said. "When is my life going to begin?"

Well, it was true. This had been their one night out in months (they had just come from the new hit musical *Jubilee* by Cole Porter — it's young star, a stringily handsome new actor named Henry Fonda), but he was busy, so busy he simply couldn't sit in one place all night. When he got to the front of the room he glanced up at the balcony. Eve was looking self-conscious at the table, her delicate tilted nose dilating disdainfully. Next to her was a table full of laughing women and attentive men. He had hoped she wouldn't notice them, but she was staring with envy. She looked beautiful, he thought. She was dressed in the height of fashion, all sorts of plummish colors, giving a ripe autumn look to her chestnut hair. How lovely she could be, he thought.

He stood for a moment at the entrance to the room, dressed in the latest fashion, pearl-gray spats on his shoes, and surveyed the pulsating mass on all sides of him. His eyes darted nervously into every corner of the huge room, ignoring the compelling beat of the music, unabsorbed by the atmosphere. He was really only interested in the volume of business, the night's take, though occasionally an individual customer was a source of interest to him. He asked Jan, the maître d', "Who's here tonight?" Jan seemed to know exactly what that meant and reeled off a small list of celebrities. In the corner, a famous Hollywood actor was seated alone, helplessly drunk, dribbling onto his stiffly starched shirt front, his black bow tie twisted comically, his handsome face flushed, distorted. Aaron stared unabashed. The orchestra launched into "Isn't It Romantic." He shook his head in disapproval. "Jeeze, I don't understand, what the hell do they get out of it?" The headwaiter smiled discreetly, knowledgeably. Drinking and drunkenness fascinated Aaron. The idea that a person was not the master of his own soul but had to yield to the caprices of an inner self terrified him. Aaron was an ardent believer in autonomy. At least for himself, control was *all* in his world — the terror of losing it often drove him down to the Bowery with relentless curiosity.

He remembered once piling the three kids into the Cord. Slowly, the long impressive car would insinuate its way through the gray and the dirt of the Bowery, looking like an antediluvian monster in the darkening shadows of the Third Avenue El. Most of the men, gray as the backgrounds, blending into the walls that propped them up, or against which they spilled in all directions, were too lethargic to notice this sudden invasion of affluence. Those few who did clustered around the car, chattering, begging, cajoling. Aaron bantered with them good-naturedly, flashing pieces of silver at them, then making it disappear up his sleeve with the snap of a finger. At home this little bit of legerdemain would delight the children, here it terrified them. An old boozer loped over to the car to wipe the windshields, holding out his black-fingernailed hand for tips. A pair of wild eyes were suddenly thrust through the open window at Aaron's goading, and palsied hands made a feeble grasp at the coins close to Jennie's face. Her eyes filled with tears. Evan trembled. "Please, Daddy, let's go," they wailed, but the man was persistent. The sound of the motor warming up didn't deter him. "Please," he said, "just a dime for some coffee an' . . ." "Coffee and what?" Aaron asked encouragingly. "Jus' coffee an'," he repeated, attempting to charm with a gap-toothed smile. The children shrieked in terror. Aaron awarded the dime to the thirsty man and put his foot on the gas, still chuckling, relishing the trapped and guilty look on the face of the old drunk.

"He's had enough to drink," Aaron said to the headwaiter, now indicating the celebrity with a toss of his head, and then officiously, "I don't like it — doesn't look right — get rid of him."

It was only a weeknight, a Wednesday, but the place was packed. The room glittered and swayed with the women's jewels and gowns, the shining instruments of the band caught the light from the myriad overhead chandeliers. Ragtime and jazz had reluctantly made room for a beguiling new sound, appropriately called swing, and the Big Bands, the biggest the world would ever see, were filling up the night with music by Weill, Kern, and a socially prominent New Yorker with the melodious name of Cole Porter. And the capital city of sin and syncopation was as always — New York. Aaron thought how lucky he was to be sitting right on the pulse of the good old New Deal, just at the right time. He was beginning to think that that cripple in the White House was a f—— genius!

It was a little before show time. The show that Billy Rose had brought over from Paris was a daring, rowdy revue full of half-naked girls in assorted sizes. Tall or short, they had one thing in common — full breasts. Aaron's girls walked up and down the narrow aisles hawking their wares out of brightly decorated trays heaped high with favors, "Mementos of a night out in Paris," they called out as they stopped at the tables. They were doing especially well with a little doll, a flexible rubber likeness of a daintily curved nude woman. The rubber was buffed and treated so that it approximated, even improved upon, the smoothest, peachiest, and tenderest human flesh imaginable. They had been artfully displayed in subtly lighted fish tanks at the entrance to the room, giving the oddly erotic impression of tiny naked mermaids coyly nestling among the flora and fauna in the water. When it appeared that everyone was seated and there was a few moments' calm before the orchestra introduced the show with a great blare of trumpets, Aaron made his way back to the checkroom. When he got there, the girls were standing in clusters like black daisies, in black lace stockings and abbreviated little French maid uniforms like tutus. He saw Banti just sitting inside, waiting.

"Well, well, look who's here. Haven't seen you around for a while, how the hell are ya?" Aaron said in a jovial voice that came out flat.

"Okay, okay, Abel." Aaron put his arm around Charlie Vallone's shoulder and steered him away from where the girls stood, toward the back of the club where it was still a little noisy but where there was a comfortable sofa.

"So what's new?" Aaron asked smoothly.

"What's new is that I owe you an apology," Banti said sheepishly, but getting right to the point. Aaron studied his face for sarcasm or sincerity. It revealed little or nothing. "I discovered what happened to the dough, the fifteen hundred dollars, you know. I foolishly borrowed it from myself and forgot to put it down in my books. I feel like an awful *putz*, really jerky," he said. Charlie was smiling in a relieved way now, but Aaron wasn't smiling. What the hell did this crook think he was pulling, put him through hell for two weeks, wipe up the floors with him, scare the shit out of him, then calmly come in and announce it had all been a mistake — he was sorry. That's the way these guys operated — and up until now he had had no choice, had to break in where he could. Oh, from now on it would be different. Aaron put on a bland face, feigned benevolence. They leaned back against the sofa now. Banti lit a cigar, seemingly satisfied, pleased with his clean-breast-of-things attitude.

"Did ya know," he said casually, watching the smoke curl up and over the thick atmosphere of the club, "that we're in for some stiff competition now?"

"What do you mean?"

"Well didn't you hear that Cliff Fischer just sold the Earl Carroll Theater on Fiftieth off of Broadway? That's diagonally across the street from this joint, in case you don't know."

"Yeah, so they bought it; that should be good for the neighborhood, for business," Aaron said.

"Not if they turn it into another club, huh. With a French motif, yet — it's a hell of a lot bigger than this joint, ya know."

Aaron squinted to understand. "Well, is that what they're planning to do?"

"That's exactly what they're doin' there. Two boys, Shapiro and Blumenthal, strictly legit, I hear." Aaron had the feeling he had been about to say Jewboys, but checked himself.

"You know those boys, Aaron?" Vallone asked. Aaron thought, Why is it these guys somehow figured a Jew automatically knew every other Jew in the world.

"No-o-o-o, not really, but it seems to me I've heard of them, big shots from Chicago or something," he said musingly.

"Well, Shapiro's a New Yorker," Charlie said.

"Uh, huh," Banti continued the narrative. "Well anyway, they've completed the transaction for the building and are going ahead with the work. There's a lot of money going into it."

"Whose?" Aaron asked.

"Oh, their own mostly, and well, maybe Cliff Fischer's, a coupla big shots here and there."

"Well, sure, it stands to reason that Fischer would like to get something out of it, he took a bath when he closed up the theater."

"Yeah, well, anyway, they'd like to get Rose in there but . . ."

"Whaddya mean? Rose has a contract here with you boys," Aaron said.

"Yeah, I know, but it don't hurt 'em to try. After all Rose's contract runs out in a year, don't it?" Banti said, pinning Aaron with a level look. Aaron got the message: His contract ran the full year also. It was November already, that meant only another four or five months of cold weather in which he could make a buck and after that, well, the new club would probably be ready and who knows, it could put them out of business. But Aaron could always defect. When his contract was up here there was nothing to cry about. In fact, for him it just might be a blessing in disguise, a chance to get a concession in a top joint run by legitimate guys, to work with the kind of businessmen he'd been planning and scheming to meet. But what was Banti's platform on this sort of thing? Almost as if reading his mind, Banti said, "They'll take a big play away from us, you understand that, don't you? The boys ain't gonna like it, not at all, ya know they've sunk a barrel of dough into this place, a barrel of dough," he repeated only half-aloud.

"Yeah," Aaron said, conciliatory now, "but they're not night-club people over there, they're real-estate men. What the hell do they know about running a club?" He was excited, thinking ahead, the wheels already click-clicking in his brain. They couldn't make him renew his contract here, he knew that; his mind was jumping back and forth to extricate from his overstocked memory the names of friends who might help him get in there, alone, no partners this time. Now was the time to make his bid, before they gave it to one of their buddies, while they still needed money for financing, but he couldn't really know what to bid, he wasn't sure what he was going to come out with here — he might end up just breaking even. Not that he didn't have the money in the bank, but he preferred not to touch that, it was sacrosanct.

"That's the least. Understand they're talking to Monty Proser now, there's plenty, and a guy by the name of Benny Marden who runs a joint over in Jersey. Helluva entrepreneur, and then there's Rose," Banti said. So far Aaron hadn't had any trouble with Rose but there was something about that ratchety little guy that bugged him, maybe it was the way he had of enveloping things and squelch-ing people.

"By the way, where did you get all of this information?" Aaron asked, annoyed that neither he nor any of the people who worked for him had their ears to the ground.

"Oh, I read it in Walter Winchell's, of course," Banti said. Vallone laughed richly. Aaron looked up to check their faces for traces of sarcasm, but as always, their expressions revealed nothing, so he laughed sparsely, along with Vallone — it seemed the safest. He was suddenly restless, suddenly remembering Eve. The show had started and she would be furious. "Oh Jesus, I nearly forgot. You guys have got to excuse me, my wife is waiting for me. She's all alone at the table." This was something they could understand, it fitted in with their strange code of ethics. What you did when you were away from your wife was your business, but when "the wife" was with you she must get the highest respect, was entitled to the most elaborate courtesies. "Would you care to join us?" He didn't know why he even suggested it, just seemed like the only thing to do at the time. He never knew how Eve would react, especially now that he had been gone so long — his "minute" had turned into forty. Well, maybe there was an element of pride, maybe he had wanted to show off his wife. They surprised him by accepting and followed behind him in the dark.

Apprehensive, his stomach was beginning to knot up. He'd have to order a glass of milk when they got to the table, warm milk, just the thought was soothing. Let them kid him about not drinking, being a health nut, how could he drink with his bum stomach? He walked fast toward the back of the room, head down, shoulders thrust forward as if to form a spearhead with which to cut more rapidly through the mob. Halfway there, he saw that the table was empty, Eve was nowhere in sight. He didn't know whether to feel relieved or humiliated. Maybe she had just gone to the ladies' room, but there was no use in kidding himself. Of course he could say that she was probably sitting at another table somewhere with friends she'd run into, or something, but he knew it would be crazy to try to con these con artists. The show was in its final moments, girls were draped all over the stage in varying degrees of gorgeous undress, the music was loud, grandiose. They slipped quietly into the empty seats, which looked even emptier to Aaron now that the three of them were there alone. They looked at him quizzically. He raised his hands in a helpless gesture and shrugged, an indulgent smile on his lips that said fraternally, you know women, what can you do with them, so I'm in the doghouse for a change, are there any of us who haven't been in the same place from time to time . . . but inside he was thinking that she was the damnedest, most exasperating woman. How was she going to get back to Brooklyn alone at this time of night? She had only some change in her evening purse. But he knew that her anger would propel her. He saw her sitting in the subway, the plumes in her hat, all her fine feathers drooping sadly, her face registering her brain's exhaustion, pursuing vainly those wistful dreams.

(17)

PAULINE HAD BEEN WORKING at the Elks' Club in White Plains off and on for the last three years. In the beginning, she complained to Aaron that she was bored to death out there and didn't like the girls she worked with, particularly that roommate of hers. He was firm with her for once and told her that it was here or nowhere if she was going to work for him. At least it was a controlled environment of sorts and she wouldn't be exposed to the big city and its night temptations. Once, she had disappeared for a while — six months or more, no one knew where she was — then she surfaced, looking peaked and tired. She had tried a job as a chorus girl; a perfume salesgirl; there was even a stint with Ina Ray Hutton's All-Girl Orchestra. She had worn a tight satin suit that made her feel like an organ grinder's monkey and stood in the back row and clashed cymbals on a signal from Ina Ray, until she began complaining of a constant ringing in her ears. But she was always either fired or laid off and she was beginning to think of Aaron as the last bastion of stability. You had to admit there was a certain security in working for your brother-in-law. Checking really was better and easier, too. In fact, she was beginning to appreciate her job, and Aaron hadn't heard any complaints from her lately. She had, indeed, been strangely quiet.

One Saturday evening, Aaron stopped by the Elks' Club on a routine check. It was almost midnight of a cold December evening, close to the hopeful new year of 1936. What had begun as a random powdering of snow had become in the last half-hour an absorbent white blanket, shutting out all outside sounds. So when he entered the club the only sound that could be heard was the Big Band music playing inside the ballroom and it seemed intensified, by contrast.

The music was sweet and slow and hot, it seemed to warm the cold vestibule and the blood in Martha Voccek's veins because she was leaning over the counter invitingly and swaying her lower body while tapping her feet. Aaron grinned appreciatively as he approached the checkroom, and then caught himself. After all, he was the boss. "What's doin' kid?" he said, trying to sound casual, but if she heard, she pretended she hadn't and continued to sway in time to the music, eyes closed ecstatically. "Okay, okay," Aaron murmured, "that's enough," still trying vainly to sound businesslike.

"Oh, uh, Mr. Abel. Hi," she said, and flashed him her radiantly dimpled smile.

"How's business tonight?" he said, brushing past her intently, going in behind the counter, and looking up her name on her work card. As many times as he saw these girls in a month, he invariably forgot their names, though he realized that this girl was Pauline's roommate and he had met her a few times before.

"Oh, not bad, considering the weather," she said, in a slow, tough way she had of talking.

"Doesn't Pauline work tonight?" he asked her.

"Yeah, well — "

"Well, where is she now?"

Martha looked confused, then vacant. "I don't know for sure. She probably knocked off early."

"Early," he said incredulously. "She's not supposed to knock off early because I especially want two girls in each checkroom here for the checkout rush, which should be any minute now."

The band was playing a haunting number. He could hear it in the background, "Smoke Gets in Your Eyes." "Christ, that kid gets me sore sometimes," he mumbled, half-aloud. "Well, you're supposed to be the pro here," he said. "Don't you know any better than to let her go?" He was referring vaguely to her reputation for turning in very heavy tips, even more, on the average, than from some of the hottest spots in Manhattan.

"Mr. Abel," she said, with mock indignation, "I can't tell her what to do, after all, she *is* your sister-in-law." Aaron reddened a little. Martha had just delivered her little speech with the greatest of relish and in a tone of acid sarcasm.

"Not exactly news, is it?" he said, eyeing her now as if for the first time. He'd never really had any occasion to talk to her before this, and he could see he hadn't missed anything. She seemed hostile and kind of tough.

"Well, not exactly," she said, dragging out the word "exactly" in a maddening manner.

"Well, what's that gotta do with the price of tea? She's supposed to be working here like anyone else."

"Yeah, but she ain't anyone else," she said.

Aaron was suddenly mad. Red-faced, he said, "Well, where the hell is she now?"

"I wouldn't know, Mr. Abel," she said, lighting a cigarette casually. She sat down and crossed her long legs provocatively. She was wearing a tight black silk-crepe dress. They didn't wear costumes at the Elks' Club and the black of her dress set off her blonde hair dramatically.

"What are you doing, you know there's no smoking on duty."

"Well, Mr. Miller lets us smoke behind the checkroom as long as there's no business out front." Aaron looked confused and made a mental note to talk to Jason about it.

"You're Pauline's roommate, ain't you?" He lapsed into her speech defects unconsciously, as if unwilling to appear too overbearing, too much the boss. "Well, in another ten minutes this place'll be alive with people and I want her here. Now gimme the key to your room and I'll go over and find her."

"Sure, Mr. Abel," she said, smiling pleasantly, erupting in dimples. "Second floor." She was enjoying this, he could tell. Damn these snotty little tramps he had to work with.

He knew the little rooming house where the girls stayed was nearby but he didn't know exactly where and how to get there, so he asked her for directions.

"I don't think you'll find her there," Martha said knowingly. Aaron hadn't worn a coat as usual but he realized he was sweating. He lurched past the girl and out the front door. He was thinking angrily that Eve was right — that kid just couldn't be trusted to do anything. Where was she when she was supposed to be working?

Sleeping maybe. Sure, that figured, taking advantage, probably she thought on a night like this nobody would come around and check.

When he stepped outside he felt the sudden blast of cold against his heat-moistened skin. The snow had intensified now, a regular blizzard, he thought uncomfortably. How was he ever to get back into town tonight, back home? He hadn't even put on tire chains. Well, nobody had expected snow, he thought defensively, without quite knowing why.

He trudged over to the small, white, wood-framed house that seemed to be sagging on its underpinnings. No one was in sight. He walked quickly up the stairs. There was a side entrance that the girls used, right up onto the second floor. He was pleased now that he didn't have to cut through the living room, wake the landlady, explain his presence, or have to stop and make small talk with her; he wasn't in the mood. He opened the door of the girls' room noisily and groped for the light — nobody there, but the room reeked of the combined odors of cheap powder and cologne and looked like a cyclone had hit it — on one side only. The bed nearest the door was rumpled and covered with odds and ends of assorted attire. Dark hair pins showered the pillow like jet beads, and a familiar hat of Pauline's lay on the blanket in a sea of underthings. The one dresser in the room was a hopeless confusion of all the aids and nostrums of female insecurity. Aaron was struck with how much this resembled his bedroom at home, that look of sweet disorder, of disarming chaos that was typical of Eve — and her family. The room seemed, in fact, divided between order and chaos, as if someone had drawn a very strict line down the center — Martha's side was neat and orderly, but somehow, that only served to remind him of how hard she was. He wanted to get out of there fast, he felt that he was trespassing, this was an intimacy to which he had no right, he was embarrassed.

Walking back to the club building, he wondered what had really happened to Pauline. Where could she be on a night like this and with whom? After all, he was somewhat responsible. No, completely responsible, he thought, with a dull thud in his belly. It was snowing heavily now, a small blizzard. The winds pushed at his slight frame, buffeting him mercilessly. He would've liked to be home for the weekend, to romp in the snow with the children — which reminded him that his car might not start, the ignition was weak and leaving it out in the snow wouldn't help. Aaron didn't take very good care of his cars. In fact, from the moment of the sharp impact of acquisition, his interest in cars had deflated, collapsed almost into disdain. A car was simply a means of transportation, a pain in the neck to keep up, to drag around and park. He really preferred to walk, his feet were his favorite means of transportation. Of course, a car, a good car, a Cadillac, for example, inspired confidence, and was a necessity of sorts.

He noticed the crowd was streaming out through the large doors of the ballroom now. There would be a terrible crush at the checkroom. He couldn't see even two girls handling it alone, much less one. He must make a note to Jason to send another girl or a kid, a young boy, in there to help when there was a big affair on Saturdays. But Martha seemed thoroughly in command. He had to admit she appeared undaunted. There was a fearless quality about her, defiant almost. She made him strangely uncomfortable. He had grown accustomed to Eve's demands for protocol, good manners, "just common courtesy in public," dues owed a wife: Opening heavy doors for her, helping her in and out of the car, putting her seat down in the theater — things he would usually forget to do, but with a girl like this one he didn't know how to react, what to expect. She wasn't really feminine, not in the way his wife was, no not really feminine at all, but sexy, somehow, sexy in her hostility and her sly anger.

"She's not there," Aaron said in a surprised tone.

"No kidding," she said smiling broadly now as she helped a man on with his coat and received a dollar tip.

"Well, it looks like it's you and me against the world, kid," he said as he walked into the checkroom and slapped the counter for emphasis. He began immediately taking the checks from the hands of the packed and restless mob.

They worked together quickly and well, and in less than twenty minutes the place was cleared and empty and suddenly chill from the constant opening and closing of the huge doors and the loss of animal heat. It had been a good few years since Aaron had stood behind a counter and personally checked out a rush hour. Jerking those coats, raking in those tips, he had felt buoyant, every nerve alive. Now he felt suddenly as depleted as the hall itself. Maybe he was just tired, he thought, but he felt strangely depressed, as if the tension of the last half-hour had forced his mind to where he really didn't want it to be, on business. He had to admit there was something stimulating about working with that girl, Martha, like taking a cold shower. He loved cold showers.

"Wow, my feet are killin' me," she said, slumping down carelessly in a chair, blowing smoke out of her nose and mouth at the same time. "Hey, boss, you must be tired, bet you're not used to doin' this sort of thing, huh?"

Aaron just laughed sheepishly. "You did a good job here tonight," he said, "great, in fact. No wonder you girls are turning in so much money out here. Which reminds me," he said, "where the hell is Pauline?"

There was a silence and then she laughed a sardonic, abrupt sort of laugh. "You're askin' *me*? She's *your* sister-in-law." She said that like it was some kind of malady or affliction she hoped she wouldn't catch.

"Does she disappear like this often, and on a Saturday night yet?" The last part he said only half-aloud.

"No, she works most of the time."

"Well, what does she do when she's not workin'?"

"Listen, boss, I don't keep tabs on her, why don't you ask her yourself?"

"Okay, okay, and you can stop calling me boss."

"Yeah? Would ya like me to call ya Mr. Abel?" she said archly. "Why not?"

"Okay, Mr. Abel."

There was a small, strained silence and then they both began to laugh. He looked at his watch and whistled. "Jeeze — ya know what time it is? It's almost 1:30. How am I ever gonna get home tonight? I don't even have chains."

"Looks like maybe you're not," she said matter-of-factly. He looked at her to see what she meant, but her face was closed, expressionless.

"I better go out there and see what's doing." He went to the door and stepped out, but he was back again in a second.

"Oh Christ, I can't drive into the city in this. Wonder what most of those poor bastards did," he said.

"Well, they're mostly from up around here."

"Where are you from?" Aaron asked.

"Well, you know where I live," she said suddenly, a warm and sensuous quality to her voice.

Aaron felt silly. "I mean where did you used to live?" He looked at her and thought her broad-boned face gave away her Slavic descent, Polish probably.

"Oh, Detroit," she said. "But I been working for you for the last three years now, so I been here and there."

Three years, Aaron thought, my God, how old could she be? He figured that she must be considerably older than Pauline, there was such a world-weary quality about her, at least twenty-five — but that seemed very young to him, now, at thirty-five.

"How old are you, kid?" he asked, trying to sound offhand.

"I don't tell my age to men," she said, making a pout in an effort to look sophisticated and mysterious. Aaron knew she was play-acting for his benefit, but he didn't mind. In fact, he was flattered. He couldn't remember being wooed or flattered since his courtship days with Eve and now those memories were half-bitter, half-sweet. Now she mostly criticized him, or complained, but she hardly ever had the time or ease of spirit to flirt with him. He felt vaguely guilty now, though he didn't know why.

"So, where you gonna sleep tonight?" she said, and although she said it in that flat, unadventuresome way she had, he felt a sharp stab of excitement.

"Jeeze, that's a good question, I'm just sitting here and I hadn't even thought about it. It's getting awfully late to go looking around for hotels on a night like this, and on a weekend yet."

"Well, I'll call up one of the other girls. Maybe I can bunk in with her for the night and you can have my place all to yourself." As she said this she looked directly at him, her blue eyes assessing him carefully.

"That's awfully nice of you."

"Don't mention it, nothing too good for the boss." He pretended not to hear that little bit of sarcasm and said, "But what about Pauline?"

"Oh, I wouldn't worry too much about her, if she's not there by now she ain't coming, at least not tonight, and even if she did, so you'd bunk in with her for the night." Aaron didn't seem to hear that.

"I wish you'd tell me what she's up to," he said. "I'm sure you know something."

"Something, me? Listen, I don't know nothing, certainly not about the boss's sister-in-law," and she began buttoning her coat and took an umbrella out of the stand. He wished that she'd drop that boss routine and the "boss's sister-in-law," but she seemed addicted to it.

"Don't you want to call your friend first and see if you can arrange something?"

"She has no phone. I'd have to call the landlady — wake up the whole house. I'll go over there after I pick up my things and get you settled." Aaron had a brief flash of that room and felt uncomfortable.

They trudged over through the snow and cut across the street diagonally, and then with a stab, he realized he hadn't called Eve. Sure, she had grown accustomed to his crazy hours, though she had never learned to accept them. But staying out all night until the next day without a word — that was a different thing altogether. No, he'd have to find a phone, wake her up if necessary.

"Is . . . is there a phone in your place?"

"Sure, and I got a bar and a swimming pool, too. Whaddarya kidding?"

He passed the parking lot where his car was almost half-hidden under a mound of snow. The last one left, it looked like a lopsided polar bear. He was half-tempted to try to start it; if it wouldn't turn over he'd feel much better, he'd have no choice — but this was madness. He really had no choice anyway, the snow showed no sign of relenting and if it wasn't for that dizzy kid, that crazy, wild Pauline, he would have started back hours ago. Where the hell could she be? Tramping around with some guy some place, no doubt, but who? And why was this roommate of hers acting so damn mysterious? You could tell she didn't like her, had no use for her, with that boss's sister-in-law routine, yet she was protecting her in some odd way.

The only phone in the place was on a stand in the checkroom and he felt embarrassed in front of her. He kept stalling.

"Look, there's an all-night bar down the street, you can go over there and make a call from the booth." For some unknown reason he asked her if she'd like to come along, and she accepted readily. "Matter of fact, I could use a nightcap," she said.

When Eve finally answered the phone she was fuzzy with sleep and annoyed at being awakened. She hung up the receiver angrily without saying good-bye. Aaron felt strangely depressed; maybe it was the hour, he was probably more tired than he realized. As he walked out of the phone booth, he saw Martha perched on a bar stool with a drink in her hand.

"Why don't you join me?"

"Thanks, I don't drink," he said flatly.

"Oh, well, I do. Mind if I finish mine?"

"No, it's just that it's awfully late . . ." and he trailed off lamely.

"So what, we ought to be used to that, we're in a night business, ain't we?"

It seemed to Aaron that it took her maddeningly long to finish her drink. All the while he just stood there shifting from foot to foot, examining his carefully manicured nails. When they got to the door of her room she fumbled with the keys for what seemed an abnormally long time. When finally the door opened, it was as empty and disheveled as before.

"Well, one thing's for certain, that kid's not coming home tonight," Aaron said. For an answer he got from her another of those quick laughs that was a sort of grunt.

"I don't have to ask which is yours, I'm sure it's this one," he said, pointing to the neatly made, orderly bed near the window.

Aaron threw himself down on the bed, exhausted, and she busied herself collecting a few belongings. He didn't feel as if he could sleep; he wasn't much of a sleeper, as it was, and his nighttime hours had predisposed him toward morning sleeping. She leaned across him provocatively to get something — slippers probably, from the other side of the bed, and her perfumy scent filled his nostrils, her hair brushed against his face. He had half expected her to smell of tobacco and alcohol but that one brief moment of contact told him otherwise.

"Well, sleep well," she said. "I'll go down the street to my friend's. I hope I can get in," she said half-aloud. But he heard her.

"I hate to throw you out of your bed on a night like this." There was a momentary pause in which neither one said anything and then she was gone. He lay there in a state of confusion, his thoughts suddenly centered in his groin. What a fool he was, why had he let her go? He had wanted her in a way — he wanted her this moment. Probably under different circumstances he wouldn't have looked at her twice, but now — tonight — and she was a looker, a good-looking broad, sexy, with those come-hither dimples and blue eyes, a little "Polacky" looking but not bad, he thought, in the torpor of half sleep mixed with desire. And then he heard the fumbling with the lock again. Oh Jesus, was he going to have a scene now with Pauline, not now, he was just beginning to relax . . . the door opened and Martha threw her keys down on the dresser and said quietly, huskily, "There's no answer, I can't get in, so I guess . . ." and she kicked her shoes off . . .

"Come here for a minute," he commanded in a half whisper.

She walked over to her bed. "Will you unhook my dress for me?"

He fumbled with the hooks and suddenly her bare back revealed only a thin black band of brassiere, which he also undid. She turned and they were kissing now, her hair had come loose from its neat bun and they were rolling over in the bed. Aaron was overcome with a sharp and overpowering urge to subdue her, tame her, to wound her. But, in what seemed like one instant, he was inside of her and the sensation of her obvious enjoyment, warm and clinging, encouraging instead of rejecting, was so beguiling that he could think of nothing but the sound of his heart beating in his head, and when all too soon it was over, she lay with her head on his chest and he saw with surprise how very young and fresh she looked without make-up — more vulnerable now that her hard mask had melted away.

"Gee, you're something," she said to him.

"Is that good?"

"It's good enough!"

He wasn't sure what that was supposed to mean but he was flattered in a way he hadn't been with a woman before. The very memory of her pleasure warmed him, he wanted her again.

When they awoke it was around nine-thirty in the morning and he was reluctant to leave. "Listen," he said, jumping up abruptly, "Pauline's liable to come in at any moment. I'd better get the hell out of here."

"What are you afraid of, afraid she'll tell your wife?"

Aaron felt suddenly annoyed with her, with himself. Why had he allowed himself to be put in this position where this girl, a typical checkroom kid, had something on him? He was usually too clever for that sort of stupidity.

When he left — walked away in the cold, snow-washed Sunday morning — he felt strange, a combination of distaste and a voluptuousness, a leaden feeling, as if his brain's signal to his legs were being intercepted.

*

Less than an hour later, Martha was kneeling before the confessional booth at the Immaculate Heart Church in White Plains, clutching her rosary beads in a shaking hand.

(18)

ARON AND JASON were sitting in an all-night Horn and Hard-art automat, a few blocks from Broadway. Aaron was fascinated by the click-clicking of the little slots that a nickel or dime opened miraculously to reveal appetizing cakes and sandwiches in all their pristine beauty, their peculiar magazine-cover perfection. Aaron hunched over his steaming cup of Ovaltine. He had been on an Ovaltine kick ever since he had heard the radio commercials guaranteeing a full eight hours sleep; he would gladly settle for half, he was getting desperate. As it was, he had only five or six hours in which to sleep and at least half of that time was spent in fitful tossing and turning and twisting of the bedclothes. Opposite him, Jason sipped at his coffee and puffed on a cigarette. There were yellowish circles under his dark eyes.

"Why the hell do you smoke so much, don't you know it's poison?" Aaron asked paternally.

"Yeah, I know, but I'm not a health nut like you. I don't care if I don't live to be a hundred."

Ignoring that, Aaron persisted, "And doesn't that coffee keep you awake?"

"Listen — I'm so tired now, there's nothing going to keep me up." Aaron didn't understand that, he couldn't understand that kind of tiredness. Here it was almost four o'clock in the morning, only three hours sleep the night before, and he really wasn't tired, not physically, and certainly not mentally.

"And at your age — Jesus. I don't know, you must be screwing around too much, that's your trouble!"

"Who me?" he said in mock surprise. Jason squinted beyond Aaron through the circle of his smoke ring. He blew beautiful rings.

"No, not really," he said, denying the charge. "There has been a little blonde . . ."

"Oh, you mean Dolly whatever her name is, that cute little blonde who works for us over at the De Paris?"

"Yeah, yeah. That's the one. How'd you know?" Jason seemed surprised. Aaron liked getting an unfamiliar rise out of him.

"I think my sister-in-law told me. She's a sweet little thing, kind of kittenish." There was a silence, Aaron looked cryptic. "Yeah, Pauline told me."

"I don't think she even knows Pauline."

"I guess she's big friends with Pauline's roommate out in White Plains." Aaron didn't know why he'd said that. He hadn't really wanted to.

"Oh, you mean that blonde kid — er — Martha, with the Polish name?"

"Yeah, yeah, that's the one. She works like a demon, like she's been doin' it all her life."

"Doing what?" Jason asked archly.

Aaron was determined to keep the conversation on a business level now, at all costs, because it was getting away from him. He felt strangely uncomfortable.

"Even if she had, that wouldn't be very long, unless she started checking at twelve," Jason continued. "I don't think she's even nineteen yet, or maybe just — at least that's what her work card says — " There was a silence like a thud. Aaron hoped his face didn't give him away. He felt taken, foolish, angry — helplessly, terribly angry. For one mad moment he was thinking of coming clean; yes, that was it, clean, he felt soiled now. It would feel good to unburden himself to the younger man, the whole silly, sordid evening. Jason would understand, he had a pretty relaxed live-and-let-live attitude — you had to, in this business. You saw so much at nights, in this town, the night spewed out so much swill and garbage. He was thinking of a thousand questions that he wanted to ask Jason, but somehow he couldn't get out one. He was conscious of his position, the boss, the proper respect he must command, and he knew Jason's real attitude toward these girls — but he must say something, continue in his usual style.

"I worked with her one busy Saturday night over at the Elks' Club in White Plains. It was the night of that blizzard we had a couple of weeks ago."

"You worked with her, what do you mean?" Jason asked, suddenly very much on guard to preserve the protocol of a business little known for its formalities.

"Pauline forgot to show up, just when I needed her. That's what comes from hiring in-laws. We got stuck for a girl and I pitched in — what could I do?"

A Negro porter was mopping up near their feet. Aaron compulsively pulled his feet away, he didn't want dirty water sloshed on his spats. He felt somehow he should change the subject, let it go, but he couldn't seem to stop himself.

"Well, I don't know where the hell she was, or what she's been up to but I'm sure it's no good."

There was a strained silence as Jason flicked his cigarette and looked down deep into his cup of coffee as if reading the dregs there.

"Look Jace, if you know something, tell me for chrissakes, don't play games. I thought we always leveled with one another."

"Yeah, I know, Aaron, I know, but this is touchy. She's your wife's sister and you know how your wife is, well, kind of high-strung."

Miller — the eternal diplomat, Aaron thought. That was probably the understatement of his life.

"Look kid, what are you trying to say?"

"Well that crazy kid's been running around with a guy — a musician, I think."

"Well, I figured something like that and a musician would be just the kind of guy I figured, too."

"Yeah," Jason said quietly, "but, but there's more — he's colored."

"He's what?"

"He's a nigger," Jason said quietly, regarding the glowing tip of his cigarette from all angles.

"What, are you kiddin' or something? If you are you ain't very funny," Aaron said.

Jason raced on, talking faster than Aaron had ever heard him talk before. "Aaron, the poor kid's lonely, she's been dumped here and there ever since she can remember — "

"Look, don't excuse her to me, she's gotta be crazy, what is she, crazy or something," Aaron said, his already bloodshot eyes dilating. Jason tried to expand a little but Aaron rushed on, impervious. "I gave her a home, I took her in, I gave her a job."

"Yeah, and your wife threw her out." Jason was a stickler for family loyalty. He was his parents' sole support, he worked tirelessly, denying himself even the most minimal luxury so that he would have to deny them nothing. He didn't even dare to think about marriage, and anyway, the kind of girls he met in his work — he wouldn't even dream about insulting his mother and father with such girls.

"Oh my God. Eve musn't know. My life wouldn't be worth living, Jason."

"Well, you can be damn sure I'm not going to tell her."

"Is, is she sleeping with him?" Aaron managed to nudge it out in a hoarse whisper.

"Listen, what the hell do I know? I don't sleep under her bed. Listen, it's 1936, anything's possible, I suppose, so — "

Aaron gave a long, low whistle. He was silent for a moment, digesting the information. He thought to himself that Jason was a mine of checkroom information, just ask Jason Miller, he knew what was going on on all levels, in all places, but he'd never volunteer, didn't gossip — thank God. He seemed disinterested. He could be trusted with secrets, was himself a secret.

He thought of Eve with a sinking feeling, of how she would absorb this as part of the personal tragedy of her life. As if there hadn't been enough personal damage already. She would look for more, add it to all the other pain of her life; he could see her now, trembling at the sordidness and humiliation. She would immolate herself. Eve, the moralist, unrelenting, with an archaic mind full of *bobbemysehs* and legends and *dybbuks*, supersensitive to the constant battle between good and evil. He barely heard Jason's mumbled comment, "Well, they're a good pair, those two, both of them jailbait. How did she get hooked up with that Polish kid, anyway?"

"I sent her there when I heard there was a job vacancy out in White Plains." He couldn't stop himself: "Why, what's wrong with the Polish kid?"

"Oh, she's just been around, that's all," he said cryptically.

"She's a friend of Dolly's, I thought — "

The barbed nonsequitur left Jason unruffled. He shrugged nonchalantly. "Yeah, I suppose so, but they don't see much of each other anymore. Dolly's working here in town, the other one's out there — I don't know — I only sleep with her. I'm not married to her. So what's the difference?" Jason said with an odd sort of detachment.

"What are you, twenty-six or twenty-seven? So what's the hurry?" Aaron's mind raced around wildly trying to sort out the information Jason had so offhandedly supplied. Hmm . . . a Catholic girl. He thought to himself, by way of a curious salving of conscience, that the Catholic girls were "faster" than all the rest. All that mumbo jumbo about the Virgin Mary, all the warnings against the perils of the flesh — Oh, the whole thing was ridiculous, he wouldn't see her again.

Jason refilled his empty cup from a nearby coffee stand, but Aaron could tell he was tired.

"C'mon, Jace, I'm gonna let you get some sleep, I can see you're dead on your feet — " Aaron rose without waiting for him to finish his coffee. When he was ready to go, it must be that moment and no other. His own legs felt stiff, heavy when he stood on them, wobbly suddenly. He felt uncomfortable about going home, to his wife; he felt that way often lately, for special reasons — for no special reasons.

They walked toward Broadway where their cars were parked. Aaron had gotten used to nightscapes, had learned to love their sharp contrasts, the shadowless, shining beauty. He simply could not understand sleeping it all away as most people did. He'd sooner sleep through a Broadway show, which is what he usually did, than through a night. A show was planned, contrived; a New York night just happened, fell together in haphazard patterns, like a kaleidoscope.

Twice a week now, Aaron rented an armored truck that went

around to his places and collected the receipts. First they were counted carefully by Aaron, Jason, or some of the other boys now in his employ, and kept in the vault on the premises. He might have to start using it nightly, less chance of stealing by the girls. He thought about this now as they walked toward their cars. "Jason, have you thought about what I told you concerning the new place?"

"You mean the French Casino?"

"Yeah, I've got a good chance of getting a concession there, it's as good as in the bag. They can use the cash in front now, and the guy who introduced me there is a good friend of Shapiro and Blumenthal."

"Well, as long as you understand you can't work them both, you can't stay on here at the De Paris and go over to the French Casino, too. You understand that, don't ya? — because there's gonna be a war, a regular little war."

"Sure, I understand that, and who wants to stay with those hoods? One year's sentence is enough for me, the sooner I get out, the better I like it! I don't mind telling you I was scared shitless when he threatened me about the lousy fifteen hundred bucks. Who needs it — the little bastard!"

"Anyway," Jason said, "I'm not sure, but I think it'll be a classier operation all around, and no partners, I presume."

"No, no partners for me from now on, if I can help it; I don't care for partners. They're usually crooked and only out to screw you."

It was almost as if the fact of his 'twinning' had left a permanent hostility to partnership of any kind. He had been rudely separated from the first, from the original, he had struggled to independence, now he resented any intimacy with a facsimile. Aaron himself dimly realized that he was incapable of intimacy, tenderness terrified him. He felt deprived.

"I don't know that they'll let you go so easily, even now," Jason said.

"What do you mean?"

"Well, they've got a load of money sunk into the club. They're not about to be satisfied with a one-year tenure and then out. They couldn't possibly make back that kind of money in a year. You and I know that the new place will have put them out of business by this time next year."

"Yeah, yeah. So what're you trying to say, Miller?" A growing sense of panic enveloped him, he tried to block out what Jason was saying, what he had known from the beginning.

"What I'm trying to say is that they're not going to like your financing the French Casino, that's all."

"What financing?"

"Whatever you pay up front for the concession, and I figure it's going to cost plenty, they'll consider another nail in their coffin and they won't let you get away with much, they'll fight you for every nickel — the same as you would." Jason's irony was not altogether lost on Aaron. "Look how they carried on over fifteen hundred dollars, which wasn't even your fault. That should tell you enough." They had come to Aaron's car, but neither saw it, they were so absorbed. They were standing at the corner of Lindy's restaurant now. The full moon looked wrinkled through the curling smoke from the huge electrified Camel sign across the street. People were straggling out onto the sidewalks, talking fast, kibitzing in bunches. Aaron glanced at the full-length glass windows that were brightly lit to show patrons lingering over huge pale slabs of golden cheesecake or giant sandwiches bloated with various spiced novelty cuts. Aaron groaned unconsciously and felt his stomach turn over — that's all he needed at this time of the night.

He looked frazzled. He knew he wouldn't sleep for whatever remained of the night. That cool, know-it-all Miller had just fixed that for him, for sure, with that superior manner of his, as if he were Moses on the mount, or something. Who the hell did that kid think he was anyway? Why, if it hadn't been for me, where would he be?

"Aaron," Jason's deep voice shook him out of his reverie, "don't worry, we'll be able to handle it." Aaron looked at Jason carefully.

Jason looked tired suddenly, terribly tired. He ran his hands over his eyes, large strong hands, different from Aaron's fine-boned, delicate hands with their clear-cut, pale half-moons strangely translucent now under the white street lights. No one would have guessed that they had handled soiled money all night long.

Broadway Rose sidled over to them and pushed her tray of apples in between Aaron and Jason, and cackled, "Hello there, Abel, what's new with the hatcheck king?" Aaron loved to be called that; he grinned and put a dollar on her tray.

"Hello, Annie, how's my favorite hooker, catch any live ones, baby?" She grinned appreciatively and smoothed one of the many fraying strands of hair back from her hollow face with a densely liver-spotted hand. She jostled a few more familiar faces, cackled fraternally, and disappeared into the night.

A FEW WEEKS LATER, after Aaron had tried in vain to reach Pauline on the telephone, she caught him one day at the central telephone number he gave out for business. He had rented a tiny office in a small, run-down old building on Sixth Avenue. A sign, Wingfoot Enterprises, hung above the door of the second-floor office. He had agreed to meet her at the Elks' Club on an afternoon of that week, "to talk," she said. At three in the afternoon the checkroom was peacefully deserted. Aaron hung around waiting for Pauline to arrive, already feeling tension beginning to close in as his muscles tightened all over. She arrived late as always, breathless and distracted, her hair a shambles of experimental colors, her mascara already smudged beneath her eyes. She put her large purse down on the counter and began fumbling in it nervously, objects spilling out of it every which way. It annoyed him. It flashed across

Aaron's mind how much like Eve she was, always bubbling up or boiling over, her heart scattered helter-skelter like the contents of her pocketbook.

Pauline didn't look well, he thought, aside from her generally sleazy get-up. She looked unhealthy.

"You haven't seen or talked to your sister for a long time. How come?"

"Oh, come on, Aaron, you know why. For what? She'll only lay into me."

"So? You've gotta answer to someone, everybody does. And she cares about your welfare, you know that."

"She makes me feel crummy."

"C'mon, we can't sit here and be uncomfortable. We'll go into the dining room and you can have some coffee or something."

They walked into the big empty room, closed officially until evening. It seemed as yet strangely unprepared for the banquet that would take place that evening.

Jeremy, the old Negro waiter, bustled around Aaron. "Can I get you something, boss? Coffee, maybe?" he asked.

Aaron sparred and jested with him. His voice raised an octave, he said, "Sho' nuff, now ya knows that I don't drink that Java Jive, that's pure poison. Why, that stuff'll kill ya faster than corn liquor. Git me some of that thar Postum stuff and some buttered toast."

"And you, Miss?"

"Just coffee, thanks." She wasn't laughing at Aaron's routine, in fact, it didn't appear that she'd heard.

"Oh, just some o' that thar poison I was just talking about for the lady."

"Okay, boss," Jeremy grinned, showing white teeth brightly checkered with gold.

Aaron turned to Pauline.

"So what's going on with you, kid? You don't look too good, I'll tell you."

"I don't feel too good. First of all, I haven't had any place to live for the last few weeks." Pauline lit a cigarette. Aaron waved the smoke away with annoyance. "Yeah, that bitch Martha threw me out, bag and baggage. I came home late one night and found all my stuff sitting on the front porch. Who the hell does she think she is, anyway?"

Aaron suppressed a smile, but he was angry beneath it. That smart-ass little bitch is getting out of line, he thought to himself. He wondered at her supreme self-confidence.

"Well, wasn't she afraid of losing her job?" he asked, though he already knew the answer.

"Evidently not. Listen, she's afraid of nothing, that one, *nothing!*"

He felt weak. He knew she was taking advantage and he was overcome with a fury of helplessness.

"Well, why the hell did she do it?" he was probing, hoping to learn *nothing*.

"How should I know? She's kind of crazy, if you ask me. But that morning she picked a fight about something or other, and worked herself up. I couldn't have stood her much longer, anyway. She's been getting worse lately."

"So there must be other girls you can room with," he said blandly, but all the while he was thinking to himself that Martha'd been itching to get rid of Pauline for months now, ever since their affair began. "I don't need your wife's sister breathing down my neck," she'd said, "and anyway, she's a lazy slob. Half the time she doesn't even show up for work, and I'm covering for her, doing double duty." Martha wanted the place to herself — "needed" was a better word. Also, she was a compulsive neatnik, and Pauline was a threat to her sense of order.

Aaron was confused. "How come you didn't tell me right away . . ."

"I couldn't."

"Why?"

"She threatened that if I told you she'd tell you," she faltered slightly, ". . . tell you about me."

"*What* about you?"

"That, that I have a boyfriend."

"Oh, that, Christ, I've known about that for a while. I've been meaning to talk to you about that for weeks, in fact, but I don't know . . ." his voice faded. "I guess I just couldn't believe it, couldn't bring myself to talk about it."

"Who told you?"

"Oh, I don't know, maybe Miller."

"That rat, that's all he's got to do is spy on me — " she mumbled, but sounded relieved. "God, you're not going to start lecturing me, are you?"

"So it *is* true! You must be crazy, too, like the rest of your crazy family. You oughta have your goddam head examined."

"Why, what the hell's so terrible about it? We love each other, and he makes me feel good, he makes me feel like I'm a movie star or something."

"And you make me feel sick."

"Oh, stop it! It doesn't mean I'm no good 'cause I'm sleeping with a Negro, does it?" she said. "You and my sister are Victorian, you think everybody's no good unless they live according to your particular rules and regulations. You even think Mama's a whore . . ."

Throughout this tirade Aaron had withdrawn into a stubborn silence of disapproval that only succeeded in further inflaming Pauline.

"Well, there's nothing wrong with Andy Cole." Up until now he had been nameless, and Aaron hadn't bothered to ask. "He's a very talented musician, he plays the trombone, and he's handsome. He's not really black, I mean he's so light-skinned you'd hardly even think he was . . ." Her voice trailed off and she lit another cigarette.

"Do you have to smoke so goddam much?"

"Yes."

"Jesus."

She blew an angry puff of smoke in Aaron's direction. "On top of all of this, I'm pregnant."

"What? What did you say?"

"You heard me," she said, more quietly now.

"Oh Jesus," Aaron groaned.

"He's got nothing to do with this, I assure you," she said, hoping for a break of comic relief.

"I'm glad you can sit there making jokes — why, that dirty black bastard, I'll have him killed, I'll get some guys I know and have him

killed, or I'll kill him myself." It seemed to her that he was trying
hard to make all the right noises.

"Oh, stop it, Aaron, for God's sake!"

"Are you crazy or something, getting yourself mixed up like that
and letting a nigger knock you up?"

"That's checkroom talk, just filthy checkroom talk," Pauline said,
tears streaming down her cheeks like sudden shafts of light. "Eve
should hear you."

"No, she should hear *you*, except I wouldn't do it to her, I
wouldn't humiliate her like that. But *you*, couldn't you get a white
guy to fuck you??" Aaron had been working himself up gradually
to what he considered an appropriate pitch.

Pauline was sobbing now, her head down on the table, her shoulders heaving, the coffee sloshing on the table.

"Where is he now? Does he know?" he asked it all in one gasping
breath and then ran on to answer his own questions. "Oh, what the
hell is the difference. You can't marry him anyway."

She sat up and began mopping the table with a napkin and talking
through her tears.

"I was lonely, he was so sweet to me . . . He's intelligent, a talented musician, he's . . ."

"Wonderful, wonderful," Aaron said. "Then why don't you
marry him and save me a big headache, huh?"

"I don't want a baby, a colored baby," she whispered, "any kind
of a baby!" She was crying. "Please give me the money for an abortion, Aaron. I'll work it off, honest I will, I'll pay you back every
cent."

"I got a choice? If your sister ever found out about this, whose
fault would it be? Mine — I had to throw you into the checkroom
at barely seventeen; I know it by heart. I'll call Jason, he'll get you
another place to stay."

"No, no! I don't want to work up here with *her* anymore!"

That presented a problem. He really didn't need her underfoot up
here, spoiling his party, his romp with Martha. On the other hand,
he didn't particularly want her in town near Eve, either.

"Maybe I'll put you on another shift here, an afternoon shift.

Well, you won't be feeling much like working for a while, anyway. Jesus, don't say a word to anybody, you understand, not *anybody*. I'll let you know about the doctor in a few days." And suddenly he wanted to get out of there, he had to get out of there, far away. Her presence embarrassed him, it was unclean.

He got up as if he'd grown suddenly impatient, signifying that the conference was at an end. He walked quickly through the old, solid-looking dining room with its slightly sweet and sour odor. The stale smell of old cooking was pierced sharply by occasional bursts of fresh new aromas of the evening's dinner. He felt as if his feet couldn't carry him fast enough. It figures — she with her spoiled, greedy, self-gratifying nature, and *him* — well, that was only to be expected — irresponsible creatures. But he had long ago clouded his mind to the connections between cause and effect, and he really couldn't see that this might well be part of his own machinations, his favorite game of *noblesse oblige*. He enjoyed the *noblesse* part, but the *oblige*, well, that was something else again! Not that he didn't enjoy the power of obligation, he did, it was heady, dizzying, delicious, but it was almost too easy, the pawns he played these games with didn't have a brain in their heads or a coin in their pockets. No, the challenge would be to win the game with equal opponents — well, almost equal . . . Well, he'd have to find Pauline a husband of sorts, get her out of his hair, out of trouble.

*

Two weeks later Pauline was dead. Andy Cole phoned Aaron. Aaron, in a cold sweat, went to an obscure part of White Plains to reclaim her body from the rooming house where she had been staying with Cole.

In a haze of tears, he cleaned the walls and floors while Cole tried in vain to make the lifeless body appear normal for the undertaker. It became an impossible effort because of the drastic seepage of blood and the already sodden sheets. In desperation, they carried the body to the bathtub just outside in the hall, where Cole washed the blood off while Aaron took the sheets out to the back and burned them. He kept murmuring while he worked, "There must not be a trace, not a trace of anything around here. Gossip — my wife — my God!" He wasn't making any sense, his speech was disjointed. Sweat and tears ran down his face while he worked, and he was fighting the nausea that had welled up in him the moment he entered the room. He seemed not to see Cole at all. It was as if he were alone. He couldn't keep his mind from racing jerkily from past to present and back again — memories — like Broadway neons flashed in and out of his head. He kept seeing Eve's face on Pauline's body, Fredda's white arms, a black fag at Webster's Hall who wore make-up. Then he was back again to the horror of the present.

Until now Aaron had moved like a mechanical man, a robot, wordless, mindless, efficient. In spite of the shared intimacy of the last few minutes, he only seemed to see Cole now, as if for the first time.

"I got her a good doctor, what the hell happened?" Aaron said, his voice a hot whisper of rage.

"We went to someone else, she wouldn't listen; he was seventy-five dollars cheaper, said she could use the difference — I begged her — " A tall man, he appeared to have crumpled, and stood slumped in the shadows of the corner of the room, a cigarette trembling between his fingers.

Aaron walked over to him and grabbed him by the collar. He spit hard in his face. Then he began to bang the man's head against the wall, over and over, it seemed to him a hundred times. The man offered no resistance, his body loose as a rag doll. Aaron kept hitting the wall with the man's head until he slumped to the floor, then with an unfamiliar strength he dragged him back up to his place on the wall, and holding him up with one hand punched him hard with the other, a sure, short punch to the gut that his brother Bennie had taught him to use on the neighborhood kids — the kids that used to lie in wait for him outside the big Catholic church on Vesey Street on Saturdays and yell "get the dirty sheeny," and snatch his silk *yarmulkah* and stamp on it in the gutter until its delicate blue and white colors blurred to gray.

Still panting hard, he said, "You dirty, cock-sucking, murdering bastard, get back to Africa where you belong — if I ever see that black face of yours again anywhere in this world, I'll personally see that you're strung up from the highest tree."

The man who drove the truck for the undertaker arrived, put the small, soaking-wet body in the wagon and directed Aaron to follow him to the funeral parlor. Aaron wanted to get completely away, to run, but he could barely get his legs to move. Like a sleepwalker, he forced one foot before the other until he reached the door.

As he drove, following the undertaker's truck, he tried to get his mind riveted on Eve, on what he would tell her, what kind of story. This would be the finish for them, somehow he knew it — the final excuse she was looking for. She'd blame him — damn her family! It seemed that they were around for the single purpose of laying bare her soul, exposing its raw, red underside, victimizing her as her father had done by his irresponsibility, his careless spending, his failure to provide for them in the event of his death, his profligate ways. Yes, it was her father's fault to begin with — why should he feel responsible?

*

Even at the end it seemed that Pauline could not stir a ripple of interest from the powers that be, and the skies didn't even afford her the appropriate mantle of rain. The sun continued to shine down spitefully on the little cortege as it inched along in traffic over the Fifty-ninth Street Bridge into Queens. There was no way to have hidden the facts from Eve completely, he knew that, so he cleaned them up as much as possible and gave only a rough outline. He said he didn't know the man, had never met him, and that Pauline had died in a hospital in Westchester. Eve said that she didn't believe a word of it and would get to the bottom somehow. Aaron was lying as usual, covering up again for his own horrible machinations; not only had he viciously victimized *her*, but all of her poor, unfortunate family.

She refused to talk to him, or to ride in the same car with "my sister's murderer." Aaron drove a small borrowed Ford, a discreet distance behind. It was Jason's car, but she would not permit Jason or any of the other checkroom "low-lifes" to attend. They had done

enough to Pauline in her life, she said, she didn't need them there to
gloat at her death.

Eve rode in the long dark green Cadillac, chauffeur-driven, with
her mother beside her, her brother Jules, and her half brother Albie.
The chauffeur was Aaron's latest acquisition, precious to him, not so
much for the impression he made as for practicality. He hated driving, invariably got lost, and was constitutionally unable to park a
car because it required a moment's mechanical concentration and
patience that he simply did not possess. Eve sat woodenly, just staring out the window.

"Eve, darling," her mother said, "stop killing yourself, what could
anyone do?"

"That's what you said when Freddie died too. You could have
tried being a mother, a real mother, that's what you could have done,
but instead it was more important to be a wife to him." She said the
word "wife" with bitter irony. Lisa was silent; the boys stared out
the window, seemingly unmindful of the charged atmosphere.
There was another long silence. Tears spilled down Lisa's loose
cheeks onto her deep bosom, which lost itself somewhere in the ample waistline. Eve relented. "Here, Mama," she said more tenderly,
"let me fix your hair a little." She tried to arrange the thinning
marcelled waves around her mother's face. The little pocket comb
trembled in her hand.

They alighted for the meager service, to be delivered by a hurriedly hired rabbi, and the disparate group stood around the little
mound of new earth. Eve did not glance once in Aaron's direction.
After the *Kaddish* was read in a monotone, the rabbi closed his book,
took some money from Aaron, and moved on to the next grave.
Aaron came over to put an arm about Eve's shoulder. She pulled
away — "Don't come home again," she said evenly. Aaron looked
puzzled. "Anyway, I've changed the locks, your things will be down
in the lobby — " The first words she had said to him since she learned
of Pauline's death three days ago.

"What — are you crazy — Eve, please — " He spoke in staccato
bursts now — undigested words causing him to choke — "It wasn't
my fault, you can't blame me — "

"I knew it would happen, I begged her not to get involved with you — "

"But, Eve, I don't want to break up my home, our marriage — the children. What's the good of adding still more loss?"

"Oh, don't pretend that Pauline is the only reason."

"Is — is that all?" he said, "Aren't we going to talk about it more — discuss it — ?"

"Since when have we ever discussed anything — you've never had the time. Anyway what is there to say that we haven't said before a thousand times — "

She was right, he knew it. There was nothing different to say now, they had said it all through the sad and disappointing years of their mutual confusion — almost from the beginning. What could more rehashing bring but scandal, remorse, and disgruntled children.

"Take heart," she said, "there's always the checkroom — there's always that consolation."

"But the business would mean nothing without you and the children — it's all been for you — "

"I don't want it, have never wanted it, it's tainted money. See what your checkrooms have wrought," she said, looking at him now without really seeing him. "They've lost me a sister and gained you a mistress — "

"Stop, you two, stop," Lisa cried, running up behind. "You tore at her before she died, the two of you fighting over her, over everything and nothing — you who have so much — now at least let her rest in peace, for God's sake!"

They rode in silence on the way home, until Eve said, staring out the window, as if to herself, "All I ever wanted was a little beauty in my life — I've never found it anywhere but in books."

(20)

THE OFFICES OF CARTON AND BIRNOFF were on the twenty-third floor and commanded a broad view of Murray Hill and the twin banding of rivers that battered their misty fumes back and forth at each other across the city.

Aaron hadn't been to the new office. When he needed any legal advice, which wasn't often, he usually spoke to Sy Barche, though he'd always had a profound respect for Al's legal acumen and his integrity, and often promised himself that when he became a really important account he'd give it exclusively to Al. Aaron was impressed; Al Carton had done okay. It wasn't a big office, but it was well appointed, had a quiet air of elegance. Aaron thought without much interest that Al's wife, Edith, might have had a hand in the decorating. He thought that Edith was clever and that she adored Al, but that was about all he could say for her. He considered her almost too bland for comment. Aaron was late, as usual, but was annoyed at being kept waiting. When the receptionist suggested he take a seat, he refused, preferring instead to stand or to pace back and forth restlessly, cracking his knuckles. Now and then she glanced up, giving him sour looks.

Finally the door to Al's office opened, and a fat man with a fleshy lower lip emerged. Aaron looked up as he passed him closely, and hurried into the office even before the receptionist gave him the go-ahead signal, thinking nervously to himself that the man's underlip resembled a piece of raw filet mignon, blue-red and flabby. Ugh! How he hated ugliness.

Al and Aaron greeted each other warmly and Aaron took a seat in front of the large, efficient-looking desk. The walls were properly lined with legal books and other works, richly bound in red leather, heavy and impressive. There were pictures on Al's desk, too, but he couldn't see them from the back. He assumed they were of Edith, maybe even the baby, a year-old girl. Al had only been married a few years — maybe four, and Aaron had just about completed ten. The thought of the word "completed" sent a shock wave of confusion through his entire well-disciplined body.

Aaron felt a fleeting stab of envy for the orderly office and desk, for all of Al's traditional and well-adjusted life. He, Aaron, with his office in a hat, behind any checkroom counter at which he happened to be, or any restaurant telephone — he really needed a decent office, a hub for all the spokes of his business that radiated across Brooklyn and New York, a central place where he could be found — where he could scheme his schemes, dream his dreams.

There was a brief uncomfortable silence. He was beginning to feel sorry he had come. For what? To throw himself on Al's mercy? To ask him what?

Al said, suddenly businesslike, "Aaron, I guess you know that Eve asked me to represent her, don't you?"

"Yes, are you going to?"

"Well, I don't know. I want to help in a way, but I don't like to be put in the middle."

Aaron leaned forward urgently and said, "Al, don't take the case, please, it's crazy. She doesn't know what she's doing. She doesn't need a lawyer, she needs a psychiatrist!"

Al smiled blandly. "Why?"

"Why?" Aaron's voice was incredulous. "Whaddya mean, why? It's a crazy whim of hers, just a crazy whim, with three children. Why for God's sake, I don't think the baby is four yet. What the hell's wrong with me, what's so lousy about me? What did I do? Work my goddam fingers to the bone, stay up nights until I'm dead on my feet. I've made a good living for her." He thought for a moment that that was silly, it didn't really follow. He had always worked hard, from the earliest time he could remember, when he was a kid on the Lower East Side. Stealing ice and selling it, delivering newspapers. He and his brothers, the four of them, toting, carrying, charming for tips, begging. Jesus, he was still begging for tips. After all, in a business where the sole commodity was other people's money (he made nothing else, produced nothing, offered only a service), what else was it? Now he was sitting here in his old buddy Al's plush, correct office and begging for his wife. Aaron was frightened for the first time. He thought that his life and his work had completed the process of induration, but he was wrong. He was vulnerable still. He felt a panic of disappointment.

"You know what I took her away from, Carton — she . . . her mother was . . ." Aaron sputtered, growing red in the face.

"Yes, I know," Al said slowly. Then he said, "Look Aaron, you don't have to convince me — can you convince her?"

"Convince her of what, for chrissakes, what the hell is she looking for — a few lousy bucks a month?"

"For one thing can you convince her that you are blameless in her sister's death?"

Aaron seemed to be taken off guard. There was a pensive silence while he gathered his defenses, and then he said in a voice barely audible, "You know that's not fair, Al. All I did was give the kid a job when she begged me for it. But it was a terrible thing to have happened — "

Al appraised Aaron momentarily, as if deciding whether to speak or not. His soft brown eyes were sad and guarded. When he looked down, Aaron noticed his lashes seemed sandy, almost as if they were powdered. Al still didn't say anything, but got up and walked over to the window and looked out as if he were searching for something way out there beyond the tall bridges and the tiny ships. A police siren screeched by; it sounded tinny from the twenty-third floor. Horns peeped in sour, urban disharmony.

Aaron found Al's personality curiously nebulous. No wonder Eve had chosen him over Al. She needed direction, he had decided that long ago. Why then was she so resentful about taking it, rebelling so ferociously, turning on him so bitterly? It had to be out of contrariness. After all, he was a good provider, a fine figure of a man in the prime of health and wealth. What more could she want? What in the hell did she want from him? He squirmed in the oversized leather chair and shrugged off these thoughts with characteristic impatience.

Without turning around, Al said to the window, "Remember the Italian guys who lived in our neighborhood, how they used to talk about the 'biting of the thumb,' remember that?"

"Yeah, so?"

"Well, it's like that with Eve. She's bound on turning the marriage into a lifetime vendetta, to pay you back for something. I don't know what — I don't even think she knows — but I know she feels left out of your life."

So that was it, Aaron thought, it's back to this — her basic loneliness and her resentment about it. Al turned around then and looked at Aaron. For once Aaron couldn't seem to find anything to say, so he studied his nails. Al continued, still standing by the window, barely audible: "God, how she stood out in that neighborhood, a beacon in a blighted area" — Aaron looked annoyed. Al turned back to his desk now and sat down. "She'd always wanted a career. Just when she was about to have it, to be a star in Hollywood, she suddenly dropped everything to come back and marry you. Why?"

"Why?" Aaron tried on his amazed look for Al. "Because she loved me, of course, why else? She came back to live in a two-dollar-a-day room with me, didn't she? You know how she is — an idealist, a romantic — you oughta know that, Carton."

"I do know it, I always knew it," he said, his usual florid color deepening. "I think she still loves you. Yet why is she leaving you now? There's nothing out there for a divorced woman with three kids."

Aaron shifted uncomfortably, then slumped low in his chair, his legs stretched out in front of him. "Oh who the hell knows her? She probably wants to be sure that she never has to get laid again." Al produced an uncertain smile, but Aaron continued his catharsis. "Who knows, maybe she thinks she'll have money *and* independence. She's always going on about independence — which I don't really think she could handle anyway." He waved his hand in a deprecating gesture. "She's crazy; I don't think she knows what she wants."

"Well, maybe it is a kind of crazy, because what she really wants to do is to destroy herself. Like most depressives, she's self-destructive."

Aaron looked up, torn between being impressed and annoyed by Al's glib labeling and his omniscient attitude about *his* wife. "Hey, Carton, since when did you become a psychiatrist?"

"When I became a lawyer."

Aaron smiled. There was a pause. "Even the act of marrying you was self-defeating," Al continued, as if against his will. "She needed time, attention, understanding, all the things you couldn't give her, couldn't find the time for — "

Aaron looked up into Al's flushed face — smug bastard, he thought, so there it is; never really forgave me in his heart.

"Listen, you can't have it both ways, can you, Carton? Work like a dog and be constantly at your wife's beck and call."

"Remember, Aaron," Al interrupted, "she never really had a chance, she's had one trauma after another, loss after loss, since her father died — pretty tough on a tender psyche."

"She had a lot of bad breaks until she met me, but I was her one lucky one and don't you forget it." Al looked dubious but answered nothing, further irritating Aaron, who now began tearing at his fingernails.

Then Al said casually, "She says you're playing around with a checkroom girl. Is it true?"

"Oh, that's ridiculous! A guy gets laid on the outside once in a while — doesn't mean a thing, not a goddam thing."

"Well, why did she have to know if that's all it was? How would she have found out about it, her name, everything, if that's all it was?"

"She doesn't really know anything."

"By that, I suppose you mean she couldn't really prove anything."

"She puts two and two together and gets five." His eyes suddenly felt tired. He had been up most of the night working, and he'd spent the rest of that night in bed with that crazy kid; he hadn't slept much. Under his half-closed lids he began to examine his feelings in regard to Martha. An ignorant kid, coarse, tough, sly, but there was an earthy, unselfconsciousness about her that was appealing. No hassle, he didn't have to think about cause and effect with her, as he did with Eve, about the amenities. No standing on ceremony. And it had been kind of fun — exciting — a different sort of excitement than he had had with Eve, even during their courtship. There was a certain greedy, selfish quality to this thing, he couldn't exactly call it a relationship, it really wasn't much of anything yet. A husky, healthy, athletic-looking kid, casual, informal, wise-cracking, yet — just thinking about it now, trying to debunk the whole *shiksa* myth, he grew strangely excited. What was it that the boys used to say back when he was a kid, about *shiksas* — "Ya screws her, ya use her, and then ya lose her." Well, that was the jist of it. Anyway, what could Eve expect with her high and mighty airs and the favor she conferred upon him by letting herself be taken now and then. He was always in a hurry to get it over with lately, to relieve her of the annoyance.

"Aaron," Al said sharply, as if to bring him up out of his thoughts, "she says that you've been staying with her in a room down the hall from your apartment, on the same floor with Eve and the children."

"Are you crazy, as if I would do such a dumb thing! Would I do something like that, something completely stupid?"

"I don't know. Maybe you're working on a little unconscious vendetta of your own."

"Why? For what reason?" Aaron's blue eyes looked serenely innocent.

He shrugged his shoulders. "How would I know, I don't sleep between you."

Aaron stole a glance at Al's face. Aaron laughed. "You might just as well, for all the sex she generates on that mattress." Then he added magnanimously, "Not that I really cared about that, that wasn't the problem. To me, she always seemed the most attractive woman in the world."

Al wasn't to be so easily deflected. "Well, where do you suppose she got the idea then?"

"What idea?"

"That you've been sleeping with that kid," Al said with rising irritation, "and that you bring her to a room down the hall."

Aaron's voice was loud, drowning out even the frequent buzz of the phone in the outer office. "I had to take a room down the hall because she threw me out on a moment's notice. Where was I supposed to go on a dime? To the Y? Luckily the manager of the Towers is a friend of mine, gave me another room."

"I don't know how lucky that is, or that he's much of a friend of yours. Eve says he's talking about it all over the hotel, and she's the butt of gossip throughout the whole joint."

"Jeeze, Carton, I thought you were supposed to be smart, but you sound like a jerk. You know how she is — everyone's out to get her, everyone's staring at her everywhere she goes. I had to move to this hotel in the first place because she was suddenly miserable at that beautiful house on Albemarle Road, the neighbors were 'hostile, anti-Semitic,' or who the hell knows what else."

Al, in an effort to bring the conversation back on target, continued listing her allegations doggedly. "And she says you won't give her any money, every penny is a fight, and she knows you're a rich man, Aaron, after all — "

"Yeah, I know, and if it wasn't that, it would be something else — I didn't put the seats down at the theater, I didn't open the doors for her fast enough, I didn't take her out at night, or I did take her out and left her sitting alone while I attended to business." All this narrative he delivered in a flat, singsong style. Al sighed, tapped his fingers nervously on the desk top, pulled his upper lip thoughtfully.

Aaron leaned forward and said, "Al, no divorce, do you understand me? I'm not going to pay her a load of dough so that I can live like a hermit in the Y."

"What is this fixation you've got with the Y?"

"What am I going to do, set up housekeeping all by myself? I haven't got the time or the patience; and then there are the kids, I don't want to lose Jennie and the boys. Jeeze, Al, I don't want to lose the kids! — to pay that way because I made a mistake, because I married the wrong girl — or maybe we were wrong for each other. Who knows? She should have married you, Al — Al, don't take the case. If you don't take it she'll have a tough time finding a lawyer who will. She really hasn't any grounds, and I'll fight it."

"I'm not so sure you're right, Aaron. Other lawyers will figure they can make a barrel from you on a case like this. They figure you for a rich man. And then there's adultery. If she can prove adultery, she can clean you out, and you'll be lucky if you get visitation rights at all. There is, of course, a legal separation; she'd consider that, you know."

"Whose side are you on anyway?" His stomach had begun acting up again. He actually felt the knots, the hydrochloric acid swimming around.

"I told you I'm not taking sides. Well, here's what it boils down to now, Aaron. She's pretty determined. She's made up her mind, and you know Eve when her mind's made up."

*

Al sat in his solidly comfortable swivel chair for a long time after Aaron had left the room; that is, after his physical presence had left, because the room still seemed to vibrate with that peculiar current of electricity that Aaron managed to generate by his presence and to leave behind in his wake — like aftershocks from an earthquake. Al sighed. He knew that no matter who would represent Eve, she didn't really have a chance at independence. Once Aaron owned something, he didn't surrender it easily. He didn't relinquish his holdings, even his mistakes — they were *his*, so they were tolerable.

Al's hand rested on the receiver thoughtfully for a moment. He had made up his mind, almost from the beginning — not to take the case.

(21)

JENNIE WAS NINE when her parents separated. After Aaron left, there was a sudden emptiness. The break was inevitable; even the children knew that. But it was only 1937, and it was embarrassing, very embarrassing, especially for Jennie. The kids at school looked at her strangely, as if she were different. She felt different.

For one thing she lived in a hotel. They had moved there hurriedly from the house on Albemarle Road about a year ago. Eve said that she didn't want to be alone nights in a big house, and it was too much work. Besides, the neighbors were "hostile." Aaron had the concessions here at the Towers Hotel and had an arrangement with the management — a due bill, the hotel expenses, would come out of his profits.

Jennie wished they could stay on at the Towers forever. She loved room service, with its luxurious odor of Sterno and the mystery of those domed silver dishes. She loved the water that almost surrounded them — it was soothing. She felt safe, way up there in their turret on the twenty-first floor — a medieval princess in a tower. Nothing could ever touch her here.

Not that the apartment was anything remarkable in itself. It was just an ordinary, furnished hotel suite, with an extra bedroom opened for them on the other side of the living room. It was the dazzling view of the East River, the Brooklyn Heights harbor and its magic flotilla of toy ships beneath, that captured Jennie so completely. She loved to play adventure games on the little balcony that hung precariously over the water. She felt a perverse thrill of excitement when her mother chided her about leaning so far over the railing — but she was not afraid. No, nothing could touch her here.

*

A few months later her mother began apartment hunting, dragging her around from one colorless Flatbush apartment to another. They all seemed dark and disappointing after the shimmering beauty of her Island in the Sky.

In the fall they moved into one of those nondescript apartments. Eve was living on money from a temporary settlement, pending a legal separation, her financial future precarious. "What the hell am I supposed to do, reward you for this insanity?" Aaron had said, indignant at what he considered to be her irrational defiance. Children or no children, he wasn't going to make it easy for her. But nothing had ever come easy for her, she said, certainly not with Aaron. War erupted. His first reprisal was to cut off any and all credit — gratuitous spite, she said. Her gorge rose.

Jennie really wasn't sure which apartment it was that her mother had decided on, and it didn't seem to matter much, if only she could sleep. She was so tired every day. She had trouble paying attention at school. All during the day she felt leaden and dull. Thoughts nipped at her brain like mosquitoes she couldn't quite catch. She tried very hard to fall asleep at night, but instead she lay in her outgrown youth bed, crowded in by the sides, and strained her eyes until they stung, staring at the light that hung from the ceiling in the narrow hall outside her room, listening for night noises. She wanted to close off the silent, empty foyer from her view, but she was afraid of what the darkness would bring. If only she could switch off her imagination, like the radio when it grew gravelly with static.

The radio! — how its magic voice transfixed their lives, brought them pleasure and even pain sometimes. Like those Sunday evenings when Gabriel Heatter's funereal voice proclaimed, "And that's the way the world turns." Jennie knew that meant 7 P.M., and almost the end of visiting day with her father. Back to Mother and her sadness.

The radio — radioator — no, radiator — she was afraid to stay awake alone and afraid to fall asleep, because sleep might bring the same dream. The one where she stood frozen in the middle of her mother's bedroom, while a sepulchral voice that seemed to come from the recessed radiator issued forth a stern command, which she followed, hypnotized by terror. She could never remember what the voice said, but always she fled down the long, narrow corridor of the apartment. Yes, it was this apartment, she was certain of that. The very same rooms unfolding, slowly, foggily, like a camera panning a scene in slow motion, following unseen behind her. She was terrified to look backward. As she approached the living room, very slowly, very cautiously, the terror grew until she felt as if she would burst — then she woke in a cold sweat and lay still, rigid.

Soon after they had moved here to the Flatbush Avenue apartment, Jennie heard a loud scuffling noise coming from her mother's room early one morning. She walked up the hall to the room, and looked in. Her father was there; it seemed odd, so early in the morning. It was not a visiting day. He had Eve pinned up against the high chest of drawers, and was pressing her body so tightly with his own that she seemed about to scream but was unable — couldn't get the sound out. Aaron's face looked different to Jennie, like the face of a stranger; for a terrible moment she wasn't sure. His eyes were wild, his face contorted. Then she noticed that he held a small metal object to her mother's ribs.

"Go ahead and pull the trigger," she said. "Go ahead, you're a murderer whether you pull it or not, you're taking my life piece by piece."

"So help me, I'll do it if you don't shut up." Her mother began to yell, "Help, help me, he's trying to kill me!" She was crying hysterically now. Aaron drew back and placed the gun on top of the bureau. His hand was shaking, but he began to laugh in that nervous and jerky way he had when he was pretending something.

"You're crazy, crazy. I was only joking, only kidding, trying to scare you a little, that's all." Eve continued to cry hysterically.

Jennie stood trembling behind the door, undiscovered.

Sometimes at the point where night becomes smudgy with day, in a half sleep she thought she heard her father coming home, fumbling with the keys, juggling a few packets of coins that for some reason were separated from the rest, the bulk of the night's take.

But the sound would die away — just the icebox recharging, or the reverberation of a lone truck rumbling in the silent street below. Then there followed the deep, loud silence of wakefulness when everyone else in the world was asleep. She was wide awake then, her eyelids feeling sandy and prickly. She'd push her pillow around impatiently, a hot, angry hurt in the pit of her stomach.

*

"The children are like cheese worms, jittery and overstimulated. Whipped up by their father," Eve complained. Jennie, a thoughtful child with a fiercely bleeding heart, alternated between reveries of life with parents reshaped to fit her dreams, and bouts of hopelessness born out of the sure knowledge that it would never be any different. Bemused, she often drifted above it all, or became very thick with her brothers, whose detached and disinterested company she found strangely satisfying. Jennie sensed her mother's misery, and felt vaguely responsible. She became the barometer for Eve's precarious emotions, whose histrionics bounced off the boys like rubber balls — they hardly noticed it seemed.

Then they moved again. Jennie was happy to leave the Flatbush apartment; she had never really liked it. It was melancholy, like her dream. Six months later they moved again, to a similar apartment on East Nineteenth Street. There was always some perfectly good reason. Eve would say the landlord was rude, or the woman down the hall was crazy, or there was a much better value in the building on the next block. So they'd be off again, the boys clutching passionately their collections of stamps, butterflies, marbles, rubber bands, or whatever they were collecting that month. Reid was hysterical about his wooden cars, Evan in a state of panic that a tiny metal soldier might remain behind — his eyes red and tearing from the fresh paint — all three noses running, and Jennie as always, tired, so tired.

No matter how much their lives changed, Eve's bedroom remained the same. Apartments came and went, but Eve's bedroom went on forever. To Jennie it seemed a fragrant and mysterious bower of

celadon green and peach, a place of shabby splendor, which she regarded from the threshold like Alice in Wonderland, always a little
afraid. Eve's tastes, like her loyalties, were not capricious, and besides, she had to bear in mind the peach and green antique Aubusson
on the floor. "That might be the only one I'll ever have in my lifetime," she said. Jennie saw her mother arranging and rearranging
the furniture in hopes of achieving an elegant effect. She knew that
she loved beauty, so with each new arrangement she prayed it
would become beautiful. But it always came out the same way,
somehow — confused and harried-looking, instead of cool and
serene like the living room of her school friend, Betty Louise Morris.

Betty Louise was the only other Jewish child in the class — in the
entire school, Eve suspected. The whole student body comprised
maybe eighty-five boys and girls, kindergarten through sixth grade.
Most of the children started in kindergarten on the first floor and
burrowed their way up through the building, like moles, to the pin-
nacle of the sixth grade, which was in the attic. The Kirk School,
the only small private school of its type in Flatbush, was run by two
spinster sisters, Mary and Isabelle Kirk, who wore long Victorian
dresses, choker collars, and did their hair alike in elaborate birds'
nests. Jennie often wondered how a comb could possibly find its
way through the tangled terrain.

The rickety old wood frame house stood on a quiet tree-draped
street. It boasted four stories, joined by a trembling stairway that
threatened to give way completely every Thursday, on Assembly
Day. Jennie loved assembly, when everyone lined up on their floors
and marched downstairs to the rousing music of "Country Dance,"
played on the tinny old piano, with great gusto, by the "other sister."
Miss Isabelle taught kindergarten and spoke in a rich falsetto voice.
Her hands were usually dripping with clay, and she carried them in
front of her like a surgeon after scrub-up. She was called the "other
sister" because Miss Mary was the principal. She was also Jennie's
fourth-grade teacher. On Thursdays Jennie felt reckless and free,
and she cracked clever jokes that made everyone laugh and caused
Miss Kirk to frown and smooth up her wisps of hair. She felt drunk
with a heady sensation of conspiracy. She belonged. School was a

warm and friendly place, smelling of clay and paste and hazy with chalk dust.

Behind the school, through a private entrance, was a tiny clapboard cottage. It stood in the middle of a secret garden, as tangled and overgrown as the sisters' hairdos. Eve said it was a real English garden. (The fusty Victorian charm of the school and its owners appealed strongly to Eve — was, in fact, a soft whisper of the England she remembered as a child.) This was where the sisters lived, and were lovingly ministered to by their housekeeper, Miss Theresa, the third unmarried sister. It was a mysterious treat to be invited into this inner sanctum, and one that would be the subject of much whispered conversation in class the next day. The only time Jennie had been inside the sisters' magic cottage was when the upper grades were invited in to listen to the broadcast from London, when the Prince of Wales announced to the world in a pallid voice, without inflection, that he would renounce the throne for the "woman I love."

*

Betty Louise was very settled, Eve always said so. Her family was very solid, and the large, elegant building they lived in looked very solid, too.

Jennie lived in terror that Betty Louise would learn her guilty secret.

Going home from school one afternoon, Betty Louise asked in her usual superior tone, "What business is your father in, anyway?" Jennie's heart skipped a beat. She didn't like that "anyway" at the end of the question.

"Oh, he's a concessionaire," she answered, matter-of-factly.

"What's *that?*" Betty Louise asked, as if it were something unclean, and then before Jennie could offer her rather uncertain definition, she raced on. "Does your father eat dinner with you every night?"

Jennie quickened her pace to keep up with her friend. Betty Louise was skimming along on one roller skate. Jennie's were broken, as usual. She was glad that Betty Louise was a bit ahead of her, it gave her time to gather her resources, to think out her answer.

She wanted desperately to give the right answers to these dreaded inquisitions that came up from time to time, so Betty Louise wouldn't suspect anything and perhaps tell some of the other kids, or maybe even the entire class. Maybe she would even organize one of those "hate clubs" against her, as she did to Marge Demroch. The club was called A.M.D. — "Against Marge Demroch." Jennie dutifully attended the meetings to assure herself of acceptance, rather than risk becoming the next target, although she was never quite certain when the tide would turn. She really did want Betty Louise to like her.

"Well, not every night, but some nights."

"Why not?" Betty Louise persisted. "My daddy does."

"Well, my father's in a night business. He works until very late at night." The small truth she had injected somewhat ameliorated her troubled conscience.

"Do you see him in the daytimes, like in the morning? My dad brings me to school every morning."

"Well, he sleeps in the morning. I told you, he works all night."

"How come he never comes to school, then, to pick you up or anything?" She was unrelenting. Then she said cryptically, "My dad has to go out of town sometimes, too."

She had seen Betty Louise's father a few times. He was tall and heavyset, with glasses. Comfortable-looking — the way an accountant should look, she supposed. He looked like the pictures of Father she remembered from their third-grade readers.

"Why does your father work so much?"

Oh, that's easy, Jennie thought, and said simply, "Because he wants to make a lot of money."

"Well, does he?"

"I think so."

"Well, don't you know? Don't you hear your parents talking? You don't seem to know much about what goes on in your family."

Jennie knew what went on all the time when her parents got together. There was an awful lot of yelling and shouting about money, but she never quite understood whether each clash was a new incident or the same old themes hashed and rehashed. Besides, she had learned to turn them off lately, like a radio program that she didn't understand, or that was too complicated and confusing for her, or that made her feel sad.

She was glad when Betty Louise crossed over at Prospect Place to begin her long trek home, juggling her books and lunch box. Jennie lived only a few blocks from school. It was a relief to be alone after the tension of those last few minutes. Still, it was better than having to be picked up by Eve. She was never quite sure who would come for her. Would her mother come, with her nervous, intimate attentions, always slightly breathless, as if she had been rushing from somewhere to get to nowhere in particular? Or worse still, her father might pull up outside the playground in that long, black, chauffeur-driven car of his, acting awkward and impersonal and somehow embarrassed by the teachers and children — even his own. She was relieved that he collected them quickly and stayed out of the way of the teachers, especially the principal. Eve said he didn't want to make small talk with the staff, and was too bored to ask how the children were doing.

Jennie managed somehow to keep him out of the way of Betty Louise — that's why she had never seen him. God forbid she should see that car and tell the others about it! She'd die. Once when her parents arrived together she was jubilant and searched high and low for her. But unfortunately it was late, so there was hardly anyone around to notice the golden moment, and anyway, Aaron was, as always, in a hurry.

*

Jennie went out of her way today to pass the creepy little witchlike house on the corner of Crook Avenue. It reminded her of stale gingerbread, and the narrow windows looked like the angry eyes of its occupant, an old lady on constant vigil. The house fascinated her, drew her in. It was surrounded by a mean and scrubby patch of dirt — a sorcerer's garden. Sumac bushes that seemed to have sprung up in protest grew roughly and at random. Jennie stopped to pick a tiny orange lantern. She had to pop it to see what was inside. As if on cue, a window flew open and the old woman scolded her, threatening to get a policeman. She had done it a couple of times before.

She felt strangely excited. The little mischief, the scolding, were somehow reassuring. It reminded her that she was still a kin to childhood, had lived too much in an adults' world.

She wondered idly if Grandma would be at their apartment today. She hoped so; things always looked better when Grandma Lisa was around. Things were orderly and bustling, the way a home should be. There was always a delicious hot meal, and her mother didn't fuss at them, nag at them. Jennie felt free, relieved, as if she could turn over the responsibility of Eve. Grandma seemed to soak up Eve's anxieties, and there wasn't much left to spill over onto the children. But when she got home, Grandma wasn't there. The boys weren't there, either. Aaron had taken them somewhere or other. Eve was sitting at the kitchen table, drumming her fingers on the printed oilcloth.

"Why are you looking so glum?" Eve asked.

"I'm not." Jennie thought with satisfaction about all the homework she had. She could close the door.

"Now what?"

"Nothing."

"Betty Louise again, I suppose." Eve knew about the grand inquisitor.

"She's an awful snoop," Jennie admitted grudgingly.

"She's a regular *yenta*. I have half a mind to call up her mother — "

"Oh, God, please don't, Mother, please don't!"

"Well, I'd know what to say. It wouldn't be just like that — I wouldn't come right out and say it just like that, but these are things she must hear at home."

"Just don't, Mother, promise me you won't."

"Oh, all right, but why do you have to look so tragic about it?"

If only she had said to Jennie instead, "Oh, never mind Betty Louise. There's no special secret about us. It happens all over the world that people aren't happy together, and they separate. It's no shame, Jennie, it's not a secret thing." But Eve couldn't say that — couldn't explain away Jennie's anxieties. Her best defense was always an attack.

(22)

THIRTY THOUSAND DOLLARS up front to help finance the extravagant new French Casino on Seventh Avenue bought the key to the washrooms, the checkrooms, and the latest innovation, the darkroom for souvenir pictures. To Aaron, thirty thousand dollars seemed a staggering sum at the time, it was now 1937 — and considering the fact of the depression, it even seemed foolish, but he kept telling himself, "You have to spend money to make money." And it was, after all, just a more deluxe edition of the methods he had been using in his business since the start. Buy, earn, trade off, buy again, augmenting, always augmenting what he had. The only trouble was, he hadn't really made any profit over there at the De Paris. For reasons he couldn't quite figure out, he had just about broker even, and felt grateful for that, and relieved to be rid of a partner, particularly one of "them." He was surprised they had let him off so easily. Well, what did they need him for really; they didn't need the money. He supposed they only let him in to begin with to teach them the knack of running the concessions. His contract was up, and that was that — at least he hoped so. He knew about *their* kind of contract, and hoped there wasn't one out on him. Well, so what the hell, if his number was up, it was up. But that was pure nonsense, whistling in the dark, and he knew it — he wasn't about to give it all up, not that easily, not now when everything was just beginning to fall into place . . .

He had thought that the De Paris was the grandest, most gorgeous place he'd ever seen. Now he knew that it had been small potatoes, amateurish, next to the huge new place. In less than a year from the time of purchase he had seen it transformed miraculously into its present undulating, shimmering magnificence, the pleasure dome plucked from Xanadu and dropped on Broadway with the accompanying fanfare, the attendant publicity, at which New York columnists were so adept. Fifty crystal chandeliers seemed to stream upward into the tiers and various levels of the club, as far as the eye could see, giving the impression of a Busby Berkeley-style heaven. Rich red carpeting throughout sopped up the sound and fury of the world just outside its golden doors. The walls were solidly mirrored — gorgeously garish. The place was doing phenomenally well since its opening in November, and suffered no competition, not even from its neighbor, the Casino de Paris.

New Year's Eve was expected to be a sellout, with some double bookings in case of cancellations. All week long the maître d's had been juggling and rejuggling tables in order to make room for more. The holiday visitors, as well as the usual smattering of good old café society regulars, had reserved every table that December night. A kind of sorcerer's vapor hung over the city, immutable, a cold smoky mist created by its own peculiar combination of geography and noxious elements.

The dinner show was packed, but the real bedlam began when the Broadway theaters let out at around eleven, and in resplendent evening attire they flocked in for the late show.

By ten-thirty that night the crowds converging on the club created traffic jams that snarled Broadway and Seventh Avenue in a hopeless tangle. The two doormen out in front of the French Casino were nearly stampeded as they tried to hold back the mob in some sort of order and were soon joined by three or four musclemen in elegant evening dress. Reservations that until now had been scrupulously honored gave way to first-come (with a ten dollar bill), first-served, creating little pockets of fist fights here and there, to be efficiently squelched by one of the many bouncers.

Inside the oppressive confines of the checkroom, Aaron worked feverishly with Jason and three girls who were considered crackerjack. Jason's little blonde, Dolly, was there and Martha Voccek and a brunette called Bernice. (Aaron had misgivings about Martha; he generally preferred to leave her in White Plains, in spite of her repeated complaints.) He had promised that he and Jason would also be there all night. Jason, with an eye to symmetry, had seen to it that the hair color ratio was attractively balanced. The girls wore little French maid costumes similar to those worn at the Casino de Paris, but more elaborate. All of them worked quickly and efficiently, but the lines at the checkroom seemed endless. Bennie Abel was posted out front on this occasion, to make sure no customers slipped away to their table with their coats. Every so often he called out loudly, "Ladies and gentlemen, please check your hats and coats before being seated" or "Hats and coats here." He corrected sternly the few mavericks who straggled up to the headwaiter still defiantly wearing their outer clothing.

Six or seven cigarette girls, also headquartered at the checkrooms, stopped in now and then to refill their rapidly dwindling trays with cigarettes, little packages of French chocolates, and various assorted pastel stuffed animals. For this night there were free samples of Shalimar in tiny bottles — not just vials, but miniature replicas of the graceful half-heart-shaped flacon, flown in from Paris by arrangement with the French government. On every table a centerpiece of tiny silk French flags waved in the breeze of the women's swishing skirts, and on the stage a raucous, gorgeous, naked revue straight from the Lido in Paris. The New Yorkers expected as much — the out-of-towners went wild!

The orchestra returned from its break, the lights were dimmed, throwing the huge, cavernous room into secret shadow. Female forms slithered back and forth in the half-light. The constant rich rustle of taffeta, like wind in the trees, was punctuated by audacious clicking of jewelry, compacts, and cases, staccato chirps like cicadas in a night forest, and overall the women's fragrances mingled with the heavy air. There was a quick silence, broken only by a few stubborn revelers who preferred their own jokes to the action up front. Then the band began with an uproarious roll of drums to announce the last show of the evening, the crowd having finally paid, fought, and stumbled their way to their respective seats.

The checkroom area looked strangely deserted. The coats, topped by fedoras and Homburgs, hung limply from the hooks like giant puppets. Aaron felt nervous and worried. He felt a heavy lump of anxiety in the middle of his chest, and it was beginning to spread to his belly. He was sure his old ulcer was acting up again. It hadn't bothered him for the last few years, but it was back now with a screaming pain that all his sour cream and cottage cheese couldn't assuage.

"What's eating you tonight?" Jason asked.

"Who, me? Nothing. It's just that I'm tired, I guess. So much excitement." He made a mental note not to bring Martha into town for any more openings. Her presence somehow combined to irritate and excite him at the same time.

The girls were still stationed out front to catch the latecomers, stragglers, and bar patrons. They were tired — it was beginning to show through the make-up. Martha looked pale and drawn. She lit a cigarette and walked to the back of the room where the two men were talking softly. She sat down wearily on one of the folding chairs and stretched her long legs in front of her, puffing on her cigarette. Aaron looked uncomfortable. Well, this was really only an experiment. In a moment's weakness he had promised that she could work the opening night in the new jewel of his collection here at the Casino, but now with Jason and Jason's little broad on top of them, he felt strangely ordinary, somehow cheap. "Just a wise guy, sharpie from Delancey Street," Eve would have said, "not fit to kiss the ground I walk on, right at home with that vulgar checkroom element." Well, maybe water did seek its own level after all.

"So, ya tired?" Martha asked of one or both of the men, they were not sure which, so they answered in unison and then laughed nervously.

A minute later Dolly came back, too. She made no secret of her feelings for Jason. It was unmistakable the way she smiled at him, searched him out with her eyes, colored when he spoke. Jason fumbled for a cigarette, Dolly jumped up to light it and her hand trembled slightly. Jason barely glanced at her over the match. Aaron pretended not to notice, but he was thinking, How businesslike he is. Guy's got nerves of steel, or maybe this kid doesn't really make any difference to him after all. But he knew the affair had been going on for some time now. "A love like that is hard to resist," Jason had told him in his laconic way. He looked at Dolly appraisingly now. She was small and very feminine, with lovely blue eyes and natural, soft honey-blonde hair, kind of blowy, like milkweed, and her mouth was full like her breasts. He could understand a guy going for her in the sack, a cute little trick, probably Russian or Czech, a bohunk with her rosy cheeks like the fresh outdoors, a Sonia Henie type, he decided. You half expected to see her in a ski parka instead of a tight black dress. He wondered why these kids ended up here, in this work. Maybe they loved the night life or maybe they thought they'd meet a millionaire who'd marry them, these girls with their Mary Magdelene complexes, confused in their role playing between whore and virgin. Aaron thought how anxious they were to get into the big time, the bright lights, to get the stuffings kicked out of them by life.

Jeeze, if Jason's parents knew, they'd die. He was brought up in an Orthodox home, his parents *frumme yidden*, the only child, the only son. But Jason was a good son; he could never do anything to hurt them, anything dumb, like marrying that kid. But where else could he meet a girl, Aaron thought, in an uncharacteristic burst of sympathy for Jason, he's here in these joints every moment he's not sleeping. Where is he going to meet a respectable Jewish girl, and if he met one, what the hell would he do with her?

"Still smoking so damn much, eh, Miller? You and her," he indicated Martha with a toss of the head in her direction.

"Yeah," he said with that funny half smile of his, keeping his head down over something he was busy with. "You think I want to live forever, like you?"

"Some night! You'd think it was New Year's Eve or somethin'," Dolly said in a breathy whisper, as if unsure of the effect of her humor.

"Yeah, it'll be the new year before you know it," Martha said, shooting Aaron a meaningful glance that appeared to go unnoticed by him. But he had heard her, figured it was some sort of silly sentiment, not that she was a particularly sentimental girl, romantic or anything like that; a far cry from Eve, the girlish, coquettish Eve of long ago who threatened to fill in with kisses the deep cleft in his chin. He kept his head down over the little orange coat tickets with the large *A.A.* carefully imprinted on the face. A little touch of class for the new place — his initials marked boldly on the stubs. He was pleased with his handiwork.

Aaron moved restlessly back and forth in the small enclave like a caged lion, then streaked off to check with the camera girls. "Souvenirs of a night out in Paris," they called as they went around clicking their cameras — flashes of sudden white light in the surprised faces of the customers, assailing the senses. The camera girls were carefully chosen to attract, but never so attractive as to make a customer's wife or girlfriend uncomfortable. They must never compete; that might make a woman feel self-conscious, unbeautiful, so she'd refuse to be photographed.

The orchestra played "Auld Lang Syne" at midnight. People kissed and toasted, some shouted and yelped in the darkness, enjoying the excuse. In the checkroom Martha sat alone and ground her cigarette down into the brass cash tray kept on the counter to collect tips. She had sent Bernice to the bar to bring her a drink. Lately she was ordering the other girls around left and right, and they acquiesced, grudgingly sensing the relationship between her and Aaron, or having been set straight by Martha herself.

As Bernice approached the checkroom bearing Martha's drink, a terrible sound exploded from the area of the washrooms, causing her to trip and fall, splattering the glass and its contents, and showering the heavy red carpet with coins. Those that remained in her dress she clutched with a hand whitened by tension. Jason, pale and serious, running in the direction of the noise, pulled her roughly to her feet, barely slowing his pace — "Thirty dollars a week — and all you can steal," he said sardonically over his shoulder — and made a mental note to have her fired tomorrow —

There was general confusion and murmuring in the audience, but the noise had not been so readily audible down in the theater area, and had been much obscured by the tumultuous sounds of the orchestra that had accelerated to an ear-splitting pitch, as if providing a cover.

Dolly and Martha were standing in a huddle with various other employees, all talking and gesticulating wildly. A moment later there was another deafening explosion, this time from the checkroom itself. A steady stream of water flowed down the carpets from the men's room and the air smelled sulphuric. Plainclothes detectives materialized from out of nowhere, forming an invisible cordon around the dance floor area. Some of the patrons began scrambling for their coats, though not all were aware of the explosion, depending on where they were seated in the huge room. The show continued undaunted; the girls were in the midst of a frenzied, half-naked cancan.

Aaron rushed breathlessly up to the checkroom and surveyed the disaster. The men's coats were completely covered with white plaster dust, the carpet underfoot a soggy amalgam of water and debris. Some racks had been broken by the blast and a few ladies' furs lay sodden on the carpet. Heavy smoke was rising from the checkroom and customers were holding handkerchiefs to their noses and mouths, pushing and shoving and clamoring noisily for their coats. Fist fights had broken out in line. Two men rolled around in the dirty, evil-smelling water that flowed down the hall from the toilets, now clogged with plaster of Paris — an old gangland trick.

Jason and the girls worked fast dispensing the clothing that was salvageable, taking down names and phone numbers of those whose belongings were damaged. Aaron checked out feverishly whatever was still intact, even overlooking the fact that most people grabbed their coats angrily without tipping. Suddenly he remembered to ask if anyone was hurt, if the girls were okay. But no one was injured, only nuisance damage, fear created in the minds and memories of the public. Maybe a warning of sorts. Well, those miserable bastards could take their threats and shove them up their asses. Aaron's stomach screamed in pain as the crowd grew heavier, murmuring and complaining. He was trying to rationalize what had happened. So those bastards celebrated New Year's Eve with fireworks at midnight, so what? Didn't they know he was insured? But — hadn't they tried to murder him! How could they know who would be in the checkroom and when? He knew instinctively that they were omniscient, and he was scared out of his mind.

(23)

EVE AND THE CHILDREN had moved to yet another apartment, this one nearer to the school. But here Jennie had to share a bedroom with her mother. Finances were getting tighter and tighter, Eve was threatening to sue for more money, but nothing came of it, only long, agonizing arguments with Aaron over the telephone and in front of the children, in restaurants, in movie theaters, and on the street. Aaron was determined to keep up a charade of family unity, perversely insisting on injecting himself into the picture, or begging Eve to join him and the children on his visiting times. Then he spent most of that time convincing Eve — and he hoped, incidentally, the children — how much he had done for them, how much he was going to do. But later Eve and Jennie would look for the tangible difference and find that it was all hot air — promises, but no changes.

*

The first time it happened, Jennie lay in her bed frozen, unable to move, covered with cold sweat, wanting to call her mother, but terrified of breaking the terrible silence, not really certain if she were waking or sleeping. She listened until her head hurt and her eyes smarted from staring upward into the blackness, but the cry stuck in her throat. Still she heard the shuffling and a shifting around under her bed, and now and then the mattress seemed to move slightly from beneath. She thought of those scary radio programs, like "The Shadow" and "Inner Sanctum." Maybe a neighbor's cat or dog, some strange little animal, had somehow managed to crawl under there. But she grew more confused when she heard what seemed like even breathing from beneath her bed. She could not bring herself to look, and finally fell off into a fitful sleep, from which she awoke completely exhausted the next morning. Dear God, she thought, I hope Miss Kirk doesn't call me to the blackboard to solve a long-division problem today. I can't think straight.

She told Eve what had happened during the night.

"Now, Jennie, you know your sleeping problems," Eve said distractedly. "Anyway it was probably just a nightmare, or you imagined it."

"No, really, I heard it, that's why I'm so tired this morning. I stayed up for hours unable to sleep . . ."

"Well, how come I didn't hear it? I'm in the bed right next to yours."

"Because it was under *my* bed." She was afraid to say that her mother didn't hear it because she was such a heavy sleeper. Don't you know you sleep like the dead, she thought. All day Eve was excited, every nerve wide-awake, too much awake, but at night she was as exhausted from her anger as a laborer from his day's work.

"Oh God, I hope it doesn't happen again tonight."

"Well, if it does, dear, call me," Eve said, as if that settled the matter once and for all.

For the next few weeks she grew used to this eerie pattern, and with habit there came acceptance and the fears began to diminish. But in their place grew curiosity, wild, gnawing curiosity. One night during the third week of this phenomenon, she called her mother softly, fearfully, but Eve was sound asleep, making funny little clicking noises with her mouth. When Jennie finally shook her up out of her unconsciousness, she said irritably, "If you're going to disturb me like this every night, Jenna, you can go and sleep in the other room with the boys." She kept threatening but she never followed through. Jennie was dying to sleep in with her brothers; the boys always had so much fun. But Eve wanted Jennie with her. "You have to learn to be a companion to your mother; after all you *are* the only girl."

"Mother, please look under the bed. It's that crazy noise again."

Eve pushed herself heavily up from her bed, put on the small bed light next to her, and peered under the two beds, which were pushed together to make more space in the small room.

"My God!" she said. "It's Evan. He's under your bed."

Jennie could not look down at him. She felt shaky all over. She
didn't understand why, but somehow she didn't feel any better than
she did before the mystery was solved.

Eve pulled him out from his Spartan hiding place; his body was
like lead. She carried him gently to his crib.

Jennie wanted to hide her face in her mother's heavy breasts, in
her nightgown crumpled into a thousand angry creases by her shattered dreams, and say, Why is everything so hard, so confusing?
Even sleep, which is meant to soothe, has become pained and fragile.

No matter how long Jennie stayed awake, she was never able to
catch Evan in the act of going in or coming out. He just seemed to
materialize, like a barnacle on the bottom of a boat he just grew there
under her bed. Eve had high bars put on the top of Evan's crib, and
Jennie breathed a sigh of relief because not even a monkey could
hurdle those bars, she assured herself. But a couple of nights later
she was calling to her mother again in disbelief, "Mama, he's doing it
again." No answer. Jennie wished she could sleep like her mother,
"the sleep of the innocent," Eve said.

She thought of her brother lying in the cold, narrow blackness
beneath, staring up into the bedsprings, lost and alone, and only six.
The bedsprings became the conductor of his terror — she felt electrified through the mattress. She wanted to talk to him at those times,
but he was so silent, trancelike, it was as if he were not really there
at all, but had gone somewhere with his dreams, where his nightmares had led him. Each night Jennie entered that unfamiliar world
of sleep clutching her stuffed animal, a monkey. She lay sleepless
and on guard, listening to Evan grinding his small even teeth beneath
her bed.

One day she did talk to him on the subject of his nightly sojourn,
but he ran away and hid. When she found him, he refused at first to
answer, then he said, matter-of-factly, "I don't want the b-boogie
man to g-get me." He had begun stuttering lately . . . She decided
that he was a mysterious and unchildlike child, silent and sulky with
his round blue eyes brimming liquid. For one moment she touched
the cornsilk that fell in ringlets all over his head like a rag mop. She

buried her face in the soft golden mist of her brother's curling hair. His body was trembling.

Lately her parents were arguing more often and more loudly than usual. Eve wouldn't allow Aaron upstairs in the apartment anymore; he had to wait downstairs like a delivery boy. Eve's screaming followed her even through her dreams — her nightmares. It's been almost a year, why couldn't she stop screaming at him — at them? What was her father saying that provoked such fury? Sometimes she thought the delicate blue veins in her mother's forehead would burst, and there would be blood everywhere, drops of her mother's scarlet blood, sharp against the contrast of her milky white skin, Snow White and Rose Red.

The arguments were usually at the dinner table. The Jewish dinner table — once sanctified as a joyous and holy family gathering place, had been transformed through the generations into a battleground. After dinner, her stomach hurt, it felt tight, stretched taut as a drum. She wondered if her father had really heard Eve screaming at them. She hoped so, it would serve her right. She remembered snatches of a conversation she'd overheard between them recently . . .

"I stand outside the door and listen some nights — I hear the riots. You screaming at them and hitting them. I get sick inside, sick, I tell you — I'm going to take them away from you . . ."

"You just try it. You'd have a hard job proving that you're a fit parent, between your dirty checkrooms and your not-so-private life."

"I don't see you refusing the money from that business you're always moralizing about."

Jennie tried to sleep, but she kept thinking of her father standing outside the apartment door — listening — perhaps even peering through the keyhole, as if he might once again become part of the scene by absorbing the sounds from within. She felt strongly the impropriety of his being so humbled, skulking around the fringes of their lives like an intruder, scratching at the front door like a puppy.

The doctor has told Eve that she may give Jennie a sleeping pill with a glass of warm milk before bed, to help her sleep. Taking sleeping pills and warm milk at eleven makes her feel self-conscious, a little old lady of eleven. She hopes that Betty Louise will never find out. There is no change — still she tosses and turns every which way. Her brothers are long ago asleep, their shrill voices quiet. Only the sound of her mother's rhythmic sobbing as she washes socks in the bathroom basin, her tears mingling with the navy blue water.

24

THE CHILDREN LIVED under the constant threat of abduction by one or the other parent, especially when summer approached.

One summer when Aaron spirited them away to a house at Spring Lake with his mother and sister, Eve yanked them out of there and sent them to camp. Another time Eve sent them to camp and, refusing to pay the bill, Aaron withdrew them in mid-season and took them to the seashore. They were deposited and withdrawn with the alacrity of an overworked bank account.

Eve had custody of the children, but Aaron had weekends and summers. *Custody* had become a new word in the children's vocabulary. Jennie thought the word sounded soft and creamy, "custardy." In the beginning, when her father had summers, she became painfully homesick for her mother and sometimes had to go back to her in the middle of a weekend or a summer holiday. When Eve had custody, during the greater part of the year, she'd miss her father with a sore ache at the back of her throat. But in either case it meant leaving her brothers, another painful choice —

Eve claimed *he* got the cream off the top, the leisure time unencumbered by school problems and winter colds. On Saturdays and

Sundays Aaron didn't exactly know where to take them, or what to do with them. Sometimes on aimless spring weekends he'd take them to Atlantic City, but the sand was still clammy with cold and the winds raw.

The summer before, Aaron had taken the children to Long Beach to a house he had rented near the ocean for his mother. Sometime in the middle of the summer a pretty blonde woman came to live at the house, too. Jennie thought she was very glamorous. Sometimes she wore her hair in turbans, and even wore a blue velvet suit in summer. Aaron said she was his mother's distant cousin, from out of town, visiting for a few weeks; but she stayed on and on.

Grandma Abelson seemed practically a stranger to Jennie, and Eve had wanted it that way. So Jennie wasn't much surprised that Grandma had relatives she'd never even heard of. Of course, Cecile did seem very American, too young and modern to be related to her grandma, who still spoke very little English and wore long skirts that touched the floor. But who cared, they were having such a good time with her. Cousin Cecile was fun, and she beamed adoringly at Grandma and Aunt Rachel. She waited on them hand and foot and catered to Aaron so much that the children giggled with embarrassment, not being quite sure whether to treat this rare find, this new-found cousin, as a nursemaid or a friend. They had never seen a woman act that way with a man before — coquettish and fresh and deferential, all at the same time. Jennie felt torn between admiration for the svelte, beautiful blonde lady, and stabbing jealousy.

Aaron's room in this old-fashioned stucco house was only a little larger than the rest, and was crammed full by a huge bed that seemed to touch wall to wall. Jennie suddenly wanted to sleep in with Aaron; she said that her brothers were noisy and kept her up. Her sleeping was still a problem. When she let Aaron hug and kiss her, and call her "Becky" in that half-tender, half-teasing way he had, she felt vaguely guilty and disloyal. Sometimes she pulled away from him roughly, and kept her head down, so as not to see the hurt look on her father's face, though he laughed and teased her all the more.

She went to sit on her father's lap more often than usual. She placed her finger in the cleft in his chin and asked, "Why do you always call me 'Becky,' Daddy?"

"Because you *are* a Becky and because I love you," he said softly. But she jumped up quickly for fear of being seen, feeling awkward and clumsy there, not quite decided as to whether she wished to be a little girl or her father's sweetheart. No matter what her mother said about Aaron, Jennie thought that he was very handsome and exciting, though she tried to keep it secret.

One morning the door was partly open to Aaron's room, but he wasn't there. He'd gone out for the newspapers. Instead, Cecile was draped languorously in the bed, wearing a pink satin nightgown. Jennie was furious. She wondered if Aaron had given her permission to use his room. She waited impatiently for Aaron's return, feeling angry and exploited. An uncomfortable sense of restless excitement had spread over her, settling somewhere in her loins. As soon as Aaron returned she said, "Daddy, do you know that Cecile slept in your bed last night?"

"Oh, did she?" Aaron said, smiling. "Well, never mind, it's okay."

"Well, where did you sleep last night?"

"I slept in Cecile's room. We exchanged rooms."

"Why?"

"Why?" he repeated. "Well — because her room was too hot and mine was cooler. You know, I have to be polite to a guest." This was punctuated by a conspiratorial laugh from Cecile down the hall. Secrets, Jennie thought, how she hated secrets.

The next day Jennie went along for the ride to the train station, when Aaron dropped Cecile off. She had to attend to some business in town, she said, with an air of mystery and importance. Aaron closed the car door after her and said, "Goodbye, don't do anything I wouldn't do," and winked broadly. She laughed and said something like, "That leaves me plenty of leeway." She threw him an intimate smile over her shoulder, flashing her dimples, her blue eyes deepening beneath her blue velvet turban.

Jennie was dazzled. She wondered casually and without much curiosity if it was all right for Daddy to fall in love with his own cousin, especially since he kept telling Jennie how much he loved her mother. Well, a distant cousin was probably all right. If she were ever going to fall in love with a cousin, it would be her first cousin, Steve, Uncle Max's oldest boy. He played the saxophone and was gorgeous.

But for a long time after that summer, Jennie had a curious feeling of having been misled.

ON SATURDAYS OR SUNDAYS, Aaron would come for the children, but exactly which day or when was a subject for their guessing games. He was usually so late that often they thought he had forgotten all about it. Sometimes he didn't come at all; then the boys were disappointed, but not Jennie — she was relieved. These afternoons were really for the boys, Jennie thought. They always did the things boys liked to do, like playing ball in the park, shopping at a sporting-goods store, or worse still, swimming at the public pool. Standing around those steamy, hot, confusing pools, she felt somehow foolish. She knew that her sweater and skirt looked incongruous there, but she wouldn't get into a suit, not in front of all those strangers, all those men; she with her half-woman's figure, her beginning breasts above a still uncurved waist. She just stood there feeling sweaty, clumsy, and lost.

Sometimes Aaron would take them to visit his mother in Williamsburg. Jennie didn't much like going to Grandma Abelson's house. It was dark and scary and smelled funny. She wasn't certain that Grandma could see her, and if she could, she got the feeling she didn't know who she was anyway. Aunt Rachel kept mumbling "*klug, klug, bist du,*" in such a ferocious way that Jennie wasn't sure if it was a threat or a compliment. Anyway, they never asked for Eve, and Jennie just knew they didn't like her.

"I like the other Grandma better," Reid blurted out one of those times in the car. The children looked at each other in silent consent. They all liked Grandma Lisa better — well, anyway, they knew her better, and she spoke English. They liked the idiosyncratic way she puffed on her cigarette, holding it down right near the tip between thumb and forefinger and sucking at it, puffing the smoke out in cheerful staccato bursts. They liked her loose, brightly-rouged cheeks, that looked like they were dabbed with gentian violet. In school, at Thanksgiving time, they sang, "Over the river and through the woods, to Grandmother's house we go." Over the city and through the slums — no matter how hard Jennie tried, she could not substitute a horse and sleigh for the Third Avenue El, dark and dingy as it roared past lighted apartments that looked overly lived in.

At first she hated the occasional trips to Stillman's Gym, but her father seemed so happy there, and the boys so absorbed into the atmosphere, that their excitement was catching and she found herself almost enjoying it. The boys jumped and bobbed up and down in imitation of the jabbing and weaving movements of the fighters working out in the various rings. Clutches of fast-talking men in too-long overcoats and snappy fedoras, tough-looking types, Jennie thought, pressed up close to the rings. It frightened her a little, but it was thrilling, too. Aaron emerged from the locker room in a blaze of metallic blue shorts, bouncing lightly on the balls of his small feet, and jabbing at the air like the rest. Jennie was enthralled. An attendant helped him on with his gloves; he had brought his own. Jennie assumed that was just another mark of her father's importance, it was only fitting in his position. She felt her skin prickling into goosebumps. They took turns on the punching bag that hung from a hook on the wall. She dutifully took her turn and punched at it dully, feeling silly with her stiff Sunday felt hat falling across her eyes slightly, like a drunk. She'd have much preferred a turn on the running board, but that was unlikely. Her father didn't approve of it for a girl; her mother would not approve of it for anybody, she knew that.

On other visiting days there would be a series of stops and starts while Aaron disappeared into impressive-looking restaurants and nightclubs.

"I'll bet he's talking business," Evan would say, trying to look very stern and adult. But the exhausting waits would grind them down, pulverize them into an amalgam of tantrums and tears.

The only neutral agreement that they could come to on these weekends was the movies. Funny thing about the movies, Jennie thought, always that feeling of sanctuary, of delicious anonymity there, a few hours of relief from choices, decisions, mother's crankiness. Lately it was getting more and more difficult to find a movie they hadn't seen. It had become their single source of recreation when they were with Eve. It was "a place to go, somewhere to keep them quiet," she said, but Jennie really didn't believe it. She saw the total absorption, the fixed rapture with which her mother watched the films. So the children would drag Aaron from movie house to movie house, rejecting one after another, a sinking feeling of hopelessness washing over her when the last theater was ruled out.

"I'll see it again," Jennie would say, almost hysterical now with frustration, her heart set on escape, a hiding place, but the boys usually vetoed it in favor of the park. Radio City Music Hall, although *first run*, was a last resort. Aaron and the boys always got restless during the long stage shows, and the enormous art deco palace with its soaring lobbies overpowered Jennie so that she felt a little lost and lonely there.

On cold, gray afternoons, as refuge from the elements, they would often have to settle for a local Trans-Lux newsreel theater — *The March of Time*, Jennie could usually talk her father into *The March of Time*. Looking very serious and forbidding, without his usual playfulness, he would say, "You've got to learn about what's going on in the world, kids." He didn't have to work very hard to sell it to them, they loved the grainy newsreels with their sense of immediate adventure, their solemn musical accompaniment, the stern-voiced narration. Here Jennie saw a world that was beyond her apartment house on Crook Avenue, inside here where it was cozy and dark. She dreaded the sepulchral voice announcing "Time Marches On." It gave her the shivers. She wished it had been a longer program, like a double feature or something. A newsreel left you feeling sort of half-filled, half-empty. Emerging from the protective darkness she felt let down, vulnerable. Sometimes she half dreamed that she stayed there all night or until she fell asleep. Lately any place seemed easier to fall asleep in than her own bed.

*

On a particular Sunday in March, crisp, bright, and windy, spending itself into April with a final suspiration, Eve decided to go along on Aaron's Sunday with the children. She didn't trust him to take care of them. The boys raced around, got sweated up, then he didn't put sweaters on them, she said, or Jennie sat bundled up in the car, waiting for him to conduct business on their time — the children's time — sweating, overdressed as usual. No, Eve was determined to go along. Anyway, she wanted a ride in the car. "I never have the opportunity to ride in a car, not a car like yours. Mind you, I'm not crazy about driving with *you*, but I have to have a change of scenery." Jennie heard her mother's deep voice on the telephone, talking to Aaron, ". . . something else besides dirty floors and dirty dishes . . . plenty of money for everything you want, but for me nothing . . ."

Jennie thought to herself, why must she say things in that tone? After all, if they were all going to be together for the day, couldn't she begin by making it pleasant for a change? She prayed her father wouldn't be late as usual, that would only infuriate Eve, give her the chance to work herself up to a fever pitch, get down on them all. Well, maybe it would be all for the best; at least they'd have to do something specific, concrete, rather than floating in that haphazard limbo, the way they usually did with their father. But when noon came and went, and when station WQXR, Eve's favorite, announced one o'clock between Schoenberg's *Verklärte Nacht* and Mahler's Fifth, Jennie's stomach began to tighten up. At one-thirty, Aaron called. More tense talk on the kitchen phone. The boys were downstairs playing ball, oblivious to everything, as usual. She felt a fleeting stab of envy. She hardly ever had a date with a friend on weekends like the other girls, she had to wait around for her father. It seemed to her that weekends were for waiting, long arid stretches of suspended animation. Would Monday never come!!

At last the bell rang. Aaron was at the door with Evan and Reid; they must have met downstairs. She felt left out. Her father had probably stopped to play catch with them, while she'd been upstairs sopping up Eve's complaints. Jennie came out of her room, walking toward the foyer. She heard the laughter, jokes, guffaws — practicing their boxing again, she supposed. The same jerky darting and weaving motions every week, it made her dizzy. Didn't they ever tire of it?

They piled into the green Cadillac, the boys scuffling for the jump seats, flipping them up and down frantically. But once they were settled, Jennie found herself in the back with Eve and Reid, Evan up front with Aaron.

"So where do you want to go?" Aaron asked uneasily, assessing Eve narrowly through the rearview mirror, a glint of sarcasm in his canny blue eyes.

She didn't answer at once. Then grudgingly, "Well, it's really too late to go much of any place . . . Well, I suppose we could drive into Manhattan," she said dubiously. "Let's see how the other half lives. Of course you're there almost every night, but for me, it's a novelty, a luxury."

The boys were exchanging seats recklessly, sliding back and forth over the seat tops. Jennie tried to ignore their display of agility, their chameleonlike antics, but Eve was becoming annoyed now, and her voice was growing increasingly shrill, "Will you stop that before one of you gets thrown from the window . . ." Then back to Aaron: "I rarely get a few uninterrupted minutes with you, you're always so busy. So while I think of it, where is the tuition for the children's school?"

"Oh, Eve, this is our Sunday out together for a change — "

"So let's not spoil it by talking about money," she said, finishing the sentence for him. "And why should paying for your children's school be an unpleasant discussion?"

"I didn't say it was. Just that talking about it, you get yourself all worked up . . ."

"Just pay it. Then we don't have to talk about it," she said, her voice beginning to rise from the deep tone of a tuba to the metallic streak of a reed instrument. She's still angry about his being late, Jennie thought. God, didn't he know what would happen, why did he have to be so selfish?

They were beginning to approach the Brooklyn Bridge. Jennie breathed a sigh of relief. The bridge, its neutrality, relieved her anxieties. For these brief moments they hung as if suspended high above the world. Nothing could ever touch her here, nothing that was imperfect or unbeautiful. Flanked as she was by the twin towering harps, she heard only their special music and for a moment it drowned out the din of the green plush interior.

One of her earliest recollections of her father was their walks together over the Brooklyn Bridge, her five-year-old chunky legs hurrying to keep pace with his athletic stride, all the while he talked to her of wondrous things, funny things that made her giggle. She knew that he was clowning for her benefit, and she was an appreciative audience, with her hand enfolded tightly in his dry, assured palm.

Jennie pretended to hear nothing. No, she *really* did not hear. She had reverted to her cocoon, the one she saved for these occasions, forcing herself to think pleasant thoughts, warm, sunny pictures of far distant places where she could be happy alone, or better still, with the boys. They would be happy there, together. She would take care of them as always. She'd learn to cook; really cook. No ketchup soup that the boys pretended made them vomit, but real soup like Grandma Lisa would make.

But lately the sounds of her life were becoming increasingly hard to blot out, to erase. Would Aaron give Eve the money for school? For their clothes? Would she really take him to court and sue as she always threatened? Would she, Jennie, be packed off to some boarding school? Her mother had often talked about it.

The intensifying sounds of her parents arguing ripped through her cocoon like lightning, her mother's strong voice grew shriller, the boys were suddenly silent . . . "Don't you dare to mock me," and she leaned forward and smashed her large, overstuffed handbag over Aaron's head.

"Ouch." He ducked his head instinctively. The blow caught him offguard. For a split second he seemed stunned. Then he yelled in surprise and rage rather than pain, and the wheel slid dizzily in his fingers. They were driving fairly slowly now to keep pace with the steady flow of Sunday traffic. He usually drove very fast when he was angry. If it weren't for the traffic he would have been speeding now, sixty miles an hour maybe. That would have been better, Jennie could handle that, it was familiar. But his pent-up anger scared her — she didn't know what he would do next. Her father had a wild temper once it was roused. She could see his face in profile, engorged with dark blood, the color of fury. "Are you nuts? I'm driving. You'll get us all killed. What the hell's the matter with you?"

"Let me out! I want to get out of here this minute! I don't want to breathe the same air with you one more minute! Now let me out! Slow down and let me out!"

"What are you, nuts?" he repeated incredulously. "We're still on the bridge."

"If you don't let me out, I'll open the door and jump."

Reid was hunched down in a corner of the seat as if he were trying hard to squeeze himself invisible, his eyes shut tightly, his hands pressed over his ears. Jennie caught a glimpse of her father's face in the car mirror, it was a deep purple. He whirled around, his eyes staring wildly. "Go ahead. Jump, why don't you? I'd like to see you do it." For one moment Jennie thought she saw her mother shrink back in her seat. Aaron turned back again and screamed tauntingly, "Go ahead. Here, I'll help you." He twisted his arm to the back door awkwardly, the car careened wildly from lane to lane and suddenly they were rushing to the foot of the bridge in a great whoosh of chill air . . . one side of the car yawning wide, the door strained by the March winds as though it would break off. Eve screamed loudly. Horns honked, brakes shrieked. Aaron finally drew to a lurching halt where the bridge's glitter ended in grayness.

There was a sudden deep silence, and then Eve said in a chill voice, "I'm glad you did that. I'm glad the children saw you try to murder their mother."

(26)

PROHIBITION HAD MADE IT DIFFICULT for Aaron to gain a foothold on Broadway. It was pretty well sewed up by the Boys. The toughest guys in town had the nightspots, and they hadn't wanted outsiders inside. So up until now he had crept up on Broadway stealthily, on cat's feet. Now he was ready to move in on the big time.

"Cash in front, that's what they want, that's what it takes to make a deal today," Aaron said, with a philosophic air, staring into the bottom of his glass of milk. He was seated at Jack Dempsey's Restaurant with Jason and another of his deputies, Morris Grissman. Morris had been working for him for over a year now, and in spite of his sallow, unhealthy pallor and his kinky hair, Aaron found him likeable. He seemed to understand the business well, and he and Jason had a good rapport. Generally Aaron disapproved of friendships in the ranks, it could create problems for him. Of course, they had something in common. Each one had a little *shiksa* checkroom girl that he lived with, and the girls were friendly already.

Aaron stared around the walls, with their pictures of celebrities and the large portrait of Dempsey in the ring, and could barely contain his admiration, his envy. Boxing was his real first love. When he wasn't thinking of what a good lawyer he might have been if only he hadn't been too restless to study, he was thinking of what a great fighter he could have made. But a lightweight, that was the trouble. Whoever heard of a great champion lightweight! He had gotten to know Jack Dempsey pretty well through the years, having first met him at Stillman's Gym, then here and there around Broadway. Now he had the concessions at his place, as well as at the two big Brass Rail restaurants across the street — the very thought of those enormous slabs of underdone roast beef stuck in his throat, made him gag, but what the hell, that's what the people paid for. And the more people that could pay for it, the better tips they got in the checkrooms and washrooms.

The nightclubs and meeting halls, of course, had no luncheon trade, but Jack Dempsey's and the Brass Rail restaurant did a terrific luncheon business. So the three men were talking business over lunch while observing it in action.

"So, Aaron, are you going to Chicago with the new Casino?" Jason asked casually.

"Well, you know I'm not crazy for traveling. Maybe you'll go for me."

"That's okay with me, but what do you think of the whole idea?"

"I think they're crazy. We're making a barrel of dough here. Why press your luck? Chicago still ain't New York!"

"Yeah, but they think they've got a formula and they're dying to try it out," Morris said, eyeing the coatroom all the time he talked.

"Dying, ugh, don't even use the word. I'm afraid that's how the Chicago French Casino just may end up."

"Do you *have* to put up the dough?" Morris asked.

"Well, sure. I have no choice, thirty Gs. I couldn't afford to get them sore now, that's all I need, to have them down on me, *too*. It's bad enough I've got those other crazy bastards on my tail. Jeeze, they still scare the daylights outa me."

Jason smiled tolerantly. Sure, what the hell has he got to worry about, Aaron thought. It's *my* hide they're after.

"Well, I warned you that they weren't going to lie back quietly and let you finance the competition," Jason said, lighting yet another cigarette, to Aaron's apparent discomfort. "On top of which they're going snow-blind from the tablecloths over there since our new joint opened."

The French Casino had been thriving for over a year now, and the management had planned openings for it in three or four other big cities where they felt nightclubs were a prospering business. Chicago was to be first, then Miami, followed probably by Boston. Aaron was always reluctant to go out of New York. He knew his own town backward and forward but was not so sure of the opportunities in those other hick towns, which is how he thought of any city outside New York. Besides, the Chicago Mob had most of the clubs sewn up there neat as a pin, and more than anything he wanted to disassociate himself from them completely. He was growing important in his own right now, he didn't need to have anything to do with those *mumsers*, not if he had his way, anyhow.

"Yeah, Jason," he said musingly, "if we gotta go, we gotta go, except I *can't* go to Chicago. You'll have to go, I'm just too damn busy here. Anyway, as you know, I'm right in the midst of finally getting an office set up for the business. It will be better for all of us — you'll have a big office, a place to telephone, to interview girls, to count the take. We have no room over there at Wingfoot, the place is a dump. And besides, it doesn't look good for people."

"What people?"

"People, just people," Aaron said, shoving his empty glass of milk around here and there on the table, early signs of the return of his usual agitation. Jason had learned to recognize them; his antennae were enormously sensitive to the reactions of this strange, abrupt, charismatic man he called boss.

Aaron jumped up, signifying the lunch meeting was at an end, although the boys still had their coffee cups half-full and cigarettes burned in the ashtray.

"Miller," he said, "I'm going over to the old Manhattan Opera House on West Thirty-fourth Street now, wanna come along? It's an awfully interesting building, and you'll see some fun. I want to buy it some day. It could be the Abel Enterprises building — upstairs the offices, downstairs we could use the ballrooms and meeting halls for affairs."

"That's some commercial location," Jason said, "fantastic. But they'll want a barrel for it. It's a landmark."

"A white elephant, you mean. Oscar Hammerstein's folly," Aaron said, with a wave of his oddly delicate hand, his fingers fluttering, a sharp contrast to the disciplined, muscular body.

They began to walk down Broadway now at a brisk pace, Aaron in the lead, in spite of Jason's longer legs. It was early in spring, and the air was warm and full of the greasy odors of gasoline and fried foods. As many times as Aaron had walked this crazy, ugly, beautiful street, with its hectic advertisements and squatting theaters, he never tired of looking and commenting. Now and then he'd stop briefly, stepping into a grimy doorway to joke with a half-sleeping drunk, or spar with a punchy boxer he'd recognized from some gym or other, or maybe kibbitz with a comedian that Broadway had long ago forgotten. Today, however, he seemed in a hurry to reach his destination.

"Yeah," he continued, "Hammerstein died broke. When he opened that opera house in 1906 it looked like big competition for the Met, so they gave him a million dollars to close down, and he took it, can you beat that, where was the guy's spirit? Ah, he had to be a deadbeat, anyway, because even with the million they gave him, he died broke. I should've been around to show him how to wheel and deal. Yes, m'boy," he said, holding onto Jason's shoulder paternally, "ya gotta get up early in the morning to outfox the next guy."

As they pushed their way through the garment district, dodging the rolling racks heavily laden with dresses and coats, the choking noise and clattering din were horrendous. Huge trucks disgorged their merchandise up and down the streets, and Aaron found himself jumping over metal chutes, but nothing slowed their pace. They were propelled by a mutual inner excitement, the one's enthusiasm charging and recharging the other.

Aaron loved Jason, in a way. They'd been together almost from the start; there was a nostalgia about that, a hurt almost like a toothache. But he couldn't admit it, not even to himself. Admitting it might suggest he needed somebody, was not wholly responsible

for the realization of his own dreams, and most of all it might suggest that he was at bottom vulnerable. He really did not trust Jason
— not completely. He knew that Jason had it in his power to steal
from him much of what he owned (what he owned was really only
borrowed) especially the goodwill of the proprietors. What was
to stop him from going to the various club owners and syndicate
bosses whom he knew well (some of them better than Aaron did)
and getting them to renew with him personally, maybe even making
a deal to pay off out of profits, or even offering to run the concession for nothing for the first year? No, it was crazy thinking. Jason
simply didn't have the money to pull off anything like that (unless
he had been steadily stealing, which Aaron considered, but didn't
really believe). No, the places needed solid financial backing, with
the secure feeling that there was more where that came from. He
alone could provide that security — Just the same, consciously or
not, he kept Jason on the same salary, moderate for the time, the
hours, the work.

So Jason wasn't getting much out of all of this, personally. But
he was making what *he* considered to be good money, very good
money, maybe twenty thousand dollars a year, sometimes more, and
if he weren't so scrupulously straight he could have made twice that.
Anyway the money didn't really bother him. He loved the work,
the life, the challenge, the opportunity to work with Aaron. It was
to him that management turned in times of crisis. The only time
they got to see Aaron was when he made the initial deal, and maybe
now and then when he whisked by on a token appearance, or when
he made the rounds in Jason's absence, which was rare. No, he
never complained about money, he wasn't a whiner. But Aaron had
heard faint echos of dissatisfaction drifting back from his sister-in-
law Neva — "He's worth so much more, he's being underpaid —
exploited . . ."

He wondered about Jason. Was it just that he didn't have a
gambler's instincts? Or did he? He played the horses, he knew that,
pissed a lot of money away there, ran around with some pretty
tough characters, went ahead and did exactly what he wanted about
Dolly, over the intense objections of his parents. Maybe he didn't

know Jason at all — didn't really know *what* he might do. He didn't comform to any special mold, a bit of a crazy, that kid, he thought uncomfortably.

Jason had enough money to support his parents, and to take care of himself and Dolly. He wanted Dolly to quit working now, he took care of all her needs, except one — the need, the terrible, urgent need she had to be married to him. But how could he do that? His parents — and then there'd be the problem about raising the children. She was devoutly Catholic. He and Aaron had discussed it a hundred times, and always came to the same conclusion: It was unfeasible, impractical. Even now Jason was getting weekly workouts from his mother, who kept threatening to throw herself from a window if he ever married that *kurveh*. It was already a *shande* that he was living with her, instead of home where he belonged, with them.

Aaron and Jason approached the old Manhattan Opera House, a great pile of cement smoothed into an oblong mold, as innocent of adornment as a child's clay model. It had been remodeled in the new romantic art deco style some five years before. Artistically, it was not a success.

"The 'Scottish Rites' have it now, but they can't afford to keep it up. I think they'll sell it for a song if I want to buy it, but I'm not sure about that just now; I may only rent. It's a great piece of real estate, why, for Christ's sake, it's bordered by the Hotel New Yorker on one side, Macy's on the other, and just around the corner is Madison Square Garden and Penn Station. Not a bad location, is it?" he asked, chuckling.

"That depends what you want it for, Aaron. For commercial uses, it's great; for a theater or for dances, I just hope it's not too far downtown."

"Miller, you're crazy. You worry too much, let me do the worrying for a change. And speaking of worrying, are you still all upset about that little broad of yours? It's a shame the way they mess up their lives. Pretty kid," he said musingly.

Jason knew that was supposed to be high praise, coming from Aaron, on the subject of girls.

"It's not a question of being upset, it's just that I have to make a decision. I owe it to her, it's been a long time. She's got a right to a decent life, too, and well, after what she did, I see how unhappy she must be."

"Oh, admit it, that suicide business just appealed to your ego, didn't it?"

"Not really," Jason said matter-of-factly.

"What will your mother say?" Aaron asked, still tied to his own mother's fraying apron strings. Without giving Jason a chance to answer, he said, "Don't tell me, I know what she'll say, that she'll put her head in the oven."

"Look, I'm twenty-eight years old, what can they do?"

"Ah ha, so she's wearing you down, you son-of-a-gun. I haven't heard you say that you love her yet. What about love?"

"What about it? You were in love, really in love. What happiness did it bring you?"

"Yeah, I suppose you're right, but that's begging the question, kid."

"I'm used to her," Jason said. "She's an awfully nice kid. Yeah, I suppose I love her in a way. I love her loving me the way she does."

"That's what I said in the first place," Aaron said triumphantly. "And the kids?"

"What kids? I'm not even married yet. Anyway, I don't want any kids."

Aaron looked at him incredulously. "Then why the hell get married?" But he knew Jason had made up his own mind already — she had won him over at last.

They entered the building, still absorbed in conversation, and rode the elevator to the fifth floor where they waited for the building manager, a dour Scotsman by the name of Danny Delmar. They found him sitting at his desk in a bare office that was much run down at the heels. Aaron stole a glance at Jason to catch his reaction, but he had already slipped on his business mask and was looking convincingly bland. Aaron offered his hand, then introduced Jason.

"Listen, can you put the bottle in the bottom o' the box," Aaron said, trying out his best brogue for the Scotsman.

The man didn't smile, but looked at him as if he were mad.

"Ah, you think the mon e daft, do ye. Well, just watch your step, this old mon is crazy like a fox," still in dialect. He restrained himself from using the old bromide about what Scotsmen wear under their kilts, although it danced invitingly on the tip of his tongue.

"If you're all through clowning, Mr. Abel, I think we can talk some business."

*

An hour later when they emerged from the office, Aaron had rented the top floor of the building for five thousand dollars a year with an option to buy, and the main ballroom thrown in besides.

"Let me show you some of this building," he said to Jason. "It's really fantastic. It's enormous. There are at least four ballrooms and a gorgeous theater with a seating capacity of a thousand." He was almost unable to contain his enthusiasm, his new pride of acquisition.

Aaron seemed lost in the huge, cavernous lobby of the building and tried doors, poking here and there, searching for the ballrooms.

"Jesus, this place is in some lousy shape, it'll need plenty of work," Jason said, whistling and looking around the building. "And plenty of maintenance."

"What are ya worried about, that's their problem. If I buy it, my brother Ben'll handle the maintenance; he's an old hand at fighting it out with the unions. I only leased it, remember." Aaron had finally found the entrance to the main ballroom. "Now if I can only find the lights." They were standing in total darkness and Aaron was groping around for the light switch. Just as Jason reached for a match they both turned in answer to a scuffling sound, and before either could say anything, two men had stepped out of the blackness with flashlights. One held a gun to Jason's head, the other said, "Don't move or I'll shoot." A third hit Aaron hard in the gut, and then a fast uppercut to the jaw. Jason made an involuntary move toward Aaron and felt the cold muzzle slide around his temple. Aaron let go with his famous left hook and for a moment it looked as though the other man would crumple, but, incensed at the unexpected attack, he began to slam Aaron around hard until the blood was running freely from his forehead and nose. Now the other man cracked Jason over the head with the butt of his gun and pitched into Aaron. Jason slid to the floor unconscious. Aaron had used everything his brother had taught him, and more that he had picked up from the pros at the gym, but he was no match for brass knuckles. The last thing he remembered hearing before he passed out was, "Just a little reminder not to screw your friends, smart ass, next time you won't get off so easy."

*

Aaron didn't consider the syndicate's assault on him a bad omen, or else it would have turned him completely sour on the deal with the Opera House. On the contrary, he was still alive, relatively unharmed. They had let him live and that was all that counted. He was lucky. He had gotten off more easily than Joe E. Lewis, in Chicago, the one-time singer. He knew Joey, had met him often at the clubs. He really got cut up bad, they had severed his vocal cords, and for no less trivial a defection — the same thing: He had wanted to change clubs, press his opportunities, further his own career. And Jason — Aaron felt closer to him now since he, too, had shared the risk. Maybe he ought to consider giving him a raise. Why did he have such a paternal feeling for Jason, they weren't really all that far apart in age, maybe ten years or so . . .

No, the Opera House would be lucky for him, he had willed it.

In Aaron's first year there, the great showman Max Reinhardt rented the huge old downstairs theater for his colossal biblical extravaganza, *The Eternal Road*. Building three revolving stages and completely remodeling the theater at his own expense, he insisted on ripping out all the lovely old red plush seats, to Aaron's shocked disapproval.

Although it was hardly a financial success for Reinhardt, it certainly didn't hurt Aaron any and it gave the old place plenty of much-needed publicity — free. But while Aaron liked having a building to call his own, he was already running headlong into the next project.

*

The Casino Group opened in Chicago and then Miami, as planned. Aaron didn't go along with them on that. He told Shapiro the truth: He wanted to live, was crazy about living, and furthermore, he honestly didn't believe that they would be good business ventures. He felt that they should keep their energies and investments concentrated on the club that was burgeoning in New York. And within six months of the opening in Miami he was proved right, but with a result he had not exactly counted on. The New York club began to suffer. The attention and money siphoned off from it to sustain the others had gradually begun to show. Monthly earnings were starting to drop drastically.

The club closed less than two years after its gala opening, leaving Aaron angry and somehow frustrated. But out of his anger a new tactic was being formulated. Why pay some other guy for the privilege of running a club into the ground with his poor planning and lack of shrewdness, when he could, with some backing, afford to take over the place himself and make it all work together to his benefit? Especially now that the pressure was off him from the competition down the street. They had been forced to close down some six months earlier.

For a while he would just mark time, give the competition time to forget a little, a breathing spell that he could use to his advantage, to concentrate on infiltrating some of the remaining places he didn't already have and which were proliferating up and down Broadway. He wasn't afraid of competition. He really didn't have any, no one else had organized this thing into a real business. As the country tried to pull up and out of the depression, people wanted fun, loud and frequent. Competition in the entertainment business was growing fierce, and the club owners needed money and backing. Aaron was right there with it, cold cash in the form of concession money as each new club opened up and down the Great White Way. It was for this that he had been carefully scrimping and saving through the years.

The concessions were run coolly, efficiently, and to the point, even artistically, like the arrangement of the sample quarters in the brass dishes on the counters. The organizational talents of Jason Miller and the six or so underlings (Eve called them "hoods") Aaron had spawned through the years, were a fine foil for his less precise but more inventive qualities.

He was determined to reopen the Casino. He felt there was still a fortune to be made there, but he needed a great showman — the Greatest. Aaron thought immediately of his previous associate, Billy Rose. Impossible though he considered him, difficult as he was to do business with, he *was* talented. He had to give the guy that much, and he was shrewd, a *landsman* of sorts; another Lower East Side boy who was making it big, bigger than all of them, Aaron thought uncomfortably. He estimated that he might be worth a couple of million already. Well, he wasn't too far from that mark himself, but his own fortune was liquid — flowing gold, all cash. He decided to invest some of that cash in the Manhattan Opera House. He exercised his option and bought the building for $7500, taking over mortgages totaling almost $342,500. The price in itself was lucky. Now Abel Enterprises owned their own building.

(27)

EVE WAS SITTING in the kitchen of her Flatbush Avenue apartment with Mama Lisa, and between them on the floor rested a sizable tub of benzene. Eve had just finished treating Reid's infested head, and Lisa was carefully combing Jennie's long blonde hair with a fine comb. The slow, oozy smell of the gasoline made

Jennie giddy; lately everything made her giddy. But she had to have her scalp clean by the time boarding school began. She could hardly be sent away to boarding school with a head that was alive, Eve had said.

"How did they catch such a thing?" Grandma kept repeating, and clucking her tongue. "Private schools," she mumbled disapprovingly. "Not in my day. What did you do, wear someone else's hat?"

"No, Mama," Eve cut in, "towels are a more likely possibility."

Grandma turned Jennie around now and commanded that she face her, head down, while she drew the fine comb forward through the golden jungle of her hair, making the final check. Jennie was happy to be rid once and for all of the agonizing itching and smarting caused by the unwelcome guests her scalp had played host to for the last six weeks. She studied Grandma's cameo-styled face through the strands of her hair. She thought it was sweet and slightly petulant, as if unjustly treated by life. Soft, round features, like a squash blossom — a fat person's face. She reminded her of a Jordan almond, a candy-sweet pastel shell on the outside, all shiny and pink like her cheeks, but inside she was tough, and just a tiny bit bitter. With her head wrapped in a large towel, Jennie was excused from the ordeal, and Grandma officially declared her clean.

From the bedroom down the hall the boys could be heard screaming and fighting over their electric trains.

"Ugh — those screams, they go through me like a knife," Eve said.

Lisa looked up at Eve, as if to answer, and then, as if she thought better of it, back down at the combs and brushes she was cleaning with the fluid.

"I don't know why you are sending them away again. What will you do with yourself all alone, anyway?"

"Well, quite frankly, I've got to have some time to myself, Mama. I'm so involved with the children's lives that I have no time for myself. I feel numb, only half alive."

"Well, if you resent it, it's wasted time, not good for either the children or yourself."

"I'd like to get to know myself all over again, get reacquainted with some of my old dreams — get back in touch with life and people. Maybe I could find a job, do something, be somebody. I've got the education. I'd like to put it to use."

"Humph, you think it's such a bargain to work out there? Take it from me, you're better off where you are — a woman without experience in a man's world — "

"Oh, Mama, I don't believe that anatomy is destiny, though men try to browbeat women into believing it. You used to make a living, supported yourself, and *him*" — she said *him* with a strong, sly emphasis.

"So what? I had no choice — *you* do. And where did it get me? I still have to come to my daughter for handouts and bite my lip in the bargain, so as not to kill the goose that lays the golden egg."

"Mama," Eve said, genuinely hurt. "You resent me, too."

"No, dear, I don't, but I resent your being so ungrateful. You really have everything a woman could want — "

"Except for the children — and they've been very difficult lately, I don't mind telling you — what have I got?"

"You could have had your husband and security, but you — "

"Oh, you really make me laugh. What husband, what security? I never got anything out of his success but loneliness."

"Well, I guess you can only appreciate financial security when you've never had any," Lisa said in a faint, tired voice.

"Well, I never had any either," Eve said.

"But that's the way you chose to have it. I had no choice. Look, Eve, he must be a millionaire by now. You should have stayed with him — "

"Why, for what?" she cut in, her voice rising, loud and shrill. "I wouldn't have had any more financial security than I have now, you know how cheap he was with me — "

"He was on the way up, he was frightened about money — "

"And what's more," Eve continued, forging ahead on the steam of her anger, "no emotional security of any kind, no emotional satisfactions — "

"So emotionally you're satisfied now? It doesn't look that way to me. You know it takes two to make a marriage satisfying. Are you sure you did your part?"

"That you can even ask that question, knowing me as you do, knowing the depth and intensity of my feelings in relationships, only shows me that after all you're on his side, that you — you — resent me, maybe because of Lubowitz, maybe because of Freddie, how she loved me, how we loved each other, or how much Papa loved me. Maybe you felt excluded, I don't know, but — " she was crying.

"You are like your father — he used to wallow in self-pity too — Eve, look what you're doing to yourself. You're killing yourself, and you have this terrible habit of building up your martyrdom on the bodies of those around you."

"You were always callous, didn't feel things the way Freddie and I did, that's what saved your life — "

"And yours," Lisa said gently. "I'm not callous, dear, just tired." She heaved herself up from the kitchen chair heavily and walked over to the sink.

"Well, I want to be my own person again, I — "

"You want to be little Eve Levinson again, with a father alive to pamper you and dress you up in kilties and have you do a Scottish pipe dance on a table top for company. Well, nobody can ever go back. You want a second chance, like a kid in a candy store. You want to take a bite, try it, if you don't like it give it back and get another. If it were that easy, nobody would ever be satisfied or enjoy what they had."

"Oh, stop your mid-Victorian philosophizing, please. I only want to go back as far as meeting that man is concerned. From there everything started falling apart — " She paused and said bitterly, "Yes, my *family* — my sisters, oh God, Mama, three sisters, our lives all snuffed out before thirty. Do you think I can ever forgive Aaron for Pauline's life — for mine — both of us his victims, the victims of men."

"But, Eve, Pauline's gone, it happened years ago, your punishing him — yourself — can't bring her back; besides it wasn't really *his* fault."

"So," Eve interrupted fiercely, her voice rising to a shriek, "so eight years wipes out a sister, a daughter — ?"

"But what's the use? The more you resist life the more it seems to come down on you."

Eve looked up quickly, but not surprised. "I sometimes wish I had your placid temperament instead of Papa's chaotic one — "

"Mine you've always considered dull and insensitive."

"Well, where did your quiet resignation get you? At least I unburden myself. It's healthier."

"For you, maybe, but for the children, I'm not so sure."

The one thing Eve could not tolerate was any criticism of her treatment of the children, who now dominated her life, though somehow joylessly.

"Well, it's not easy bringing up three children alone, worse than alone, when he's there pulling in the opposite direction. They won't listen to me, that's why they have to go away for a year. I need a rest — a long rest. Anyway, I've got to get out of Flatbush. I'm going to Manhattan and take a beautiful apartment there, right by the middle of Central Park, and gorge myself on theater and restaurant food and Carnegie Hall. I've been isolated with children for too long. I feel like a paper doll with only one dimension."

"Well," Mama said from the sink, her elbows deep in suds, "maybe you'll take that time off to try to work your marriage out."

Eve jumped up, shoved her chair angrily under the kitchen table, and said, "I don't want to, Mama, and what's more I don't think he wants to now either, not since he's got her. Anyway, marriage isn't a panacea for all things. At best it's no great bargain, and ours was 'at worst' — Loneliness frightens me, it's true," she said, momentarily reflective, "but what frightens me even more are the stifling effects of a bad marriage. For me it was like putting a stopper in a bottle of scent — it seemed to dull all the senses."

"All but one for you, it seems — anger."

"Yes, I'm angry all right. Aren't you, deep down inside? What the hell did you ever get out of marriage? Of course I'm talking about Papa. I don't call this — this mess you're in a marriage."

Lisa let that pass unruffled. "Companionship, for one thing. As you get older it becomes awfully important."

"The worst kind of alone is to be alone with someone in the house," Eve said. "Although even there ours was not the usual marriage. He was never *in* the house, only for a few scant hours to sleep or talk on the phone, and even when he was there physically, he wasn't."

"*Your* marriage is not unusual," Lisa said unperturbed. "No unhappy marriage is unusual, it only seems that way to you; what is unique is a happy marriage."

Eve went over to her mother, she turned her around, her soapy hands dripping wet onto the floor. "Oh, Mama," she said fiercely, "I need you on my side, why aren't you on my side?"

"But I am, *kinderle*, I am," she said, astonished.

*

After the children were neatly tucked away at boarding school in Darien, Connecticut, Eve had meant to get down to the business of living her own life. She kept promising herself that she would look for a job, but she reasoned that she had no work experience and didn't have the proper credentials for teaching — sub-teaching perhaps, but what was that after all? Each day she awakened breathless and knotted with fear, and as the day wore on she either felt too ill or was too depressed to go anywhere except maybe to Lord & Taylor's, where she wandered aimlessly among the lingerie. The days dragged by pointlessly now. She was neither wife nor mother, and yet she was both. Perhaps she was only meant to spend her life fighting at service entrances, screaming down back elevator shafts after recalcitrant handymen and day workers or wooing reluctant pediatricians to her children's bedsides. Erudite, asexual men found her attractive, and she'd use them as occasional escorts to the opera, but she felt uncomfortable, always assuming that they wanted something from her that she could not give, so she eventually drifted out of contact with them. She had more time than ever on her hands, yet her heels were run down and her hems began to droop.

Now she had the time to think, and all she could think about was
the coming of night and her lonely meal at Schrafft's or Childs or
the possibility of waking up in the middle of the night desperately
ill — alone . . . Loneliness is a killing disease, she thought. This
was no life. Maybe mama had been right. She usually was.

(28)

WHEN JENNIE WAS ELEVEN, Aaron decided they would
go to Canada for the Christmas holidays from the Greenlawn School. It would be a cozy old-fashioned white Christmas in
the bosom of a cozy old-fashioned family. At least that's the way
Aaron saw it and that's the way it would be. He was after all, a
traditional man at heart —

"All of us together. Mother will go too. How'd you like that,
Jen?" he said. "We'll take the train to Quebec direct, then drive
down to Montreal. That way we won't miss a thing!"

Jennie couldn't help noticing the looks that crackled between her
parents lately, and Eve even allowed Aaron upstairs when he came
to get them Sundays, instead of having to wait down in the car as
usual. She saw them kissing in the kitchen one afternoon, but even
their embrace was somehow like a combat, Eve squirming in his
arms, feigning annoyance, and Aaron's embrace hunched up, teasing,
taunting, never relaxed. But he was saying cajolingly, "Relax,
darling, relax. I'm your friend, your best friend, you'll see." Jennie
had heard this before. She always wondered if she'd see, too, and
when and how.

That this was to be a reconciliation of sorts she had no doubts.
After all they weren't divorced yet, just legally separated. She'd

heard that expression for years. Now she knew exactly what it meant. Her mother told her every chance she could get.

"I've got to get that agreement changed, it's ridiculous. I have to go to your father every other day like a beggar with my hand out. That's what he wants, to keep me begging, to humiliate me, to make me the bad one, to turn you children against me." Or with even greater frequency: "He's making money hand over fist and what do I get? The same paltry sum I got five years ago during the height of the depression."

When Jennie was out with her father he took her aside and said to her, "You know, I pay for your school and all your clothes, and all the vacations. You know that's not in our agreement, it's all extra."

Jennie nodded uncertainly. She wasn't at all sure of her ground and could never quite decide whose side she was on. Sometimes when she was home and her mother would scream and yell at them and slap her, she'd hate her and wish she could be with her father. He was lucky to have gotten away from Eve's bitterness and temper tantrums and uncontrolled outbursts everywhere, even in public. How Jennie hated to go to a restaurant with her. She always made a loud fuss about where they sat, changed tables a number of times, either because of drafts, a hostile waiter, or worse still, "The people at the next table were staring." Of course they were staring, Jennie thought, who wouldn't stare? How strange they must appear to an outsider, she thought, a crazy chattering woman with too much rouge and a silly hat loaded with fruit and flowers, and there with three children and no man, no husband. No wonder she gets no respect, poor service.

Now it would be different, her father would be with them. But somehow she wasn't convinced. She felt a cold lump in her belly. Nothing ever really changed for them. Her mother wouldn't permit change. She was relentless in her persistence, hammering at the same arguments, the same old complaints and threats. She didn't seem to care that nothing ever got solved. It only seemed important that she be heard, and heard and *heard*.

"Christmas is a wonderful time to see Canada," Eve said bubblingly. "It has the European flavor I loved when I was a child in London." For days now Jennie had been watching her mother fussing and primping and unwrapping packages carefully, saving the tissue paper. "If you pack in tissue paper, nothing will get creased," she said confidentially to Jennie. Jennie thought of her few outgrown sweaters and time-worn plaid skirts, a little too long or a little too short, and didn't much care if they got creased or not, but she somehow sensed the importance of her mother's wardrobe for this trip and was glad of it. This was normal, for once they would be a normal family like others all around her, like Betty Louise Morris's. Maybe for once she wouldn't feel freakish.

Twelve days with her parents together filled her with a terror of anxiety that was as bad as the condition she usually lived in with her mother alone. And the boys, their wildness, their jumping around usually made Eve nervous, and if Eve was nervous, that might trigger off more scenes with their father.

As usual, Aaron changed plans a hundred times before departure and they had to end up meeting him at the train. Eve complained all the way down in the taxi, "It's always the same, nothing ever changes. I've got to grapple with the luggage and the porters and you children, all alone, with no help from your father, from anyone." Jennie made a mental note to help her mother when they got out of the taxi. Aaron arrived just as the porter was calling "all aboard." Eve pretended not to notice him at all. Jennie thought this was an improvement over the usual noisy quarrel. Perhaps this trip wouldn't be so bad after all.

The day passed quickly. The children colored ferociously in their books. Jennie liked especially the magic coloring book, the one where secret pictures seemed to spring up out of nowhere the moment her crayon touched the rough cream paper, like a distant mountain suddenly in sharp focus after a rainstorm. Had it been there all along, just hidden by the fog? At times she delighted in ignoring the carefully planned color key at the bottom of the page, and grass would come up orange, and trees blue and sky pink. Anyway, it was better than playing those endless boring card games with her father and brothers. She loved to look out the window, particularly at sunset, when the flat eastern landscape rushing past the tracks turned a melancholy blue and was dotted black and red with wistful little hobo fires. It made the Pullman with its night bustle of porters, its dinner sounds, seem all the more cozy and protective. But Aaron was fascinated with the hobos. The "knights of the open road," he called them. When he spoke about them his eyes seemed bright and far away and he was suddenly free from tension, on a romantic journey, over the tracks, under a bridge, or out in one of those wheat fields they'd just passed. Jennie thought of mulligan stews, though she didn't exactly know what they were, and thick loaves of unsliced white bread, of how fragrant they smelled, and her mouth watered. Yes, she had to admit to herself there was a certain comfort in having her parents together. For one thing, she didn't have to worry about her mother wandering around alone, or eating what Eve called "lonely meals at Childs, the food sticking in my throat, to be washed down by my own tears" — a familiar litany.

The porter knocked on the door to make up the berths. Their compartment opened into the one Aaron was sharing with Evan. That made perfect sense to Jennie. After all, she was the only girl so she should sleep with her mother, and Reid of course was just a baby.

They went to the dining car while the porter made up the beds. The dining car smelled sweetly of soot and steam and mashed potatoes, and seemed to her in all its purity to promise perfect peace, if only for one glorious hour. Usually Jennie didn't have much appetite, but tonight she was ravenous. She bolted the heavy cream soup, then roast chicken and stuffing, candied sweet potatoes, green peas, then scraped the mashed potatoes from her brothers' plates. "They always waste everything anyway," she said by way of explanation. Her parents looked on amused. Aaron looked tenderly at the boys. He was very proud of his sons, Jennie knew that, but she didn't mind because she had to be special, singled out, the only girl.

They arrived in Quebec early in the morning of the third day. Everyone felt train-stiff, tense, and tired. A poor sleeper normally,

Jennie did much worse on the train, alternating from roasting hot, choking in her upper berth, to freezing cold as the heat was turned down toward morning. The spastic jerking of the coupling and uncoupling of the cars during the night was the topic of disgruntled conversation the next morning.

Snow, thick and velvety, everywhere seemed to absorb their irritations like a sponge. The blanket of white blotted up the profusion of colors and images of the long trip.

No sooner had the bellboy put their luggage on racks in the two large rooms, than Eve began to complain about the view — "the wrong exposure," she said. Aaron announced that he was taking the boys tobogganing. As always, the boys' super-charged, untapped energies left Jennie feeling strangely deflated, excluded, a fit companion for her mother.

They walked around the huge Gothic-style lobby of the Château Frontenac. Eve was in bubbling high spirits, and when Aaron and the boys unexpectedly joined them for lunch, red-cheeked and excited, Jennie was quietly happy. All throughout lunch Eve was gay, charming, the movie star she might have been, erudite, witty, the way Jennie had seen her sometimes with her friends from the old days, especially after a few glasses of champagne. But why did her mother speak in phrases as if she were a character drawn from a book or a stage play? In a way she thought she knew the answer. It was because her mother was playing at being all the many things she was not and would like to be.

"I want the boys to take naps after lunch," Eve said. Reid greeted that remark with a Bronx cheer. But after lunch, Jennie went tearing outside with the boys, determined to enjoy this unusual vacation.

The whiteness and the glitter seemed to pulsate, to grow all around them until it enveloped them in its fragile beauty like the shimmering Christmas ornaments on the huge tree in the lobby. It made her hesitant, fearful of crushing it. She tried to sell herself the idea that her parents were acting differently together, calmer, more natural, but in reality she felt that they blew past each other like a cold breeze.

It was near midnight when Jennie woke to hear loud voices from her father's room. She was surprised to see, by the shaft of moonlight on her brother's bed, another sleeping child. It was Evan. What is he doing in Reid's bed? she thought groggily. She almost rolled back into sleep when the voices grew louder. Her mother's sobbing was punctuated by bursts of words.

"But why not, why not? You say you love me . . . You're lying again. You're a liar. It's that Martha, I know it. You can't give her up, that checkroom tramp."

"That's not it at all. She has nothing to do with anything."

"Oh, so you don't deny it then?"

"Eve, you didn't want me, you threw me out of the house, and no matter how I begged, you wouldn't change your mind. Try again, I begged you. I had Al Carton intercede. Al's a lawyer you trust; you wouldn't listen. I had to go over and stay at the Y. I'm a millionaire and I'm living like a goddamn hermit at the Y. So what did you expect, I'm not a monk."

"So I was right, it's for her you'd give up your wife and children you're supposed to love so much. What a phony bastard you are." Now the sobbing came in hard, angry chunks.

"She doesn't mean a thing to me, not a goddamn thing."

"Why did you bring me here if not to try a reconciliation? Why do you humiliate me in front of the children? Oh, I knew it couldn't work — it never worked, and it never will." Aaron was silent now.

Jennie sat up in bed. She was wide-awake now, her heart pounded with excitement and expectancy but she didn't really know what it was that she was expecting.

She got up and walked to the door of her parents' room. From the angle behind the half-opened door she could see her mother lying on the floor by the bed, her head propped on the bed. Aaron was sitting on the edge leaning down to her, conciliatory, uncertain. Eve was wearing a filmy negligee. Jennie thought she looked very beautiful, different somehow. Eve was moaning softly. "I've been so lonely," she said, "so terribly lonely."

"Take the kids back from boarding school."

"Children are no real company for a woman."

"Well, you always said *I* was no company," Aaron said. "Too busy for you, that's why you left me, you said."

"All that you're saying is that you don't want me back under any circumstances. Isn't that it?"

"I'm not saying that I don't love you, Eve, only that I don't know. We ought to think about it some more."

"No, it can't work because you don't really want it to, and because you've already got someone else," she cried.

Jennie crept back to bed, hoping that their voices would wake the boys, then they would talk about it together, maybe even laugh. That would block out the sounds, somehow laugh them away. But instead she just lay rigid in her bed, staring unblinking, straight upwards. All the next day Jennie stayed with her brothers, as if for protection. More tobogganing and sledding, screaming as their long sled tore 'round the corners, looped, zigzagged. The boys bellywhopped down the sled chute. Jennie remembered that Eve had said it was dangerous. They were not supposed to go, but Eve had been nowhere in sight all day. Jennie had seen her early in the morning, dressing, in and out of the bathroom. Evan was back in the room with Aaron, everything as before, as if it had only been a bad dream. Yes, perhaps it had only been a nightmare. Jennie wondered if her brother was aware of his nighttime journey. Probably not, he sleeps as intensely as he does everything else, she thought, and envied him that ability. Her mother said very little to them. She was silent, in itself alarming to Jennie — one terse question only:

"Do you want to go into town with me today?"

Her mother's nearness unsettled her. She desperately wanted not to stay with her today. No answer from Jennie.

"It doesn't matter. I know you'd prefer to be with them, you always do."

She went back into the bathroom. Jennie hoped that it was to fix her hair or her face or something. She never knew what to expect from Eve.

So Jennie escaped and played feverishly all day with her brothers, but she had a nagging headache. She woke with it in the front of her head and it slowly spread to the back. Even her ears ached, or maybe that was from the biting cold, though she didn't feel in the least bit cold.

They didn't go back to the hotel for lunch, having it instead at the ski lodge near the activity center. Aaron was back to his old Sunday self, Jennie thought, preoccupied, distracted, but nonetheless attentive to them. He made jokes sheepishly and ran to the telephone only a few times.

Around four-thirty they marched through the staid lobby, red-cheeked, jabbing and pushing at one another restlessly, and then Jennie spotted her mother sitting alone in a far corner of the lobby, her head bowed low over a book, as if trying to hide her identity between its covers. She was having tea. Here and there tea carts were being wheeled by with tempting pink, yellow, and brown iced cakes, large chocolate ones, piles of scones with little tubs of jam and butter. Jennie's mouth was watering but she was torn between having them and passing through the lobby unseen by Eve. Just then, Aaron caught sight of her too, and pulled them all in her direction. Ah, good, now the decision would be made for her, and she wouldn't have to be alone with her mother. When they got there, Eve turned away silently. Her face was closed up inscrutably, as if a thousand different furies were tumbling in her brain, each one annulling the other until it all came out neutral, blank on her face, dead. I'm a fool, Jennie thought, I deserve this. I should have stayed with her today.

The boys and Aaron drifted away, but Jennie stayed — rooted there. Her mother has become a frightening stranger. She enters the scene before her objectively as if it is not happening to her at all — she is someone else. *She sits down next to her mother, unsure of what to say. Maybe I'd better say nothing, she thinks, but says,* "How was the town?" *Silence . . . then after a long pause:*

"*I didn't go.*"

"*How come?*"

"What's the difference? You're selfish just like them," in an even tone.

Jennie looks all around her to see if her mother has been overheard. The smiling waitress wheels a cart near them, but Jennie hardly notices it now, her head is pounding and her stomach feels full, but she takes a cake, two, another, mechanically. She is astonished to see that Eve does also, picking at it daintily, disdainfully — again she has the detached feeling of not really being there, she is watching a movie, scary.

Through the huge windows Jennie sees it is beginning to snow again, a cold, driving snow. Somehow it makes her feel better, evening creeping up, snow blowing, a comforting sensation of surrendering to the elements, of giving up and letting fate do with them what it willed, resigned, relaxed. They gulp their tea in silence. The lobby seems to her to be filled with the noise of normal people laughing and talking normally. Finally her mother gets up and they walk toward the elevators, but Eve veers off in a different direction, saying only in a hollow voice, "I'm going out."

After a late dinner in the dining room with Aaron, a very quiet dinner, unboisterous, they return to their rooms. Their mother is there, bent over the writing desk. She seems not to notice them and is silent. The boys are frightened by their mother's odd behavior.

Aaron herds them into the other room and goes into the room with Eve, shutting the door. The voices grow louder, louder, deep, throaty, chokingly angry screams from her, hacked out like coughs between clenched teeth. The door bursts open. Eve seems to be running away from Aaron. Then she puts her face close to his and spits into his face, foam still on her lips, her eyes wild. Aaron wipes the spittle from his face, grinning, trying to make a joke out of it and Eve rushes for the paned window and hurls herself at it wildly. With a great rush of strength, the window is thrown wide and Eve prepares to jump, only Aaron is faster. He pulls at her arms, and as if by some inner command, Evan rushes over and pulls her back too, he is suddenly in possession of enormous strength for an eight year old. She flails wildly and pulls free. Aaron wrestles her to the floor with one hand and, in a half crouch, closes the window with the other, all in one quicksilver motion. "Get a doctor, get a doctor," he commands the children, but they seem transfixed, white and cold as marble. Jennie, trembling, stares fixedly at Evan, though at first she doesn't really see him, then she sees that he is green, but standing perfectly still, like a statue, his eyes staring straight ahead.

*

After the incident in Canada, Aaron made up his mind absolutely to gain custody of the children. He had toyed with the idea often, but now it seemed blindingly clear to him. He threatened of course to prove her an unfit mother, but he could hardly do that. After all, he had taken away from her so much, left her with so little (she had at least convinced him of that through years of grinding accusation), that he worried about taking the children. In spite of the fact that she had grown incapable of demonstrating her love, beyond her overanxious ministrations, he knew how deeply she cared. Underneath — underneath, at bottom, there was love. For years he had begged her to see a psychiatrist; she would not go unless he went also, she said. Finally they went together to see a famous man; the psychiatrist threw them both out of the office. Sporadically there were other doctors, but nothing ever came of it.

(29)

THE DEAL BETWEEN AARON AND BILLY ROSE was only in the talking stage, but the showman had agreed to go along with Aaron on a partnership basis for the reopening of the new French

Casino. The deal would be fifty-fifty, all the way down the line.
Aaron wasn't crazy about acquiring a partner again, particularly a
shrewd one like Rose, but what could he do, he needed a showman.
He needed someone whose forte was nightclubs. Unquestionably,
Rose was the man of the hour now on Broadway.

On a late spring day in 1939 he headed for the Casino and his
appointment with Rose to discuss their contract, which was due to
be signed the following week. He was dressed in his snappiest pin-
striped suit and vest, gray satin tie, the ever-present silver spats, and
a wide-brimmed fedora. He was as usual coatless; he needed none,
his anxiety generated its own heat. He pushed the heavy doors open
— no doorman there now. The club had been officially closed for
more than six months, but inside the place was ablaze with lights
and sounds — workmen, stage hands, and girls, girls, girls. Rose
had just finished running some of them through a routine from the
last show, to see if it would be salvageable, and at the same time
was interviewing new girls. They were mostly tall, long-legged
beauties, with creamy skins, gorgeously made up. Aaron wondered
angrily at the way this man took over. They hadn't even signed
their deal yet, and already he was rehearsing a show — Christ, he'd
have to watch this guy like a hawk.

Aaron was standing next to the seated Rose, who acknowledged
his presence by bobbing his head, and with a perfunctory wave of
his pudgy hand, indicated that he be seated on a nearby folding
chair. Aaron, annoyed, sat down and found himself staring up into
the leotard-bound crotch of a sky-high blonde showgirl, one of
Rose's long-stemmed beauties. He ducked his head self-consciously
and cleared his throat, but wherever he looked, there were beautiful
girls. He was not unaccustomed to beautiful girls, nor was he
immune to them, it was just that business was business, and well,
anyway, showgirls were not his cup of tea — too tall, for one thing.
Just then Rose jumped up from his chair. Aaron got up also, anxious
to be on his feet, where he felt more in control. He approached the
irascible showman. Rose was shorter than Aaron, an agitated, sedu-
lous man. He needed to move his hands in order to speak. He
wore his expensive suit buttoned closely over his beginning paunch,

only his crooked tie, stained and slightly askew, gave any clue to his frantic energies. He shouted orders and talked constantly as if into a telephone receiver. Aaron wondered if he was crazy.

"Okay, girls, take a break. Those of you I haven't seen yet, please remain. Yes, Abel, how are you? Let's go into the back office where it's quieter." All this in one breath.

Aaron followed, irritated. He wasn't used to feeling like an underling in this business, particularly since he had started advancing money to the clubs — he was patted, petted, and flattered, a little like the old days at Harrison Avenue.

"See you're preparing a show already. No grass grows under your feet, Rose."

"No. Well, we planned to reopen the club, didn't we? I'm sort of feeling my way around."

Aaron looked up and grinned. "Yeah, so I noticed."

"Oh, Jesus," Rose smiled, "not me. I couldn't make a buck in this business if I fooled around with the girls. Uh-uh, never touch the stuff."

Rose was currently married to Fanny Brice, and her superstardom didn't hurt him at all, Aaron thought to himself, though rumor had it that the marriage was headed for the rocks. Well, that was the way most Broadway marriages ended up, didn't they, he thought gloomily. Something about a cute young swimmer he was planning to star in his *Aquacade* at the Fair. Eleanor Holm, yeah that was it . . . Eve was incensed about her. She didn't even *know* Rose, but she'd read all about it in the Broadway columns, and she just kept on mentioning it to Aaron, as if he were somehow responsible —

"So, Maestro," Aaron began, "the deal was that we're not changing a thing in the way of décor or backgrounds. The joint's a showcase just as it is, and it stays that way — so does the show, same general format as the De Paris — is that all agreed?"

"Yeah, generally," Rose said noncommittally, brushing some invisible speck or other from his lapel with agile, pudgy fingers. "But I think you can safely leave the show to me."

"Well, when do we get together with the shysters?"

"Hold it, hold it. What's your hurry. The more we have worked out between us, the less we have to pay the bloodsuckers." There was a brief pause in which Aaron stared over at his perfunctorily arranged desk and noted a picture of Rose with his arm around the shoulder of Grover Whelan, New York City's official diplomat and greeter — two cherubs, Whelan with a fresh gardenia in his button-hole, the other with a rose, of course. Often seen with the Little Flower himself, Fiorello, they made a colorful bouquet, bacchana-lian figures, with their frantic efforts directed always toward escape, the consummate entertainment. Whelan was in charge of the whole 1939 New York World's Fair.

"That reminds me, Bill, what are you doing at the Fair? Are you bidding anything?"

"Oh, hell, it's a little too early to think about that now, they haven't even finished filling in the land yet."

"Nevertheless, my money's on you." But he was thinking, Phony character, why he's already put a deposit down for his own pavilion, and has started rehearsals on a water show.

"Well, that's all everybody's talking about nowadays, I admit," Rose said, looking his most casual. He shot down his snowy cuffs and regarded his soiled tie as if it were some scrofulous stranger there.

"In fact, the only European country that's not being represented is Germany. Those dirty cock-sucking Nazi bastards tried, but they were turned down."

"Turned down, my ass. They were accepted for a pavilion, but they withdrew at the last minute. Better to save their money for armaments and for money to build enough death camps until they exterminate every last Jew in Europe — maybe the world, who the hell knows," Aaron said vaguely. "My mother and sister are afraid, they think it's like the old days of the pogrom — the tsar. They go around muttering 'a finster yoren eim' — the tsar, that is, not Hitler."

"Yeah, well, maybe they're smarter than we are, maybe they know something we don't," Rose said. "After all, if they could have been invited to have a pavilion here in the first place, what does that say for the condition of democracy here — and the Polish pavilion is there, too. They've been murdering the Jews by attrition for years. They'll relish helping the Nazis if they can get the chance, and they'll get the chance, mark my words."

"Well, there's plenty of anti-Semitism right here in the good old U.S. of A., it's nothing new. In fact, the American Nazi Party tried to rent my place at Thirty-fourth Street for a meeting and rally last month."

"Well?"

"Well, what? I ain't *that* hungry — You got anybody left over there, Rose?" Aaron asked as an afterthought.

"No. I haven't got anybody anywhere," he said lugubriously.

That seemed to close their brief sortie into current events — the newsreel clip before the main attraction — the fleeting moment of kinship had passed. Rose was more businesslike than ever.

"Now, exactly what's the story on the checkrooms, kid?"

Aaron looked surprised and yet he knew that if they were going to be partners in the club, it included the concessions.

"Well, I run them, of course, but we'll have to split everything down the middle — "

"How do I know what's the middle? I don't know a damn thing about your business."

"Look, Rose, we'll just have to trust each other. I don't know anything about putting on a show or much more about running a club either, for that matter, but — "

Rose interrupted, "How much did you put up in front for this concession last year?"

In his enthusiasm to impress the other man with the growing importance of *his* end of the business, Aaron answered immediately, even adding thousands onto the price.

Rose whistled. "That much, huh?"

Aaron had a sudden prescient feeling of having made a mistake. He felt very warm in the close little room. He looked down and uncrossed his legs.

"Well," Rose said quietly, not looking at Aaron, "I suppose if you put up that kind of money for the concessions alone, there must be as much money in your end of things as there is in the whole club, so it seems self-defeating for you to put up the same money to get a pig in a poke."

Aaron narrowed his eyes now, as if to squeeze out the image of the little man across the desk from him.

"Why not give me the forty thousand dollars, just as you gave them, and I'll run the whole club. You'll run the whole coatroom scene for yourself, just as always. After all, you can't argue with success."

"Jeeze, you're a greedy little bastard, aren't you," Aaron said, trying to sound playful — but it just didn't come out that way at all.

*

As it turned out, Rose did remarkably well at the French Casino for a year and a half, but Aaron didn't make a dime, he *said,* "not a plugged nickel." "I just ended up as Rose's sugar daddy," he complained to colleagues. That bastard was out to keep him from earning a living. Rose had insisted that cards be on every table that said, "All Tipping is Discretionary," and he would not permit any girls (or the usual bevy of bouncers on Aaron's payroll) to call out, "Check hats and coats here, please." Nor would he permit signs in the washrooms that requested customers to tip the matron for handing them a towel; they could reach for it themselves, if it came to that, Rose said. Why that little bastard wanted it all, wouldn't let the next guy make a living.

Aaron spent the year and a half vacillating dizzily between elation and a cold fury. Elation with the mobs of revelers who nightly thronged his checkrooms and grinned sheepishly into his cameras, and fury at the money he imagined he was losing because of Rose's spiteful manipulations that he insisted were all in the name of elegance and good taste. If he was such a stickler for good taste, why had he insisted on a show called *Let's Play Fair*, an obvious attempt to put Grover Whelan into the limelight. Most nights Whelan sat ringside, lapping up free booze and the compliments heaped on him from the stage. At the show's big finale the girls were dressed in the costumes and headdresses of all the countries to be represented at the Fair, in the center, rising some three feet above the others, a six-foot show girl bearing the pure white and hopeful symbol of the Fair, the Trylon and Perisphere, on her head. At this glorious moment, as cymbals clashed and the lights flickered, Whelan was introduced and he put in a plug for the Fair. Wonder what that costs Rose, Aaron thought. Probably got that gardenia-sprouting clown on the payroll for fifty G's. Well, if he does, he must have a damn good reason — no wonder he didn't want any partners in here (not that partners exactly wanted him either). He's cooking up something, and whatever it is, I'm going to get a bite of it this time.

What he had been cooking up was a contract for the show at the French Pavilion, as well as his own building to house a mammoth water show, the *Aquacade*. There was a fortune to be made at the Fair, and Rose was going to get it all while the getting was good.

Aaron spent the eighteen months at the Casino, berating himself for ever having become involved with Rose in the first place, having known what he was, and for ending up back in the checkrooms, which he secretly disdained, instead of an owner-entrepreneur. He had thought that owning the Casino would be good for his image, his reputation on the street would soar.

Whether out of a sudden excess of conscience or some devious plan of his own, Rose got Aaron the concessions he had wanted at the French Pavilion where he was producing the show. Garish, glossy programs, cigarettes, toys, French souvenirs, photographs, and of course, the ubiquitous checkroom flourished there amidst the Gallic splendor of fountains and columns. Each night the orchestra closed the show with the rousing Marseillaise, and there was in the atmosphere a tempo of urgency, a precarious nostalgia, that drew the people like a magnet, as if there was a collective foreknowledge of what 1940 would bring to France and the world. But for the time being, Billy Rose and Aaron Abel were growing rich.

(30)

JASON STOOD ALONE on the top step in front of the mall that led to the Lagoon of Nations at the World's Fair. Behind him the fountains soared and plunged dramatically to the man-made grottoes beneath. It was a pleasant day in May — the 150-million-dollar Fair had been open less than a month.

Looking up at him from the bottom he appeared to Jennie heroic in stature, as if on stilts, all legs, carefully encased in pearl-gray plaid. She drew in her breath with embarrassment and crossed her arms over her already full breasts, which she suddenly wished were less visible. She felt sharply the shame of adolescence.

"Well, I'm glad we found you with no trouble. I was afraid we might miss you, but it's not crowded today and you're not hard to find," said Eve.

Jason laughed and inclined his head toward Eve when she spoke, almost reverently, his politeness easy, not feigned, as if careful not to miss a word, of which there was a steady torrent, like the lagoon in the background.

"It's very nice of you, Jason," Eve continued, chattering away nervously, "but actually it would have been nicer if Aaron had come himself. After all, for once he could tear himself away from business to show his children around the Fair."

"Well, that's what I'm here for," he said amiably. "I'll get you right into the General Motors exhibition without any waiting in line, and into a whole list of others I have right here. And, as you know, he will meet you for dinner at the French Casino — " Lancelot the knight errant of Broadway come to escort Guinevere back to the arms of the waiting king — but Eve was not to be so easily mollified.

While the boys, in their carefully matched Best and Company

coats, jumped up and down the asphalt stairs and kept disappearing
somewhere into the Borden exhibit for ice cream samples, Eve
talked on, her conversation peppered with occasional comments to
the boys like "Be careful," "Don't, you'll fall into the water," or
"You'll slip on the steps." But she would not move, so involved
had she become rattling off a long list of complaints about Aaron,
and the checkroom and "that woman." Jennie couldn't understand
why suddenly Eve had elected to take Jason so closely into her confidence; she had only today referred to him as "one of your father's
hoodlums."

Jennie stole a glance at Jason out of the corner of her green eyes.
She had been standing apart from the boys in an effort not to be
lumped together with their puerile antics. Usually when she en-
countered him at the office or somewhere with her father, he treated
her with a sort of tolerant amusement. He always seemed uncomfortable in the presence of children; he was, after all, not a family
man, a father, and seemed to want it made very clear that he had
no wish to be. But in front of Eve his demeanor was solemn; yes,
solemnity was the word to describe his attitude today.

They began walking now in the direction of the exhibits. In only
a slightly quieter voice Eve continued without a breath, as if determined for some secret reason to enlist this man's sympathy. "A
family belongs together, a husband with a wife, particularly when
there are children. After all, Jason, you could help. You could talk
to him, he'd listen to you, you could be an influence for good."

Jennie couldn't decide whether Jason looked embarrassed or
bored, but she was uncomfortable with her mother in the position
of supplicant. Eve continued listing her complaints about Aaron's
misdemeanors, his lack of generosity.

"And do you think that was right to bring *that woman* to the
house to live, with the children, when Jennie here was approaching
adolescence?" Jennie closed her eyes, now praying her mother
wouldn't quote her age.

"An impressionable child who was little more than ten at that
time, mind you."

But I'm almost a teenager now, Jennie wanted to cry out.

She trailed along behind, miserable. Eve ignored her and continued undaunted. "And that mother of his — why the old hypo-
crite. Anyone, *anyone* is better than me — even a *shiksa.*" Jennie
thought she saw a sudden spot of color in Jason's cheeks.

"Look, Eve, you're talking to the wrong guy," Jennie heard him
say, irritation finally getting the better of him. "I worship the man,
he's been like a father to me. What do you want me to say?"

"I want you to save me your loyal employee routine, Jason Miller.
Anyway, what has he done to elicit such dogged devotion? Such
blind adulation is both ridiculous and unbecoming to you. With
this kind of talk you are condoning his actions and reinforcing his
behavior."

Having been duly and severely trounced, Jason stopped in front
of the General Motors building and stared at Eve in disbelief. Eve
was using archaic three-syllable words now — a sure sign that she
was growing agitated. "Now it's time you heard my side of it,"
she said.

Jason still appeared to be listening intently, but had obviously
made up his mind to stay out of the fray, no matter what, and remained silent.

It was not that Jennie was unused to her mother's obsessive injustice collecting, it was just the incongruity of her mother's proselytizing — of the attempted conversion of this man so wholly devoted to her father, his own life so much a shadow of the older
man's. But Eve as always was so convinced of the justice of her
position that she could see nothing out of place in this strange conversation. Absorbed as she was, the neglected boys grew wilder by
the minute. Reid had lost his hat in the lagoon and Evan had left
his coat on the steps of the mall.

"What — what is this person like, Jason?" Eve asked, her voice
strong as always. "Is she attractive? I know she's very young, a
friend of your wife's," she said flatly, without accusation.

There was a long pause; Jason tight-lipped now, his fleshy face
looking drained and heavy, said, "If there is such a woman — and
I have no knowledge of this fact — who do you think created her?
Only your actions could have made it possible for her to exist."

Without waiting for her answer, he turned on his heel, murmuring some comment about getting the passes for the *Futurama* show — they were to wait, he would be right back. They stood around on the street, waiting in the gum-wrapped canyon between the General Motors and Ford buildings — Eve stared into the faceless crowd.

When he returned after what seemed an extraordinarily long time, walking quickly, his head thrust slightly forward like Aaron, he told Eve they could go in in time for the three P.M. show, and that he would, of course, have to run along, as he was very busy. She appeared amazed, frustrated that she'd be left without the last word.

The afternoon hadn't exactly been a success, and there was tonight yet to cope with, her parents together, ugh — Well, at least there'd be those beautiful fireworks to see from the terrace of the French Pavilion. She prayed that they would be the *only* fireworks!

Jennie watched Jason's tall form slip away, until it was lost behind the giant Trylon and Perisphere — she shuddered and made a mental note to wait downstairs in the car from now on anytime her father stopped off at the office. She couldn't bear to see Jason again. No, it would never be quite the same, the casual teasing, the banter. Mother had burst the bubble. She had a way of doing that, of taking the froth off the top of life and replacing it with a heavy sediment of guilt.

That first summer of the World's Fair, "The World of Tomorrow," where nations had united for peace on the filled-in sump of Flushing Meadow Park, drew to a close on September first, with Hitler's march into Poland.

(31)

A MONTH LATER, Jennie sat beside her mother in the rear of the Cadillac and felt a vague sense of foreboding, but was unable to locate her feelings. The glass partition was tightly closed. Eve stared out the window silently, leaning forward every so often to roll down the glass and talk to Vic Chase, the chauffeur. Chase had completed a record of sorts. He had been driving for Aaron for about six months and managed to tread successfully the tightrope between Eve and Aaron without too much trouble. That was where the others had fallen down; they had become involved, talked too much and then left out of embarrassment or were fired by Aaron. Eve always said, "When servants become too familiar, too interwoven into the family fabric, that's the end of the relationship."

"Why are we going out to Long Beach, Mother?"

"Because it's a nice day to take a ride to the seashore," Eve said, looking straight ahead.

"Oh," she said, but somehow she wasn't satisfied. Nothing her mother ever said or did was quite that simple. Something told her that there was more to it than met the eye. Eve was acting funny. Jennie had noticed that she had spent a lot of time on the phone this week, back and forth to Grandma and a lot of mysterious phone calls to this one and that one, and she sensed that they had something to do with this drive. She tried probing, but Eve was silent. Her heart skittered along her ribs like the gong on the xylophone at Loew's Flatbush. She wished that Grandma had come along with them, things would have been easier then. But Grandma had refused this time, had argued with her mother about going.

"What's wrong with bringing Jennie along? It's time she learned what her father really is," Eve had said. Eve had also tried to get Al Carton to join them on this Saturday, but he too had dropped out at the last minute with some excuse. It almost looked as though they wouldn't go, but here they were. When Eve made up her mind, it wasn't easy to change it. No, she was strangely silent for her, secretive, as if she knew something special and wonderful, or awesome. Jennie thought probably it was awesome; she knew her mother's sense of drama. A frustrated actress, Aaron always said so. Like those evenings when Eve entertained her few remaining friends. She could hear them discussing Shakespeare or Dryden or Donne loudly, shrilly, she heard it all through the door to her bedroom. The guests were usually a sparse assortment of old friends — an occasional lawyer, a spinster teacher assuaging her loneliness. Eve had been running out of friends gradually, through the years. "A woman alone," she would say, "couples don't want to drag around a lone woman." She was aware, too, that the caliber of her friends was dwindling along with the quantity. There were fewer and fewer professional people, more flotsam and jetsam she'd meet in the lobbies of those women's hotels that housed a discarded army of broken lives tucked away in anonymous cubbyholes.

When Eve quoted from Shakespeare she sounded very different. In fact, any time that she talked about subjects far removed from her husband and children she sounded very different. Her deep voice became majestic and her diction markedly British. "Intoning," she called it. Her guests would applaud appreciatively, then she would bow low, cavalier style, sweeping an imaginary feathered cap from her head, and blush becomingly.

Jennie felt free and reckless (the way she imagined other children felt) when her mother was happy, which was in itself a novelty. She felt temporarily relieved of the burden of responsibility for her, when she had these little soirées. As if she were the mother, dropping off a difficult child at a party, she breathed a sigh of relief. "She'll be fine for a while" — no guilt about foisting her off, after all she's having a good time, out of mischief.

They sped out over the Fifty-ninth Street Bridge toward Queens and onto the Grand Central Parkway, a beautiful Saturday in June, warm and sunny, but not yet the usual New York oven that June could be in another few weeks. Trees rushed by, the little white boats on Flushing Bay looked festive and exclusive. Even though Jennie thought her father was probably rich, she felt excluded from most things that were sociable, the things that rich people did. It seemed to her that they did things in units, groups united in pleasure seeking. But *her* family was always splitting off into disparate twos and threes, fragmenting into lonely little entities — Mother and Jennie; the boys and Daddy; Grandma, Mother, and Jennie; and so it went, just like today. Jennie was tapped into service. The boys were God knows where; well, wherever they were, she wished she was with them, anyplace but here on this strange mission. There were heavy responsibilities connected with being the eldest.

She could see the towering white Trylon and Perisphere in the distance — the 250-foot parachute jump, she was dying to try it just once, but her mother would never permit it. She thought with a curious nostalgia about that day last month at the Fair with him, Jason, and the very warm and special evening they had shared with their father at the French Pavilion. That night they were a "real" family.

They must be approaching the Long Beach Bridge. Jennie could smell the sweet, salty air, the soft, spicy, fishy odor that she found stimulating, promising, that reminded her of last summer and Cecile. Eve leaned forward and began talking softly to Vic. He pulled the car over to the curb and stopped. He said in a whine that begged to be excused from this embarrassment, "I don't know where that is, Mrs. Abel, I really don't. I never been here, I don't hardly know this town." As they approached the bridge, they slowed into the converging traffic. Everything looked clean and sun-washed in the bright afternoon light, like an overexposed negative. Only the most intense hues jumped out of the white-washed facades, the rest were washed out by the blinding sun and the blue-white sky. The resort town, usually crowded, seemed denuded on this preseason Saturday.

Over the bridge the car was forced to slow almost to a standstill to allow for an endless procession of black limousines, heavily laden with flowers. The people hardly noticed; gorgeous gangland funerals were commonplace in this resort town which was home to an assortment of elite Jewish and Italian Mobsters. The procession snaked its way solemnly down the quiet streets.

They pulled into a gas station. This time Victor rolled down the window, and turned to talk to Eve.

"Now that we're here, Mrs. Abel, is there anything special you'd like to see, like the ocean or the boardwalk or something like that?" he asked ingratiatingly.

"Boardwalk? Oh, you *have* been here before then, Vic."

"Er, no, not that I can remember, but I think this town's got a boardwalk. Most seaside towns do, you know."

"Well, since you mention it, I'd like you to take me to this address," she gave an address that sounded raw and new to Jennie. The driver stiffened visibly, and Eve said, "Well?"

"Er, well, what, Mrs. A.? How do you get there? Do you have any directions?"

"No, but it shouldn't be hard, it's not a very big town and we can ask at a gas station."

"Where are we going, Mother?" Jennie asked, "Whose house is it?" For some reason her heart was beating wildly.

There was something about this town, this place, that made her feel just a little wicked and giddy. There was an air of abandon in this summery seaside world that reminded her of her father. Eve seemed out of place here, like a teacher at a kid's party. She wondered who this mysterious friend was that her mother wanted to visit. They pulled up into a gas station. They were still on the ragged edges of the town, where it was barren, just before it smoothed itself out into breezy green and powder-blue squares of lawn and sky.

"Maybe we'll visit your father. How would you like that?" Eve asked in a low voice, obviously meant to exclude Victor.

"Daddy?" Jennie said with a proprietory air that she knew annoyed her mother. "What makes you think he's here?"

The gas attendant poked his red-spotted face in through the front window. "Can I help you?"

"Oh, yes, can I have some gas, please?"

The boy looked at the gauge and said smartly, "Won't take much, you're more than half-full." He jerked the long arm and nozzle down and connected it to their car. Jennie could hear the boy cracking his gum loudly as he worked. He was finished almost before he began, or at least so it seemed to her. But still Victor didn't ask for directions. They sat in the stuffy car now, inhaling the solid odor of the gasoline. When the boy poked his head in again for payment, Eve leaned forward and asked for the directions. The boy seemed unsure and sketched a hasty and uncertain route. But Victor made no move to go, and for a moment the three of them just sat there, wooden, frozen into uncertainty.

"Victor, you know how to get there, you must. You know where he's taken a house; you must have taken him there a dozen or so times now."

"I know," Victor said, "that he was going to be in Long Beach for the summer."

"But it's really not summer yet," Jennie whispered hopefully to her mother. "Anyway if it was summer we'd be with him, wouldn't we?" Jennie was on the verge of tears now. She was trying very hard not to understand anything.

"No, you would not," Eve replied tartly. "And I doubt that you will want to, after today."

"Ma'am," the attendant thrust his head through the window once again, "please, you're tying up my place. I've got to make a living here. Could you have your discussion somewhere else?"

Eve was about to put her head out the window to tell the boy off, when Vic started up the engine again and shot out to the left, as the attendant had directed. Jennie thought she ought to be relieved, but somehow she wasn't.

"No, I won't go," Jennie said very loudly.

"What?" Eve said.

"I'll stay here at the gas station while you go to Daddy's house, or wherever it is . . ." she trailed off.

Eve leaned forward, ignoring the outburst. "I think he said to make a left here." Vic made a sharp left on a street called Almont, and they kept on going and going, but couldn't seem to find the street they were looking for. They drove around for a while, aimlessly, like a wounded fly, buzzing first here and then there, looking blindly for a place to land.

"It's getting real late, Mrs. A., and we're going to get caught in terrible traffic going back if we don't start soon."

Eve's face had that stubborn look on it. "Victor, I did not drive all the way out here to be so easily put off, and don't think I'm not wise to you. You know exactly where that house is, but it's all your job is worth not to take me there."

"That's not true," he demurred, "but if you believe it, why would you do this to me? Do you want me to lose my job? We're in the midst of hard times, you know, ma'am."

"Are you going to drive there this minute, or am I going to have to call back the agent for the precise instructions?" She had gotten the address originally from the rental agent.

There was no answer to this from the front compartment, and they just continued speeding along toward nowhere, it seemed to Jennie. No one said anything for a few minutes. They turned into a residential street, and then suddenly pulled up with a determined screech of brakes to a nondescript-looking pink stucco house that seemed just like any number of others up and down the barren, tree-sparse street. Victor alighted spryly and opened the door for them.

"Mrs. Abel," he said, "would you step out for a moment? I'd like to talk to you."

"What do you mean? Aren't we here?"

"No, this is not the street, but please step out for a moment."

Eve looked confused, and then reluctantly took the hand that Victor offered. Jennie felt uncertain, but began to follow her mother.

"No, Jennie, I just want to talk to your mother, alone," he said.

It was growing very hot in the car. She longed to jump out and catch a whiff of the ocean-scented air, feel the cool breeze on her face. She felt hot and prickly all over, perspiration was running down her legs into the short white bobby socks she wore. From the car's window all she could see was the hem of her mother's dress and her trim legs beneath, and Victor's dark trousers. She rolled down her window, and although they had moved a little away she could hear them talking.

"No, this isn't the house, Mrs. Abel, I just stopped here because I can't go on any further. I'm sorry, you understand my position."

"I'm not at all sure that I do, exactly. Where are we now?"

"We're around the corner from Mr. Abel's summer house. You can walk down there if you insist, but please leave me out of it — Please."

Jennie felt both annoyed by Victor's sniveling and embarrassed for her mother. She wondered why her mother was always getting herself into these predicaments that usually came out the worse for her. Why couldn't she relax and leave things alone for once? But, no, one or the other of her parents was always turning up the light under the cauldron, so that the pot boiled incessantly. She suddenly felt immensely tired of their schemes, their endless plots and counterplots, and wished ardently to be relieved of involvement. But at that very moment her mother came back, opened the car door, and told Jennie she was to come with her.

"Where are we going, Mother?"

"I told you, while we're here we are going to see the house your father rented."

"For us, this summer?" Jennie asked again.

They were walking rapidly now, down the street, a completely different street from the one they were on last summer, Jennie thought absently.

It was growing late in the afternoon, the sun's rays had suddenly cooled and the chill ocean breeze sent little shivers through her damp clothing to her skin; she felt the tiny goosebumps tightening the flesh of her arms and shoulders. When they found the house it looked much like the others on the block. It was of an undefined period — early boardwalk, Aaron might have called it — pink stucco with an unmatching brownstone stoop, two steps up or so. Eve pressed firmly on the bell. No answer. Jennie hung back and said in a choked voice, "Well, let's go, Mother, he's not in, I'm sure he's not there." Without answering, Eve tried the handle, and it didn't surprise Jennie to find the door opened easily. Well, that was just like her father, she thought, careless, with a haphazard heart about everything but business.

Eve immediately began to mount the stairs. Wordlessly, as if in a dream, she seemed to sail up the shadowed stairway propelled by an outer force. Jennie, behind her, could see a thousand tiny dust particles dancing crazily in the amber slants of late afternoon sun. It was obvious that no one was home, and Jennie thought it odd that her mother didn't call out to announce their presence. She could not, dared not — her voice stuck in her throat. Her mother poked her head in here and there, until she found what Jennie guessed was the master bedroom. They walked in slowly, but Jennie held back shyly on the threshold, thinking suddenly about the way her father had of putting his hand on her hair when he kissed her head and calling her "Becky."

Jennie felt like an unholy traitor. The windows were open and the late afternoon breeze was flapping the shades gently. The smell of ocean mixed sensually with the faint perfume odors of the room, with the quick, clean smell of Noxzema, a smell that brought to mind other summers and sunburns, and stirred sharply her child's memory.

"This is somebody else's house, a lady's house. We can't just walk around here like it's ours. It's the wrong house. Quick, let's get out of here!"

"No, Jennie, it's the right house all right, I'll show you your father's clothes, they're right here in the closet." She marched Jennie over to the closet that displayed a few men's suits hanging neatly.

"Oh, that could be anybody's suits. Why do you want them to be Daddy's, why?"

"You're old enough to know what he is. It's time you knew."

Eve approached the dresser slowly, and stopped as if she had reached her destination. Neat as it was, there was a profusion of pots and jars of creams and make-up. A well-squeezed tube of sun-tan cream lay topless on a tray, an open jar of Noxzema, a comb, a few lipsticks, and some sample vials of perfume. Everything about the room suggested a scurrying from one activity to the next with a certain air of careless abandon. For a moment Jennie envied this strange young couple; they seemed to be having such a good time. A brownish photograph of two faded old people looked out at them hostilely from an ugly metal frame. Eve picked up a brooch and stared fixedly at it. It was an old European design with large initials, meant to look like pavé diamonds, but on close scrutiny proved to be only tiny beads of metal — marcasite.

"Jennie, come here," Eve called in a rich contralto, that seemed to echo excrutiatingly through the empty house. The child approached the dresser uneasily.

"Here." Her mother thrust toward her the bulky brooch with the large initials *M.V.* "Do you recognize this pin? Did you see it somewhere before? Last summer, maybe? Are those initials familiar?"

Jennie jumped back as if she had been burned. She thought jaggedly of the vampire in the horror movies when confronted by the cross.

"Me? Of course not! I wish I knew what you were talking about. I never saw it before in my life. Anyway, it's ugly," she said, sulkily, as if in some mysterious way that would solace her mother, protect herself from — she didn't know just what. Eve dropped the pin in her voluminous handbag.

Jennie seemed on the verge of tears. "Mother, what are you doing? You can't do this, that's stealing, you're stealing from strangers. Please! Let's go."

"Oh, dear, go outside and wait for me then."

Jennie bolted from the room, relieved. As she left, her eye caught a pair of wet bathing trunks thrown on the floor near a corner of the bed. They were in a certain shade of bright blue that her father always wore. They looked like the ones they had bought together last summer.

She wanted to feel sorry for her mother, but somehow could not summon up any sorrow. Her mother seemed too relieved, free suddenly, as if relieved of a great burden. She was redeemed, the confirmation of Aaron's basic evil was somehow a catharsis for her. Yes, she alone in all the world was pure of heart. But she had always said that. Now it would be Aaron who would toss fitfully at nights.

She would sleep the deep, untroubled sleep of the innocent.

Back in the car Eve complained that Victor had probably run to the beach somewhere and tipped Aaron off, but after that, everyone seemed lost in his own thoughts as they inched along slowly in the heavy traffic. Victor had turned the radio up loudly, as if to block out any further conversation. The radio announced that they were listening to Larry Clinton's band. Bea Wayne was singing "My Reverie" in a voice lush with emotion. Eve was gazing at the sea of traffic, hypnotized by its sluggish ebb and flow. She began to talk in a flat voice, as if to the car window or an unseen audience beyond.

"Waste," she said, "all wasted. I could have had a career, could have been an actress, a professor, a translator, something, somebody, but he took everything and left me with nothing. And all of it for what? From the day I met that man my life was over." She paused briefly and then said, without inflection, "It never really began."

All the way home in the silent car, Jennie thought about Cecile, of her honey-blonde hair, her blue velvet turban and her smooth, tough ways, and she wondered if she would ever be so . . . so . . . female.

*

They didn't go with Aaron that summer, of course — Eve wouldn't permit it, not now, not after what she had seen that spring at the beach. His punishment would be the loss of custody that summer. For weeks after that day he tried telephoning her, to ask her out to dinner — to talk — but she just kept hanging up on him.

He came to the apartment, and rang the bell one evening after the children were in bed. She looked through the peephole and saw who it was.

"Go away, I have nothing to say to you."

"Please, just let me come in for a moment."

"If you don't go away I'll call the police." She could not use the immediate threat of a doorman. There was none.

"Just for a moment, please." There was silence, he did not know if she was still within earshot.

"Look, she was only staying with me for a while; it was off-season," he argued plaintively through the door.

"I got a deal on the house this summer — had to take it for three months. Please, are you listening, Eve? I wouldn't have her there with the children — not now — that Jennie's growing up and —"

"Really? What do you call 'Cecile,' yes I think that was the name, very French, 'Cecile'?" she mocked. "You're lucky that I didn't take you into court for undermining the morals of a minor." He was relieved that she had been listening.

"Please, that was before, that was a mistake —" A neighbor, Mrs. Freeman, poked her head out the door. "Meshuganah," she said. "Be quiet; don't you know it's ten o'clock at night —" She slammed the door loudly. He dropped his voice to a hoarse whisper.

"Let me come in and talk to you."

"What do you want with the children anyway — *you* won't have to be alone, you'll have *her*, only *I'll* be alone without the children, wandering the deserted street like I do every summer, eating alone in Childs." Childs was becoming her symbol of defeat, much as the Y.M.C.A. was for Aaron.

"I'll give you extra money, you can go away somewhere — rest up."

"Give me money to take the children somewhere."

"Let me in, we can't talk with a door between us."

"Why not, when was it ever different?"

"Don't punish me through the children." He was growing angry, finding himself begging again — he cast about in his mind for some neat turn of phrase that might win her over, but he was not eloquent, never had been. He stood there mutely for a while, pulling his thoughts together. Then he saw the light go out under the crack in the door. He was overwhelmed with impotence. In rage he screamed, "Eve, I warn you, I'll have you put away, you're crazy, can't get along with anyone. I'll get the kids. I'll prove that you're an unfit mother!" He leaned against the door, sobbing.

He'd learned his lesson, he was very careful about his priorities from then on.

(32)

AUNT RACHEL STAYED WITH THEM that summer by the sea, the summer of '41. A plait of thick, dun-colored hair hung down her back, baring her tough, weathered face — a large, Jewish Indian, she lumbered when she walked. She brought with her her lifetime shadow, her mother, who appeared neither older nor younger than before, but seemed to have been frozen into permanent old age. Aunt Rachel took loving care of them, the three of them, that summer before the war. Jennie was to think of it as an in-between summer, tentative somehow, wedged in between her first year of high school and the big move to New York. There was an expectant quality about it that filled her with an overwhelming nostalgia, not for what had been, but what was yet to be. She brimmed with a vague, restless excitement that had no particular goal, no beginning, no end. In years to come, she was to think of it in a bemused way, as a shimmering hiatus, a time for knitting up the loose strands of her childhood into womanhood.

The boarding school experience had been a big success. There Jennie had discovered *Gone With The Wind*. (She would practice before a mirror, slanting her own green eyes like Scarlett's, but they didn't stay that way.) And the Big Bands. She had become addicted to the slow, sweet tunes with their themes of loving and losing — "*Careless, now that you've got me loving you, You're careless, careless in everything you do.*" All day she played her records, drifting and dreaming with half-closed eyes, dancing alone, bent slightly forward as if leaning heavily on an unseen partner. The rich sounds of Glenn Miller's band, and the brown velvet voice of Tex Beneke could be heard throughout the small stucco-cooled house all the way to the corner where the beach began, in heaving weed-clumped peaks. Swing made her feel dreamy, jazz made her feel itchy — restless. Aaron teased her mercilessly, and insisted that she didn't have enough to do, she should get out more, go to the beach just across the way.

Sometimes, she took long walks on the beach. The vast aloneness, the muted, sweet, tangy smell of salt and seaweed cleared her mind, allowed her to think up through the confusion of her childhood into clear, sunny stretches of hope and the pure joy of being young and healthy and completely unenlightened about the future.

At the end of July, Steven, Uncle Max's son, came to stay at the house too. He was sixteen, six feet tall, and slender, and played the saxophone beautifully. He played "Blueberry Hill" along with Glenn Miller's record. It made Jennie cry. She cried easily lately. Aaron was usually swimming in relations, playing the patriarch was something he had grown used to, had come to expect after years of family obeisance. Only his brother Bennie resisted slightly, having succeeded through his own nefarious methods in amassing large amounts of real estate, some of which he owned in partnership with Aaron. He also maintained an office, rent-free, of course, in his younger brother's building on Thirty-fourth Street, and undaunted by his modest successes, he continued to live above his mother and sister in the same three rooms on Harrison Avenue, much to Neva's despair.

Jennie and her cousin danced close and did a lot of kissing on Steven's big double bed in the "maid's" room. Aunt Rachel made it her special, secret assignment to police the romance that was ripening into forbidden fruit before her very eyes, following them around, clucking and murmuring, "it's a sin for cousins." Not that Aunt Rachel was opposed to fruit in general — all day she went around offering it. "Here, take a piece of fruit." Under her breath she muttered in Yiddish about the angel of death (*malach-ha-moves*) and other dark doings, lending an air of comic opera to the whole proceedings. Festive almost. Jennie felt giddy and lightheaded all summer. And then Uncle Max came down in August, and, with that sly, worldly smile that he reserved for things sexual, he took Steven home. Jennie wept a little more.

For a time Aaron seemed oblivious to all this — playing ostrich.

As Eve always said, when he was presented with an uncomfortable situation, he buried his head in the sand.

Aaron was a strict moralist with a God-given certainty of the justice of the double standard of morality. It was of no consequence to him that his own life and work were not paragons of virtue. But he had a daughter now, approaching womanhood — as Eve would say, "trembling on the brink" — and he was going to make damn sure that she didn't fall in. He'd seen too much, too many beautiful young girls not much older than Jennie run amuck . . . didn't he deal with these girls daily . . . who was better equipped to bring up a young daughter? Yes, he was determined that Jennie have a father in the picture, now that she was becoming a woman and would begin to go out with boys, and his sons needed a father image too. They were getting too old to hang around the house and listen to Eve's constant complaining. Eve was beginning to crack a little here and there. He might just have to take advantage of this opportunity.

It was inevitable; there was a deep, dark vein of melancholia that ran in her family. She had grown up with the thinly veiled rumor that her mother's sister, Aunt Vi, had taken her own life; even Lisa sometimes complained of depression. Eve's goals were impossible, her principals unrealistic. She had done her research for living in the story books of her youth and she was poorly equipped. Aaron had studied at the school of hard knocks (his favorite expression) and could pass the tests with flying colors, he always said.

At the end of two years alone, Eve *needed* to have the children back from boarding school. She couldn't be alone any longer, it was even becoming difficult to find someone to take to the opera. She was sitting on the horns of a dilemma: She couldn't be alone — and she couldn't be with anyone for long, especially the children.

(33)

THE WORLD SEEMED TO UNFOLD for Jennie when they moved to Manhattan and she began high school at the Royalton School for Girls. Suddenly she found herself ensconced in the Centennial Apartments on Central Park West, a fabled and celebrity-spangled building whose twin towers, thirty-two floors above the city, could be seen glinting through the trees from all sides of the park. It was far enough from the Upper West Side to be within the pale, and near enough to Broadway to catch the reflection of its nighttime neons. On clear days they could see the old Tavern on the Green restaurant, dropped like some archaic Christmas bauble in the middle of Central Park.

Jennie was in love with New York from the beginning. Looking out of her window, she felt as if she'd just had a full meal. Mingling in the carnival of streets, she felt a contagious excitement passed from one pedestrian to another. Each morning the school bus picked her up, together with Reid and Evan (they attended the lower school, which was co-ed), and brought her to the still loftier Upper East Side. She considered the bus babyish and was embarrassed in front of her classmates who walked or took public conveyances, but Eve prevailed.

The first time Jennie saw the hushed and hallowed halls of the executive floor of the Royalton School she was awestruck. The corridors were richly carpeted and were calmly surveyed by grandiose china Fu dogs who sat on pedestals at discreet intervals.

Until now, school had meant a rickety clapboard building with a groaning staircase (even at boarding school the old buildings seemed to be made out of matchsticks), but here, in the imposing all-brick building, the six floors were joined by twin elevators and boasted a swimming pool, double gymnasiums, and a real theater (even a mysterious backstage) with red plush seats.

Here amidst such capitalist splendors they sang with fervor the Russian national anthem in Housemeeting and in Chorus the "Stabat Mater" in ecclesiastic Latin. In study hall, they cracked jokes about the teachers, at lunch they cracked jokes about the food, and at gym everyone seemed to have her period at the same time and refused to change into gym clothes — As far as Jennie could see, progressive education was a great innovation.

*

On a Sunday in early December, thick with vapor and surprisingly warm for five o'clock of a December evening, Jennie emerged from the Rivoli Theatre with her newly acquired school friend, Emma Joseff. Emma was making an effort to keep up with Jennie's long-legged stride but her own short, chunky legs made it impossible. They had just seen *How Green Was My Valley* and were still unaccustomed to the reality of the day, after three magical hours with the Welsh coal miners and their turgid stories. The book had been circulated through the freshman class, gobbled down, digested, and recirculated. Eve strongly encouraged reading, but had in mind books by Dickens and George Eliot, or Thomas Hardy. She had pressed upon Jennie unflinchingly books like *Tess of the D'Urbervilles*, not current novels whose appalling length and sensuous subject matter she considered unfit for impressionable adolescents.

Columbus Circle seemed busier than usual. People scurried to and fro with an air of urgency that mixed ominously with the newsboys' cries of "Extra! Extra! Read all about it! Japs bomb Pearl Harbor!"

Emma looked suddenly serious. "God," she said, her favorite expletive this season. "That sounds awful."

"Why, where is Pearl Harbor anyway?" Jennie asked distractedly.

"I don't know exactly, but it's somewhere in the Pacific. Something to do with Hawaii I think." Students in progressive private schools never knew anything exactly, but nevertheless Emma's "superior" Royalton education often made Jennie feel inadequate. Emma had worked her way up through the entire Royalton system right from nursery school on. She even went to Miss Viola Wolfe's dance classes, and while Jennie was impressed, she secretly thought that such lofty luxuries were wasted on the lumpish Emma, and that she herself would have benefited far more richly. Jennie was, at fourteen, already fully developed, with a startling figure and a kind of fresh blonde beauty. Emma popped foul-tasting yeast tablets like cookies to control her acne and looked raw and rather square. But Jennie's sensitive antennae told her that she dare not ascend, at least just yet, to the polished heights of Miss Wolfe's for fear of being thought a pushy intruder, or worse still, a social climber. That was definitely frowned upon in the quasi-liberal, superdemocratic atmosphere of Royalton. She'd have to tread gingerly in this first year. She had heard it rumored that membership in this dancing class elite automatically ensured a social life of sorts, but she rationalized by imagining sweaty little boys of fourteen stepping all over her feet and immediately relinquished the idea.

Socially, life just didn't seem very profitable for her during her freshman year. She consoled herself with the fact that she was after all a new girl in town, was attending an all-girls school, and besides, most of the really attractive older boys were being drafted daily. She decided that it looked rather patriotic, even mysterious and romantic, to be seen only with the girls — as if she were hiding a secret love lately departed for foreign shores, or better still, just lately departed. She had the ability to romanticize everything and everyone, to infuse each aspect of her daily life with drama and a special delicate beauty. She saw herself in flashes, like the heroine of a novel, from far away — objectively. She waited restlessly for her story to begin, and until then, she would weave her own, out of the stuff of dreams.

Neither she nor Emma stopped to buy a paper. They didn't want to spend the money — better to save every cent for their usual Saturday cosmetic hunts. They'd hang over Rexall's or Liggett's cosmetic displays for absorbed hours on end, and Jennie was inwardly amused at Emma's addiction to Heaven Scent — though it was deemed most correct for teen-agers, the salesgirl had assured them.

They turned the corner at Columbus Circle, where the zigzagging and monumental building, 240 Central Park South, reigned in newborn splendor, and crossed over.

As they progressed up Central Park West, the wind began to blow suddenly cold from the open fields of the park across the street. Newsboys were calling "FDR speaks tonight — Expected to declare war on Japs — Read all about it — War!"

"War?" Both girls looked instantly skyward. A number of planes roared by overhead. "My God," Emma said, "could it be an air raid already?"

Jennie was thankful that they had arrived at the warm and brightly lit canopy of the Centennial. George the doorman was handing people graciously in and out of taxis and limousines, as always running his hand, groping deftly, over the seats and floors before allowing the next passenger to enter — checking for loose change, bills, diamond rings, or forgotten wallets — who knew what (Eve said he was a millionaire from this and from the tips he made here, and that he lived over on Park Avenue). Everything seemed normal, routine, nothing changed. Jennie breathed a sigh of relief, kissed Emma good-bye warmly and headed for the elevator — and then thought suddenly of her mother upstairs, and of how she would accept the war! Only now did fear begin to nudge itself into her consciousness.

(34)

MEATLESS TUESDAYS at the Tiptoe Inn, Jennie toying with something on her plate called protose steak — an imposing name for an amalgam of pulverized vegetables. Vegetable hash, she thought, why disguise it? And victory layer cake — that was the pièce de résistance on Tuesday nights at this upper Broadway emporium, chocolate cake filled with wartime "whipped cream." But that was fine, they weren't complaining. It was a real treat for Jennie to get out of the house at night, to see lights and people, to smell the bakery smells. And it was a pleasant change from canned tuna fish, Spam, and the loaves of cottony white Silvercup bread they ate at home.

The boys were running up and down the aisles annoying the solid-looking, mostly Jewish clientele (who came and went, carrying greasy brown bags). Why couldn't they sit quietly for once, like other children? Eve, unresigned, her nerves lacerated to the edge of anger and Jennie dreaming, doodling hearts all over her napkin, open hearts, innocent of initials, yawningly open, painfully so, she thought with a pang. Sometimes the hearts became stars, Jewish stars, Mogen Davids. The geometrics of the Star of David fascinated her. She often had trouble getting the triangles just right; she hadn't the patience to concentrate on details. "No follow through" — the tennis teacher at Greenlawn had told her that. She wondered if that would be the pattern for the rest of her life, inconsistency. Well, it figured — hearts and stars, stars and hearts, they were all over her work pages, scribbled everywhere. She was aware of the reasons for the preoccupation with hearts, after all she was *nearly* fifteen — Juliet was married at that age, Heloise deflowered — but the sudden emergence of the Star of David? They had never had a particularly religious bringing-up, they were reformed Jews in the true sense, but the basic fact of her Jewishness, that they were God's chosen people, had been impressed upon her by her parents. Lately, she wondered what God had chosen them for, besides suffering and persecution. Did he love them so well that he would wipe them from the face of the world, that he would permit genocide never before perpetrated on those he loved less? No, it wasn't possible. The reports she heard must be false, exaggerated. Eve and Grandma were always talking about Rumanian aunts and uncles over there, "fed to the ovens." The Jewish girls whispered of even darker atrocities in the sunny privileged corridors of school. But this was medieval barbarism, simply could not be true in modern times, in the age of enlightenment — wartime propaganda, that was all. Jennie tried to dismiss it from her mind, her conscious mind at least, but she thought, there but for the grace of God go I. With terror she began to consider the other possibility — defeat. What if Hitler were to come here, to America? And suddenly she had become a Jew and looked at life with Jewish eyes.

Aaron had already arranged for Evan to prepare for his bar mitzvah, less than two years away, but any sort of formal ritual seemed a travesty to Eve in the light of their familial situation. However, if there was one thing in the whole of life that Eve and Aaron agreed on, it was the basic sanity of Judaism, at least as compared to other religions. At heart Eve was an agnostic, but she felt that if she had to follow even vaguely some form of organized religion, if only for the children, it might as well be Jewish. It seemed to make the most sense, asked the least of you, didn't demand that you strain the bounds of credibility, become a child again. There was an earthiness, a pragmatism, about Judaism that she found acceptable.

Eve's old friend, Ellie Baker, was now teaching at a convent school in the city. Her father was Jewish but her mother had been Catholic and Ellie had followed in her faith, without much conviction. Ellie was a sweet, quiet, cultured, and pedantic girl (Eve always called any *unmarried* woman a "girl") and at forty was fairly well adjusted to spinsterhood. When she talked she measured her words out slowly like medicine on a spoon, as if each word were another step toward the edge of disaster from which she must hold back at all costs. A couple of nights ago, Jennie had heard them from her bed, talking loudly in between the rattle of teacups.

"My hostility, as you call it, toward Catholicism is completely intellectual, mind you; there is nothing at all personal in it," Eve said with apparent honesty. "I just consider it a glorious hoax, a beautiful show that sucks money from the poor and fills them full of guilt in return (we share *that* in common; Jews and Catholics have an enormous capacity for guilt) not to mention that it's held society back some four hundred years. Did you ever take a good look at a church, its architecture? Straight out of the Middle Ages, all those points and turrets reaching heavenward in pure Gothic horror." Jennie, lying in her bed awake, thought of tithes and pardons sold in the plague-ridden streets of the Dark Ages.

"Eve, nevertheless, it's sustained countless people through crisis, giving them hope," Ellie protested weakly. Jennie felt no particular sympathy with the subject matter, only a kind of sadness for her mother, who seemed never to be living life, but only lecturing on it to one dried-out fossil or another.

"False hope," Eve continued dauntlessly. "Oh, yes, Mother Church can be sustaining, I suppose, if you don't ask too many questions. Virgin Mary, Mother of God — *imperatrix infernorum* is a damn sight closer to the truth — the empress of hell indeed!" There was no stopping her now. "I've always said that people who wear crosses, Jewish stars, Phi Beta Kappa keys are frightfully insecure — they need something to grab on to."

"But you're getting all worked up about it, you see," Ellie said. Eve invariably sought the company of meek and mild people; she wouldn't tolerate what she considered opinionated women.

Eve smiled tolerantly. It always irritated her when people tried to clip her wings in mid-flight. So what if she did wax enthusiastic about subjects that moved her? She must react, that was her nature, it was never a passive one, and she was annoyed at often having to apologize for it in the name of good manners.

"Well," Eve said, more quietly now, "it's really just that Catholicism is so bad and so beautiful at the same time — a heady combination, I must admit."

"Like some people we know," Ellie said, without great interest. She never discussed religion with the clergy and was not herself much up on Catholic doctrine, but it worked for her, filled in some of the vacancies left by the impersonality of her life, that was all. She was far more impassioned about her sweet tooth.

THE PRIVATIONS OF WAR on the home front had worn Eve down to a frazzle. Standing on endless ration-book lines, fighting for the last item in a store, no possibility of getting or keeping a maid (they could make three times as much money on the swing shift in the war factories, and come out heroines). As Aaron intensified his campaign to get the children, there was little or no chance of obtaining any extra money from him for these things that were growing more expensive by the hour. He had her boxed into a corner. He had made up his mind now to smoke her out, one way or another. He was ready to implement the plan that he had been formulating vaguely from the beginning of their separation — custody of the children. Eve could keep the five hundred dollars a month, he decided, in what he considered a burst of generosity, she'd need it now with the inflationary prices; he'd keep the kids. It was obvious that she hadn't been able to handle it, ending up sending them away to schools and camps. Well, he'd be damned if he'd pay for that when he could enjoy the children for the same money and at the same time they'd make a home for him.

It was as if Aaron had said aloud, it's time we changed places now. His time had finally come to repay her for immuring him in the epicene confines of the Y. Looking over into the broad, smiling windows of the Centennial Apartments across the street, he felt like a pariah, a millionaire holed up alone in a cell. What had he really done to deserve this isolation, this solitary confinement? He loved the children — why, they were his whole life. Hadn't he always said so? He had begun feeling sorry for himself lately; all the old dreams were pretty well dreamed out and there were no new ones to replace them. He was past the point of dreaming. It had all happened so fast, so furiously, that he didn't even have a moment to savor it along the way. By now he had a piece of almost every restaurant and nightclub in the city, and a few in other cities too. Cities that were considered hot, like Miami and Boston and Chicago. The money he had made at the Fair, together with other compiled profits, had enabled him to buy himself what virtually amounted to a monopoly up and down and around Broadway. The ballrooms and nightclubs were doing a phenomenal business, with waiting lines all over. The maître d's were growing rich overnight, and Aaron was raking in as much as a quarter of a million a week — all cold cash.

At dawn, armored trucks went around the town collecting the cash, bringing it to a secret destination that only Aaron, Jason, and his brother Bennie knew about. But, perversely, he had holed himself up at the Y. Before, it had been the Brooklyn Y, now he had followed his children to Central Park West and to the Y across the street from them. Well, he liked the easy access to the gym, and the all-male environment was soothing, noncombative. He couldn't possibly set up housekeeping now, he reasoned, at this time of life, in his kind of work. He was never there anyway, he only used the room for sleeping. Eve said that he was just too cheap to pay two rents, theirs and his own. Perhaps even *he* didn't understand his motives entirely. Anyway, most nights he'd go over to New Jersey. He maintained a suite in a large commercial hotel in which he had the concessions and a sizable interest, not the least of which was Martha, whom he kept there in the musty splendor of a suite. She was now virtually retired from work, with the exception of filling in on heavy evenings at some strategic place or other. He liked her to be available, whenever he might be able to grab some time off.

Aaron vacillated between disengaging himself completely from this alliance and holding on for dear life. Martha was beginning to give him a hard time, what with her constant whining about divorcing Eve and getting married, about leaving her alone so much and wasting her life, and now she was livid because Aaron had elected to take on his three children. She saw her chances dwindling. She had begun to drink heavily. When she was drunk Aaron despised her, himself, the world at large. Aaron was embarrassed by his attraction — and possessed by it. His feelings for her were as ambivalent as Eve's had been for him. But at least Martha did not — *could* not — compete with him. While he relished challenge in business, he had long ago run out of patience with it in his private life.

*

On a late October afternoon, with the children in school, Aaron stood uncomfortably in the lovely, bright living room of Eve's apartment in the Centennial, one of the rare times he had been permitted access to the grandeur he had made possible, he thought with annoyance. He looked around hesitantly, as if he really didn't want to see those same old shapeless lumps of Eve's, left over from their early years in Brooklyn Heights. He had to admit they looked incongruous here, with the impressive spires of Fifth Avenue poking through the autumnal russet glory of Central Park. Still he could not bring himself to give her, willingly, anything but the basic minimum of their agreement. He wholly subscribed to the old adage, "Why feed oats to a dead horse?" She had put herself in a deep hole already with this fancy rental; he knew it and was capitalizing on it.

He had been allowed in only to discuss the arrangements for the transfer of custody and where Eve would live now. He had been telling her softly, and for a long time, that she needed a rest, from housekeeping, from responsibilities. Aaron tried to let her feel that it was optional, but secretly he believed that it was mandatory. She simply couldn't handle her life, the children. She was turning them into nervous wrecks. She needed the tranquilizing atmosphere of a hotel, a kind of custodial care. It would be better for everyone all around, Aaron told her.

"Especially for you," she said levelly.

"What's that mean?"

"I don't understand this sudden glow of paternal longing. Could it be that you are afraid of the draft? This way you can say that you're the guardian for your three children, and what with your age you'll surely get an exemption."

"Ah, Eve, at my age they're not drafting me anyway."

"I'm not so sure about that. You're in good physical condition. Forty-one isn't exactly over the hill yet — "

"Look, they're not even taking the younger guys who work for me, like Grissman and Miller and — "

"Well, they're not in your shape. Anyway, I heard the story about Jason and the draft board — "

Aaron looked alternately puzzled and angry. "What story?"

"Oh, how he went down to enlist, and while they were considering his application you paid someone off down there to turn him down — "

"What! Are you crazy or something? Where in the hell did you hear that, why would I do that, for what goddamn reason?" His face was ashen with suppressed rage.

"Why? I'll tell you why. Because with the kind of business you're doing now, since the war, the kind of money you're raking in hand over fist, you need Jason out there running the show for you, organizing."

"Oh Christ, you're crazy. He's no genius, ya know, and I don't need anyone. I could hire someone else to do the same damn thing. Guys like that are a dime a dozen."

"You *are* an ungrateful bastard," she said venomously. "Look, he's not exactly my cup of tea, but he's been a good and loyal employee, and God knows for some strange reason he's completely devoted to you."

"Eve, he's thirty-two. They're not taking thirty-two-year-old guys now, to begin with. He's got a bad back, he's the sole support of his wife and aged parents, *and* — *and* he's in the entertainment field, which is in itself, in most cases, an exemption," Aaron said triumphantly.

"Yeah, I know," Eve said drily. "Checking's very important to the war effort — "

"As a matter of fact, it is. Anything connected with *morale* is important."

"Aaron, please spare me your hypocritical patriotism, it doesn't become you. And the word *morale* is entirely too close to *moral* to be used for anything concerning the checkroom."

He looked at his wife now, as if for the first time. He wondered why they seemed destined to be locked in this mortal combat forever. He had developed through the years such an idée fixe about her, that no matter how she abused and reviled him he kept coming back for more. No one else in his life had ever gotten away with that. Eve said it was guilt — or *gelt*, or perhaps a little of both (he knew that she could haul him into court on a moment's notice for additional support), but she recognized his ambivalence and used it mercilessly.

Without the confusion of the children around and the excitement of the usual playing off of one against the other, he was able to appraise her silently and objectively. She had grown heavy lately, fat — hard and obtrusive — accumulated through the years like her anger. He thought with distaste of her mother. Eve said it was the result of undigested, lonely meals. Still, there was the echo of that special feeling that he simply could not resurrect with any other woman. And though he couldn't dream of living with her again after all these years, he could not imagine life completely without her either; he had grown used to her chanting somewhere backstage of his life like the voice of conscience in a morality play.

He moved toward her to embrace her, to kiss her, as he often tried to do at incongruous moments like this, but she pushed him away, her deep hostility unabated by time, further inflamed now by what she considered his devious tactics to render her completely useless.

"Now that the children are out of the baby stage, are almost grown, now that Jennie can be companionable, *now* you want them, when the worst is over — "

"I always wanted them, and I don't know if the worst is over. Teen-agers are a big responsibility, particularly a daughter."

"Well, you don't have to worry about that, you can afford the best help. And the first time you bring that whore around, anywhere near the children, I guarantee you I'll know about it and I'll exercise my legal rights and take them back, this I promise you."

While she spoke with such intensity, he had a sudden picture of Eve with hat and cane, performing for him alone one evening early in their marriage — "Burlington Bertie from Bath" — one of her parents' old London music hall numbers. How charming and gay she could be. Where had that girl gone, he wondered, and taken with her her marvelous sense of humor. He really understood very little, only that before him stood this thickening middle-aged woman, still sweet of face, but always preaching the milk of human kindness, and her own had soured in the process.

"You are hounding me into a corner, like a rat in a hole — " were the last words he half heard as he went out the door.

*

Two weeks later, Aaron had signed the lease for an impressive nine-room terrace apartment in the building — in exchange for Eve's five. It had a spectacular view of the park and the city. If he was at long last going to get a chance to woo his children, he would do it in style, he could well afford to. That this was part of the renowned "golden ghetto," where most of New York's richest Jews huddled in hard-won contentment, troubled him not a bit, anymore than did the label of *nouveau riche*. He was not an iconoclast, *riche* was *riche*, and for *most* American Jews it was *nouveau*.

One month later he had the apartment decorated. Eve said he

was at base a cheap hood, but everything in this apartment said he
was not.

It was fine he thought, with just a dash of flash — had to have a
touch of the good old razzle-dazzle!

So during Jennie's second year of high school Eve gave up the
children to Aaron, reluctantly. Perhaps she simply gave up and
moved out of life, into a tiny one-room at the Hotel St. Moritz.

"Going with Dad," the boys expected, would be a great adventure, and they were quite blatantly joyous about the change. They
had a kind of casual, raucous relationship with their father, and had
never been able to fathom the depth of Eve's devotion to them, it
had been so clouded and spoiled by her anxieties. But for Jennie it
was different. She felt strongly guilty and strangely excited. Her
relationship with her father was awkward and tenuous — she was
always trying not to tread on her mother's toes, and never quite
sure when she might be hurting her father, who was so much less
articulate and was capable only of rough signals of affection, like
teasing or teeth gritting — and in his unconscious effort to ward off
the age-old seduction of father-daughter, he had almost let tenderness slip by unnoticed. She could not imagine herself living in one
place while her mother was almost within reach in another. It just
didn't seem natural, it was unjust to Mother, "who had given up so
much," to put her out to pasture just because she was unable to
cope. No, she wouldn't go. Her place was with her mother, what
would she do without them? She could not remember her mother
doing anything that didn't somehow or in some way involve the
children; planning their carefully chosen wardrobes, their birthday
parties, talking earnestly to teachers in that specially cultivated
voice, taking them to doctors and dentists, organizing dance lessons,
and fencing lessons for Evan (he was so graceful, she said — this
made Aaron squirm). None of these lessons did they stay with for
long. The children were inconsistent, like their lives. "Exposure,"
she always emphasized to the children. She insisted on exposure, it
was one of her prime reasons for moving to Manhattan, so that the
children could be exposed to the arts, the ballet, the theater, mu-
seums. At nine she had Evan conducting Wagner at the Met; stand-

ing up in his red plush seat (much to the annoyance of the people behind), he waved his lollipop stick in soaring arcs, rolling and tossing his curly head behind Leopold Stokowski's shaggy one, while his free hand tugged at the drooping trousers on his nonexistent hips. It was her dream, she often said, to have Jennie play the harp (an instrument openly disdained by Jennie), perhaps even in concert at Carnegie Hall. She imagined her dressed in pleated gold lamé, like a muse, her honey-colored hair cascading down her back. Jennie wondered why so many Jewish mothers were bent on turning their daughters into angels so prematurely; it was, of course, an established fact that they would reach heaven eventually.

Part II

Camelot

(36)

IN THE BEGINNING of Eve's forced "retirement," Jennie visited her at the hotel. Her heart heaved around in her chest, her throat closed over, swollen. She felt as if she were visiting a patient in a hospital. Her mother looked strangely stuffed into the tiny room that was choked on all sides with piles of books and papers, the cherished collections of her lifetime now reduced to stacks on the floor. She had a fleeting image of Poe's "Cask of Amontillado." If it continued like this, she would surely be entombed in a cell of books and papers. Jennie sat in the only chair in the room, small, straight-backed; her mother was forced into bed out of necessity, but it wasn't only for lack of space. Eve had retired to bed almost permanently now, out of defeat, and the kind of depression that only a bed and quarts of ice cream seemed to assuage.

"This is only temporary, isn't it, Mother?" Jennie asked hopefully, not knowing quite what she expected, only that she wanted to bolt from the room.

"I hope so, but you know, there's a war on." (Oh, that expression again. Jennie hated it. It was, she knew, a conscience irritant, and hers was already rubbed raw.) "Anyway, I don't think your father will spend any more for me, and right now living space, *if* you can get it, costs blood — and this is all there was to get, your father was in such a rush."

Jennie sat there vainly trying to blot out pictures of their beautifully decorated nine-room apartment. She had never been able to accept having a poor mother and a rich father.

Eve was threatening to expose Aaron and his illicit "love nest."

"I don't know how you can stay there with him, seeing how I'm forced to live. That's because you're so selfish and so greedy."

"Mother, I didn't ask to go with him. You and he arranged it —"

"I didn't see you fighting to stay with me."

"I offered to, but where would we have gone?"

"Nonsense, you wouldn't have gone anywhere without the boys, and you know it. You like to steam each other up — against me." She was pulling at her hair now, hair that had grown oddly frizzy through the years, and salted with gray already before middle age. Jennie thought her mother still beautiful, but she had grown heavy, strange, hostile. She had been falling to pieces lately, she thought, into a million tiny fragments, ice splinters — like Gerda, in Hans Christian Andersen's story "The Snow Queen," one had gotten lodged in her heart — sometimes the ice melted and she cried; even now her eyes were tearing . . .

"Last night I ate my lonely meal at Schrafft's with all the little old ladies. You should see how they totter in alone, gulp down their martinis and glimmer through the rest of their dinner with their trembling, liver-spotted hands — life's discarded remnants, like me.

"The irony of this whole fiasco will be," her mother continued, "finally having to go to work to earn a living when I am too old to do any of the things I've always wanted to do — I'm liable to wind up as a matron in one of your father's washrooms —"

Jennie stifled a wild desire to burst out laughing and she looked up quickly to see if her mother was smiling, but her face had crumpled into new lines of martyrdom. Jennie began to giggle helplessly. It was June, the tiny room was airless and suffocated with the faint sweet-rotten odor of face powder, stale perfume — of decay.

*

Out through the large, impersonal lobby of the St. Moritz, with its neat clumps of luggage awaiting departures, imparting a lonely feeling of transience — out onto Central Park South — diamond-spangled pavement under night-white lights. She passed the Essex House hotel; she could see its huge lighted sign from her bedroom window. The ES had been out for a week — tantalizing — that was *all* the girls at school had been giggling about — over the glittering Manhattan skyline, SEX HOUSE, in lights. She felt strangely excited and excluded. Beneath the striped awning of the outdoor Café de la Paix, a young couple sat close, as if fused together. Jennie looked longingly at them, not so much out of personal envy — her time would come — but for what she knew her mother had missed.

AT SCHOOL SHE FELT FREE, fluid, deboned, as if a tremendous weight had dropped from her shoulders — she began a love affair with life that grew richer with each day. She breezed through the well-kept corridors of school with a careless giddy joy, laughing gaily, giggling recklessly with the girls, a kind of heady expectation in the air. She floated when she walked, as if keeping time to some inner music, its secret rhythms rising and falling in golden crescendos that sometimes caused her to close her eyes and slow her usually hectic pace to a momentary standstill, as if to regain her balance. Conscience told her she should fight it, it wasn't fair, it was disloyal to her mother, but the hedonist in her took over almost from the moment Aaron did, and she allowed herself to be beguiled by her new life, the good life. In school the girls called her "dizzy," but it didn't bother her. Dizzy was how she felt. She was forever losing or leaving things behind, as if wanting to go back to the apartment, to be sure it was really true, not a dream.

But it was a good life with Aaron, calmer and more peaceful, Aaron putting himself out to please, the three of them very much on their own for the first time. For Jennie, it meant a novel sense of delicious autonomy that made her feel that she must succeed both in school and at home. Above all, the heady sensation of money surrounded them. The Abel children were no different from most; they could be bought, charmed — the grand apartment, the vacations, the good times, the free and easy jokes, and a plenitude of marvelous food that made her conscious of "the children starving in Europe" and of its probable source, the black market. The new epicurean miracles were prepared with a great casual élan by Aaron's treasure and rare find, Mamie Todd, without whom the whole complicated household could not have run so smoothly.

Mamie was an upright, pretty brown woman of an indeterminate age, somewhere in the vicinity of forty. She had caramel-apple cheeks, a squash blossom nose, and skin like beige satin. She wore her hair angelically in a heavy coil around her moon-shaped face; at night she let it hang down her back in a wild black storm. In her tasteful gown and robe she would send them smartly to bed, all the while massaging a mysterious white cream into her skin, which she confessed to them was definitely responsible for turning her already golden skin at least a shade lighter. The kids restrained themselves, but Aaron teased her mercilessly about it. She took it silently, cracking her gum omnisciently. She was intensely moral in behalf of her young charges, a martinet, particularly with Jennie, but her own private life was shrouded in mystery. Aaron had found her, in a sense, in the same place whence all his recent blessings flowed, the big hotel he owned in Newark. Green Park Court provided the most elegant cuts of meat for his table (through the hotel's commercial purveyors), a home for Martha Voccek — and now Mamie Todd. She had been head housekeeper there for some years, going home at night to the boarding house she owned in a good Negro section not far from the hotel. Aaron had persuaded her to give up this somewhat loftier lifestyle by appealing to her business sense. He promised to put her in a position to buy the property that surrounded her boarding houses. Some said she had been a madame before she had been a housekeeper, others said she was one still, but the children adored her and Jennie was fascinated by her. When she was in a good mood she called them "Sugar Babies" in a way that sounded like maple syrup. When she was angry (and she had a terrible temper) she didn't call them anything at all, just cracked her gum loudly and decisively through closed lips. At these times the children trembled because of the double threat, the one so often heard from Aaron, "If she leaves — " and their own terrible fear of loss.

In the beginning, Mamie did some of the children's chauffeuring and kept the household books. After a year she ran the children and the house, and stage-managed the lives of its occupants, answering only to Aaron, who didn't watch too carefully the domestic mechanics of his home. He was preoccupied with the wartime skyrocketing of his business and the maze of confusion in his personal life. A rising hostility was growing in the children toward Martha (that is, toward Martha's telephone presence). They had never really met her but that one summer four or five years ago, and even then they had a hard time reconciling Daddy's rather charming "distant cousin" with the mystic Martha of their mother's scurrilous descriptions.

The telephone became an object of incessant wrangling. During the war it was impossible to get a second phone, but Jennie was sure Aaron could have swung it if he really wanted to — she was sure Aaron had the power and mysterious connections to do almost anything. But she didn't much care right now, there were no boys around. Just the girls from school would call, and they would talk an hour at a time about the latest cosmetic on the market, the new teacher, the new girl at school. Usually the phone was tied up by Eve talking to Jennie on the average of one to three hours an evening — actually Eve was Jennie's only real problem right now, and Mamie Todd's too.

⟨38⟩

HIBISCUS BLOOMED WILDLY that spring of '43 in Miami, the spring of Jennie's sixteenth year. They burst upon the senses without amenity, violently colored, stubbornly scentless, as if their brash beauty were excuse enough for existing. But the twilight was fully scented — honeysuckle, wisteria, seaweed, mixed with the faint green smell of ripening coconuts.

There was an added seduction in the air this Easter. The sound of "Wild Blue Yonder" was everywhere. Every four or five blocks, phalanxes of handsome young fliers seemed to proliferate in perfect marching order, their approach invariably heralded by the tantalizing sounds of the Army Air Force anthem. From the way they sang, their style, their gusto, their whole panache, each group with its perfect musical accompaniment, Jennie had the odd feeling that they must have spent the entire day rehearsing for these perfect miniature parades — that they were all really extras on a movie set — that this unreal city was their backdrop and she might somehow wind up the heroine of this whole musical extravaganza. When she could no longer contain herself, at the peak of rapture, she'd lean three-quarters of her body out the window of the conservative old Palm Plaza Hotel and wave passionately to the oncoming herd. She had made a singular discovery — the male sex — and had fallen in love with it. Sometimes she would catch the eye of one particularly handsome cadet in the front row and dedicate her wave especially to him. She often received a dazzling smile in return. Their susceptibility only spurred her onward to bolder feats, and she finally ended up tossing kisses in the air instead of waving her handkerchief.

Toward sunset, on the beach or gazing from the window of her room, the heavy tropical air made her feel restless, left out, too young. She had become painfully aware of her body now. She assessed it carefully in the mirror from all angles and tried tossing her head like Rita Hayworth, but somehow her long hair just didn't toss in the same way. She noticed joyfully that her waist was beginning to curve, finally and most of that hard, stubborn baby fat had disappeared. But still, how would she ever be able to undress in front of a man, with those unruly breasts spilling all over, and she'd always have to wear a bra under her nightgowns when she got married. She really didn't approve of her heavy breasts; the girls at school said they were definitely unfashionable, models didn't have them (neither did the girls at school). But now they appeared less loathsome to her, because she knew men admired her breasts, and she could find no fault with her tapering thighs and long, shapely legs. She picked up a bunch of pink silk flowers from the bureau. She tried them on one side of her hair; some of the more daring girls were wearing them on both sides. But, no, she'd better start with one; you really had to have a center part for two, and a perfectly symmetrical face — like Hedy Lamarr's. She had neither. She wore her hair in the classic Veronica Lake side wave.

She heard her brother Reid rattling around with his keys. He opened the door and fell into the room in his usual condition, breathless and dripping with water from the pool. This feverish hysteria over his swimming is beginning to get ridiculous, Jennie thought to herself. Okay, so he's the swimming champ at school, but God, enough is enough, and I have to room with him yet. But she was genuinely fond of Reid — they had grown closer lately. In fact, the three of them had become closer since Aaron had taken over. She didn't have to feel guilty now about gossiping and bantering with her brothers as she used to when Eve would accuse them of banding together against her. She had shared a room with Reid because he was the youngest. It was more fitting, she thought properly. As it was, Reid was getting a little *too* precocious lately. Sometimes she thought she saw him staring at her body, and once, when she casually wrapped a towel around her waist after the shower, she saw his eyes drop to her thighs. Sometimes she let the towel open a little in front to allow a brief glimpse of the tangled golden-brown hair, feeling curiously excited. He's not even thirteen, she thought, not even bar mitzvahed, and already he thinks he's a man.

"Hey, you still looking in the mirror? That's where I left you this morning. You're always either looking in the mirror or hanging out the window," Reid said, a large, ever-widening puddle growing beneath his feet.

"Yeah," she sighed distractedly. "God, look what you're doing, what a slob. You know I live here, too. Do you mind — get out of those wet things."

He threw himself down on the bed in his wet suit, in defiance and the hope of evoking a scream from his sister.

"Oh my God, how are you going to sleep in that tonight? You'll drown."

"It'll be dry by then, or maybe the night maid will take pity on me and change the sheets."

"You know Dad wants me to go over to the Y tonight," she said absently. "There's a U.S.O. dance there — an April Fool's dance. The joke'll be on me for sure. He says I should sign up as a junior hostess, can you believe it?"

"You? Ugh!" he said, in feigned disgust. "No, I can't."

"He's rushing me right into the middle of it all, it's not like him, but a Y dance, ugh, it'll be a drag, I know it. Besides, I have nothing to wear."

Reid's back was turned to her in his bed. She called to him, "Reedy, do you think I should go?" but his even breathing told her that he was fast asleep. Not that she cared so much for her brother's opinion, but she felt an urgent need to talk to somebody, anybody. She knocked at the door of the room Evan and Aaron shared. Nobody answered, so she poked her head in. They weren't there. Strangely disappointed, she closed the door. She had set her hair, done her nails; for the time being there was nothing else to do. She threw herself down on the bed, but she couldn't sleep; she'd never really gotten the knack of napping, or sleeping either for that matter, couldn't seem to disconnect. She thought, what have I got to wear, nothing really, just that floozy pea-green print with the black flecks on it. Too tight, anyway — too Celanese-looking. Well, what could she expect for twenty dollars. Even her father had commented on it the other night, "Jeeze, don't you have a decent dress to wear? What kind of dress is that?"

Jennie's cheeks flamed. "A cheap kind," she answered archly. "I buy what we can afford."

Aaron realized his mistake in mentioning it but was willing to rectify it. "Well, you go ahead out tomorrow and buy some real good-looking clothes," he'd said, "something — I don't know, more cheerful-looking." Jennie knew he meant more showy, more expensive-looking. The next day, at her father's prodding, she had bought a beautiful suit in shocking pink at Henri Bendel, but it was still being altered, and anyway, that's not what you wore to a dance in the tropics.

In the end she wound up wearing her old favorite pink sharkskin playdress, a kind of one-piece tailored romper, covered discreetly with a little skirt buttoned down the front. She'd leave the buttons open flirtatiously, offering a glimpse of the pink shorts and a long expanse of suntanned thigh and leg beneath. Nobody would notice that it was faded and laundered to death. She sat at dinner in the hotel's large, vaulted dining room feeling self-conscious, and completely without appetite. Her pink lipstick exactly matched the shower of pink silk flowers in her hair.

"You're eating them," Reid said, disgustedly. "Who do you think you are, Ferdinand the Bull?"

"Yeah, you're watering them, too, in the soup," Evan added.

She pretended to ignore them. Aaron didn't seem to notice much; he was wholly absorbed in dinner. She wished that he'd look at her, make some contribution one way or another; she needed his approval, but rarely got it. In fact, the greatest personal interest he'd shown lately in her appearance had been that negative comment about her clothes. More frequently it was, "You don't look much like your mother, you know. She was far better-looking when she was your age."

Aaron came to life when the waiter came by so that he could do his famous "I'll have a hot bowl of cracked ice" number, which never failed to send the boys into gales of laughter. Jennie just looked down at her plate, embarrassed at her father's corniness and the waiter's confusion.

The orchestra swung into a gentle rhumba, a lovely girl in a bare midriff dress sang "Amor, Amor, Amor" and shook maracas, and the dance floor blossomed into white — white dinner jackets, white gowns, white gloves — traditional for the spring season in Miami at the Palm Plaza, one of the few hotels not commandeered by the air force for barracks. The war outside had changed nothing here. Jennie turned her attention to the dance floor now (if only out of a need to concentrate on something other than the evening ahead) and thought about the special look of wealthy New York Jewish women. Attractive, snappy, like the click of their gorgeous compacts, put together a little too tightly, with that peculiar aggressive quality, a self-confidence that amounted almost to hostility. It reflected itself in the deep, urgent voices, their intensely self-involved expressions. Jennie saw them all the time going up and down in the elevators of her building; she wasn't sure if she was glad or sorry that her mother didn't fit into that mold. She wondered if it was inevitable that she would grow into that look one day. Well, maybe, if she chose the right man. "It's a charmed life that gives those women that special look," Eve would say with a certain unmistakable envy.

*

The doors were open wide, letting in the tender night, and forcing out the warm brown sounds of the saxophone. The large gymnasium was still almost empty, and standing near the door Jennie could hear the restless ocean close behind. The swing band, surprisingly complete for a U.S.O. group, had just finished tuning up, and now began to play a lovely, lilting ballad — "Spring Will Be a Little Late This Year." She felt an unfamiliar sensuous tug at the pit of her stomach. Caught up in a curious aimless rapture, she closed her eyes and let it wash over her like a sudden sun bath.

There was a long table at the back of the room where a group of girls of about eighteen to twenty-one were seated — obviously the hostesses. The girls wore large paper flowers pinned to their dresses. On tables at either side of them were spread platters of the ubiquitous sugared donuts. They must be senior hostesses, she decided; they appeared so cool and poised and carefully groomed. Still pressed up against the open door, she thought how easy it would be to slip away unnoticed. She could walk back to the hotel, spend the evening with the boys and Daddy just hanging around — yes, she liked doing just nothing with the boys. But somehow she began walking in the direction of the hostesses. A few cadets could be seen here and there, but there still seemed to be more girls than servicemen. One of the girls, a brunette with dark lipstick and a soft Southern accent, asked her name and if she had signed up as a hostess.

"No, but I will now, if you like."

"Well, you're supposed to sign up in advance, and you have to be seventeen to be a junior hostess. Are you seventeen?" she asked suspiciously but politely.

"Well, yes," Jennie said, unconvincingly.

"Okay, sign here — your name and address and age. We're gonna need all the hostesses we can get."

"Not by the looks of it so far," Jennie said.

"Oh, don't worry 'bout that, honey. In a little while this place'll be mobbed — ," and she winked knowingly.

*

The dance was going into its second hour and Jennie realized with amazement that she was having a wonderful time. She had been jitterbugging wildly, doing breaks and complicated improvised steps. Each time a partner whirled her out a group of admiring cadets applauded, whistled, and cut in. She was flushed and damp and the pink silk flowers were beginning to droop like her hair, but it didn't matter; she wished that the music, the dancing, and the men would go on forever.

On her many trips around the dance floor, she kept passing the small staircase that was by now a virtual jungle of khaki, groaning with cadets. She noticed one who was particularly handsome, studying her intently, and his radiant smile suggested that he really was enjoying himself just watching her; certainly he made no move to get down through the seething obstacle course. His smile followed her through the rest of the dance. When she passed that way again, it began to annoy her, so she decided she wouldn't look up there at all. But his smile was infectious and she found herself returning it — boldly and directly.

Her dancing partner continued with the usual polite "Where-are-you-from?" narrative, but now somehow she couldn't concentrate under the relentless gaze. The trumpeter came forward to the mike and blew his trumpet as if he were auditioning for Harry James, and the room seemed to get hotter.

"Ah, mahself, am from Okeechobee, ya'll know whereabouts that is — not at all far from heah — "

Without taking his eyes from her face, he pushed his way down the crowded staircase. Jennie tried not to slow her pace now, and to keep smiling during the open breaks in the dance. They were still near the stairs; it wasn't easy to move quickly on the clogged dance floor. She was breathless from the fast Lindy, and she felt weak in the knees.

"Yeah, it's not at all far from heah, ya know, sugah."

She thought, if he passes me by, goes toward another girl, I think I'll faint. She wanted desperately to sit down somewhere, but was afraid to move from the strategic spot. If only I wasn't so damn nearsighted, she thought, I'd know exactly what was going on, I'd even know what he looked like; all she could remember seeing was a dazzling smile and a deep suntan. The orchestra had slid into a ballad now — she wished that he would cut in in time to dance this slow number with her.

The change was barely perceptible, he handled it so well. Almost naturally she found herself reaching up on her toes to better follow her new partner. He held her lightly, but very close to him. Her face felt flushed, hot, and she was embarrassed to lay her wet burning cheek against his dry and freshly shaven one. She pulled back a little and he took it to mean that he was out of line and eased his hold on her. Neither spoke. At first she hesitated to look at him directly, but her curiosity got the better of her and her eyes met his as she assessed him. His eyes are soft and amber, warm, she thought, but there's something else that's more compelling. It was the lower half of his face that held all the expression, the excitement; the full mouth, with a delicate trace of scar above the upper lip, was framed by dimples that deepened when he smiled and lent an air of insolence to an otherwise candid face. He must be conscious of the effect, Jennie thought, because he smiles so often. He was a little under six foot, and neatly built and looked wonderful in the snappy uniform. He immediately asked her name, then used it as though he had known her all her life.

"Jennie, do you know I've been watching you all evening? You seem to be having such a good time." He said that easily, charmingly, as if he were taking in a breath of fresh air.

"Yes, I am. Are you? By the way, what *is* your name, or do I just call you Sir?"

There was a pause, and then he said, "Pete, Peter's my name." He seemed resistant.

"Oh? Peter what?"

Again he hesitated. "Peter Schore."

"Okay, Peter Schore, why such a mystery about names?"

"No mystery," he said, with detachment.

She thought he was . . . moody. She was beginning to think he looked better from the staircase — things and people usually looked better from far away. When you got right down to a thing, it always seemed to evaporate a little.

"Where are you from, Pete?"

"New York."

Oh, too good to be true, she thought. "Me, too. Whereabouts in New York?"

"The Bronx."

"Oh?" She would have never guessed it from his speech. He spoke with no particular inflection, just a deep, soft voice.

"Where do you live?" he asked casually.

She was about to answer Central Park West, but instead answered more generally, "Oh, right in town, on the West Side." He didn't pursue it.

Once again the orchestra changed ballads — "It Could Happen to You," with its knowing and worldly-wise lyrics — but the mood remained the same, sweet and hot. Jennie was pleased, she had no intention of doing one of those silly jitterbug numbers with *him.*

He didn't say much for the rest of the dance, and she was praying nobody else would cut in, but it wasn't likely — the boys seemed to sense when not to. She inclined her body toward him gently, testing a little, but drew back in embarrassment when he seemed to move slightly away.

"How long have you been in the service?" she asked politely.

"Well, I signed up right before my nineteenth birthday — about six months now."

Oh God, Jennie thought, he's too old for me — nineteen. What if he finds out?

"How old are *you*, anyway?" he asked, as if reading her thoughts.

This time it was Jennie who paused uncomfortably, "Er, going on sixteen." Why hadn't she just said sixteen, outright? Why was she so damned honest?

"Uh, uh, jailbait," he said softly in her ear, still holding her close, seemingly unperturbed by her disclosure.

"This must be a pretty great place to be stationed."

"You bet, particularly for the officers," he said ruefully. "But this is only our basic training. We go on for special training from here; probably be leaving any day now — Arizona or New Mexico."

Oh, no, not that, she thought, that must be the oldest routine in the world.

The air was heavy with the scent of overripe gardenias from the corsages the girls wore pinned to their clothes, their wrists, their hair; it blended with the more primal odors of hair and perspiration. Pale girls clung to their partners limply, like honeysuckle. The molten *V* for victory over the bandstand shimmered in the

thick atmosphere, throwing spasms of light on the brass instruments
— the allied flags draped beneath, held by a pair of large silver
wings — all the trivial glitter of wartime.

The orchestra stopped playing suddenly in the middle of a number. An announcement over the loudspeaker broke the mood
harshly — "This dance ends at 11:20, one-half hour from now. No
serviceman may leave with a hostess. *Repeat,* servicemen may not
leave with a hostess. The girls will remain here until the hall is
cleared of cadets." Jennie felt trapped — thwarted. He whispered
something to her quickly; at first she did not understand him, then
she thought she heard, "I'll meet you out in front, right after it
ends. I'm going to grab a couple of beers with the guys, and anyway, I'm dying for a cigarette." And in an instant he was gone —
she almost put out her hand to stop him, reflexively, but she caught
it in time. She found herself alone, pushing through the dense
crowds; she felt suddenly depleted, and very tired. Was it all over
so quickly, she thought, as she made her way weakly to the ladies'
room. She didn't for one minute believe that he really meant to
meet her, he had seemed so vague, had disengaged himself so
neatly.

She hid out in the ladies' room so that she could organize her
thoughts and her appearance, and so that she wouldn't have to dance
again. Oh God, she couldn't have withstood another of those home-
spun assaults, not now, not after Peter. When she finally emerged,
the orchestra was announcing the last dance. It was "Silver Wings."
She tried to make her way over to the door, but it was still difficult,
though the room had emptied out considerably. On her way someone asked her to dance; he was standing with a group of boys —
some of them looked vaguely familiar. She was about to refuse, but
was struck with the notion that he just might know Peter.

Unlike most of the others, this boy wasn't very talkative, and it
made it harder for her to broach the subject. "Let's dance over this
way; it's cooler near the entrance," she said. There was a cool, soft
breeze now coming from the direction of the open doors.

"Sure thing," he said, obligingly, and began to propel her rather
clumsily in that direction.

So here she was, dancing the last dance with some stranger, and longing for another.

Outside, in the thick tropic haze, after the overbright lights of the gym, she groped uncertainly, afraid to look either right or left, unwilling to have her worst fears confirmed. She just walked straight ahead of her, and then realized she'd have to turn in one direction or the other; so with a heavy sense of defeat she turned toward her hotel. As she did so, she heard her name called softly, and she found herself near the outside gate of the building, and there was Pete waiting for her, smoking and leaning against a palm tree. She had the impression that he was not alone, at first, but in a hushed rustle the others seemed to evaporate as if on cue.

"Oh, so you're here."

"Of course, I'm here. Didn't I tell you I would be? What do you mean?"

"I don't know," she said, feeling more gauche and childish than ever.

They both began to talk at once, then stopped and laughed. He had a soft, rich laugh, pouring out velvety and slow, like heavy cream from a pitcher.

"In which direction is your hotel?" he asked.

She showed him. "But it's an awfully long walk," she said, apologetically.

"Good. It's a lovely night." He came up close beside her now. She could smell the beer on his breath; she shivered a little with the night on her still-damp skin. He put his arm around her shoulders, as if answering her need, and the sudden warmth lifted her skin in tiny bumps. They walked quietly for a while, deeper into the fog that blocked out everything but their touching bodies. Then she said, "What shall I call you?"

"What would you like to call me?" he asked teasingly.

"Well — I mean Pete or Peter?"

"Pete is fine."

"Why did you disappear so suddenly?"

"April Fool's, maybe?" He looked at her out of the corner of his eye to calculate the effect. "No, I didn't really think so — " Then he continued ingenuously, "Well, besides the fact that I was dying for a beer, it seemed the safest way to get out unnoticed to meet you. You heard the announcement —" She was warmed by the flattery and felt foolish for hassling him.

They talked casually at first, the amenities, all the bright, timely things men and women say to each other during a war, all the surface fluff that negates the uncertainties beneath. She found herself staring at his mouth. It was both beautiful and ugly. She thought that there was something decidedly ungraceful about him; it was his walk, his whole manner — it was too abrupt. She was used to the more properly bred boys from the prep schools in her neighborhood, whom she thought she hated, but now —

They came upon a small private park between the street and the ocean, sheltered by majestic coconut palms.

"Come on, let's sit down for a few minutes and talk," he said. There was a gentleness about him that irritated her, gentleness that produced a slackening of tension. She thrived on tension, had grown up on it. His relaxed and easy manner created a letdown for her, a lack of drama, without which she felt the theater of her life couldn't succeed. Quickly, quickly, she must sell herself on the idea.

"What time is it? My father, he'll be very worried" ("furious" was the word she had in mind). They sat down suddenly, "Well, what shall we talk about?" she said.

There was an imperceptible pause, and then he drew her close and kissed her on the mouth. Her first instinct was to pull back as if from the touch of fire — she had been so conditioned by her reading, her mother's lectures — most of all, her father's admonitions, those printed sermons he dredged up out of the Kotex box — What a Girl Should Prize above Rubies — it was her virtue, of course. Why didn't they just come out and say so, why all that allegorical mumbo jumbo?

She had been kissed by other boys before, many, at boarding school — experimental — furtive — summers at the shore — the more worldly kisses of her cousin, Steve. But this time she felt that she must be on guard, watchful — at first.

She is thinking — His mouth feels strange, resilient, almost like rubber — the underlip so fleshy; and she chokes down the impulse to laugh, to giggle wildly. There is the unfamiliar, sophisticated taste of cigarette smoke; it excites her. She tries to draw back, unconvincingly. He tells her that she is beautiful, whispering to her, but never beyond the warmth of her mouth, careful always to insulate her mouth with his, as if a speck of outside air might pollute — break the spell. They pull apart. She finds it difficult to look him in the eye (anyway, the light is precarious now, only moonlight really), making apologies that force her to think of the heroines of True Confessions *magazine* — like, "I don't know why I'm doing this," "I never do this sort of thing," or "What must you think of me?" — *her eyes again fixating on his mouth with its amalgam of suggestive indentations, the paper-thin white scar above his lip. If you wanted a boy's respect, wanted his love instead of his lust, you didn't neck on the first date — you never, never let him touch your body, anywhere. As for — well — anything else, forget it.* She wished she could. She jumped up from the bench, hoping that the slight physical separation might give her strength, but he pulled her back down, gently.

"I — I've really never done this before, do you believe me?"

"Of course I do," he murmured against her mouth. *Random kisses, growing wild, wilder than field flowers. Her whole body feels exquisitely sensitive, as if it is melting to liquid gold.*

When they finally rise from the bench some two hours later, Jennie is chilled and trembling, her legs unsteady, her buttocks sore from sitting, and her mind in a state of euphoric confusion — thoughts darting here and there like gnats. She cannot decide if he is really very usual, very ordinary, or if she is shaping him into something very extraordinary in order to fit him into the niche she has carved for him. She hasn't had time to find out — they've hardly spoken in the two hours. Her lips feel bruised, her face rubbed raw by his beard; she notices vestiges of her pink lipstick rubbed into his lips, into the early stubble growing in around his mouth. He cups his hands to light a cigarette. As he looks down she notices his lashes, straight against his cheeks, they seem to fold like moth wings.

She is fascinated with the way he has of compressing his cheeks and expelling tiny bits of tobacco from the tip of his tongue, making his dimples more pronounced and his mouth look richer. She wonders if he consciously does it for its calculated effect. She looks away quickly, embarrassed. Two-thirty in the morning. Collins Avenue is transfigured — a sixteen-year-old girl with gold-flecked green eyes, in a pink sharkskin dress, in love for the first time. Suddenly alone in the world, bemused they walk toward the hotel in a warm, humid daze, everything under a spell.

"Jennie, when will I see you again?" he asked.

She was surprised to see that he seemed as affected as she was. She had expected, almost looked for, all the pangs of unrequited love. When the time came, could it be that it would all fall together — right for her, just this once? It had to, there was no time.

"Well, I'm leaving in three days for home," she said.

"Can I phone you tomorrow?" he asked.

She felt disappointed — he was being vague again.

"Yes, of course. My room number is 402."

For a minute more they stood together uncertainly on the empty street in front of the hotel, trying not to stare at one another — and then he was gone.

When she entered her room on tiptoe, she noticed a sharp crack of light in the adjoining room and realized the door was partially open. Her father had waited up for her.

He opened the door and called her into his room, loudly, as if unmindful of waking Reid, then closed her up with him in the tiny bathroom. "Where in the hell have you been?" he said, his face suffused with blood, his eyes bloodshot. She wondered, detached, if it was fury or the lateness of the hour, but the funny thing was that now she really didn't care.

"I was worried to death, where the hell have you been till two-thirty in the morning?"

"Daddy," Jennie said lamely, "you know where I've been."

"At the dance until two-thirty? Don't hand me that, it was over at midnight. I know that." Trapped.

"Now I want to know where you were." And with whom, she thought, but he didn't ask that.

"At a late-night movie," she murmured, barely audible.

He was standing in his pajamas, blue like his eyes, which stood out luminously against the reddened whites, the suntanned face. He moved forward in a quick athletic movement and slapped her across the face. But she didn't feel it, she was a sleepwalker in a state of euphoria, cushioned against all the slings and arrows.

"If you were with a soldier" ("soldier" struck an old chord, it sounded archaic to her), "remember he's just that and it's wartime. Anything can happen to a young girl —"

"Nothing happened, Daddy," Jennie said with her hand up to her face defensively. "If he had thought anything of you, he wouldn't have brought you home at this hour" — Think anything of her? She was deciding that he must already *love* her; he hadn't even *tried* to take from her What a Girl Should Prize above Rubies.

"You're not going out anywhere at night for the rest of the time we're here." Only three more nights, she thought numbly. "Now go to bed, for chrissakes, without waking your brother. I'd like to get a little sleep, if you don't mind."

She didn't cry until after she got into bed, but they were really only tears of exhaustion and a curious feeling of depletion, as if all the intricate internal mechanism of muscle, bone, and sinew had turned to jelly.

*

Jennie woke up the next day with a heavy cold. She wasn't surprised. Sneezing and with bleary eyes, she was almost glad that Aaron had forbidden her to go out that night, but what worried her was that she didn't exactly know when Pete was leaving, or for where.

She stayed in bed most of the day out of torpor and because of her cold, but mostly to be near the telephone, which didn't ring all day. But she wasn't too worried yet because no matter what happened now, she felt sure that he'd call before she left.

The next afternoon around four-thirty Pete called. He seemed breathless and harried, not at all the laconic dreamer of the other night. She had no idea exactly how she would handle it, or even if Aaron was serious about carrying out his threat, but Pete made it very clear that tonight was the *only* one that he could get out of the barracks, and it would be an early curfew. He didn't even mention the night before last. Jennie just figured she would make it somehow.

When he hung up she felt hurt that he hadn't asked her if she'd gotten into trouble because of the lateness of the hour, hadn't asked her much of anything really. Was it only she and her family, alone in the world, who were so consumed with the mechanics of sexual manners and mores? Wartime was supposed to informalize things, she thought, make life more adaptable to the pace of the human heartbeat. But now it was becoming more and more complicated. Brought up on the sentimental ballads of the day, with everything heightened, magnified, by the sensual atmosphere of the times, she believed in senior proms and the philosophies of the popular songs. And in the power of true love with its ultimate goal of marriage — now she felt truly enlightened. But in her world they taught that love and sex could not possibly coexist — at least not until marriage. That and that alone would suddenly fuse the two. She thought it beautiful in theory — ideal — but in practice, she did not know . . . Her mind lingered over the words of the song they played — "It Could Happen to You."

JENNIE STARED out the tall paned windows of the study hall. A late June rain beat against the glass sharply and sloshed the American flag out in front, but she felt warm and safe here. She'd felt that way about Royalton almost from the first. She belonged, felt included in its special intellectual atmosphere, this slightly superior, somewhat complicated mechanism known as the progressive private school.

The girls were sprawled out in all directions over the tables and benches that doubled as the junior-senior lunchroom. Black and white speckled notebooks and textbooks were spread out haphazardly, unattached to their owners.

Jennie continued to gaze out the window. The girls had grown used to her latest tragic heroine pose. This time she was "the girl he left behind" and they didn't even tease her today by asking if she'd received a letter from overseas.

In the first couple of months after vacation, she had received frequent letters from a couple of air force bases on the West Coast. Then nothing for a while, and then a new batch with an exotic, unheard of, coded address in the Pacific, and that was all she knew of his whereabouts — all she really cared to know, just as long as he wrote.

Almost half the class (of which there were only forty in all) had waited with bated breath for Jennie's letters from Pete. In fact they had become the collective love letters of her less-fortunate, lessloved classmates. But lately she had stopped bringing them to school. She suddenly considered it infantile, and anyway, the letters became more precious that way. The sudden refusal to share them made her feel all the more mysterious and important — secretly Jennie considered Pete's letters less than promising. They were often flat and conversational, colloquial even, with very little personal message. Now and then when he included some allusion to their two evenings together, it seemed self-conscious, pompous, and the letters often left her wondering what she had seen in him in the first place. She had felt the same confusion that last evening they spent together in Miami. She wanted to shake him up and to force a reaction, any kind, good or bad, just some sort of spontaneous, combustible reaction. Just remembering the scent of the hotel dining room on that evening made her feel strangely restless and uncomfortable. It had smelled not of food alone, but beachy, of suntan lotion and stale ultraviolet, the residual odor of tropical sun, and tangy with ocean. The languor she felt that night came back to her now for a moment.

She had used all of her charged energies then to plot her escape from the hotel, to slip away with Pete, unnoticed. She had been sitting at dinner, the bellboy had brought her a note on a small silver tray telling her that Pete was in the lobby. Right under Aaron's nose — why had he done such a silly thing, she couldn't understand it at all. They had *agreed* to meet downstairs in front of the hotel, but it had all gotten confused. She had had to lie, to say the note was from a girlfriend who had stopped by to say hello. But Aaron seemed to have lost interest in the whole thing and had probably forgotten his scolding of the other night. She excused herself on the pretense of the ladies' room. In the lobby she thought she'd die, that her legs would give way under her. He was nowhere in sight. He'd gone, after all; she hadn't answered his note and she'd taken an eternity (actually it was about ten minutes) — and then she spotted him in the back of the lobby, pressed self-consciously against a corner of the reception desk, his khaki cap folded neatly in his hands.

They had taken a walk, talked a little about the war, his plans for the future, hers for college, and then they found themselves in the lush, tropical gardens of the hotel, dark and protective with all of its moist secret places like those of her own body, she thought. She was embarrassed by her complete lack of experience; how wooden she must seem to him, like a puppet. She really didn't know how to react now. She knew what she felt, but she had never before seen a man and a woman together in an attitude of tenderness, certainly not her parents. Her actions were preconditioned mostly by the movies of the day, and in most of the love stories she saw girls acted prim and terribly sweet and held back their feelings with discipline and just barely allowed themselves to be courted and flattered, pursued and idolized by the grateful young men. And here *she* was falling all over this virtual stranger and putting her tongue inside his mouth as if to extract from him his very soul, to suck out every bit of sweetness that she sensed was there but couldn't quite touch.

"Jennie," he said sharply, as if calling her back from somewhere else. "Jennie," he almost pushed her away from him. Had she gone too far, was he disgusted with her already? "I have to go, do you know the time? I'm A.W.O.L. already." It was only ten P.M.

"Please, darling, can't you stay a minute more? You'll be A.W.O.J. for so long."

"What's that?"

"Away without Jennie," she answered matter-of-factly. Both laughed a little self-consciously, but she loved to see him laugh, he did it so beautifully.

"Pete," she said, suddenly formal and subdued, "when will I see you again?"

"Oh, Jen," he said in a quiet voice, "I don't know, and if I did, I couldn't tell you. You know we're not allowed to tell our movements." She had thought then, with a sudden, sharp intake of breath, that his voice was like his eyes, deep and warm, and golden brown, and gave him away in spite of that rather cool veneer. They kissed again. "Write," he commanded, and he was gone before her breath came back.

*

There was a great slapping around of books and a scuffling of worn-down-at-the-back moccasins, while the girls gathered their things together to make way for the lunch crowd, which was soon flooding in with paper plates and cups in a kind of orderly disorder.

"Oh, God, not tongue again," Janie Newcombe complained.

"Ugh, *another* mute in the kitchen," Janice Seberg quipped. Everyone was primed to laugh at Janice's celebrated rapierlike wit, but today she wasn't doing so well, Jennie thought.

She wasn't hungry, or was hungry and was dieting as always, but whichever it was today, she didn't bother with lunch. Instead, with her friend Emma, she drifted upstairs to the gym, where the girls danced together closely while the juke box played the satin harmonies of the Ink Spots or the Mills Brothers. Today Billie Holiday was warbling in her rich nasal whine, "Lover Boy, oh where have you been?" Dana Lessower was bragging about having seen her show with some guy who took her to the new Cotton Club on Broadway.

"He's either a baby, or he's 4-F, I'll bet," Emma said, goaded by envy.

"No, as a matter of fact, he's neither" she said with great hauteur.

"I got it, he's a fag," Emma said brightly.

"*No,* he just *happens* to be an ensign on leave," Dana said, she with her brown hair and correct bangs, and perfectly tailored skirts and cashmere sweaters with creases in all the right places — like the sleeves. Jennie's sweater sleeves always managed to look stretched out somehow, as if she had slept in them. Emma looked crushed, Jennie enigmatic. Dana was very sophisticated; she knew every number on the Hit Parade and gave the strong impression that her knowledge came from firsthand experience, "live from the lovely ballrooms of the Pennsylvania Hotel" or the Glen Island Casino.

Jennie wondered with a stab of terror if she would ever get to places like that with Pete, if he would ever really materialize into something tangible, or simply remain a ghostly flutter of V-mail across the blue Pacific.

All around them the girls were dancing in twos, a slow fox trot, sloshing around in their oversized loafers, wishing ardently that their partners were boys, that precious commodity, and each thought, in her own private way, Oh, what a wondrous thing is man.

*

The war went to school with Jennie. At night it came home and went to bed with her. She would place her pillow beside her vertically and hold in her arms her phantom flier.

At school they knitted shapeless khaki scarves for the U.S.O. Jennie's had no beginnings and no visible ends but went on hopelessly because she didn't know how to finish it. She hated working with khaki; it was no challenge, she told the girls, and she was considering smuggling a scarlet one overseas to Pete when she realized that he might not be overly pleased with it, on some remote island in the Pacific where it was a hundred and twenty degrees in the shade.

Then there was Alice Duell Miller's *White Cliffs of Dover*. They wept when they read it aloud to one another at recess or during lunch. They wept when they rose in assembly to sing "God Save the King" and when Mrs. Farmer read Keats' *Ode to Melancholy* during Junior English. The class of '45 wept easily these days. In fact, it seemed to Jennie that she was quietly crying and knitting her way through the war.

The teachers at Royalton were a cosmopolitan and international potpourri of cloak and dagger variety (or the girls had dreamed it that way).

Mrs. Farmer was a beautiful and impassioned Englishwoman in her early thirties whose lashless, heavy-lidded eyes and alabaster complexion gave her the look of a Renaissance portrait of nobility. She wore her golden hair piled smooth and high in front and pulled into a chignon at the back. Her slim body was fragile beneath her impeccably tailored suits. Only when she read her favorites to the class, like Browning's "My Last Duchess," did the hidden fires (undoubtedly an asset in the begetting of four children) burn in her eyes and send rosy blotches of color to her hollow cheeks. Sometimes there would be a slight edge of redness at the corners of her tiny flaring nostrils suggesting the rheumy British climate that she spoke of so nostalgically.

Her husband, a Rhodes Scholar, was serving in the R.A.F. and she was left with four young children, and a hundred papers to mark every week. The girls ached for her wasting genius. The rolled-up handkerchief that she wound and unwound, the box of cough drops she fingered constantly, her legs like rubber that wrapped and unwrapped themselves about her chair were the only outward signs of tension that disturbed her otherwise glacial exterior, exposed what the girls had assigned as her secret torment, gave a presentiment of the tragedy that would ensue.

Mrs. Farmer *believed* in Jennie, looked with her lashless blue eyes into Jennie's fiercely bleeding heart and told her that she should channel the droplets into creative writing.

She read Jennie's poetry to the class and took it to faculty meetings and teas. Jennie was not sure if this was a good sign. She was mesmerized, and inspired to creative heights she had never before scaled — crashed to depths never before plumbed.

American history was taught by Miss Butler, a handsome and impressive-looking spinster whose heart (the girls said) was left behind on the fighting fields of Flanders and in the long-gone trenches of 1918, where her famous poet-brother and her fiancé were buried. She taught the history of World War I with a kind of quiet hysteria, interweaving it with the present war, and in her delicate, tremulous voice she read to the already dazzled school girls Rupert Brookes' "The Soldier":

> "*If I should die, think only this of me:*
> *That there's some corner of a foreign field*
> *That is forever England . . .*"

The aristocratic Madame de Landé taught French and was said to have mysterious connections with the Resistance. She was always talking about the Free French (Jennie had *always* thought of the French as free). Her husband was a celebrated artist, Jewish, and hiding out somewhere in France. Madame was said to have fainted in class when France fell, and when the Germans marched into Paris.

Mrs. Ricajee-Rau, the charming American wife of an Indian statesman and philosopher, taught Latin and was whispered to have been his mistress for years before they were married. Their two youngsters, attending the lower school, were considered somewhat "exotic," particularly since the girls carefully calculated that they were somewhat older than the marriage.

Art was taught by a mysterious and handsome Mexican Indian painter, already celebrated in his own country and quickly gaining world prominence, and the girls said he richly nurtured the genius of his most talented student, who studied "under" him.

All were *avowed* liberals in the full romantic sense of the word, all subscribed to the then celebrated words of Paul Robeson's song, "All races and religions, that's America to me."

Afternoons after school, Jennie rushed home and looked for a letter from Pete. Sometimes she ran into an out-of-work comedian from a defunct show, standing around the foyer of the apartment, waiting to see her father (who usually failed to show up), or a black group practicing in the "bar," noodling with the piano keys, laughing and smoking. Ordinarily she would stop to exchange jokes with the comedians; excited, impressed, she would let them do their *shtiks* with her to help them pass the time. But lately she only wanted to get away to the cool blue secrecy of her bedroom, flip on the radio and, to the music of an appropriate ballad, read Pete's letter — and dream. She'd close her eyes and try hard to remember the rapture of love, but she could not. She seemed able to resurrect only faint nuances of feeling in a detached sort of way. She wondered sadly how long the war would continue and worried that if it went on indefinitely she might fall out of love with him completely, and then what? Back to emptiness, and her former impoverished heart. The air force officers were romantic, with their peaked caps pulled daringly low over their eyes, like the doomed young fliers in the current Broadway hit *Winged Victory*. Peter Schore was romantic, but somehow not nearly doomed enough, she decided, no one could really consider him doomed, sitting out the war on a tiny atoll in the Pacific, in interminable boredom, safely out of harm's way.

In between the love songs were the realities, the endless bulletins totaling up the casualties, the fatalities in Europe, in the Pacific, all over the whole topsy-turvy world, in little-known places with unpronounceable names like Kwajalein, Guadalcanal, Iwo Jima —

exotic sounds, exploding suddenly, quickly assimilated into the daily conversation — They brought the war closer, and Pete with them, but it was a bitter way of reaching out to him — So she often turned back to the dance music.

Pete's letter today was a strange one, unusually serious and introspective, not casual and bantering, as they often were. He told Jennie that he had given her name and address, together with his parents', for notification in case of death or if he was missing in action. He told her also that he had sent her his wings. Her joy in this was tempered by the earlier part of his letter. It was hard to contemplate the death of a boy you loved, but hardly knew. She had rarely contemplated death. Why should she? For what reason? Besides, hadn't her mother always promised her immortality! When they were little she had promised them a heaven so perfect that it would far exceed anything Jennie had experienced here on earth, and when they grew older and asked the same time-worn question, she would say, "You're lucky to be young, by the time you're my age they will have discovered the secret of eternal life. You will never have to die, dying will be out of fashion."

40

CHRISTMAS SWIRLED DOWN Central Park West in furry white drifts. This year the children had defected from Jewish family tradition and chipped in their savings for a spectacular tree. Jennie felt sugar-coated all over with a delicious sense of Christmas. The songs from the Christmas pageant, oddly provocative with their sweet dissonance, filled her brain, pushing out even her favorite love songs and lush thoughts of Peter Schore.

They planned to decorate the tree on Christmas Eve, and Mamie would make one of her "gorgies," as the children called the huge company-style dinners she prepared, even when there was no company. Aaron, himself a small eater, insisted on it. An abundance of food was comforting to him. Eve said that was part of his campaign to woo the children, but it was more likely the ghetto-bred Jewish fear of an empty table. Jennie was terrified of getting fat, but could barely resist the temptations, particularly when her brothers and father went downstairs to the drugstore in the building and came back staggering under quarts of the rich, French ice cream that they carried exclusively. Then each sat down at the table with his quart container before him, his "castle," and proceeded to erect walls and battlements out of glasses and other table props to defend it from attack. A kind of Jewish jousting ensued, with spoons instead of lances. The boys and Aaron never seemed to put on a pound, but Jennie feared she might take after her mother and grandmother, and tried with Spartan will to keep out of the fray.

Eve spent much of her time now on the telephone, lecturing Jennie for hours on her duties toward a mother and her disloyalty for enjoying the benefits of life with father. After two hours of hanging on in a state of suspended animation, while homework loomed and the possibility of ever being contacted by the outside world dwindled, Jennie would hang up, her forehead drenched with perspiration, her head reeling from her mother's persistent suicide threats, only to face a refreshed onslaught of disapproval from Aaron, who had goaded her all during the conversation to hang up. As if she could ever get a word in even to say good-bye. Not even after the first hour had dragged by on leaden feet. Eve had long ago adopted the habit (she had more than adopted, it had begun to grow on her like an extra limb), common to Jewish mothers, of constantly whining and making of herself the martyr, the better to gain the attention of the children. But with her sons, especially, it produced the opposite effect and they succeeded in turning her off entirely.

Eve visited the apartment sporadically, but the kids usually had to clear the coast first. If she found Aaron there usurping her little scraps of attention from the children, there would be a blow up. Everyone had to tread tenderly when she was around to avoid extra confrontations.

Now, sitting around the elegant satinwood table in the dining room with the snow blowing about outside, Jennie felt for the moment, reckless. She didn't have to feel apprehensive about the ominous ring of the telephone because Eve was here with them, safely at the table, and she could enjoy her dinner without worrying where her mother was and what she was doing (she would probably have been *alone* on a night like this when everyone else had something planned with someone). Jennie did feel a bit guilty about making her father stay away from home tonight. It seemed that she would have to choose her guilts carefully these days.

Mamie bustled out with dessert, a huge apple cake smothered with whipped cream and she placed it ceremoniously on the table. At Mamie's entrance, Eve stiffened visibly.

"Is this the way you eat every night?" Eve said picking uncomfortably at the apple cake. "It's a wonder you don't get fat, Jennie. But I guess you don't really eat it, you just pick at it — and I eat my lonely meal in my room (or worse still, downstairs in the dining room, alone), afraid to order anything but the cheapest item on the menu." Jennie, in a last desperate attempt to sidetrack her mother's avalanche, said, "How do you like the tree, Mother?"

"Well — I thought you asked me over to help trim the tree, Jenna, but I see it's all done already. Did you do it all by yourselves?"

"Well, Mamie kind of helped us too," Reid chimed in.

Eve pursed her mouth, tightening her lips over her teeth.

Jennie felt trapped. As if to compensate her mother somehow for this disappointment, she hurried on. "You know I told Daddy he can't come home tonight, that it was *your* night."

"M-m-m, I'm sure he was heartbroken," Eve remarked drily. "Well, Christmas is *her* holiday anyway, it's only fitting that he spend it with *her*."

Jennie didn't like the way she said *her*. It always made her fidget. Who was *her* anyway, just some figment of her mother's febrile imagination.

"He breast-stroked in three!" Evan was shrieking.

"He did like heck," Reid said. "*I* swam the only record last week and you know it!"

Jennie thought, annoyed, those two at it again, Reid so competitive, Evan so bookish, always lagging a little behind, trying to keep up, to impress his father, to get a rise out of him. It seldom worked, only Reid seemed able to do that. Little happy-go-lucky Reid who just couldn't seem to grow up without his props — dragging his toys and *collections* behind him all the way.

Eve leaned over to Evan and tenderly pushed his floppy hair out of his eyes.

"Have any Latin homework tonight? Maybe I could help you with it."

"No, it's a holiday now, you know, I'm all caught up on it, anyway."

Eve looked disappointed again. "Still keeping up that 95 average?"

"Yeah, specially in Latin," Evan said falteringly, ever anxious to play down his scholastic achievements, lest it detract from his athletic ones.

Eve had just transferred them to a fine, all-boys prep school and Evan was doing extremely well. She made no secret of her preference for this child, who, she declared openly, "is much like me," and had tried through the years to stuff him with opera, ballet and art. His feelings for these lofty enrichments seemed ambivalent, although he was the only one that Eve could find to sit all the way through a Wagnerian opera with her — a five-hour stint with the *Ring of the Niebelungen*.

As soon as they had bolted the dessert the boys asked, "Can I be excused?" (already half out of their seats), on their more formal behavior with their mother who was, after all, a guest.

"Can't you just sit a bit and talk to me for a while — infrequently as I come to eat here." They sat down reluctantly, teetering back and forth on the chair legs.

The boys began to talk about the ice cream jamborees (as they called them) with their father. They talked about basketball on the beach in summers and jumping the big waves with Aaron.

"Hey, I bet you two dopes don't even remember the summer when we drove to New England and Daddy got so lost and Mother wanted to ask directions at the gas station and he said 'No, we'd find our way somehow' — and we ended up back in New York."

Jennie turned toward Eve. "You remember, Mother, don't you?" she said urgently.

"*I* remember!" Evan said. "That was fun, and Da-Daddy made a contest with li-little colored kids eating watermelon with their hands tied behind their backs." Evan still stuttered when under any sort of pressure.

"No, no, it was blueberry pies," Eve said, suddenly alive. Jennie looked at her mother, happy at her inclusion.

"I wish it had been lemon meringue," Reid said, bobbing up and down and rubbing his stomach. "And, and remember," Eve said, laughing, "that funny little rooming house we stayed in where the curtains were all torn and there were only two big beds in the room for the five of us!"

"Like a haunted house," Jennie took up the narrative, fearful of letting it dissolve. "And — and the boys got terrible sunburns, and all three of us had to sleep in one bed — except nobody could sleep because of the pain and the smell of Noxzema." Jennie stopped breathlessly in midstream. She thought she saw tears in her mother's eyes. Eve put her head in her hands then and began to sob. Her shoulders shook, the overbright chandelier above spotlighting her harshly.

"I just don't want to go back to that room again. I'm so — so lonely. Being here with my children, it's — it's just all the more painful," she said between sobs. Jennie wanted to ask her to sleep here tonight, but feared Aaron's reaction.

Just then Mamie came in to remove the dessert dishes.

"Mrs. Abel, is everything all right? Is there anything I can do?"

"It seems to me you've done enough already!" Eve said, straightening up.

"Now, what do you mean by that?"

Oh God, Jennie thought, please God, not these two, it would be dreadful! Decisions, choices — the divided loyalties were now beginning to break down into insolvable fractions.

"You know damn well what I mean."

The boys murmured a hasty "May I be excused" and ran from the room. Mamie slammed back silently into the kitchen, leaving Jennie, as always, to stem the tide.

"Mother, let's go into the living room where there's some privacy. Why does Mamie have to hear all our business?"

"Oh stop your shivering for her. I don't give a damn about her," Eve said extra loudly. "The hell with her. Don't feel sorry for her; feel sorry for me. I'm the one on the outside looking in — She lives better than I do — She has a place to be and a *family* to be with on holidays — my family."

Jennie got up, feeling weak, and began walking quickly down the long foyer toward the living room, the bright lights and baubles of the tree beckoning sanctuary. She thought dizzily of the Christmas pageant, the way the lights of the Inn must have looked to Mary, "great with child." She heard her mother stomping after her. She could hear Eve's immense silence in the background.

Once in the living room, Eve sat down in a soft chair. Jennie fooled nervously with something on the tree. She didn't want to look at her mother right now. Eve had lately developed a different way of sitting which irritated her. Her hands resting resignedly in her lap, her thighs discarded in hopeless abandon — *Seated Defeat*, Jennie called this pose secretly, as if it were a piece of prize sculpture. "Why are you so down on Mamie?" Jennie ventured.

"Stop taking her part — take mine for a change."

"I'm *not* taking her part, but she really didn't say anything unpleasant to you tonight, Mother!"

"She's haughty and hostile, haughty because she's given too much importance here — out of all proportion — and hostile because she's smart enough to sense the family's hostility to me."

"Oh, Mother — who's hostile?"

"Being weakly defensive will not change anything," Eve replied tartly.

Mamie came flying out of the kitchen, bringing Eve's heavy, overstuffed purse, and plunked it down in the living room. "You left this in the dining room, Mrs. Abel, I'm sure you'll be wanting it," she said sweetly.

It seemed to Jennie that Mamie was being unusually sweet. She almost expected to hear "Sugar Baby" at the end of the sentence. Eve refused to look at her and just stared straight ahead.

"C'mon, let's work on the tree," Jennie said to no one in particular.

Mamie made some suggestions about the tree looking a little lopsided. "It needs more stuff around the sides and back," she said, standing off and surveying from a distance, her hands on her hips officiously.

This gesture seemed to infuriate Eve, and she said, "Do you mind if *we* decide, *the family*, just how a thing should look or not. As it is, the tree was all decorated before *I* got here!"

"Well, that's no fault of mine, I assure you, Mrs. Abel, and as far as the family's concerned, I do pride myself on being considered a part of it in a way — " Until now, Mamie had used her honey-sugared voice, soft against Eve's deep contralto, but now her voice was becoming steely and trembled slightly on the low notes.

Eve snorted. "In a way! In a very *large* way, I would say. Well, if you don't mind we'll finish without you. I'm sure there's something that can be done here without you."

"Not very much," Mamie mumbled, still standing by the tree, her back to Eve.

"In my day, servants didn't always have the last word," Eve said furiously. "They knew their place."

Mamie swung around angrily. "Well, this is not 'your day' — and listen, you, I've had just about enough, quite enough. You've been jibing at me and hurling insults around here all night. I just don't have to take this from you. You're not my boss and you're not paying me either."

Eve jumped up and went to where Mamie stood under the tree and called her a "black bitch."

"Who you calling a black bitch? Why, in your heart you're blacker 'n anybody. Shit, you're a selfish woman making everybody 'round here miserable all the time."

Suddenly Eve reached to grab at Mamie.

She ducked, and Eve found herself tearing at Mamie's hair.

"Don't you pull my hair," Mamie screamed and grabbed a handful of Eve's hair. They pushed and shoved at whatever parts they could grasp, and the tree on its delicate base swayed ominously. Jennie, weak and trembling, ran out of the living room just as the tree came hurtling down in a shower of blinding glitter.

She was torn between shame and a sickening compulsion to grab her mother and slap her face until she drew blood, to join Mamie in tearing at her hair. God, this must be madness, she thought, and was stunned by the humiliation.

The boys had run in and stood looking forlornly at the tree. "The tree — everything's broken!" Reid said. "Everything!" and he began jumping up and down and punching his brother, in a trancelike fury — like Rumpelstiltskin.

(41)

AARON HATED TO ADMIT IT even to himself, but Eve was right: He was running scared lately. Scared about being drafted (oh, not afraid of fighting; he doubted that they would send him, at forty-four years old, into the thick of things, though he *was* in the pink), but scared about leaving right in the middle of the best business he'd done, while the going was so good, better than ever before. He was scared about audits by the Internal Revenue, about the government's threat to outlaw gratuities, about the vast amounts of cash he was taking in from some thirty concessions — where could he stash it so that it wouldn't be found and wouldn't be stolen? — scared that the girls were stealing from him, no matter how carefully the checkers watched the checkers. Scared that he wasn't making it work with the children, with Jennie, whose approval he wanted more than any other single thing.

He learned in pieces the story concerning the Christmas Eve fiasco at the apartment — from the boys, from Mamie's stiff-necked silences in the days that followed (she wouldn't tell him outright — she was too wise). Aaron was furious and would have liked to do something concrete, something to put an end to the constant scenes that seemed to be eviscerating Jennie, driving Evan inward, silent in his refuge of books, or Reid to his stamps and endless collections.

But he felt, as always, where Eve was concerned, impotent, plagued by unnamed guilts. He talked to Jennie often about "what to do about Mother," sounding her out on the subject of talking Eve into getting help, encouraging her to check into a hospital, or even *imposing* hospitalization on her.

And still he really didn't want to precipitate anything quite so definite, for fear that Jennie might add this up to one more resentment. He was in the same self-imposed bind that he had trapped himself in for most of his life. His own worst enemy, he was fated to be in constant turmoil, torn between love and money.

*

Aaron had just advanced about fifty thousand dollars for the concession at the gorgeous new Latin Quarter in New York, the most he had paid for any one concession thus far. Lou Walters, the proprietor, was said to be the new Billy Rose and Flo Ziegfeld combined. Like the two men before him, he was small in stature but he had immense energy. He had recently been responsible for

producing a new Ziegfeld Follies on Broadway, in association with
the powerful Shuberts. He had come to New York after a
spectacular success in Boston, bringing with him his stunning
French girlie extravaganza. The club was grossing about a million
a year. Aaron, who had little overhead compared to management's
huge "nut," was grossing almost as much in cold cash. He did not
consider it war profiteering; the thought would not enter his mind.
After all, somebody had to do it, and the servicemen were having
a ball — so if anything, he felt patriotic.

Because of the ferocious competition, a number of Broadway
clubs were threatened with going under. Aaron was right there to
bail them out, to take over the club, often with the provision that
the entrepreneur stay on to run it. In this manner, little by little
he insinuated himself into the geography of the city. Piece by
piece he was buying up New York.

*

Aaron jumped out in front of the Club Martinique and slammed
the car door impatiently.

"Drive her around until she sobers up," he told Vic, who was
miraculously still at the wheel, having survived five years of acro-
batic manipulation between all the factions of the family. Lately
Aaron had him working a couple of days a week in the apartment,
as houseman, assisting Mamie, scrupulously following her crisply
given orders, dusting chandeliers, washing carpets. Eve's comment
to Jennie was that he was getting his just deserts for being "a
panderer to Aaron and his paramour."

In the back seat Martha smoked a cigarette furiously and complained to Vic in a voice husky with alcohol. "This is ridiculous!
I want to get out — he promised to take me with him. Doesn't he
think I like to get out once in a while too?" She was slurring her
words badly now, and she couldn't seem to remember exactly what
point she was trying to make. "Buried out there alone in the
goddamn sticks, alone day and night — I'd'a been better off
marrying Jack Hanlan, he owned a big dance hall near Philly, he's
still after me if you really wanna know — " She was silent for a

moment, as if recharging for a fresh assault. "I was looking forward to this all week, Vic — Hey, Vic, ya hear me? I'm talking to you," she said.

"Yes, ma'am. Well, we'll just go for a short drive and I'll have you back to the club in a jiffy. The boss has to talk business there anyway and you'd only be sitting around alone."

"So what's new about that? Anyway I have a couple of drinks, listen to the music, I like swing music, see the show — beats sitting in those hotel rooms alone every night." She was suddenly quiet.

After a moment, Vic looked at her in his rearview mirror and saw that she was fast asleep sitting up.

Aaron ran down the stairs to the basement club and as soon as he pushed open the massive padded doors the din hit him, a sudden, sickening drone that struck him as if he had collided with a beehive. For how many years had he been experiencing this odd sensation, this gripping in the belly each time he entered a club, inhaled the thick, sour air, ingested the frenzy of movement on the dance floor, of bodies whirling and writhing? He was really ill suited to this business, this life, these places. The whole atmosphere seemed forced, mechanical to him. He could not imagine why people fought to come to these places, scratched, saved, and bribed to get into a nightclub; he only wanted to get his business over with and get out. He would have much preferred to be home with the children. They were growing up so fast, Jennie graduating from high school, going off to college — he'd missed most of their childhood. What a shambles his life had become, he thought. Eve was just the sort of woman he could have been so happy with, yet here he was with that boozed-up broad out in the car — And still he had fun with Martha. The kind of fun he never really had before — crazy, irresponsible, sensuous pleasures he'd never even heard of — well, maybe he'd heard about them. There wasn't much you didn't hear about if you hung around *that* street long enough.

He pushed his way through a maze of people at the entrance to the room. The lines were two-deep and wound halfway up the staircase. He murmured something to the harassed captain and pushed through, almost colliding head-on with a waiter carrying a table high in the air to fill in — he couldn't imagine where, there wasn't a spot in the room that wasn't occupied. Past the bar four-deep in khaki, the air heady with cigarette smoke and perfume and lipstick odors. Everyone seemed to be tumbled on top of each other in glorious confusion. An intimate conspiracy, they struggled happily for a bite of the thick blue velvet air. Thank God for Jason and some of the other boys he'd hired. He'd been lucky with them, loyal guys, hard workers. This was usually their job, but tonight he had to talk to the boss, to Barbero. He'd kill two birds with one stone, check the receipts, let Barbero know that he took a personal interest, really cared.

Christ, it was warm for late May, thank God for air conditioning. It was a recent innovation, without it his business could die alto-gether; as it is, it nearly died in summers — and they were talking of cutting out air conditioning altogether in order to conserve energy for the war effort, the final big push against the Japs. Jesus, this was a tricky business, depended on so many outside factors, hung by so fragile a thread as the human emotions — the collective mood! Like now — wartime — every night was like New Year's Eve, as if each night might be the last, and it just might be for some of these poor bastards. He looked around at the sea of khaki. On the dance floor couples were pressed up very close to one another, as if seeking comfort from the proximity.

He knew the war was rushing to a conclusion; the Germans were expected to capitulate any day. And he knew too, that cabarets flourish in hard times. There would be another few good years of postwar boom and then, then a gentle ebbing, and then nothing. That's why he was here tonight, he wanted something more tangible than what he got at the wispy whim of the club or restaurant proprietor; he wanted the property itself: *That* — the land — wouldn't blow away after the war but would, he was sure, go up in price like a Roman candle.

The maracas were off the beat tonight, and the drums a toneless jungle throb he thought as he pushed his way into the little back office of Bill Barbero, the club's owner. Bill, a heavyset but not unattractive man, sat at his desk with his ear to the telephone while another receiver lay on the desk off the hook. Aaron was unruffled. He lived his own life via the constant rasp of the telephone and knew that everyone else in the business did the same. He sat patiently tonight while Bill finished his business and hung up both phones, only to have them begin ringing all over again.

Aaron slumped down in his chair, gave Bill a cheerless greeting, and commented on the fantastic business they were doing.

"It's like that all over the street," Bill said complacently.

"I know — so what do you need me for?" Aaron said. The phone rang again, providing a convenient pause for Barbero. When he hung up he removed the two receivers from their cradles and laid them on the desk, where they proceeded to whistle and beep irritably.

"It's not that I need you, Abel, you understand, I don't really need anyone for that matter." (That had a familiar ring, Aaron thought.) "We're making money hand over fist here, you've seen that yourself. It's just that I don't like that dumb bastard Holtz who's in here with me. I wanna buy him out, the sooner the better — he's gotta go and I ain't got the dough on hand right now."

"Why you must be making a fortune here — "

"Yeah, but I ain't got the cash, been putting every cent back into this joint — " (and into the ponies, Aaron thought to himself). "No, you're the guy with the cash, you're a walking cash register — with no way for the government to check up on you, no way at all," he said obliquely. Aaron was not sure whether to be angry or flattered at these last remarks.

Aaron said, "What seems to be the difficulty between you and Holtz?"

Barbero shifted uncomfortably in his seat, smoothed his dark hair back with a hand that displayed a prominent star sapphire. "Well I know he's been clipping me for one thing, and then, too, there are other things. He's got too many irons in the fire, don't pay enough attention to this place."

Aaron was thinking that this was a good piece of ground, he'd like to own it. It really only meant paying a little more for the concessions, but he'd have to check Barbero out first. He'd heard rumors — he didn't want, in any way, to get involved with *them* again, with the Boys. He was riding free and easy now, didn't have to answer to anyone, it wouldn't pay for him now — it would be crazy. Bad enough the government was breathing down his neck.

"You can have your accountant go over the books of course."

Aaron heard him, but was unimpressed. He knew that didn't mean a thing; there were a million ways of falsifying the books if they wanted to screw around. He'd have to check it out — Was Holtz really getting out, or would he remain a silent partner in the background? Yes, he'd have to do some careful checking. As always when he was about to make a deal, he was plagued by suspicions and tortured by mistrust. He lived in a terror of being taken, and yet it had rarely, if ever, happened. Excepting, of course, that time with Rose, and what really bothered him most about that was not that there was any dishonesty involved. In all fairness, it was mostly that he could not bear to be *outsmarted* in a deal.

In the midst of this abrasive discussion, the door opened and Martha walked uncertainly into the room. She was wearing an unremarkable dress, too long and a bit out of style. Aaron made a mental note to get her something more presentable.

He looked by turns surprised and embarrassed. "Listen," she said, "I can't drive around all night, I'm getting car sick. Whaddya think this is?" She sat down in the remaining chair.

Aaron made a hasty introduction. "Okay," he said. "Please wait for me outside. I'll only be a minute — "

"No." She was emphatic. "I don't wanna stand at that bar alone. Ya can't sit there, it's impossible — "

"Why don't we just get up and go inside and have a drink and see the show," Barbero said, grinning and obviously enjoying the whole thing immensely.

Aaron was about to protest, but what was the use; it could only become more embarrassing with her in that condition. He shot her a furious glance, his eyes looking luridly blue in a face suffused with red. She looked back at him undaunted.

"The show'll go on in a short while, and we can still talk a little there," Barbero said obligingly.

"Yeah, that's better. Let's talk a little, have a few drinks, see a show like other people," she said as she rose to go. "Ya gotta learn to live a little, Aaron," she said, touching his arm intimately. There was a sharp reek of perfume as she preceded them from the room.

Aaron was thinking irritably to himself. I should have let her marry that guy who had the ballroom business. It was all set, why did I stop her, why — He was remembering how, two years before, she had come to him, told him her plans for a wedding in a month, and how he had frozen up, panicked, begged her to stay. He had offered her anything not to go through with it, anything but marriage. He'd never even asked Eve for a divorce, he desperately didn't want it. He couldn't start all over again — not now — he was too tired. But he had promised Martha anything she wanted that was material, and he had promised security, that is, *fidelity*. He'd promised to stay with her, always. That was not necessarily an impossible commitment for him. He was not a womanizer. But it was she who ran the risk of having him bound to her, not by love, but by his enormous guilt. He remembered her crying, and then they had made love differently, gently and with less anger.

He had never thought to ask why she had made this sacrifice for him, because he really didn't consider it a sacrifice. *She* had chosen. He had never stopped to question himself about whether she really loved him; he took it for granted, dues owed for the benefits he provided. He didn't even realize that she was head over heels in love with him. When she complained about eating dinners alone most nights, having no fun, no companionship, he answered, "for chrissakes, I've got three children over there." Well, he wouldn't feel guilty anymore. Why should he? After all, how could she do any better? She got the *boss*, a damn sight better than winding up with that Hanlan kid — she would have been alone nights anyway — or worse still, standing on her feet all night working with him. Sure Hanlan was younger, not encumbered by the past as he was, torn and shredded by the duality of his life, by the cross-currents of his inclinations — to make money — to be ruthless — to be benevolent — to be father, to be son, to give and, while giving, to fear being "taken." Where a complex girl had failed to sustain the schisms of life with him, a simpler girl hoped to succeed. Aaron hoped too, even more — but so far he had doubts.

The show would feature a famous stand-up comic. Aaron had seen him a hundred times since the old burlesque where most of them got their start. As he walked toward the table, he wished devoutly that tonight he could get out of going into the pits (as he and his employees called the frenetic interior of these basement clubs), that he could go home and go to sleep. They approached a ringside table, obviously the boss's table.

Aaron tried telling Barbero that he'd seen Henny Youngman a dozen times and would prefer to let a customer sit there, that he'd be perfectly happy to sit upstairs out of the way — but Martha said this was just perfect and why not let her enjoy her night out, even if it did begin when Aaron was ready to go home. The moment they were seated, a waiter appeared like a genie. Everyone else had been frantically signaling waiters, but to no avail.

She put her forefinger in her scotch and stirred thoughtfully as if searching hard for something in the ice cubes.

Bill Barbero, in an attempt to be polite and charming, turned to her and asked:

"So, what do you do with yourself?"

"Me, huh," she said, "mostly what you saw me doin' tonight — wait around for him — " she indicated Aaron with a toss of her head.

Bill grinned, he was really beginning to enjoy this. "No, really, do you work?"

"I used to check, but I'm, well — let's just say I'm retired."

"You look pretty young to me to be retired, what do you think of checking?" he asked.

"Thinking didn't much enter into it. I mean you did your job, you know?"

"Does he really give you girls such a hard time?" he said loudly, so Aaron would hear it above the racket. "I mean, did he really watch you like a hawk?"

Aaron laughed uncomfortably. "Well, he usually gets a fair shake from us girls," she said drily. "We throw the coins up in the air, see, and whatever sticks to the ceiling is his and the rest is ours." Barbero guffawed loudly, then doubled up with laughter.

Aaron smiled a bit too, he knew it was an old joke among the girls, although it touched a sensitive nerve.

"Now let's finish our business, Bill, because I doubt that I'll be able to stick out the whole show. I'm beat."

"Gee, is he always like this?" Bill said to Martha. "He's got ants in his pants — "

"That's Aaron A. okay," she said and signaled the waiter for another drink.

Barbero had been drinking right along with her, while Aaron sucked angrily at his lemonade. "Why don't you guys use fresh lemon juice, this stuff tastes like what we use to disinfect the men's room."

"Well when *you* own the joint you can fix all that," he said, and continued to goad Martha, who had quickly thrown down the last drink and was shifting around her line-up of shot glasses like Mah-Jongg tiles.

"Guess you turned in plenty of tips in your day, beautiful."

"Turned down plenty too," she said — Another bellow from Barbero.

"Jeeze, she's in rare form tonight — she always like this?" Without waiting for Aaron's answer, he continued, "Listen, do you miss it?"

"It? What? Oh the business, ya mean — " More laughter.

"Ya know," she said ruminating, "when you think of it, checking *is* a little like sex. You can never run out of it, you just keep using the same old thing over and over again — " And she added as an extra fillip, "And then you get the tip." She laughed heartily, richly enjoying her own joke. Bill, looking over at Aaron's sober red face, decided that he'd better tone down his appreciation a little.

Aaron was furious now, but managed to control himself by shifting around in his chair, and, finally slumping down into it, he glared into his now watery lemonade. The orchestra was gathering for the last show. The Latin band was thumping and clanking discordantly while getting their instruments together to leave.

He had no intention of sitting through an hour-long show,
it was already 1:45. He could see it wasn't any use hammering at
it any longer with Barbero. He could probably get the deal if he
wanted it, and he wasn't so sure he wanted to be in partnership
with him. He could get a dozen other places like it, they'd be folding up left and right in another year or two. Maybe he could get
Barbero to sell to him outright. He always hated partnerships.

"Look, pal, I've gotta get some shuteye. We'll kick it around
on the phone some more tomorrow, okay?" Aaron said.

"Where are ya rushing, the little lady wants to see the show — "

"Yeah, I know, well that's the way it is. The little lady's seen
plenty of shows and she's got a whole lifetime more to see 'em."

He pulled her up onto her feet harshly. Barbero stood up too,
made a polite if somewhat facetious farewell speech to Martha.

Once the fresh air hit her she began to wobble more unsteadily
than before. Aaron, still wordless, was looking down the street for
Vic. He spotted him parked a small distance away.

Without stopping to give Vic the instructions, he began to talk
to Martha in a menacing low voice.

"If you ever pull a stunt like that again, humiliate me in front of
somebody from business — anybody — I'll drop you like a hot
potato, promises or no promises," he said. "You understand? You
made a goddam horse's ass of yourself, do you know that?"

"Oh yeah? Maybe *she'd* come off better with your *fancy* business
people, maybe you don't have to be ashamed of *her*."

"Who's *her*," he said annoyed.

"You know, *her*, your wife?"

"Oh shut up about her, what's that got to do with anything
now — "

"Pardon me, Mr. A.," Vic said, "but are we going home?"

"Yeah, sure."

"Naw, let's go somewhere 'n have a drink." He slapped her hard
across the face. She reeled back, shocked. He had never raised his
hand to a woman, he prided himself on that, though God only
knows he had been sorely tempted in those early years with Eve,
but now all the ambivalence of this relationship culminated in that

physical release — and it was somehow cathartic — he felt better instantly.

"Oh fix your hair," he said in a quieter voice now. "Look at yourself, for chrissakes, your eyes are all red, and you reek of alcohol. Don't you have any sense at all? A man like me, I'm ashamed."

"Yeah, I know you deserve better than me." He wasn't even sure that she was being sarcastic. "And I deserve better too, I don't mind giving up marriage — kids — a real life — but Jesus, I can't even go to confession anymore, my mother and sisters don't even bother asking me to go to the goddam church with them on Sunday anymore. It's like they gave up on me — "

He ignored the outburst, not fully comprehending. As she spoke he winced visibly. He found the combined odors of tobacco and alcohol on a woman's breath distinctly distasteful.

They were silent. She seemed to have suddenly sobered up and was looking out the window disconsolately. He thought to himself with annoyance that he probably wouldn't even be able to get it up for her tonight. He was turned off — tired — but there was always the morning. She liked it in the morning.

(42)

DURING THE SPRING of 1945, it seemed to Jennie that the entire world was caving in on her at once. All that had been comfortable and familiar in her life during these last four years seemed to be blowing away like milkweed.

At school there was a frenzy of preparation for graduation, weekly talks in the principal's office about college — "orientation meetings" was the official label. Acceptances were coming in daily, and the girls, who had grown too much together with the years (some since kindergarten), were being dispersed all over the country. Jennie had been accepted at her first choice, the University of Buffalo, well known for its literature and language program.

She thought vaguely about her future — a career as a teacher, a journalist perhaps — but her life kept getting in the way. In an unconscious effort to rewrite her parents' lives, she became obsessed by love, possessed by it, so that she could make no concrete plans for her life other than romantic ones.

The end of the war was in sight. This meant reckoning with Pete, the reality, not the dream. The war in itself had been a kind of security blanket for her, with everyone thoroughly united under one banner, united in hate, against the common enemy, toward one mutual goal — survival. There had been clearly definable limits. And the home front — bathed in the rose water of shared love and pain. She felt as if she had been wrapped in cotton for four years. For Jennie, who lived in fractions of the whole and amid uncertain allegiances, this had been security.

Her mother was disappearing before her eyes — drifting out of life — and Franklin Roosevelt, her strength and her redeemer for as long as she could remember, had died suddenly, leaving them in the hands of a virtual stranger. Jennie's security fell in triple folds of diminishing power — FDR — Fiorello LaGuardia — Aaron Abel. She felt naked, shorn.

Shortly after graduation she learned that Mrs. Farmer had thrown herself from the window of her fourth-floor apartment, leaving her husband the legacy of four children. She kept thinking of her terribly blue and lashless eyes . . . There were only rumors to go on, something about severe melancholia brought on by overwork — and disappointment.

(43)

JENNIE AND HER MOTHER descended gratefully into the cool tomb of the subway, a sanctuary from the furnacelike late June air. Jennie put a penny in the Suchard machine and retrieved her prize, a neatly wrapped tiny packet of royal blue. Bittersweet chocolate. Her favorite flavor. Bittersweet fit her mood today.

June was particularly bitter for Eve — the long, lonely summer was stretching out ahead like a desert without oasis. But for Jennie it was bittersweet. She was torn between the sheer animal exuberance of contemplating a summer at the shore — at the new beach house — and thinking of her mother in the deserted city, stifling alone in her tiny room "looking at the four walls," or floating around the thick-smelling streets with the assorted flotsam and jetsam left behind — Her own life seemed to float like sea anemones on an ocean of her mother's salty tears. She watched Eve forcing herself through the balance of her life like pulp through a sieve. God, how she too hated city summers; they were enough to break the healthiest psyche. She had a prescient feeling that all that was bitter in her life would take place under an angry broiling sun.

A few months before, Aaron had purchased a summer home, a lovely old decaying white elephant. It had come to him the way most things did in his life. Borne on the wings of distress, it had fallen into his lap for a song.

Aaron was growing to enjoy his role as father, or single parent, and he played it to the hilt. He relished hearing the oft-repeated "Isn't it sweet? Busy as he is how he drops everything at six o'clock and rushes home to eat dinner with his children." He was sorry that Jennie would be going away to college in the fall. He had fought it, gently, careful not to alienate her and always conscious of the fact that she ought to get away from the pressures of Eve and her problems.

As part of the price that Jennie extracted from herself for those guilty pleasures, like those summers at the shore, she accompanied her mother downtown on her infrequent shopping trips. It was becoming increasingly difficult for Eve to buy clothes. Her weight, combined with her financial insecurities, sent her crawling (*"Krichn,"* as she called it — a pithy translation into Yiddish) to the bowels of the stores, foraging for bargains in the Women's Department, where she would try on shapeless bags that Jennie secretly thought looked like Eleanor Roosevelt's rejects.

The BMT Local roared to a stop. They both made an almost involuntary move toward the rear of the car, where there was a tiny private compartment for two, the trainman's seat.

"Look, Mother, it's free," Jennie said with a kind of false cheer.

"Oh good, grab it."

With mixed emotions, Jennie led the way past a sea of wilting readers and rumpled newspapers.

She usually felt comfortable in the little dark cubicle; it seemed a small island of peace in the battle of the day. But today it might be the battleground instead, she thought, closeted in here alone with her mother in her present mood. She knew her habit of proselytizing in any moving vehicle, taking advantage of her captive audience.

"Well it's cool and private here anyway," Jennie said hopefully.

"Isn't it sad that things have come to this. I have to ride the subways to get out of the heat," Eve began immediately today, without the familiar prologues.

"Are you sure you want to go shopping today, I mean all the way downtown to Altman's in this heat?" Jennie asked.

"Where else am I going to go? It's something to do, and at least I'm not doing it alone for a change, *and* it's air-conditioned in the stores — my *room* isn't."

"Mother, you could go away almost anywhere you want to, you know that."

"Alone, always alone, where would I go? Besides, I can't spend the money."

"Dad would give you the money, he said so."

"He's a liar, that's just talk to impress you. He tells you one thing and me another. Anyway, I'm tired of doing everything alone."

"Wouldn't your friend Marcy go with you?" Then Jennie thought, why did I say that, that was cruel.

"Oh you know she wouldn't leave her husband for a minute — That's right, shove me off on Marcy. Just as long as *you* don't have to be burdened. Just as long as you can run away to your father's fancy home at the beach, and to hell with me sweltering here! Summers are so long," she added plaintively. "When are you going away anyway?"

A loud silence from Jennie. Then in a softer voice Eve said, "Will you have dinner with me tonight?"

Jennie was silent, staring hard into the blackness. In a tiny voice, further muffled by the carniverous roar of the subway, she said, "Well today *is* Friday, we were sort of planning to go out to — the . . ." She faltered again and almost whispered the word "house". . ."for the weekend."

"You'll be going there for over two months soon. Can't you leave after dinner, can't you give up *something* for me?"

"Yes, well, maybe, but Dad is driving out around six — "

"What if he went a few hours later? Or would it be so terrible if you took a train, you're almost eighteen years old you know — I take plenty of trains!"

They went through a tunnel for a moment, all the lights blinked out. She couldn't see her mother's face, but she heard her voice —

"After all how many meals can I eat alone at Childs, the food sticking in my throat, to be washed down by my own tears."

Eve's quaint Dickensian phrasing peppered with her earthy Yiddishisms always struck Jennie as a false note and caused her sympathies to waver precariously. We are *both* choking on her loneliness, she thought. She wanted to cry out, "Mama, I know how

lonely you are. I have ingested it for years. You will not be satisfied until I wear it like a cloak, until it envelops me, swallows up
my life." I know that I *should* ask her out to the beach house this
weekend, that's what she really wants, she thought. But somehow
the words stuck in her throat. It was as if she were afraid that her
mother's loneliness was contagious. And then, too, she was blocked
by the now open feud with Mamie. As if reading her mind, Eve
continued, "Don't you think that I like a home-cooked meal once
in a while? It's claustrophobic living in one room for two years.
But even there my children have chosen a colored maid over me."
Eve paused hopefully as if awaiting some answer from Jennie, but
there was only silence. And then in a quiet voice she said, "I feel
like a beggar, it's humiliating to have to come to one's child for
emotional handouts, to beg for companionship, but tonight I feel
that I just can't eat another meal alone — Oh what's the use — why
don't I just throw myself from a window and make it easier for
everyone concerned?"

"Mother," Jennie said, not unfamiliar with Eve's threats, "don't
say things like that."

"What you really mean is, do it if you must but just don't talk
about it, don't involve *you*."

She saw it was useless to protest — or was there a vestige of truth
in it? She didn't know anything anymore.

As they entered the store Jennie thought how much this store
suited her mother, archaic, a sort of sad place with its honest
scrubbed-wood floors, its innocent, uncomplicated counters. Eve
walked aimlessly up and down the aisles, looking at nothing in particular. They wandered around a bit more and then drifted downstairs to Women's.

Eve floundered dazedly between the racks while Jennie trailed
behind, making small nervous sounds of enthusiasm about one or
the other garments. "Look, Mother, here's an attractive black dress,
some nice detailing on the skirt." She thought guiltily of her own
snappy high-styled clothes from uptown stores like Bergdorf and
Bendel. Eve glanced at it dispiritedly. "I'm getting so tired of living in black, I'm beginning to feel like a Sicilian matron."

Suddenly Eve was weeping, standing in a forest of racks, un-
abashedly weeping, her shoulders shaking —

"Mother, what is it?"

"What is it," she said through her tears, "it's my life, that's
what it is!"

She began walking through the aisles sobbing. People were turning. A stout saleslady hurried up to them and asked if she could
help. Jennie shook her head mutely and hurried along beside Eve,
who continued walking blindly into Women's Girdles. "Mama,
Mama, stop please, stop — this is crazy, let's go to the ladies' room
or somewhere we can sit — "

In the ladies' lounge they fell into a corner sofa and, amid carbolic odors, they sat for an uncomfortable moment in numbing
silence. Eve drew a ragged sigh and tried wiping her eyes, but the
tears kept oozing out of the corners, dropping on her heavy bosom.

Jennie kept hearing Mrs. Farmer's reedy voice reciting Keats —
"But when the melancholy fit shall fall . . . then glut thy sorrow
on a morning rose . . . or on the wealth of globed peonies." Even
here Eve was foiled — it "fell" in the ladies' lounge and she was
forced to glut her sorrow on the wealth of Lysol disinfectant.

"Look, Mother," she said with a quiet desperation, "there must
be something we can do," once again assuming the role of Little
Mother that she had so often adopted or which had been thrust
upon her through the years.

"I, I don't know," Eve said vacantly. "If only I had chosen a
career, I might have had some life now — some substance, admiration, companionship, but this way — I'm so alienated from everything — from life." She seemed to have forgotten that she used
to say that successful people were usually the loneliest in the world.
"And the war," she continued, in a flood of catharsis, "to be lonely
in the middle of a war is to be excommunicated from mankind.
Everyone is so involved, the women, so saturated with it — with
their men . . . I just seem to float above it all, a bystander to
life . . . I've always felt cut off from the sisterhood of women —
never completely understood them with their man-craziness — their
predatory instincts. I've never known what it feels like to be cher-

ished by a man . . ." She dropped her voice an octave now . . .
"never even had an orgasm — "

Jennie reddened and looked about her guiltily — her mother's
voice carried in any octave. She didn't know much about *that*
either — only that it was something you were *supposed* to have,
but she did know instantly what she meant about wartime.

. . . How the women talked knowledgeably, possessively, of the
war, of its battlefields, how proudly they sported their wings or
other tokens of loving and losing. She thought of Pete's wings at
home in her drawer, nestling in her lingerie, and wondered, pan-
icky, am I as unsexed as she is . . . Or was she? . . . Perhaps that
was only her father's propaganda to cover up for his own inade-
quacies. Had passion swept through her like fire, extinguishing
itself with him, taking everything with it in its intensity, reducing
all else to ashes?

She had always suspected that her mother had been deeply in
love with Aaron, once — perhaps still was in some strange way she
did not fully understand.

As if reading her mind, Eve ran on.

"But don't worry, you're different from me, very different.
You're good and boy-crazy already and have been ever since I can
remember." Musingly she said, "Well maybe that's better, who can
say."

Jennie swallowed hard and forged ahead bravely.

"How about war work, it's at least more rewarding than closing
yourself up in a room — you meet people that way — " As she
spoke, she knew now why desperate people so often turned to
organizations.

"Oh, please, who am I going to meet rolling bandages but other
relics like myself or, worse still, satisfied, motivated war wives and
sweethearts — belonging — all belonging — "

"That's ridiculous, Mother," Jennie cut in sharply. "For example, at Temple Emmanuel there are lovely women who work doing various things to help the war effort — "

Eve looked at her sadly for a moment and murmured, "I wonder
why war is so exciting to the young."

"Please, Mother," Jennie said eagerly, "what about this — ?"

"I — I don't think I could concentrate," she said in a barely audible voice, her head inclined, her glasses beginning to go steamy again. "I guess I'm just too sick to even roll bandages."

Jennie froze at the word "sick." She knew it meant taking some action. Or perhaps it was the simple statement of defeat. She felt torn between wanting to shake Eve hard to make her care again and putting her arms around her protectively to shield her from so much pain. But she refused to give up on her, no, she would not surrender her mother just yet.

"Look, Mother, if you can spend all those hours in the library that you're always talking about, then you are able to concentrate enough."

Eve stared at her in amazement. "You think I'm really doing all that reading and research when I'm there? Oh God, not really, not for a long time. I just go to get out of the heat in summers. It's cool there — like a tomb. I just go to see faces after so many hours alone. You yearn to see faces, hear voices, reassure yourself that you are still amongst the living — But the words — I can't read the words anymore, they just blur together and drop down on the page with my tears." Jennie was experiencing a rising irritation.

"Well don't you ever go to the library anymore and *not* cry, Mother?"

Eve gave her a withering look in answer. "Ugh, you are hard. Just like your father — tough. Even when you were a child you rejected me for him. You even chose your father's whore over me — that summer when you *allowed* her to live with you — "

That accusation, out of all the many that her mother had leveled at her through the years — the gross injustice of it welled up inside. Her palate ached to cry. It rankled and burned in her throat until she wanted to scream —

"Because he meant good times and trips and money," Eve continued.

"No, dammit, not money so much, but my childhood. I wanted my childhood, was that so terrible, Mother?" she cried in anguish.

"*You* had everything, the best of everything. It was I who never had a childhood, with my father dead, and my mother almost," she cried, beating her upper chest with the flat of her hand. The women were staring, nudging each other, some giggling nervously behind their hands, but Eve was oblivious — "Me with a glorious potential — the only four years of happiness in my life, my high school days — "

Jennie, weak and suddenly nauseated as fury swept over her, was trembling. In a loud voice she cried, "God, all you care about is your own youth, your glorious past. You are wasting a whole life for four years — Well you're finished, it's over, it's my turn now. You had your chance, you should have salvaged something — !"

"Selfish, selfish," Eve said and slapped Jennie hard across the face. A small crowd had begun to gather now, murmuring and gawking.

"No, it is you who are selfish! Selfish!" Jennie screamed.

Eve picked herself up, possessed suddenly of a fierce strength, and walked quickly out the door, leaving Jennie there in an anguish of humiliation.

A minute or two later she ran to find her mother. She could not allow her to ride home alone, thinking, thinking — her head would burst open. But it was too late. She could not find her anywhere — It was as if she had been picked up and whirled away in the vortex of her own fury!

AARON HADN'T COME HOME for dinner that night and Jennie was glad in a way. But it seemed ironic to her that after all, the whole eviscerating scene with her mother, Aaron seemed to have forgotten about driving out to the beach for the weekend. He had not even called until it occurred to him around ten o'clock, and by then the boys were asleep. He said he had been detained with business and would come home late and take them tomorrow. Jenny knew anyway that she had only used their leaving for the beach tonight as an excuse; she just hadn't wanted to be with Eve. She hadn't exactly formulated in her mind just what she would tell him of the day's events, if anything, and yet she knew that only he was in a position to help.

She had been in bed for what seemed like hours now, but she was unable to fall asleep. She often lay awake like this at night, listening to the radio dance music from Chicago's Chez Paree, faraway, exotic. She knew her father had the concession there; there was an added excitement about that. Tonight she tuned into the broadcast from the Café Rouge at the Hotel Pennsylvania, a nearer mystery. Everything sounded bustling, alive, busy. The clink of crystal glasses in the background was momentarily comforting — after a day with Eve she needed desperately to think about life and living it. Awake for hours, tossing and turning, trying not to think of her mother, or her father, whom she feared she might lose any day to Martha, or of Pete either. Oh, she mustn't think of Pete now, when she felt like this — tense, brittle, a complexity of exhaustion — feverishly trying to keep her hands from her own smooth, rounded body, from the golden brown root between her thighs, where she dreamed that joy began.

She heard her father's keys fumbling in the door. She jumped up from bed and snapped on the light, perspiring, her heart hammering hard, and went into the kitchen. She could hear Mamie snoring through the door to her room. She wanted Aaron to know she was up. She liked the occasional late night "Postum parties," discussing gaily their mutual insomnia; it wasn't so bad when it was shared. Her sleep mechanism had adjusted to listening for her father's key in the door from the time she was a small child. She was a night person like Aaron, she thought. Her mother and brothers slept like the dead — "The sleep of the innocent," as Eve would say — Or what about the escape of the guilty? Jennie was silly with exhaustion.

"You still up, Jen? What's the matter, why can't you sleep?"

"Oh, I don't know, overstimulated, maybe?"

Aaron, looking tired, his blue eyes faded, glanced up at her with interest and laughed. "Overstimulated? By what or whom?" Aaron fiddled around in the cookie jar while Jennie started the water for his Postum.

"Oh, I don't know exactly."

"Is it college you're scared of — or is it that flier, or both?"

She took a long while to answer. "Neither really," she answered honestly.

"Well, it's almost all over now — the war should be completely over by summer's end, and then a lot of questions will begin to get answers," he said.

Aaron sat down at the square card table in the foyer just outside the kitchen, a makeshift table they used for snacks and breakfast. The dining room seemed too imposing for these simple pleasures, usually snatched on the run.

Eve's words, "Selfish, selfish," kept jumping around in her head.

Suddenly, spontaneously, she heard herself telling Aaron something that she hadn't meant to talk about; she had thought it was already laid to rest in her unconcious. "The other day around five, I was speeding home in a taxi, and you know the entrance to the park on Fifty-ninth Street? Well, we stopped for the light there, before entering the park. The street was a sea of faces, as it always is around that corner, and then I saw Mother's face in the crowd. She was wandering about the crowded street — so, so alone — looking tense and confused, and you know what I did? I ducked my head — it was almost a reflex action."

A short pause while Aaron poured milk into his Postum. "So," he said, "what were you supposed to do? Jump out of the cab and get killed in the midst of traffic — and what would you have accomplished? It's no use, you're just no good for each other."

"But, Dad, it was my *mother*, among all of those strangers, and I passed her by as if she was just *one* of them."

"Becky," he said, getting up from the table and going over to where she was still standing. He put his arms around her protectively, and sitting her down at the table, he kissed the top of her head. She shrank instinctively from her father's touch, the years of her mother's invectives had done their work. He was always suspect, his love was hypocrisy, dishonest, or at best, in Eve's favorite adjective, selfish. She wanted it to be otherwise, but she could not know for sure — he was slick, "a slick article," Eve said. He said softly, "I can't give you those juicy, wet kisses anymore that you used to hate so much. You're too grown up. Now it's getting so I just don't know *how* to kiss you anymore. You know, up and down Broadway they think you're my sweetie when they see us together." She thought, He still clings to those archaic words out of another era, "Sweetie," and "simoleons" when he means dollars. He too is misplaced in time. My parents cannot bend, they are too firmly entrenched in their old dreams.

"Daddy, why are you changing the subject?"

"What's the subject?"

"Mama, that's the subject, Mama!"

Aaron sat down again. Stirring his cup thoughtfully, he said, "Did you see her today? Is that it?"

"Yes."

"Ugh, that explains why you're still awake."

"She's suffering so it hurts to watch her, she's dying in pieces — of a most deadly disease, Dad — loneliness."

"We're all lonely. Anyway, what can we do? She can't live with anyone, and she can't live alone. No one can help her now, my job is to help you — to see that you get a chance at life. Why do you have to spend so much time with her, why?"

"Because she's much too valuable to waste!" Jennie cried out as if from some inner self.

Aaron paused momentarily in his nervous administrations. There was a silence and then the loud sound of sipping.

"But it's not doing either of you any good. Without knowing, I can tell you the day ended in disaster."

"I was cruel to her."

"Yeah, she has that way of making people feel like shitheels," Aaron said, with some bitterness.

"Dad, she is threatening suicide, daily, every day on the telephone."

"And I believe she means it too," Aaron said quickly. "We all remember Quebec."

Jennie was silent. For some reason, that was a subject never discussed in the family, as if by tacit agreement. Jennie and the boys had never referred to it again in the years since. That and the subject of Martha were topics never mentioned openly in that house.

"Dad, none of this is getting us anywhere. She needs help. Please, you've got to help her."

"Help her? How? She won't let anyone help her."

"For one thing, you can start by getting her out of that coffin of a room. It's shrinking the life out of her, and . . ."

Aaron was laughing and looking at Jennie — shaking his head and laughing. "Do you really think that's going to change anything?"

"And for another, she needs not to have to worry about money now, on top of everything else."

"And for a third," Aaron said levelly, "she needs a psychiatrist and a hospital. You can't take care of her. I mean one of those fancy places — very swell."

There was an uncomfortable silence while the truth hung between them like static.

"That too," Jennie said.

"But will she go? You know she won't go, Jen."

"I don't know, but she admits to the severity of her depression. She might — who knows? Anything is worth a try. I'll talk to her, I'll see if I can find out what she wants."

"Ha," Aaron said, "you do that and I'll give you a medal — I've been trying to find that out for over twenty years!"

Jennie smiled a little, in spite of herself. "Daddy," she said, "Dad, would you really give her the money if she wanted to take a real apartment?"

"Yeah, sure, but try to get one. Don't you know what the housing situation is like in the city now?"

"Yes, but *you* could swing it!"

"Look, I'm not a magician. I'll try, I'll see what I can do. Not that it will really change anything, that I can promise you. Look, you spoke before about not wanting to waste your mother — and you're right — well, if you really don't want to waste her, then for God's sake, help her."

"You mean a place, a hospital to push her away to — to take her still farther out of life? I'm not sure that would help her. It might help *you*, but her? How would it help her?"

"It would cost me some twenty thousand dollars a year, how would it help *me*? But it might just give her back what's left of her life."

"Do you care?"

"Of course I do."

"And with Mother out of the picture, Martha will feel a free rein . . ."

"Mother's been out of the picture for ten years, whether you knew it or not."

"Not really —" There was an irrefutable silence.

"Why don't we let a doctor decide?"

"That's just it — there *is* no doctor. Neither of you ever trusted a psychiatrist. You really don't believe in them, either of you."

"Well, there was that doctor — what's his name? Jeeze, I can't think of his name now, but he got about the closest any of them ever got to your mother — she seemed to like him."

"Oh, Doctor Goldbart, well, maybe — we'll see — He may not tell her what she wants to hear, then that's that, but . . ."

"I'll try broaching it to her," Jennie said dubiously.

"His office is at Payne-Whitney," he said. "I hope that that in itself doesn't scare her off."

Back in bed, she had the feeling of having been once again smoothly, deftly manipulated by her father.

*

Jennie had to begin college in summer session, a term specially added for the girls in order to open places for the returning veterans, whose applications had flooded the colleges since D-day.

When she left for college in the beginning of July, nothing had been resolved with Eve, and the thought of leaving her behind made her feel edgy — Eve had vaguely promised to call Doctor Goldbart, but Jennie was unconvinced.

(45)

WHEN PETER SCHORE RETURNED from overseas he would need much more than his sensuous underlip and flashy dimples. To begin with he'd need a decent suit of clothes. His uniform was more ill-fitting than ever, since he had lost so much weight on K rations, and the khaki color clashed with his tan. He also needed a job, but had already made up his mind to take advantage of the opportunity offered by the government, to go to college on the G.I. Bill.

During her last year of high school, Jennie had decided that her appeal was stronger for the less sophisticated and unspoiled boys of the outlying boroughs like Brooklyn or the Bronx. The smoother, more urbane boys from her own neighborhood, having grown up with glamour, were not as sharply impressed, and seemed unaffected. They appeared to prefer the more understated girls that were becoming the fashion at the small select private schools scattered around the city. She had her share of admirers among the boys left on the home front but she simply hadn't created the furor she had counted on.

There had been little of physical beauty in Peter Schore's life, that is, until he met Jennie — not in his home, his neighborhood, *or* his family.

So this was Peter Schore, home from the wars, with a nice middle-class family who lived somewhere in the Bronx in one of those faceless dirty-gray apartment buildings built in the twenties. He had an older sister and younger brother and was forever on guard to preserve the open secret that he shared with them his small bedroom. Privately his feelings were ambivalent. He struggled between delicately incestuous guilt feelings, and a certain comfort he derived from the sibling camaraderie.

He was on one of the first boatloads home, and early in the fall semester of college she heard from Aaron that he had returned and had phoned the apartment only to find that she was four hundred miles away. Her feelings seesawed dizzily between numbness — a curious feeling of nonfeeling — and wild elation. Two and a half years of waiting and writing and planning and now the real thing — Why did she find herself suddenly wishing to continue with the dream, and at the same time wishing that she were home, where he was?

There would be a long vacation weekend coming up in mid-October, in honor of the opening football game of the season, to be played in New York. Pete had left the message with Aaron that he would call back when Jennie got home for that weekend. She couldn't understand his not phoning her in Buffalo. How much could it have cost? A couple of dollars, five at the most? Was he so shy, or hadn't her father given him her dorm number? She had no number for him, and there was no listing in the phone book (she had checked that immediately). But it never dawned on her that he simply might not have the money. The practical realities of this whirlwind affair had, in fact, from time to time intruded into her consciousness, but in the flurry of excitement between her senior year, graduation, and college, she hadn't really given them much serious thought.

*

One afternoon after classes, the bell rang at the dorm. Jennie, at her usual post in the living room near the record player, opened the door. A small, round young man stood shyly at the threshold. "Yes, can I help you?" she said brightly, keeping the door only ajar slightly for safety.

"Well," he said looking uncomfortable and just a little sheepish, "I've — I've really come to see a girl I don't know. Does a Jennie Abel live here?"

Jennie, surprised, said, "You're talking to her."

The round-faced young man seemed taken aback, as if he could hardly believe his good fortune. "You mean it, you mean you're Jennie," he said with some degree of awe, causing her to pull herself up to her full height and toss her head effectively.

"What — who are you?"

"Well, my name is Phil Klurman and I'm a very good friend of Peter Schore — we kind of grew up together. Well, anyway, he knew I was coming to school here and asked me to look you up — to tell you that he's back, he's home." Jennie felt rooted to the doormat. She felt foolishly schoolgirlish in her oversized pink sweater and pristine white dickey with its Peter Pan collar, and her serious gray flannel skirt and run-down loafers — and bobby socks. She touched her hair reflexively, wished she had worn some make-up, and said, "Oh, I'm — I'm really terribly sorry that I can't ask you in, but you know the rules, I guess. We'll just have to stand out here like this and talk awhile. There's so much I want to ask you. Even so, I'm not really allowed to talk standing here, or to leave the dorm with a guy. Isn't it crazy?" But they did stand there talking for an hour, Jennie picking clean his brain for memories of Pete.

And when he left, she felt better, as if somehow she had grown closer to Pete, had learned to love him from way back, deep down, such a loving and glowing portrait had his friend painted. "He really loves you so much" he had said quietly, almost guiltily, in parting, as if telling tales out of school.

So Pete was what had come of two years of suspended animation, of breathless dreaming and prayers for victory. He alone would make restitution for all the losses — the youth lost, the fun missed, the sweet carefree neighborhood boys washed up on the beaches of Iwo or Anzio, "the six million" all gone — the children of Theresienstadt — gone — only their sad little pictures left behind on those bloodied walls to prove that they too had had a share of childhood. She knew all this, even in her ivory tower on Central Park West. So he came back to Jennie, floundering under these great burdens and unknowingly responsible for all of her heroic expectations. The trouble was that the part did not suit him; he had been miscast.

*

The evening — their first date since Pete's return — had seemed long and arduous to her. It had been work. She was suddenly terribly tired, defeated — it seemed to her that two years of her life had been wasted. Like her father, she had great respect for the years — for the transiency of life. At eighteen she had already come into a large share of that primary female characteristic, a tendency to nostalgia. Whatever happened before, a week before, a day before, was automatically more precious than the present, sweeter by the minute for having aged, no matter how slightly.

They had taken a walk, had a soda at Rumpelmayer's. She thought of her mother wistfully, and the tiny room upstairs crammed so full of her mother's presence, and then tried to drown the thought in a vanilla ice cream soda. Pastel pandas kept a benevolent watch from the surrounding shelves, and overdressed gift baskets made empty promises. One or twice she felt Pete reach for her hand — she kept looking for places to hide it. He had been talking on nervously about his friends, his old Saturday morning basketball game, his brother, his sister, anything but the war. Their only link seemed already a buried memory. This annoyed her, but she wasn't really listening.

She was too busy worrying about how she would fend off this "slathering wolf," this sex-starved G.I. whom she had encouraged so wildly — so many long months ago, another girl, a child really, in another lifetime. He caught her eyes with his for a moment and she felt a stab of that tight, sweet feeling she remembered, and then he said something inconsequential that struck her as awkward, and the feeling was gone.

She was anxious to get back into the apartment — she didn't even know exactly why. When they got to her door she considered saying good night then and there, but she didn't have the gall to dismiss him like that, so discourteously, and she still wasn't sure she wanted to. Once the heavy metal apartment door shut, the tension was loud enough to hear. Tonight she hoped Aaron would be home for a change. He hadn't been sleeping home much lately and even when he did, he returned very late from doing the rounds.

They sat down on the sofa. She hesitated to look at him lest her look be mistaken for invitation, or worse still, she might glimpse some annoying irregularity of feature or expression that would further irritate her, not so much with him as with herself.

Pete rested his head against the back of the sofa and watched the smoke rings from his cigarette climb up toward the aqua-blue ceiling. "Guess I better get going," he said absently to the ceiling. Jennie said nothing. He looked at her from under his gentle moth-wing lashes and his warm, frank gaze caused her to look up and smile a little in spite of her listless condition. "You know, Jen, I've just got to get my life into some kind of order. I — I'm just a little discombobulated right now." He said this unapologetically. She smiled at the colloquialism, it said so much: so thoroughly mixed up. She gazed at him now with an echo of tenderness.

"Aren't we all. But you know what? It will all come out right, Peter Schore," she said with authority. "You'll see."

"Yeah, I guess it will," he said wearily. He got up from the sofa and went over to the mirror across the room. His silky brown hair had fallen into his eyes, and he combed it back quickly, straightened his uniform shirt and khaki tie.

"Can't wait to get outa these and into some civvies," he said as he walked to the door in the semidarkened hall.

"You'll be even *more* gorgeous then," Jennie said, graciously, feeling sad now that he was leaving. Could two years end in three hours?

She opened the door, he took her hand in his; they stood for a moment divided by the metal barrier of the half-open door, and suddenly he reached an arm out over Jennie's head, pulled her back into the dark hall of the apartment, and slammed the door shut, all in one spontaneous movement. And they were in each other's arms as if he had just come home that moment and she had run breathlessly to greet him at the troop train. A long kiss with no marked beginning and no end, just myriad variations — murmurings and fragmentary confessions.

"I should have done this in the beginning of the evening," Pete said in her ear.

"I wish you had," she answered with eyes closed, parted mouth against his. "Would have saved a lot of time" — once again back in the garden of the Palm Plaza and the scent of sun and sea around them. She thought how incredibly sweet his breath tasted — clean, with only a pleasant memory of tobacco.

"I'm going to hate going back to school now. I just found you again."

"How often do you get home?" he asked, as if suddenly aware of the situation.

"Oh I guess as often as I want to," she said coquettishly.

"Well, that's got to be at least an eight-hour train trip."

"Yes, I know, but it will be worth it," she said. She held his fleshy lower lip between her teeth for a moment, playing with him cat-and-mouselike. He looked at her reprovingly, turned her around toward the door with more assurance now than an hour ago, picked up her long hair and kissed the back of her neck as she walked.

"It's three in the morning. I've got to go. Call you tomorrow, okay? When are you going back? Sunday?"

"No, Monday."

"Oh good, then we still have tomorrow and Sunday."

"Pete, please give me your telephone number. You know I can't get it."

"That's probably because I don't have one," he said.

"But I mean your parents, they . . ."

"They don't have one either," he said calmly.

After Pete left she thought about the candy store down at the corner of their last apartment house and how some of the neighborhood people used to receive their calls that way. It had always seemed to her a presumption, making of the proprietor a sort of social secretary. She felt uncomfortable again.

(46)

AMID THE PERVASIVE ODOR of burning leaves, Jennie spent much of that semester at college enveloped in a golden fog.

She and Pete had had more time together than either had expected — all of that first football weekend and four or five evenings over Thanksgiving holiday. And now there was Christmas to look forward to — a three-week holiday from school, that is, if anyone could dig themselves out of the heavy snows that had enveloped them in Buffalo since before Thanksgiving.

But it wasn't until New Year's Eve that Jennie found out for herself how Pete really felt. He wasn't easy to read. She hardly ever knew what he was thinking or feeling. That was frustrating to her, coming from a family where the smallest nuance of emotion was immediately verbalized.

During the long Christmas break, her relationship with him had already begun to settle into a kind of comfortable permanence. Three times a week he rode the subway downtown to the dizzying "heights" of Central Park West. Each time he entered the art deco monster building with its labyrinth of lobbies, he felt light-headed, his legs felt rubbery. He was grateful that she lived on the ninth floor. It was a neutral number, not so low that he didn't have time to compose himself, not so high that he had the time to generate more anxiety on the way up.

When he got to the door of the apartment he could feel a beating in his temples, in his pulse. Everything beat but his heart, which seemed to stop the moment he approached the threshold of 9D.

Once inside, the pattern was generally much the same. He had by now memorized some of his opening lines, delivered usually to Aaron, or to Jennie's younger brothers, who invariably jumped on him with the same questions. "Did you shoot any Japs?" "How many planes did you bring down?" "Do you have any more bowie knives?" (He had already given them an exotic assortment.) Then there would ensue a polite, if somewhat strangulated, conversation with Aaron about the war, which he wanted to forget, or about N.Y.U., which he had only just started (and didn't seem to think a challenge worth discussing) and to which Aaron referred proudly as his alma mater.

After a wait of some fifteen or twenty minutes, Jennie would burst forth from her room, breathless with apologies, and kiss him with a warmth that melted away his temporary irritation at her games.

Sometimes they went out, more times they did not. She knew that it was a strain on him to take her downtown dancing, or to dinner. They both loved to go to jazz joints in the Village. Jazz had a wonderful way of making you forget everything but the moment, but often it meant saving for weeks the small supplement he got from the government — and anyway she was just as happy staying home with him, happier maybe, because then she would spend the evening wrapped in his arms, or curled in his lap, and they were not exposed to outside influences, which somehow made her dissatisfied. As long as she was in his arms she was happy with Pete. Physically apart, though together in the same room, she knew instinctively he was not right for her.

No matter where they went or what they did, the evening ended the same way. They would come home, put on a record of Dick Haymes or Frank Sinatra and curl up with each other on the big green easy chair in the living room and stay that way in a cloud of kisses until dawn.

One such evening close to the New Year, she sat on the floor at his feet while he played with the honey strands of her hair. She rubbed the back of her head against his knees like a cat. She turned to kiss the blue serge of his inner thigh, driving him to distraction.

"Don't, don't, Jennie, please," he said weakly.

"Why not?"

"Why?" he repeated — "Well you just don't *do* those kinds of things to a man."

"Well you certainly wouldn't want me to do it to a woman — " She was laughing now, having fun with him. Then in an intimate voice she added, "Anyway, you're not just a *man*. You're *mine*, you're my *love*."

He pulled her up onto his lap and kissed her lips and eyelids and buried his face in the golden tangle of her hair and whispered how much he wanted her, how sweet she smelled, but he was afraid. She knew that he was afraid — he was not the kind of boy to rush in where angels feared to tread. He wanted — that is, half of him wanted — desperately to *have* her; he knew he could. And yet the other half, that part of him that was entangled with his soul, did not. He was no gambler, he feared the risk, was terrified of losing her, either out of her disgust, or her remorse, or his own failure. He felt the fragility of her person, of their relationship, and sensed that it could not withstand the deflowering of a "convent-bred" Jewish princess — but it would also not withstand indefinitely the denial. He knew that her body had passed through eighteen years of life, gift-wrapped, without ever having been handled and he revered her for this, felt he must protect her; he could not be the one to betray her. But the mere thought that it would be someone else made him tremble with pain. He was caught in a dilemma, one he had never had to face before, because he had never before been in love — he was barely twenty-two, and he had been at war since he was nineteen.

Some evenings they stretched out together on the guest bed in the bar that adjoined the living room. They would lie close, their lips touching, their hands exploring each other hungrily. Pete's lack of initiative irritated her sometimes, put her out of the mood — if he was going to go fumbling around in the damp crotch of her panties she wished he'd do it with some authority. But Pete lived in dread of Aaron's intrusion, and the thought that he could come home at any moment and find them like this, even fully clothed, distorted his desire. Actually Aaron rarely came home at all on weekend nights — Jennie told him so, but there *was* the possibility, and that was enough.

He was as much a prisoner of his time as she. There were only two kinds of girls in this world — "good" and "bad" — and the borders just didn't blur into one another — not if he could help it. Jennie was inviolable, she was to him all that was glamour and beauty in the world, Gatsby's Daisy, the distant green light at the end of the dock — except that the only green light he ever saw in connection with her was the one atop the engine of the Jerome Avenue Express as it plunged through the tunnel out of the silence of dawn.

He gave her an ankle bracelet, uniting them in some sort of vague bond. Golden hearts entwined with their names. She loved to jiggle her foot casually as she sat with him and talked, one silk-clad leg crossed over the other, watching the tiny hearts catch the light. He loved to watch her.

During the holidays they went down to the Café Rouge where Les Brown's band was playing. She wore a blood-red slash of lipstick on her mouth. In her ankle-strapped platform shoes she danced up close to the microphone and looked right into the face of the girl vocalist, a beautiful blonde in a slinky black dress, whom the bandleader introduced as Miss Doris Day. On the dance floor Pete kissed Jennie until long after the music stopped.

On one of these evenings he had planned a big holiday surprise. He wouldn't tell her what it was until they were in the theater district. Then he revealed that he had gotten orchestra seats for the show *Harvey*. But she had already seen it with her parents and the boys. She prayed that Pete would not find out. But as they left the theater one of the program vendors nodded to her graciously and said, "Good evening, Miss Abel. I won't ask you if you enjoyed the show tonight. I know you did or you wouldn't be back so fast — I didn't see your dad tonight . . ." Pete said nothing. Jennie kept telling herself that maybe he hadn't heard, but she knew he had.

On the eve of the new year of 1946, they went to a party in Queens given by an old friend of Pete's for all of his newly returned buddies.

Phil Klurman came along, dateless, to drive them in his small black Ford. There was no room for three up front so they sat behind him, his idolatry for Pete glowing back hotly from the rearview mirror. The party was a B.Y.O.B. party. Jennie had never heard of that before. At any parties she had been to, the parents provided quarts of elegant liquors from their own private stock. So Pete had brought his bottle, and between them in the car rested "their baby" as he called it. Jennie felt just a little square and left out.

They said that the host was an ex-marine who had been wounded at Okinawa — a bullet through the brain — and left on the beach for dead. Now he had a steel plate in his head. Pete said with a curious absence of emotion that they didn't expect him to live . . .

They pulled up in front of a typical two-family house in a forlorn section of Queens. The street seemed to be stitched together with telephone wires, like ugly black sutures.

They had not been there fifteen minutes when Pete seemed to vanish into the air. He simply disappeared from the small, square, overcrowded living room and Jennie was left with a group of strange girls. Almost all the boys had vanished. A now deepening din led her in the direction of the small, overbright kitchen, where some twenty boys in their shirtsleeves were sitting all over the chairs, table and floor, drinking and talking about the war. Pete was in the thick of it. If he saw her he gave no sign of recognition and she wandered back to the roomful of discarded sweethearts and wives. They stood huddled in knowing and worldly clusters, excluding her, the uninitiated, from their special sisterhood, seemingly unperturbed by the stag party that was raging in the kitchen.

Jennie wished that she had brought along a date for Phil, as Pete had suggested. But most of her more attractive friends were already

busy for New Year's, and anyway she didn't much like getting involved in blind dates. Only Gladys Blumberg, her friend from
boarding school days, had been free, and that was the trouble:
Gladys was too free. That was the reason she assumed Pete was
so anxious to get her for Phil, figuring she was a sure thing. Gladys
had admitted as much ruefully to Jennie one time last summer during an all-night heart to heart at the beach house. Jennie had tried
to reform her, or at least modify her extreme abandon somewhat,
but Gladys, with her coarse features and kinky hair, was un-
repentant — unsalvageable. "It's all right for you to talk, you're
beautiful," she had said. "You can afford to play hard to get, but
look at me — I can't afford the luxury of virginity." They had
ended up dissolving into giggles, Jennie begging for details of her
voluptuous sex life. But none were forthcoming, whether out of an
excess of sudden modesty, or an underdeveloped imagination,
Jennie had never been quite sure. In any case, she could have used
her now, with her salient wisecracks and irreverent jokes.

At midnight, Pete tore himself away from his drinking buddies
and told Jennie he wished to speak to her privately. Jennie, who
had little or no experience with alcohol (nobody drank *or* smoked
in her entire family, a fact they were extremely proud of, though
it mortified *her*), knew that he was a little more than slightly drunk.
He propelled her to what appeared to be the bedroom, a tiny
black room off the living room, containing only a wall-to-wall bed,
as far as she could make out. Pete seemed somehow different,
distant, as if he had aged within the last hours. She was almost
frightened of him, but he took her in his arms gently, and as if
sensing her fears, told her not to be afraid, he had something important to discuss with her. He told her, without touching any
part of her, how much he loved her (but she must know that already), and asked if she would wait for him until they could be
married. He would buy a ring — somehow (as if the ring were
the key that unlocked the gates), and they could be married as soon
as he got a job — that is, after he got out of college, which would
be in another three years.

She lay back on the bed, suddenly exhausted, in a sea of coats, and felt only desolation. The moment she had dreamed about, and talked about endlessly, with every girlfriend she had ever had since she was eight was suddenly upon her without warning — well almost — and the only certain emotion she felt was sadness. Pete continued, "Of course it would mean no more running around with other guys — no more," he was emphatic. "No more"? She had only occasional other dates to suit her father, who said she must not tie herself down. But who knew what magic lurked out there in the great delicious unknown. She saw herself waiting three years in a state of suspension while life raced by her — while everyone else was getting on with their lives. She saw it ending at eighteen and culminating at twenty-two with diapers, debts, and G.I. loans, before she had ever *lived*. Or worse still, "on the dole from Daddy," as her father used to say in his teasing way.

She moved slightly away from him on the mammoth bed, and said, muffled in the rough alpaca of someone's coat, "Can't I have some time to think about it? After all we do have a few years to wait."

"What is there to think about? Either you love me or you don't," he said. "It's as simple as that."

"But, Pete — I'm only a kid, I was only seventeen a couple of weeks ago."

"Jennie, you're eighteen now, you were eighteen on December eighth."

"Well I just *turned* eighteen, but I was only seventeen three weeks ago — Pete, I haven't even lived yet, not at all. Nothing ever — " She knew she had grown up long ago, but here she was fighting again for her girlhood — the one that she had never had.

"Well I'm not exactly asking you to leave this life with me, Jen — just to marry me," he said quietly.

She looked at him by the light of the door ajar, into his earnest, beautiful eyes. "It's sort of the same thing," she said quietly. Pete stood up slowly and walked out of the room. He never referred to the conversation again, nor did he re-emerge from the all-male security of the kitchen until it was time to leave.

Three in the morning, Phil sober at the wheel, they drove back into Manhattan. Jennie and Pete sat close together, but tense and upright. Pete did not look at her or address a single word to her. She thought about losing him now and the thought was painful.

The screech of a siren followed them. They turned quickly together to look out the back window — it was only an ambulance. As they turned back, Pete suddenly caught her mouth with his, kissing her long and hard, an urgent kiss that wandered all the crevices and valleys of her mouth.

Phil surprised her by coming upstairs with them. Pete didn't dissuade him. She was disappointed. She wasn't exactly sure why, except that she was leaving for school the next day — and she felt vaguely empty, as if she owed him something for the years and the dreams that might go unfulfilled.

The apartment was bathed in the cold blue light of dawn. It seemed intensified by the sea of shadows, through the window, the shorn branches of the park beyond. Phil disappeared discreetly into the kitchen or the bathroom. They stood together closely; he searched her face for clues — he found tear stains.

"Pete," she whispered, "send Phil home. Stay — please — "

She put her arms around his waist and kissed him through the thin fabric of his freshly ironed shirt, inhaling its fragrance, envying his mother the intimacy of ironing his things — Jennie who never so much as pressed a handkerchief.

Pete dismissed Phil, who seemed annoyed. "See you at basketball practice tomorrow, huh Pete?" he asked uncertainly.

She knew her father would not come home tonight.

She lay on the sofa, her head in his lap. He kissed her slowly. "Darling, I love you," she murmured, her tongue seeking the tiny scar above his lip.

He closed his eyes and surrendered to the moment, gave himself up to her — and wished hard that he had been born rich and didn't live in the Bronx. How often he had thought of supporting the weight of those breasts in his hands, gently running his palms across the pink bulk of her nipples, but he had balanced the momentary pleasure against her indignation, and usually stopped the train of thought the moment she moved his hand. Tonight he was reckless, he risked her indignation, but none was forthcoming — the torrent tumbled into his hands like a windfall. She only moaned gently and cupped her hand around his full one.

"Please, darling," she whispered, "I want you to be the first."

He did not seem flattered. "Sounds like you're planning on a series — no, I think I'd rather be the last, I'd be better off — *on all counts,*" he said laughing softly against her hair.

"Pete — don't you *want* me?" She wondered if he really wanted *her,* or whether he wanted to *be* her, if maybe he wanted the gloss of her life to rub off on him.

"More than you can believe," he said, serious now, his blue eyes warm on her face. "But, well, I want you forever, for always, not just for now — "

She sat up. "Peter Schore, what kind of middle-class malarkey are you spouting? Can't I love you and be sleeping with you at the same time? I expect that would be the case if we were married."

"Oh, Jen," he pulled her up close to him and rocked her gently in his arms, covering her face and mouth with small nibbling kisses. "I won't ruin your life, I promise you, everything will be fine, you'll see, but you do love me?"

She did not answer but instead said to him, "C'mon, Pete, let's . . ."

They walked the few steps into the little guest room. In the dim light she saw him begin to remove his trousers. She was momentarily stunned with the situation she had created — and yet, it was something she had to do, and with no one else, only this boy.

He seemed poised above her uncertainly. Then she thought she felt him entering her, but she could not be sure. For so long, dreamily, she had yearned to touch his body, feel its smooth sureness against her fingertips, feel it stretched out in all its boyishness against her own.

Odd noises from the apartment, the heavy tread of footsteps — the door opened with a spasm, and Mamie, hair streaming down her back in an angry black cloud, clutching her wrapper together with a whitened fist, put on the lights.

"What is going on here? You! Get out of here — *this instant,* do you hear? I am responsible for this young girl. Put your clothes on and leave," she said, her voice shaking majestically.

Jennie, blanched and trembling, could only sit clutching the bedspread around her. She wished for death at that moment — and some sort of explanation for what had gone before — certainly it hadn't been much . . . she hoped. With belated discretion, Mamie went to the foyer to wait. Peter said nothing to Jennie, he just put on his clothes and straightened his hair in that final way that suggested good-byes.

He turned to her then, as he left, and said, "I'm awfully sorry, Jen," and he was gone. She thought of running after him down into the street, into the subway if necessary where it was dark and impersonal, and asking him what happened, "Tell me, please, what happened — " But she only sat on the bed, fatigued and numb.

"Mamie, nothing happened," she said, "really — "

"Thanks to me. But I can't police you every minute. What will happen next time?"

"Would it really have been so terrible?"

There was a silence, as if she was turning the question over in her mind.

"Well it *could* have been — for me." Mamie said honestly. Jennie knew that Mamie would not tell her father, but still she felt compelled to ask her.

"Are you going to tell him?"

"I don't know — " she said, "but, God, girl, you should know better 'n that!"

But Jennie didn't hear her anymore for the crazy thoughts, the questions, that were crowding her mind.

*

The next evening, exhausted from a sleepless night, she rode back on the train with her roommates, an agonizing eight-hour trip. She had not heard from Pete. Her roommates, two rough-styled girls from

Rahway, New Jersey, chattered incessantly about their affairs with their respective boyfriends, giving juicily vivid descriptions, as if it were the most natural and uncomplicated thing in all of God's world.

(47)

BACK AT SCHOOL, Jennie wore Pete's gift around her slender ankle. Around her neck she wore her virginity like an albatross. She had always been proud of the fact before, had even considered it a jewel above rubies, but now it had become a clouded issue in which she and Pete were hopelessly entangled.

She simply could not concentrate on her studies anymore. The vertical, upstanding A's of the last semester had now fizzled into C's.

She thought about leaving school. Perhaps she would transfer to one in Manhattan, though transfers were not often granted now to women, since the boys were flooding back into college on the G.I. Bill. She hadn't been getting on so well with her roommates this semester — she felt isolated socially because of Pete. And then Aaron was calling every week, begging her to come home, bribing her with one thing or another, a house on a private island in Florida — or Havana (he knew how she loved Havana). He seemed to want her home desperately, as if to save him from something or someone. She was well aware of her father's attitude toward girls and college — "Silly, just a waste of time" (and waste of money was somehow implicit in that statement too) — "What a woman needs to know about life she can't learn in books." Eve saw this as still another aspect of Aaron's destructive attitude. His estimate of women was unconsciously base, so that even his daughter's needs were automatically considered unimportant. (In his perverse way it was only Eve that he appeared to regard with any degree of respect. It amounted sometimes to awe — and that was, she said, because she alone in all the world stood up to him.) But now only her mother, whom she knew was not at all well, let up a little on her usual emotional demands. Jennie knew that, more than anything, more than even her own need for her, Eve wanted her to stay at college, to continue with her English literature major and her intensive work in French.

Jennie sensed with growing alarm that the adults in her life were still depending on her, in a way that made her uneasy.

In early February of '46 she had an unexpected visitor at school. She received a phone call from Grandma, who was miraculously in Buffalo for the weekend. Jennie had lost touch with Grandma Lisa in the last few years, not without reluctance, but Eve's relationship with her mother had deteriorated with the years, ground down now to a fine silt. Jennie knew that things were not going well with her — the same old story, only aggravated by age. The last she had heard she had been living with Lubowitz (who appeared sporadically now) at one of those run-down hotels on upper Broadway where people go to commit suicide. Eve added this to all the other "pain and degradation" of her life. Jennie remembered when she was a child how proud Grandma was, how impressed she herself had been, with the Half-Moon Hotel in Coney Island when Grandma had lived there for a short time.

Out of nowhere in particular Grandma materialized with Lubowitz and a story about coming down from Canada, where he had gone for a business opportunity that didn't pan out (when did they ever, Jennie thought sadly). But she knew immediately that they had come for a "touch," as her father would have said. She would have gladly given her anything she had — she had always felt content when Grandma was in the picture — but she really had nothing to give, only a few dollars remaining in the school account after books and odds and ends and lunches at the Soda Shoppe.

So Grandma, with her gentian violet cheeks and great girth balanced on chicken legs, stood there in her hastily rented attic room, and begged and lied and wheedled and coaxed.

"Jennie darling, you're not a baby anymore, I don't have to treat you like a baby." (Lubowitz was looking at her greedily, his eyes on her breasts. She didn't feel like a baby.) "You know I, I haven't been on such good terms with your mother lately. Well, you better than anyone should know how she is — " Jennie felt uncomfortable to find herself allied with her grandmother against her mother. "So I wonder if you could maybe lend me a little money, that is, just until he gets on his feet."

Jennie wanted to laugh — When was he ever on his feet? He was usually on his back, what with his "confinements" for one accident or another, invariably followed by one of his unsuccessful suits.

"Grandma, I don't *have* any money. You know Dad, how he is about certain things."

"But, baby, don't — don't you have a bank account? *You* he gives, he's so crazy about you he gives you whatever you want — "

"I have no *use* for money up here."

"But something," Lisa said, desperation adding a throb to her deep, music hall voice, "*something* for poor old Grandma. You remember you always enjoyed my cooking — didn't I cook good for you, all those meals I used — "

"Grandma, stop! Stop!" Jennie shouted. "I would give you anything if I had it, but I don't know how to get it."

"You must get an allowance," Grandma cut in sharply. "Look, can you borrow from your friends, you must have a million friends here — all rich girls from fine homes, I know — "

"I — I can't do that," Jennie's gorge was rising. Anyway she didn't have many friends left this semester, and they were all in worse straits than herself. And she *needed* the twenty-five dollars that she had — "I want to help but — "

"What do you mean you want to help," she screamed. "You *have* to help, you're our only hope, we spent our last dollar to come up here by bus — we don't even have the carfare to get home — "

"Then you didn't come down here from Canada, you came here from home just to see *me* — "

Lisa nodded in defeat.

"I have only some of my month's allowance left, and I don't get another until the end of the month," Jennie said, "but I can give you about twenty-five dollars, and if you want you can wait here for the next check — it's almost due."

"No, no, I can't afford to wait here, it's expensive. Can you ask your father to wire you the money, make up something, some emergency or other? But, please don't tell him the truth — "

Lubowitz, in the shadows of the eaves, sat on the bed, drinking celery tonic and nodding approval of this plan.

"I'll try, Grandma," Jennie said, suddenly very tired, "but he's not very fast about sending money, and he asks an awful lot of questions."

"Please, Jenna, whatever you do, don't tell your mother that we were here. Promise me, *madelah*, promise me — " Grandma hadn't called her *madelah* since she was a small child, and then only when she was especially pleased with her.

The next day she went into town with the little peridot and diamond ring Aaron had bought her on one of those aimless visiting weekends in the town outside the boarding school. She pawned it for fifty dollars. That afternoon, taking the money together with what she had left in the bank, she went to the rooming house. She wanted them out of town fast, as fast as possible. Why should she feel so disappointed? It wasn't anyone's fault — the fault was life itself — yet she was uneasy in the presence of failure.

So she thought about leaving at the end of the semester. What was the sense in fighting it? They would not leave her alone. Wherever she went, something, someone out of the confusion of her life would track her down, ferret her out. Her life seemed poised in a perpetual state of animated suspension — Why did she care so much? And then there was Pete — he'd been writing only sporadically, a couple of bleak and wintry letters that suited perfectly the present climate.

An inchoate relationship — left rudely — jaggedly torn — dangerous shards that cut deep —

In the end the decision wasn't even hers to make, Pete took it out of her hands.

(48)

I N THE DREARY SLUMP OF MARCH, during the coldest and
snowiest week of an upstate winter, Pete telephoned her at the
dormitory. She was surprised and happy. She had been waiting for
him to make the first move; her rigid code demanded that it be the
boy who take the initiative after — after, well whatever it was that
had gone before. She felt as she always did at the sound of his
voice so deep and soft, excited and irritated by it, by him. She felt
that she wanted to stir him up, bring the bubbles up to the surface,
the way you did with good champagne.

"I'm thinking of coming up to your school next weekend, maybe
stay with Phil. You know he lives off campus, couldn't get any
place on the grounds. It's not much of a place but . . ." Yes, she
was well acquainted with the housing problems, the ignominious
Quonset huts hurriedly set up for the G.I's — Phil didn't live in one
of those, he assured her. Pete, she wanted to shout, what are you
trying to say to me? Surely you didn't call me long distance to discuss the deplorable housing shortage on college campuses around
the country — or did you? But she said nothing . . .

There was an uncomfortable silence.

"Jennie, I have to see you again — to — to talk about things."
She felt a sudden stab of fear.

"But, Pete, I'll probably be coming home for a weekend very
soon . . ." Some static through the wires and another pause.

"I think I'd rather come up there to you."

"Okay."

"Don't you want me to, Jen?"

"Yes — yes, Pete, I do."

"I love you," he said simply into the telephone.

"I love you too, Pete."

Because of his own college commitments, Pete arrived on Saturday in the late afternoon and was planning to leave Sunday night — sixteen hours of grueling travel to spend one evening with her. She felt pleased — and pressured.

At about six o'clock he arrived at her house with Phil. Phil had the car, and a date this time, an attractive brunette co-ed. But next to Pete, Phil always seemed somehow old and wise, like the chaperone. The girl whom they introduced to Jennie as Iris Bryce was a stranger to her, and for some reason this annoyed her. She felt disappointed that Pete had not thought to see her alone first, but she had begun to understand him a little better now. He simply did not think that way, the way she did. He did not see himself as the hero of a sweeping novel. Certainly he looked the part, but he never dramatized himself — in fact he underplayed his role. Jennie, coming from a supercharged background of emotional indulgence, considered that perhaps he could use just a little more style, the kind of style born of confidence, and still she noted that he appeared more confident with almost anyone but her.

They drove into town in high spirits, the girls dressed in skirts and cashmere sweater sets and very high heels. Iris was devouring Pete with her eyes. His supreme disinterest only seeming to inflame her further.

The snow, frozen in grotesque shapes and faded yellow, did nothing to enhance the city, not beautiful to begin with. They went for dinner to a small Italian place that Phil had recommended. It seemed filled with a peculiarly sulphuric light, generated by the smudgy reflection of the street lamps on the snow. They crowded into a corner table. Pete immediately ordered drinks, a double for himself. It struck her that he might have had a few before he arrived at her house.

On the juke box Perry Como singing "Till the End of Time," a few couples dancing, the slosh of their moccasins creating a soft whoosh. Opposite them the endless drone of varsity vulgarism from Phil and his date. Pete complexly silent except for an occasional soft laugh . . . politeness. Perplexity hangs heavy over them now, they are beginning to take life seriously. They are all bound up in futures, spoiling the present. She is happy to have Pete here beside her.

Phil and his date got up to dance to the juke box. "Kiss me once and kiss me twice and kiss me once again," they were dipping and weaving and doing fancy, silly steps — putting on quite a show. The restaurant was virtually empty, with only a few patrons here and there, mostly university students. Pete made polite conversation about college — soulless fluff. For a moment she thought, my God, he must be crazy, that boy is mad, he hasn't seen me, has hardly even spoken to me since that night. But she saw through his pain to the core of love that was there, and she was warmed by it — It was his loving her that she loved.

*

She found herself at Phil's, a small pleasant room in a private house. Phil had dropped them off while he supposedly went to take Iris home, which Jennie felt sure meant the car — and trying to get laid. In any case Phil had magnanimously donated his room to Pete and she felt angry because this seemed to her planned and because the boys had been collusive, and Pete's attitude had been strange and impersonal all evening, and Pete was a little drunk. Anyway, by this time she was quite happily resigned to her virginity.

She sat gingerly on one of the single beds in the room. In a large armchair by the window Pete sat down and in a characteristic pose, leaned his head against the chair back and pulled at his cigarette. "Pete," she said very quietly, "don't you want to talk? We've never really talked since that night." When he didn't look up or answer she wondered if he had heard. He just kept pulling on the cigarette in that tight, restrained way he had of holding back his heart. And then he said, "Jennie, I want to forget, I want us both to forget that last night — everything. It's not what I wanted for us — neither is this — " he said, looking around, indicating the small sterile room. She felt the sudden reversal of roles, and it touched her, as it so often did when he unmasked.

"All right, Pete," she said, "then maybe you'd better take me home. You know I have a twelve o'clock curfew and it's almost eleven now."

"Well, we've got to wait for Phil to come back — "

"When will that be?"

For answer he took her in his arms, and as always when he was close to her, she forgot her nameless fears and angers. Her mind might be undecided, but her body was ready for him almost from the moment he touched her. They lay on the small narrow bed kissing; they were fully clothed. She felt angry with her own ignorance — she did not really know if or when he was ready for the act of love — angry with her parents for keeping her in ignorance, angry with Pete for his inarticulateness — his reticence. Two brothers and a father — she had seen them sometimes undressed and what she glimpsed on those rare occasions suggested power, but told her nothing. She had never before seen a man's body set for love.

They seemed to be just *necking*, sort of fooling around on the bed as they had done so many times before. She relaxed. He tried slipping her underpants down from beneath her skirt, but her garter belt got in the way so that the panties were imprisoned somewhere below her thighs. She did not help him. He pressed his body up close to hers, but nothing unusual seemed to be happening — nothing extraordinary was happening to her. Perhaps it takes a very long time to get started, she thought. Curiosity was making her impatient. She waited breathlessly. Pete's shirt seemed to come open; he was bare beneath it, his chest smooth and taut. He threw his trousers off quickly and she suddenly panicked and tried to jump from the bed. They grappled for a few moments, and then he kissed her, imprisoning her, and moved his body desperately on hers . . . She felt only a mild discomfort, not unpleasant but not irresistible either. At the end he pulled himself away from her spasmodically — and she felt what love there was between them sliding down her thighs. It had taken a long time to get started but it was over quickly, before she had even adjusted to the intrusion. Lying close to him now, she wondered why he had fought her with his body. They lay there in the silence of a defeat that follows questions that will go unasked.

"I can't, Jen. It's no good like this," he said finally, getting up heavily. "It's just not the way I dreamed it for us, not knowing like this, not belonging to each other — " She understood that Pete had to have everything neatly sealed and filed away in his mind under a label marked *Jennie,* or maybe *love,* or *marriage.* She needed more casualness in her life. Wasn't that the whole point of being young? She did not want to be handed an already illustrated book of her life; she must sketch it in for herself as she went along.

For the first time in his life he had gambled, and he knew he had lost. He felt her slipping away. He had thought to bind her to him with his body, but his own body had rebelled. He did not want to accustom his body to needing her. They were young — desire was at its peak — So was ineptitude. He wondered how something so natural had grown so complex.

He looked at his watch and jumped.

"Jesus," he said, "where the hell is Phil?"

"What time is it?" she asked, suddenly responsible again.

"Oh, Jennie, it's 12:30 already — "

"Oh," she said and sat down again unsteadily on the bed. "I'm going to be in an awful lot of trouble." And then she looked at Pete and said dully.

"Pete, am — am I — is everything all right? I mean I won't get pregnant will I?"

"Ah no. No." He smiled a little, as if at her naiveté, "I didn't let anything happen inside of you." They looked at each other for a long moment and then Pete said to her softly. "Jennie, let's get married, I'll quit college, I'll get a job — "

"No, Pete, no, don't quit college, it's your only chance — Please — we can't talk about it now. I don't want to spoil it for you and I will — I'm not exactly sure how — but I know I will." In a more decisive voice she said, "There is a very strict curfew here for women, and it's midnight. It's expulsion, or suspension at best, if I'm caught. I must go immediately."

"I'll phone for a cab," he said.

"A cab at this time of night, in this weather! If we got one at all it would take a half-hour or more to get here."

"Christ," he said, "can we walk?"

"Well it will be a long, cold walk but I guess it's our only choice right now."

Hunching up hard against the bitter March wind, they trudged in silence through snow and ice made lurid by the moonlight. Jennie in her high heels slipped and teetered precariously. She hesitated to hold onto Pete's arm. More than halfway there they spotted Phil's car speeding along Main Street.

When he brought them to the door it was already well after one in the morning. She did not stop in to see the housemother, Mrs. Chalmers, although her door was partly opened, suggesting that she was still awake. The student who had night watch that evening was off duty at 12:30, but the sign-in book remained open on the desk. Everyone who was out had signed in by midnight. Jennie looked at the clock in the hall and signed 2:00 A.M. She mounted the stairs on tiptoe.

Her roommates were sleeping. She lay in her bed, unable to sleep. She thought numbly, What had their relationship ever really been but a series of good-byes wedged in between *curfews*, first his — and then hers?

The next morning an exhausted sinner, she stood before the dean of women and learned that she was to be suspended for the balance of the term, and would be expected to do the whole term over next fall if she were to continue. Her parents would receive a letter — that meant Aaron of course.

The suspension itself would not be difficult to tell her father about, only the reason for it. But her mother must not know! It would be one more nail in her coffin.

(49)

JENNIE HAD HAD TO LIE to her mother, to tell her that she hadn't been feeling well, the flu or something like that and so she had come home to recuperate, but would return as soon as she felt better. She would make up the missed work over the summer, she said. Eve didn't believe it and kept threatening to call up to the school to check her story, but somehow she didn't. She just sank into an obdurate silence, refusing to talk to her for weeks, a thing in itself alarming because of her usual verbosity.

It seemed to Jennie that nothing she had done since graduation came out right. She could not seem to make a move that didn't hurt someone she cared about. Aaron was stonily angry. Oh, she knew it wasn't the interruption of her education, or even the stigma of suspension — only the *reason* for it. He had always trusted her, he said, and now he didn't know what to think. She hated to lie to him and yet she had to, she told herself, if only to protect Pete. She assured Aaron that nothing had happened; they had just stayed out too late and Phil's car had broken down — they had had to walk back in foul weather. Aaron appeared to believe her, although he had put her through a third degree when she first got home. But after that he seemed pleased about having her back. Now the nest that he had so cozily prepared was whole again.

And Pete, she knew she had hurt him, was hurting him each time she left a letter of his unanswered. He did not phone because of Aaron, and she was glad, but he had written her a couple of letters. In the last one he said that if she did not answer his letter he would understand that it was over between them. She did not answer his letters, but it had not all gone out of her heart.

Worst of all, she had only succeeded in adding to her mother's endless roster of disappointments. She tried to raise her spirits by offering up Evan as a bribe. *Look, Mother, you can be so proud of him with his 95 average and already preparing applications to Harvard, Yale, and Princeton.* She had the feeling again of the strange reversal of roles. She felt like the mother saying to her child, "Oh never mind that broken toy. See, here's a bright and shining new one — amuse yourself." It did not work.

She felt hollowed out inside — shell-like. Already she missed the intellectual stimulation of the university. Showdowns, crises, decisions, she should have grown used to them by now; she had cut her teeth on them. But she kept trying to change things. She dreamed of order — peace — but chaos just seemed to spring up around her, like a wild harvest.

(50)

JENNIE'S FEELING about the Payne-Whitney Clinic and her mother was that it would be a short-lived union. Even in extreme inertia, her mother showed vestiges of that iron will.

Eve had agreed to go, she said, only because "I can't face another of those deadly summers alone again in the heat, aimlessly wandering the deserted city streets. Here at least I'll get to see people. Even sick people are better than none."

It was mid-April of '46, almost a year since she and her father had first discussed it. He still had not gotten the apartment he promised, "The *post*war housing shortage is too acute." But Jennie felt he could have swung it if he really wanted to. Certainly it was not the money — but the old antagonisms, the *rejection vendetta* . . . Nothing ever really changed for them, Jennie thought.

Eve seemed to be getting worse, more reclusive. She had seen

Dr. Goldbart only sporadically. He said that the one way she would be able to get concerted help would be at the clinic, where he could see her daily.

April *was* the cruelest month.

A foghorn groaned forlornly as the taxi pulled up to the famous clinic, an elegantly sprawling compound of white brick and pearl-gray granite. "Funny how people pay such fortunes to live near the East River," Eve said. "I've always found it melancholy."

Once they entered and the tall, forbidding doors closed behind them, Jennie's stomach wrenched hard and she felt unsteady on her legs. She saw her mother's stricken look; her whole body seemed to crumple in defeat. They were ushered into a room where they waited to see Dr. Goldbart. The room was wood-paneled and book-lined and had the atmosphere of the library of a great hall. Eve looked momentarily comfortable here. Her life had been lined with books, like the walls of her many living rooms. Her constant and musty companions, they provided few disappointments and above all offered no resistance, giving her only pleasure, no pain. That was much more than she could say for the people in her life.

A pleasant, matronly-looking lady who was probably a nurse hovered in attendance. Eve sat looking dismally into her lap, saying nothing.

Dr. Goldbart came, after what seemed an interminable wait, and greeted them warmly. He seemed in a breathless hurry. Jennie had hoped that this man would have some time and patience for Eve — she needed it so desperately.

Jennie had met Doctor Goldbart only briefly some months before when she had brought her mother here to his office for the first time. He did *not* have a Viennese accent, not even a Jewish one; he was not of the Freudian school so popular then. He was a thoroughly American, overly busy, harried, hurried New York psychiatrist. Tense, slim, dark, and of average height, he was somewhere in the vicinity of forty-five or fifty. He radiated the electric aura of his own closely nurtured neurosis. Some women might have called him attractive. Eve didn't like him. She didn't like most doctors, psychiatrists in particular. They were for the most part pompous phonies, a description that she extended to include most men.

"Well, Mrs. Abel," he said, inclining to Eve, who glared at him suspiciously, "will you go with Mrs. Hansen," he indicated the nurse, "and see your room? Your daughter will be along presently."

"Why can't she come with me now?" Eve asked, alarmed, her voice tremulous.

"Well, I would like to talk to her for a few minutes, just more history and routine — things like that."

"I am in a much better position to tell you that kind of thing than my eighteen-year-old daughter, I assure you. I have lived my own life — no one else has lived it for me, and I haven't lost my wits yet, just my hopes," Eve said.

"I have already taken your history. Now I need some details from viewpoints other than your own."

There was an embarrassed silence while Jennie felt like a scurrilous traitor without having uttered even a word. And then the nurse began to walk Eve down the long, dark corridor.

Once seated in the elegant office with the doctor's impressive credentials lining the wall, Jennie tried to relax.

"What do you know about your mother?" Taken off guard on a subject so vast and spectacular, she was tempted to answer, "Everything and nothing," or something slick like, "What does anyone ever *know* about anyone else?" But she thought for a minute . . . What *did* she really know? She knew as fact only what she saw before her now, this lachrymose and broken woman, so profoundly angry. She knew there was a time when she had been otherwise. But if so, when? Hardly within her sphere of memory. Only perhaps woven in and out of the fabric of her mother's life or her extraordinary letters to her, to others, were visible the skeins of a wasted singularity. What good would defending her mother's past do now; her mother was her own best champion of the past. She answered simply, "I only know that she is very unhappy, Doctor Goldbart."

"Yes, yes, that is the obvious," he said waving away Jennie's simple truth. "What I want to know is how, why, when." She noticed him fidgeting with a piece of loose wood at the corner of his desk, making clicking sounds that momentarily distracted her. "Now how do you suppose she might have become so — so unhappy, as you call it? From your father I haven't been able to get much of a picture. I don't mind telling you, he has been of very little help indeed." She looked astonished, she did not know that Aaron had seen him too. She wondered why he hadn't told her.

"All he kept telling me was, what a beautiful girl she was — "

Jennie had to stifle a smile in spite of her irritation. No one, nothing ever changes, least of all *her* parents.

After a painful forty-five minutes while Jennie groped at understanding and grasped at straws of memory, he pushed back his chair in what appeared to be a fit of frustration with her cloddishness and clinical ignorance and said in a sort of irritated summation:

"So this then is what we have to work with. A sensitive young girl who early loses the father she fixates on, in an accident that her mother holds *him* responsible for. Whether consciously or unconsciously, she longs to replace him — thinks maybe *your* father is the right man because he seems determined, forceful, but finds her needs go far deeper than that, is disappointed in her choice, her *life*. She is manipulative, demanding of her friends, insatiably hungry for attention and especially for approval and love, which she seems only to have gotten from the sister she loved and lost. She was, perhaps still is, a flamboyant romantic, capable of extreme joy and extreme depression, almost at the same moment. She is now middle-aged, the chances of turning dreams into reality are dwindling rapidly — there is the menopausal factor too — so the lost dream has turned to anger — the anger to despair — hence we have extreme melancholia or a type of depression, which, I might add, has been building up steadily through the years, like pressure before an earthquake."

When he finished this soliloquy, he sat back in his seat, suddenly relieved and calm. Jennie was breathless and excited. She felt hurt and angry that this stranger should reduce the sum of her mother's life to a recklessly labeled paragraph, marked *typical*. Or was it? She wasn't sure of anything at this moment.

"Doctor, I'm — I'm very impressed with your quick study," she said tartly. "But you don't — you can't possibly know my mother by pasting together some basic truths. You cannot know what a fine mind she had, what her intellectual and esthetic capabilities were —"

"What does that matter now? Such is the stuff that dreams are made of."

"I thought you doctors put a great deal of emphasis on dreams," Jennie said coldly.

"Well, this is not getting us any further along in helping her," he said irritably. "She wants, has always wanted, to live on her own intense terms and there is simply no one around her who can sustain her intensity — or has the time and patience to care. Little by little she has lost everyone by attrition. If perhaps she had indeed chosen an intellectual environment such as she speaks of romantically, a university post, say, or if she had become a writer" — my God, now he sounds like her, she thought — "a confessional poet of sorts, she could have gotten out her *hurts*, but this way — ," and he began to shake his head slowly and negatively.

"The question is how can you help her?" Jennie asked. "Here — in this place?" She looked around deprecatingly. "Or wouldn't she be better off at — at . . ." She couldn't say the word *home*.

"Was she? Look, she's only here for observation, to see if we can help her — there are no promises, no quick cures. There are, however, some new drugs," he murmured this, as if uncertain about sharing his methods with a layman, and only a young adult at that.

"I doubt very much if she will submit to drugs," Jennie said.

"Well that's *our* problem isn't it?"

No, she wanted to cry, it's not, it's mine in the final analysis — all mine —

"And there is always electric shock. It's worked miracles in these cases, and quickly — " Jennie blanched.

All the way down the narrow corridor to her mother's room she thought in a kind of groping terror of guilt — shock . . . lose consciousness — break the spine — humbug — drugs — zombies — Mrs. Farmer's delicate voice followed her down the corridor with its primly locked doors, her face, white and chiseled like marble, flashed before her — her body shattered in a million tiny fragments on the pavement beneath the ugly windows of her building.

The door to her mother's room was open. Eve was seated on the narrow, virginal bed. Jennie's heart sank, *another cell.* A nurse hovered, officiously bustling around in the dresser drawers.

"They took away my mirrors, can you imagine? Why my mirror? I — I don't understand — " She walked over to the window, and tried to open it, but it moved up only about an inch and then seemed to lock mysteriously.

"Ridiculous," Eve said loudly for the nurse's benefit. "If I were going to try to kill myself I would have done it long ago, all these years alone in a cell just like this one, with no one to watch me. It's just as well," she said with resignation, "mirrors are for the young. I don't want to see myself growing old — everything sagging downward toward the grave, eyes, jowls, breasts — " Jennie, who was concerned with getting through eighteen, wondered if she would ever be *young.*

(51)

ONCE AGAIN JENNIE FOUND HERSELF in the unsympathetic, teeming lobby of the Hotel St. Moritz. With dread she rode the twenty-three floors to her mother's empty room. She must go now to pore over her meager possessions. Eve had requested this and that item, and besides, Aaron had asked Jennie to organize the confusion there, so that if it appeared that her mother would stay at the clinic, he could move her things out quickly. Why should he be paying *two* enormous rentals? he said. After all, he could use the money more positively toward the fifteen thousand a year at Payne-Whitney. Two hundred a month for one *tiny* room was ridiculous. Why, his whole apartment of nine rooms only cost three hundred and fifty dollars. Jennie thought that this could be a positive factor, because if Eve had nowhere to stay whenever she came out of "that place," she would be forced to stay with them. Then Aaron would find her an apartment. Fast, she hoped — This idea tickled at the back of her brain, but she brushed it away, ashamed. She rationalized in this way as she rode the elegant brass cubicle upward with a party of boozy revelers.

The room was stuffy and warm, a blizzard of orderly disarray. Yellowed and forgotten newspapers lay in stacks on the radiator. She saw that many were carefully marked and underlined in different-colored pencils.

Jennie sat down heavily on the small bed. There wasn't much choice. The night table by the bed, a salvaged treasure, one of the originals from the peach and green period, now trembled on its rickety little Louis Quatorze legs and groaned under its weight of books and snow of papers. A series of small appointment books lay around on the table top. She leafed through two and saw that they went from year to year. On these pages were scribbled everything of no consequence — and nothing that was insignificant, the fragments of her mother's life. She searched for the current book, feeling treacherous. It was lying under the *Opera News*. 1946 was jotted in the inside cover in flaming red — the last three years of her life lying about the table top in fading reddish-brown paper booklets, the pages less densely filled with each year, more open spaces between lines every month.

January 2, intermittent rain, underlined in green.

January 8, my twenty-first wedding anniversary, an ink line through it, crossing it out — annulling.

January 11, call Doctor B. re: dear Evan's health form.

A.A. phoned, underlined in bright red — (apropros, Jennie thought).

Send dear Jennie's black shoes up to college.

Buy her charm for bracelet at Marchal's.

January 13, lunched at Stouffer's.
Studied opera libretto.
Met Jane W. at opera house.

Jennie recognized the names of the solid old reliables like Marcy Janis and Ellie Baker, but now and then there appeared the faceless names of a few women friends whom she had heard her mother mention from time to time, culled at random from here and there, the public library perhaps, the lobby of the Barbizon Hotel for women or the opera house, standees whom she had rescued, from their delicious martyrdom — invited to fill the empty seat beside her — her coveted Friday night subscription tickets that she'd held for fifteen years.

Sing away sorrow
Cast away care

(*Cervantes*) she had scribbled at the bottom of the page.

March 15, see Reid's English teacher re: last test.
April 2, go to Reid's swim meet.

She glanced through the other little books, looking intently for — she didn't know exactly what. In each, her wedding anniversary noted and underlined in red or green — according to her mood at the time, Jennie imagined. She felt a cold lump rising in her throat. 1945 — 1944 — the children — the children, everything bounded by the children — the children that she wasn't even sure were hers anymore —

On the night table, in the sea of papers and unpaid bills were dunning letters. She was always threatening to take Aaron to court to get her allowance raised in accordance with the enormous escalation of his business since the depression agreement. But Al Carton had already told her that with Aaron having custody now, she wouldn't have a chance. She called other lawyers, they put her off.

Scribbled on a note pad were a few desperate resolutions before she had succumbed to the waiting arms of Doctor Goldbart.

Go for manicure.

Jennie thought of her mother's soft and strangely peeling fingernails, like the shell of a dying baby turtle, the kind they used to flush down the toilet when they were children. *Start diet — Enroll New School re: Greek poetry — send money to Mama.* And scribbled beneath:

What is a wasted life,
Only one that isn't lived.

Jennie sat numbly on the bed. She couldn't remember what she had come for.

*

At dinnertime she came into the apartment feeling as if she had been drained of blood. It was a Thursday. Mamie was off. She was relieved. She wondered if the boys were home, and she headed gratefully for the cool, blue and silver privacy of her bedroom, equipped now with her own private telephone.

She threw herself on the bed, exhausted. Evan came to the door and seemed to want to talk. She forced herself to an upright position. He sat down on the edge of the bed. Neither spoke. Then Evan said, "So how did it go today, Jen?"

"Oh as well as can be expected, I suppose," she said.

"Do you think she'll stay?"

"No," she replied.

"Do you think they can help her if she does?"

"I don't know — " They sat for a moment, silent.

"Thanks, Jen," he said. "I mean about today and all." She reached for his hand in reply and held it momentarily. He said, still looking down, "I should have gone to the opera with her those last few times she asked me."

"That wouldn't have changed anything really," Jennie said. She looked at her brother and thought that he was handsome, growing to look more like his father every day. She remembered how many times he had been father to her dolls and Reid had been uncle and they had taken one favorite doll, Loretta, out to "the park," in imitation of what close-knit families did, she supposed. The closet had been the park and she had locked them into the closet and then forgotten all about them. They had waited patiently for such a long time in there before banging on the door — they had been

afraid to spoil it for "Loretta" — for her. She realized that without
her brothers her life would have been unbearable.

"Where's Dad?" she said.

"On the phone as usual, in his room," Evan said.

"Oh."

Aaron came and stood on the threshold of her room awkwardly.

"So?" he said with that slight borscht belt intonation, that might
translate *nu?*

"So, so what? I did it," Jennie said flatly. Aaron came into the
room, and Evan jumped up politely so as to make room on the bed
for his father. He began to walk out of the room.

"Evan, stay, let's talk. This concerns us all," Aaron said to
Evan's retreating back.

"No, I've spoken to Jen a little already. I have to finish an assignment."

"I don't understand that guy," Aaron mumbled. "He's a lot
like *her*."

They talked, hashing over the same things they'd said so many
times before. Eve, her unhappiness, her basic goodness. Jenny, for
the moment, could not tell him about the notebooks.

Aaron looked philosophical and then said, out of no particular
context, "I needed to be stronger, strong enough for two. I needed
to rise above my own neurosis, but what did I know *then* — only
to work — to make a good buck. In my house, when I was a little
kid all I could remember hearing was *gelt, gelt, alles, gelt.* Whenever anybody was hungry or cold or tired from working the question was *'Du host gelt? Neyn?'* Then, you worked, or you hun-
gered, or you froze." Jennie was silent, she knew much of this
already. What she wanted to say was, "It was not strength you
needed for Mama, Dad, it was patience; you could have been more
patient," but she knew that he was an impatient man. She said
nothing.

He said, "I was too busy — I didn't have the patience . . .
I didn't make the time — " as if talking from a long distance. She
looked at him. He looked tired. She saw that his face was set in

the lines of a man who is afraid that he is not loved. His constant feverish workouts at the gym kept his body slender and youthful, with an electric vitality, but his strong, fleshy face seemed to be growing into its own lines and seams, especially his forehead — Such an expressive forehead, she thought!

"Why must everything be someone's *fault?*" she said. "Don't some things just grow that way?"

"Yes, I suppose," Aaron said. "It's funny, though, how that doctor doesn't want me to visit her. He says it's like waving a red flag before a bull. Can you imagine?" Aaron said, laughing incredulously.

Her eyes rested indulgently on her father.

Aaron just sat there looking down at the floor, his hands clasped loosely before him.

"Whatever happened to Pete," he ventured, trying to sound casual, his eyes still on the floor.

"Oh I don't know, Dad, guess he's still at school."

"He was all right," Aaron said magnanimously. "In fact, an awfully sweet boy, very decent — " She knew that *all right* was her father's kiss of death.

"Just wasn't exactly right for you, wasn't strong enough."

"Not enough like you, huh, Dad?"

"I'm not saying that, although he *is* a very different type than I am — than I was at *his* age. Not exactly full of piss and vinegar."

"He's not exactly full of shit either."

Aaron looked up quickly, but Jennie's face showed no trace of bitterness.

"Well don't knock ambition — being willing to fight the good fight . . ."

"Oh, Dad, he's just finished two years of fighting the good fight, now he comes home and has to fight another — to get an education, to make a buck, get a job — get his girl," she said softly. "And he's not the kind of guy who'd ever take a cent from anyone."

"Oh beautiful," Aaron said explosively, "very beautiful. Then how's he gonna get it, will you tell me that? I didn't work all these years for my only daughter to wind up broke and idealistic. That's what I meant when I said *sweet* — idealistic."

She wished he would stop calling Peter Schore *sweet*. He was fine and decent and had an awfully sweet *mouth*, but, God, *he* wasn't sweet. She thought in a sudden rush of old feeling that he was serious and responsible and could laugh easily. He was, she realized sadly, probably the nicest boy she'd ever met in her life.

Aaron continued, "He's *too* fine, would have never been able to handle you. Not sophisticated enough for you, I guess."

"We just met too soon," she said, suddenly embarrassed to be discussing Pete like this with her father. "My life is in a quandary. Right now there are a million directions I want to go in at once, and marriage isn't one of them, not yet — ," she said.

"You don't have to make any commitments right now. You want to have a good time, go places, see things, broaden your horizons. I'll take you all over, we'll travel, you'll meet all kinds of exciting people — men. Then you'll be in a better position to make decisions — You know, you turned out beautiful — " She felt like a freshly baked cake. "Oh maybe not like your mother was, but you're a damn good-looking kid," he said magnanimously. A thousand times he had told her that, made that comparison, ever since she had started growing up. "You've got plenty of time."

"But then Pete won't be around," she said.

"If he really loves you he'll be around. What's *his* hurry? He's in no position to settle down and get married — to anybody."

"You know, Dad," she said wistfully, "sometimes you meet the right guy first, before you've even had a chance to make any comparisons. Beginner's luck," she said, laughing.

"Listen, you want to go out for dinner tonight?" He was clearly tired of the subject. "We can have a good steak at Gallagher's — you know it's one of my places — or if you want a quieter atmosphere, let's go over to the Algonquin. I know your mother always loved that place — " She noticed that he was speaking about her in the past tense. "And now that I have the concession there . . ."

She had often had lunch there with Eve before a matinee. In its oak paneled dining room, Eve had chattered, gaily imagining herself as part of this elegant anachronism, rubbing shoulders with the round-table wits . . . Dorothy Parker, or Bob Benchley, or George S. Kaufman, while Jennie was thoroughly absorbed by their splendid coconut layer cake —

"No I don't think I'm in the mood," she said.

"Well maybe the boys and I'll go down to the drugstore and bring up something to eat."

He jumped up from the bed as he heard one of the boys pass near Jennie's room.

"Hey, Evan. How about you and me and Reid having a catch in the park Saturday morning, huh?"

She didn't hear her brother's muffled reply.

"Reid," she heard her father's gravelly voice shouting through the apartment, "c'mon, we're going down to the drugstore, I'll need you to help me bring up the ice cream."

"We'll need a derrick," Reid shouted back from his rock collection — playful as ever.

Part III

The Errant Knight

(52)

IT WAS MORE THAN A YEAR since Jennie had left college. She was complaining about being at loose ends; she couldn't seem to find a person, place, or thing to settle down comfortably with. She was restless and bored — painfully bored. Most of her friends were either away at college, or at home and in college, or getting engaged and married.

Here she was sleeping until noon and worrying about her mother at the hospital. She often shopped for clothes to wear out at nights with one or the other of the many boys she was dating with great casual disinterest. She went to beautiful places with them, wore her beautiful clothes, smiled her beautiful smile, saw beautiful people, but it was an ivory mischief; there was no special beauty in it for her, no incandescence, like those quiet times at home with Pete, curled up in the big green chair in his arms, or the great kick of those occasional evenings that Pete had saved up for, when they went someplace grand where it was crowded and they could dance close — and be alone in the crowd.

Aaron asked her casually one day if she would like to try working for him at the executive offices of Abel Enterprises. "I could use one of my own there, to check the money when it comes in to be counted. It's all cash you know, very tempting."

"Tempting, to whom?" Jennie asked, pretending to be appalled. "You don't mean your sister Leah? She's one of your own." Aaron looked dubious. "You can't mean Joe Edelman, he's been book-keeper there forever, and you certainly don't mean *Jason Miller*," she said in mock surprise. Aaron had been silent throughout Jennie's banter. Then he said, "No, I certainly don't, but they need help there and I'd rather it be you than someone else, some stranger I wouldn't trust."

Jennie turned it over in her mind quickly. She'd prefer checking or doing the rounds of the restaurants and clubs — after all, she was doing them anyway at nights, on her own. But Aaron had always kept her firmly away from the checkrooms. Her mother's preaching must have left its mark. Or did he too really disdain the business, considering it base, beneath him? One always seemed to bite the hand that fed him. Only Jason Miller had seemed dedicated to the work. As to whether he was really suited to it remained a mystery, but it seemed to Jennie that much of his enthusiasm for the business had dwindled lately — Aaron's inability to relegate authority, his terror of losing the reins in any arena, could well defeat anyone who worked for him.

Aaron had decided that Jennie's job was to be behind the scenes at the office, to make sure no one was clipping him, anywhere, any*way*. To put an undercover agent in the midst of well-seasoned employees was, Jennie knew, to start off with a zero rating on the popularity scale.

Throughout much of her life it had been a common sight to find Jason at late breakfast with her father, hunched intimately over coffee, their heads together, talking earnestly. Sometimes she got a brief nod or shuffle of recognition, or an elaborately formal Good morning, Miss Abel." More often he hardly noticed her at all. Lately he seemed unduly interested in her *behavior* and often greeted her with a quick "Are you behaving yourself, Princess?"

But now she found it annoying to stumble out of her room in a wrapper, without make-up, groping for the breakfast table and coffee, and to find Jason there, freshly shaven, perfectly groomed and looking as if he had just stepped out of an ad for men's haberdashery — there was always that faint lavender odor of his cologne mixing oddly with the smell of her father's burnt toast.

A week or so before she was to go down to the offices of Abel Enterprises, Jason appeared at breakfast — as always unexpected, at least by Jennie. She was glad that she was dressed this morning and her hair brushed to its glossy burnished gold. As she approached the dining foyer her heart began to hammer in her chest for some crazy reason that she could not fathom. She took her coffee in the kitchen. Mamie whispered, Did she want any breakfast (she usually didn't). Mamie always whispered when Aaron was talking business with someone. She was walking back to her room with the coffee when Aaron called to her to sit down.

"Since you'll be going down there Monday, I think we should talk a little about it with Jason." She sat down uneasily. The table was small and wedged into a corner, another of her father's idiosyncrasies. Why couldn't they use the big comfortable dining room in the mornings?

Aaron began a halting and uncertain narrative explaining an absolutely simplistic pattern of fiscal sleuthing, the way they counted the coins and kept a tally on the cards that came in with the take from each girl at lunch and at the end of the long night. Jason listened quietly, in that serene, unblinking way he had, all the while watching Aaron's face intently as he talked — now and then the flick of his sardonic smile, that smile of special tolerance that he seemed to reserve for the Abel family. Jason said, *"Don't worry* about it, Jenna, it can't be too hard, or your Aunt Leah and Joe Edelman wouldn't be doing it all these years."

Jennie remembered now the rumor that there were some pretty bad feelings between Leah and Jason, but then again who could love Leah — so bitter and sour. She was remembering how she had always hated her mother through the years.

They had slipped into some other subject concerning one of the chain restaurants, the Brass Rail perhaps, Jennie thought, and they seemed to have forgotten all about her.

She sipped her coffee thoughtfully, careful not to rub her knees against Jason's long legs beneath the table; they were so tightly packed into the corner. She wasn't at all sure that she wanted to work with Jason either, although she knew that he only came by the office for a few hours during the afternoons — the rest of the time he was "at the places." She wondered about Dolly now; she hadn't seen her in years. She remembered that she used to be pretty, awfully pretty, although she had gotten fat — that's what Aaron had said (*fat* was the kiss of death in this business — anywhere on Broadway). She knew that she had been friends with Martha once upon a time, but that had waned too, probably since Martha had grown so imperious. Jennie had absorbed all of these things through the years. She had never much cared, but now suddenly she was sharply curious — The trouble was they were all too inbred, really, had been together too long, knew too much about each other. She sensed that Jason knew all about her parents, their private life, even their sex life or lack of it. Aaron used to tell him everything. She wasn't so sure about now anymore (though she sensed he knew about the clinic). Hearing Jason's deep voice in the background of her thoughts she remembered other things she had heard about his own life, his wife, his marriage. She looked at him now out of the corner of her eye and thought, how many beautiful women he must have known in his lifetime. Although if it were true, it must have been the best-kept secret on Broadway, because she'd never heard a breath of gossip about him. But it was not flamboyance that he projected. She saw a quiet man — and in the aftermath of the terrible din of her growing up, he seemed wholly desirable.

He pushed his chair suddenly from the table, his long form casting a shadow on the wall from the late morning sun. "I have to run — So long, see you Monday." He looked at her now briefly, but as if seeing her for the first time in years. "So long, Princess." He had that way of making her feel like loose change in the pocket of an old coat, unimportant, but not unwelcome —

(53)

S HE HAD BEEN WORKING DOWNTOWN at the office for a couple of weeks now — a generally dull routine, counting money, checking tallies, sitting bent over a desk surrounded by the warm metallic odor of soot and money. Aunt Leah's whining voice, cranky, sounding as if she were trying to transcend some physical pain, told her sharply that she resented the years of keeping Aaron's books, twisted and tangled but always in the black — it was this she probably resented more than anything else. It seemed ominous to Jennie that no one closely connected with her father seemed free from hostility.

After the office, she often went to visit her mother at the clinic. It seemed a miracle that Eve had stayed there this long — with constant and bitter complaints — no one had believed she would. But Jennie was troubled; she was not sure if the new-found docility was due to a real desire for improvement or just an unhealthy surrender. Jennie was allowed to visit a maximum of twice a week, to which she adhered slavishly, although the doctor had told her that for the time being, less was probably better. Sometimes the boys went with her. Aaron was strictly prohibited by the doctor from visiting, a fact which instantly set him against "that phony shrink," and the "ridiculous fees." The implied criticism that somehow he was being held responsible for her condition was a fairy tale, a myth to be laughed away.

Returning from one of these clouded visits alone, Jennie was deep in thought and didn't notice a flashy white Cadillac convertible with the top down parked conspicuously at the entrance. But as she turned to enter the building, she heard someone calling out to her and she saw her Uncle Max waving at her from the red leather back seat. He jumped out and came over to her on the sidewalk.

She hadn't seen as much of Uncle Max and Aunt Ina as she used to. She remembered how her mother used to say that he was an opportunist, not their friend — "He runs with the hares and hunts with the hounds — he knows what side *his* bread is buttered on . . . retired on the *pretense* of being sick, cardiovascular — been living off your father for years, but he's *her* friend and don't mistake it" — crazy talk from her mother, just more of her mother's jibberish from the long-playing record of their family album.

"Hi, honey, gee you look wonderful," he said. "What've you been doin', breaking a million hearts I suppose. You were always a heartbreaker — " Jennie felt momentarily confused, there was a woman in the front seat of the car, a blonde, youngish, pretty. She looked faintly familiar to Jennie, but — no — this woman looked heavy, bovine, her features blurred with weight. She could not exactly recall, not exactly. Vague, faint stirrings of recollection mixed somehow with pleasure and pain. She gave no indication of recognizing Jennie, so Jennie knew she must be wrong — decidedly wrong.

Uncle Max noticed the direction of Jennie's gaze and seemed suddenly uncomfortable. She wanted to ask him who it was, but she could not seem to locate the right words.

"Well, er, I'm waiting for your dad to come down, Jen, tell him to hurry up, will you?" Max licked his lips nervously. The woman was staring hard at her now. When Jennie turned she ducked her head quickly. Uncle Max was heading back toward the car and the waiting driver when she heard herself say, "Who's that at the wheel, Max"

"Oh — uh — huh? Oh, don't you know who that is?" While they spoke they were approaching the car, but Jennie pulled back instinctively. "Let me introduce you." Uncle Max seemed to be warming to the whole thing, rising to the occasion whatever it *was*. The woman was silent, an indolent, clumsy silence, heavy, like her body, her bloated face, and then Jennie realized that she was pregnant, absurdly pregnant, grotesquely. She had never seen a woman so distorted with pregnancy. It seemed to Jennie that she was

spreading wildly like a fungus, out of all proportion to normality —
She wants to be seen, so I will not see her.

"Come on, Jennie," her uncle seemed to be urging her to the
curb, to the car. He looked strangely crafty to her now, his small
eyes canine, vicious. The woman turned to her with a slightly sardonic smile that seemed to flicker out in disinterest, but her uncle
was persistent.

"Don't you know who this is, Jennie? Take a guess, take a
guess," he said grinning crazily. The woman offered no assistance
but looked at her unsmilingly.

Jennie was suddenly furious. "I don't want to play these child's
games, Max. Are you going to introduce me or not — !" And
then, as if by a last minute signal from the woman, he dismissed her.
"Aw, go ahead upstairs and get your father — I was just having
a little fun. You know I'm a tease like your old man."

She felt nothing at that moment, only a terrible emptiness, an
unfathomable depth of loneliness and fatigue.

At first she could not get her legs to move, she only knew that
she must put one before the other. She began walking into the
building, running fast into the elevator, breathless to escape — she
really did not know why. What had she seen? An unfamiliar car
— belonging to someone she did not know. Nothing, nobody,
— only a woman so swollen with the seed of some shadowy and unnamed man . . .

She would not even mention it to Aaron — it was too trivial.
Why should he care? It would disappear somewhere in her unconscious, locked together with some of the other dusty mysteries
of her childhood.

(54)

H E WAS KNOWN by variations of his given name. "Jace" by his friends, by the people he worked with, the checkroom girls — hard, flirtatious girls who acted silly when he came around. To his wife and family he was "Jaycee." But to Aaron he was always Jason, or more often, in a direct no-nonsense business vernacular, Jason Miller, as if it were one name instead of two. Right-hand man, shadow, thug, angel, no one seemed to know for sure, but everyone up and down that wild street knew Jason Miller.

Jennie's earliest recollections of him went back to when she was six or seven and he first began coming home with her father at dawn, and they'd sit and count the take there in the tiny living room of that Brooklyn apartment. Peeping from behind a door, to her child's sleep-filled eyes he seemed to loom up out of the shadows like the continuation of a dream, his pearly gray suit blending in, blurring into the grayness of dawn.

Sometimes she saw them do something with little metal objects the size of their hand, click something out, then lay them on the wooden table between them. They barely spoke, only in hushed tones. Jason never said much to her or her mother, and on those rare occasions when he did it was in a soft, quiet voice, gentle and assured. She hadn't paid much attention to him through the years, he was just there, in the background of her life, an enigma. She had dismissed him from her conscious mind, a shadow without substance.

She knew they didn't really like her being there, at the office. They resented her, felt she was watching them, spying, checking on them like the checkers they employed to check the checkers, she thought facetiously.

Jennie wasn't crazy about working with her Aunt Leah, either, or the embittered and balding Joe Edelman, but with Jason there it might be bearable, she hoped — that is, when he wasn't patronizing her or being overprotective and paternal, always there protecting her father's interests, and after all, wasn't she one of them, his only daughter? "The Hatcheck Princess," the newspapers had called her; Jason called her that sometimes too, in his amused, offhand way. But when he was there he managed to keep the others' steady flow of complaining and backbiting down to a minimum. She wondered how many years they had sat there, these three, in that musty, ill-furnished room, grudgingly counting her father's money, locked into a kind of fraternal hatred.

Jason ran the money machine in silence; its noise made it difficult to be heard. He filled it with coins, the machine separated, stacked, and wrapped the money into gaily colored packets, his deft fingers quickly organizing them into columns.

"The king was in his counting house counting out his money," Jennie said in mock nursery rhyme style, her head down over an envelope of money from the Latin Quarter. Jason pulled down hard on the lever and smiled. "The king doesn't count his money, we do." Leah laughed grudgingly, a short, attenuated laugh. Jennie detected the cynic behind Jason's slow smile. She wondered sharply what he really thought of her father. She was torn between feelings of pride and shame. As a child she had always thought of her father as a *king*, a mighty warrior. But years of Eve's pounding about his "vileness," and the "gangsterism" of the business, and she felt somehow culpable, unable to wash off the taint of the coatrooms, the strong carbolic odor of the washrooms.

Today was Friday. The whole long, hot weekend stretched out ahead of her, aimless and uneventful. The room was warm and close, and the acrid smell of the money, combined with the faint scent of Jason's pomade, made her feel a little giddy, stimulated. Funny, she thought, how invariably the scent of money excites.

Jason got up, turned toward the machine and stretched, yawning loudly. She had the feeling that his back and shoulders must be smooth and hairless beneath his thin white shirt — the thought had zigzagged through her mind like lightning and was gone in a minute. Crazy, she thought. Who cares?

He bent to light a cigarette, his head low over the lighter, cupping his hands against the faint September breeze that blew in from the open crack of the window.

She thought how gracefully he did that, saw the shadow of his long dark lashes on his cheek.

"Careful," she said, "or you'll singe your lashes." He put his lighter back in his pocket, took a long drag from his cigarette, and flicked a glance in her direction. "Why, Jennie, I didn't know you cared," he said, smiling slightly. Jennie reddened and returned the smile.

Leah and Joe, who were getting used to their occasional bursts of sexual badinage brightening the heavy silence like confetti, pretended not to notice, but Leah looked crafty and knowing. Jennie wanted to impress him with her worldliness, to remind him that she had grown up, was not to be treated as the boss's spoiled brat little girl anymore.

"Trust we'll see you on Monday," Jason said as she brushed past him on her way out.

"I — well — probably."

"Tsk, tsk," he made a mock reproving sound. "We must be able to count on our employees now, mustn't we?"

"Good-bye, Jason," she called, a laugh bubbling up in her throat.

The next day, a Saturday, she had planned to go downtown to Macy's and Gimbels. It was a hot Indian summer day, typical weather for the approaching Jewish holidays. She thought, God is smiling on his chosen people once again — fiercely.

Aaron stomped through the long mirrored foyer, looking harried. "Jen, whaddya doing today — "

"Going shopping. I guess I'll go downtown.

"Where?"

"To Macy's. They have some French designer imports I want — "

"That's perfect. I'm finally going to get some help from you —

I should get *some* help out of you for all you cost me, don't you agree?" he said teasingly. "I want you to bring some papers for Jason to sign."

"I didn't know he came into the office on Saturday."

He worked Friday and Saturday nights until early morning, and she knew Saturday afternoons were sacrosanct.

"He doesn't, but his apartment is right near the office, you know, over a few blocks west — "

She had dressed carefully on this day, wearing fresh white linen to fight the oppressive heat, but in the taxi she was already beginning to feel wilted and clammy. She suddenly remembered that Jason's wife and mother were in Florida for a few weeks, a situation that she found ironic, it had a sort of Ethan Frome sting — that mother who had been so opposed to Dolly from the start, threatening to throw herself from a window if he married her and Dolly threatening to slit her wrists if he didn't. But he did marry her some eight years ago and they had all remained in the same house, together under one roof. After Jason's father died, his mother and his wife had become constant companions; Dolly was almost her nurse.

The apartment building, ordinary prewar, discreetly businesslike, looked like Jason; its best exposure was a view of the Manhattan Opera House.

When no one answered the bell she was sure her father had forgotten to call him and he'd gone out — or maybe he was on the telephone. He too lived his life chained to a telephone. Some five hundred girls had to check in with him in the course of a week — no wonder he seemed to her so immune to beautiful women.

He finally opened the door, looking rather tentative and surprised. She seemed to have startled him. He must have just finished shaving, for he still had a towel around his neck and his hair and skin looked wet. His shirt was completely unbuttoned, the sleeves rolled up to the elbows as if he had just thrown it on in a hurry. The apartment was pleasantly air-cooled, and the sharp change from the suffocating cab ride caused her an involuntary shiver.

"Jennie — what are you doing here?"

"Oh, that's what I figured, my father didn't call you — oh, I'm sorry, but you know him, he's — "

"That's okay, let me just finish drying myself. Come in with me and tell me about it."

She followed him, confused, through the gloomy apartment to the bedroom, surprisingly neat in spite of its unmade double bed, and stopped at the bathroom, a large old-fashioned one. It was strangely quiet, no radio playing, just a heavy silence while Jason rattled around with a few bottles and jars in front of the mirror.

"I'm supposed to give you these papers to sign — "

"Yeah, I know what they are," he cut her off. "He wants them signed today." He finished drying his hair and neck, turned away from the mirror, and looked at her now without the usual amusement. Suddenly they were staring at each other, silently, dumbly, in the blinding clinical white light of the bathroom. Voluptuously, as if in a dream, without self-conscious preliminaries, she moved closer to him and he pulled her to him gently with a sudden surge of sweetness that she would never have believed him capable of. Her body felt at once weightless and heavy, the papers slipped from her hand to the floor. She thought for one crazy instant that he must have been drinking, but she knew he didn't drink and there was no odor of alcohol about him, only the faint rich odor of hair and skin, dark hair, swarthy skin that had its own special pungency. His hair and face were still damp, the aftershave lotion smelled woodsy, the dark brown mole near his mouth was velvety close — she saw it in a haze of blurry sweetness before she closed her eyes.

It seemed to her it was in slow motion they began undressing each other, smoothly, deftly, as if they were lovers whose every hook and button were familiar. Her arms wrapped around his neck, her lips moved to his throat, his chest. His head back, his eyes closed, he moaned a little, kissed her mouth again, undid her brassiere, bent to kiss her breasts, her navel, all the while her lips gently slipping across his hands, his fingers, with her eyes still closed. She felt him bare to the waist, yet she could not remember a single gesture of undressing, none. Walking with him the few steps to the bed seemed a hallucination that she had seen in flashes somewhere before, but to be looked at objectively, standing off on the sidelines, dreaming about some other people. It seemed to her that their mouths had not separated for an instant, and then she felt the length of his warm body against hers. Suddenly, without will, with no sense of past or present, her thighs opened, her body arched upward to meet his, and a sensation of fullness, an instant of such exquisite sensuality enveloped them that neither moved for a moment or spoke, but were transfixed mutually by the rich surprise, the suddenness of the whole encounter. She felt weighted beneath him, weighted to insensibility, and yet she was all senses, heavy, buttery with sensation. He kissed her again slowly now, their heads moving gently from side to side, his hand cupping her face, stroking her hair. Jennie whispered his name, "Jace, Jace" — the very invocation of his name seemed to draw him nearer, closer, deeper, her own wildness enticing him to a pitch of ecstasy, but even now their bodies moved only slightly, rhythmically, as if they couldn't bear even the fragmentary pulling back before the inward thrusts. Nothing was hurried, only lovely liquid movement until the moment when he instinctively tightened his grip, as if he knew she might pull away from him, afraid to surrender completely at the last instant — A moment later Jason lay on his back with his eyes closed, his arm flung across his eyes, the other still under Jennie's shoulders. She turned into the crest of his arm so that her mouth was close to his shoulder; they looked at each other briefly, mutually sealing the secret that had just passed between them. He kissed her closed eyelids and drew his arm from beneath her. Without sitting up, he reached for a cigarette by his bedside where a pack lay opened, and groped for a match. He lay on his back, one arm across his eyes, inhaling the smoke deeply, blowing it out, his lids half-closed, heavy, blue-veined. "Oh Jesus," he said, "what have I done?"

Another long, smoke-filled silence and he said, "I didn't hurt you, did I, Jen? I felt as if I would break you in two — you seem so — so, delicate to me." It came to her mind now, a remnant of conversation, something her father had confided in her once, unaccountably, about Jason and Dolly. How he hadn't been able to make love to her for a few years, that she had gotten fat and "he couldn't get it up for her" was what Aaron had said, her father so clinical and unimaginative —

"It's my father, isn't it, more than anything?"

There was a long pause.

"Jennie," he said quietly, "he's — he's been like a father to me — "

"That sort of makes this incest, then doesn't it," she said, trying to sound light and offhand.

"You really don't have much use for your old man, do you?"

She felt oddly assailed — Why was he always going on about her father? She did not want to think about that now, it was obtrusive here — nobody else, nothing that connected them, only herself and this man, detached, suddenly forged together out of the atmosphere. "Jace," she said, touching him lightly with her fingertips — and somehow she could not finish. She had just shared with him a special experience of the greatest intimacy, but the moment had passed, and although she had known him all her life, she realized that they were really only strangers. She had wanted to tell him that he had been her *first*. If he knew about it at all, he could not count what had been with Pete as anything more than what it was, an adolescent experiment in love. It was not necessary to tell him that she had never before shared with a man that shuddering, belly-tightening, explosive moment that had just torn them apart and bound them together so irrevocably — "Jen, I'm seventeen years older than you, and I'm married. It's crazy, it should never have happened — "

"Is that your last word on the subject?" she said. He looked at her now, smiling that slow, quizzical smile, and rumpled her hair, as if to remind himself and her that she was, after all, just a kid — the boss's beautiful kid. He jumped up. "Jen, I've got to get to work. I was getting ready to leave when you came in."

"Aren't you glad you didn't?"

Jennie tried to get up from the bed. Her body was trembling, her legs felt rooted, they dragged at her whole body. She lay down again. She wished she could just lie back on the bed in the cool, dark room and stay there all day — all night even, until he came back from the clubs — but she was afraid to broach it, she knew how he would laugh.

She went to him in the bathroom while he stood before the mirror, a towel around his waist. She felt awkward about her own nakedness, her large breasts unruly without their usual imprisonment, and grabbed a towel to cover herself. From behind she wrapped her arms around his waist. He had grown thicker than she remembered him through the years, but, looking at his reflection now in the mirror, he was still a handsome man. She lay her cheek on his smooth bare back; it felt cool. Her towel dropped and her nipples swayed against his back. "Jace," she said, "I want to spend every last minute with you because I know that every minute may be the last." In the mirror she saw him close his eyes momentarily, saw his stricken look, and then he turned and began to put her gently out of his way. "I've *got* to get going, Jen — " he reached over and turned on the shower, as if to strengthen his words. He got in and pulled the shower curtain around him, closing her out once again into the cold white anonymity of the room — really another woman's bathroom. But there were so few signs of Dolly in the apartment that she found it difficult to believe that there was another woman at all.

She opened the shower curtain and stepped into the tub.

Jason didn't look surprised, but drew her close to him.

"Jen, oh baby," he said, softly into her hair that was already damp from the spray. She lay her head on his chest and inhaled his heartbeat. She felt his body grow rigid, and as he kissed her mouth, drew her down into the tub, his movements seemed to her slow and hypnotic. The porcelain felt warm against her back, her hair was wet and loose about her face, but she felt nothing but him — his body — the essence of it in and all around her. She tightened her arms around his neck, caressed his hair — her touch seemed to drive him wild . . . the shower hazing the air like a warm spring rain.

When they opened the door, the phone was ringing loudly. Jason ran to answer it. It was her father.

*

She did not go down to the office and she had not seen or heard from him in weeks. She knew with a certainty that he would not call her. His work, her father, the whole story — this business meant more to him than anything or anybody, was all the romance he really cared about. She understood it in a way and knew immediately after that day that this was just something that *happened*, with no past, no present, no future — suspended in limbo.

(55)

SHE GREW PAINFULLY AWARE of her body, every ache a sensuous reminder. Lovingly, she tended her bruises like African violets.

In the weeks that followed, she developed a terror of the telephone. She would let it ring and ring, pretending not to hear, waiting for someone to answer it.

One evening Aaron, poring over some contracts, called angrily from his room, "Pick up that phone, Jenna, for God's sake." It was Jason calling for her father. Her heart raced so hard that she could barely speak above a whisper.

"Oh — Jason. How are you?" Her lips wanted to form the word "darling" but they did not dare.

Jason sounded unnaturally polite. He asked after her health. There was a silence — then —

"How come you're not working for me anymore, Princess? Did you find a better job?" he asked very softly.

"Oh I'll get down there one of these days . . ."

"We've got to be able to rely on our employees, you know — "

As always, he made her want to giggle like a kid. She felt lightheaded — a girlish girl. She laughed tightly and said, "I'll get Dad."

As soon as she said it she was sorry. Why had she been in such a rush to get off the telephone? She should have dragged out the moment, talked about — about anything. She hated herself for a coward. Her knees were shaking but she thought, he missed me, he wants me . . . Beyond that, she did not know what to think.

She knew that she could not work there any longer. But just to see him once again, to read carefully his reaction, just *to know*, would be perfect peace. This was crazy, she told herself — disgusting — sodden with love, lovesick over a man almost twice her age. Well maybe it was not exactly love, at least not the same kind of love she had been brought up to recognize.

Aaron had been asking her why she didn't go to the office anymore. She told him that she hated counting money. It was depressing and they really didn't need her there. It was a filthy job, her hands were black when she finished . . . She felt grimy all over. But that part she would not say. She knew that Aaron's defensive response would be much the same as it had been to her mother through the years. "You don't feel dirty when you spend it," or "Your hands don't get soiled when you pass it over the counter." And he was right, it was true. She had become a full-fledged hedonist under Aaron's wing. She was floating down the path of least resistance.

*

At nights, lying in her bed unable to sleep, it was not Pete she thought of any longer but only Jason and the soft brown mole near his mouth. And she staged scenes in her mind of a million different places she might meet him accidentally — fetchingly dressed, alluring. Each morning when she woke, her heart hammered in her chest until she was breathless. Maybe this would be the morning, maybe this morning she would walk into the hall to find him hunched over coffee in the foyer, his long legs tangled uncomfortably around the little wooden chair. But she knew he would not come, that he would find some reason, some excuse not

to come even if Aaron asked him to stop by. It was not that he did
not want to see her — she knew that — she kept telling herself that
— but because he knew that seeing her again would only seal in
more securely their mutual need.

*

To Aaron, bred in the chill, heatless world of the ghetto, Miami
Beach was the panacea for all things from a broken heart to a
broken leg, from pneumonia to bankruptcy. There was nothing
that its strident sun and salty surf could not mend. To this optimum
land, then, he sent his daughter on a quest for self.

It did not seem important to Jennie where she went, only that
she leave New York and the awful visits to her mother, leave her
father, with whom she felt a stranger now, leave the temptation of
telephoning Jason, or appearing one day at the office, standing on
line perhaps, with the job applicants who waited docilely to see
him outside his office door on Wednesdays and Fridays. She didn't
know exactly what (would he respond to the thrill of the unexpected)? Her mind formed crazy pictures . . .

Aaron would not be coming down this year. He said that he was
buried with business problems—an audit by the I.R.S. (*And because he's liable to be a father again any day and he'd just better
stick around* — she was embarrassed by her own crazy thought,
she pushed it from her with distaste.) Anyway the boys did not want
to go; they had their friends at home, and their swimming, and Evan
was preparing for his entry into Yale. He was a fine all-around ath-
lete, an excellent student of the classics, Latin and Greek and French
literature. He had grown tall and handsome, and was very much
like the maternal grandfather he had never known. His mother's
child, he had a strange relationship with Aaron, one that teetered
dangerously on hostility. In some perverse way, Aaron saw in him
all the things Eve wanted in a man that *he* hadn't been able to
satisfy — sensitivity, elegance, intellect. There was the chance that
he had unconsciously placed in time her faltering feeling for him
from the moment this first son was born. But he was proud of his

sons. They didn't drink and they didn't smoke. They were good boys.

She would miss them there with her, the camaraderie, the fooling around, her father sparring recklessly with all the suntanned young men who hung about their pool cabana, impressed with him — with her — But no, that was a lifetime ago, when she had still been innocent, uninitiated, her eyes filmed over by love for her father, by admiration, before Eve's bitter prophecies had proved true. No, now she was anxious to get away from him, a blessed relief — she would breathe freely without constriction. His presence was a constant nagging reminder of his treachery — of her own.

But still she did not want to go to Miami Beach alone, either. Aaron suggested some of her friends, but for one or another reason she rejected them, and then she thought of Gladys Blumberg. Of course, it would be perfect. Gladys was a reckless, raucous girl full of laughter and thoroughly lacking in illusions about herself.

*

There was surely something in the Jewish soul that cried out to the Latin beat. Perhaps its Moorish roots, a longing to return to Spain ever since the Inquisition, who knew? But the beat was ubiquitous. Jennie could not seem to separate from it, it followed her day and night, the gentle sound of the rhumba, the staccato rush of maracas — the whole Latin soul of it — exuding from the city's every corner, warm, sensuous, obvious, like Miami Beach itself.

Those were the days in Miami when every Jewish boy talked like a stand-up comic, had a *shtik*, did a routine around the pool in mimicry of what they saw at the many clubs and lounges all over the Beach. And Gladys fell right in with them, these poolside Romeos. They clustered around her, but always with their eyes on Jenna, not far away.

(56)

JENNIE HAD EXPECTED to go home with Gladys after the
New Year, but she really had nothing to do at home, and
here at the Hotel La Coquille she could hide out pleasantly with
her memories, augmenting them daily in her imagination. During
the day she lay on the beach in a scanty suit, letting the sun lick at
all her body, lull her tired mind to peace. She had only been here
for three weeks but already she felt like a lotus eater, an exile from
reality. She felt guilty — that was a family legacy — but she also
felt good.

She and Gladys were alone on the beach at Jennie's insistence,
far away from the tumult of the pool area, and as near as they
could get to the cool of the ocean, scrupulously avoiding the shimmering blue jellyfish, which looked extraterrestrial here.

"When are you leaving, Gladys?" Jennie asked uncomfortably.
Gladys kept her laughing and she didn't want to be alone at night.
Here everything happened at night; she did not want to have to go
out with men for company, and have to make the usual excuses
about a headache to get rid of them. It was all right, in fact it had
even been fun, momentarily diverting, to be with groups of people
in the evenings, to eat dinner, see a show, dance the rhumba with
some amusing, faceless partner. But beyond that, the thought that
any of these leering copies of nightclub comics might attempt to
make love to her, turned her stomach inside out. She knew Gladys
did not feel the same way, but that was an old story.

"Well, you know school starts again on the fifteenth of January,"
Gladys said. Gladys was a bright girl. She had a quick mind, was
considering going to law school — and she would be a good lawyer,
Jennie thought.

"Jennie, I've been thinking," she said, rolling over on her belly in the sand. "Why don't you apply to Hunter, it would be such fun, and they have a marvelous liberal arts department — "

"Yeah, Gladys, you're probably right, that's what I ought to do — Maybe I will next term . . . or the term after — "

"Next term," Gladys said strongly, determined not to let her slink off.

Jennie laughed, patted her kinky head affectionately, and said, "Okay, next term. Actually I may have to, for the sake of my sanity." She was not sure about how the suspension factor might affect her application and transfer.

She had not confided in Gladys about the suspension or about Jason, either. She had told her only that she had decided to transfer home because of her mother's ill health. Although Gladys would have reveled in it, Jason remained Jennie's very private property and she need not share it; she could not surrender her delicious secret. "I'll miss you, Glad," she said.

"What do you mean?"

"I don't know, I think I'll stay down awhile. What is there for me to go back to?"

"Jennie, tell me, what is it? Is it still Pete, is that it? You know you really should have married him — he was one in a million." Gladys had always been Pete's champion. She had frequently gone out with Phil and had made herself Pete's confidante.

"Why, Gladys, you always have been just a little bit in love with him yourself, haven't you?"

"You bet," she said in her exophthalmic, intense manner. "God, he was one delicious, delectable male."

"How do *you* know?" Jennie said, laughing.

"I've got eyes, haven't I?"

"Our eyes often deceive."

"Are you trying to tell me now that he wasn't great in the sack?"

"There you go again, boiling everything down to basics — "

"And are you still gonna hand me that virgin stuff," Gladys said, sitting up now, obviously agitated, "or tell me you don't know, or you don't care, that kind of crap?"

"I'm not going to tell you anything — I'm just going to change the subject."

"Listen, what the hell are you saving it for? It just turned 1948, in case you haven't heard. We're out of the Victorian era — "

Gladys lay down again with a sigh of resignation. "Well I don't know, that girl he's going with now seems to like it pretty much. Of course she's no beauty — that is, next to you, Jennie," she added with some satisfaction. "But then again who *is* next to you."

Jennie felt a momentary stab at the mention of Pete, at the mingling of his name with someone else's. She still had such a proprietary feeling about him — through the war years — it seemed that she had grown up loving him. But now it was only a fleeting sadness.

"Oh Jesus, did I put my foot in it again?" Gladys asked. "You knew, didn't you, Jen? I was sure you knew — "

"Yes I knew, I suppose I was the first to know really." There was a silence then that told her Gladys was still awaiting the full story — none was forthcoming. Jennie wasn't even sure she knew it herself. It was all tangled up somehow with the times and timing, and morals and . . . *memories.*

"Do you think he'll marry her, Jennie, do you?"

"I'm sure Pete will do the right thing. He usually does," she said, feeling suddenly very tired, as if Gladys had just put her through a wringer.

"Do you think he loves her, Jen?"

Jennie didn't answer immediately.

Then she said, "I think he does — in a way."

(57)

IN THE THREE WEEKS OR SO since Gladys had left, she hadn't been idle at the white marble pleasure dome, La Coquille. She considered that she was getting a little of the life experience that her father was always talking about, while scrupulously protecting her from it.

Out of boredom and loneliness she had gotten in with a bunch of wild pleasure seekers, mostly men, though there were occasional women (blondes only). They ran in a pack of eight or ten from club to club, show to show, gambling, drinking, dancing until four or five in the morning. Her entreé had been her name. They all seemed to have heard of her father and treated her as if she were a celebrity, a society girl made of glass. Jennie found this life amusing, and for these weeks she didn't have to think (usually a copious reader, she couldn't seem to concentrate anymore). Sharp, too well dressed, secretive about their work if not their lifestyle, they used gutter language, language which she had never heard from her father (or his employees) in spite of his years on Broad-way, his rough associations. They talked constantly about sex, and yet she saw little evidence of anything actively sexual within their ranks. The men were between the ages of thirty and forty, the few women usually in their late twenties. They seemed to be, for the most part, Jewish or Italian. When they were not down at Hialeah Racetrack during the day, they hung out in clumps around the cabana of a famous Teamster boss (who only appeared at rare intervals), playing cards, drinking and, as they *said*, "screwing broads in the cabana." She managed to stay clear of them most of the day, but in the evening one or the other of the "girls" would phone her up, insisting she come along. The men treated her with the greatest deference and never made any crude or overt propositions. And though one of them, whom they called "Babe" (a somewhat oily, but not unattractive, man in his late thirties), seemed to have developed an obsession for her, in general she got the idea that there was a certain code of ethics, a kind of private charter of morality for this dubious club, which did not permit them to overstep the bounds of what they considered decency with women of a "certain class." They seemed, in fact, mostly interested in having Jennie along as an adornment, and the women of the group were constantly counseling her in what to wear and how to look before each all-night endurance contest. "Flashy without being gaudy," was the way Flora had put it. (That described Flora pretty accurately. Flora, Jennie thought, was actually somebody's wife there. She was not exactly certain.) There was a great and elaborate show of tipping to bellboys, waiters, and other assorted messengers assigned to carry out the divine duties of keeping them in a state of perpetual fulfillment and inertia. But the situation was odd, to say the least — and she was beginning to find it more than a little distasteful. There was something *freakish* about it, about them. She began to think about going back to New York.

*

Jennie, lightly tanned, her blonde hair paled by the sun, was dressed in a white flannel skirt and a gauzy white silk sweater. It was about one o'clock in the afternoon. She stepped from the elevator and strolled toward the huge marble desk for her mail. She had grown used to turning heads when she walked through the glittering marble lobby. In fact, by the time she had reached her present age, she had fallen under the spell of her own image, and was finding it difficult to unglue herself from the mirror, difficult to believe that this ravishing creamy blonde, so closely styled on the movie stars of the day, was really she.

La Coquille Hotel had sprung up immediately after the war, together with a series of other modern white pleasure palaces on the ocean at the Beach, usually bearing some sort of French name. It did not have the charm or the weathered elegance of the old

Palm Plaza, but Aaron had made the reservations here for reasons of his own, not the least of which was his "friendship" with Jack Taglitz, the owner. They were doing some deals together, she knew that, and Jack was currently very important to Aaron. She had the feeling Taglitz was watching her — with those crafty blue eyes. She wondered idly whom her father would send in to watch the watcher.

She stepped up to the desk. The desk clerks were all busy and she had to wait a moment. Then she heard one of them say her room number. "Well just put these in her box, will you?" — a familiar voice that caused a sudden cramping in her belly. She looked down the length of the reception desk to see Jason Miller at the other end. They turned to face each other, and he said to the clerk, his eyes on her face, "Oh never mind, here she is now."

"Great timing," the clerk mumbled affably.

"Well, well," Jason said slowly, the faint edges of that quizzical smile forming at the corners of his mouth. He walked slowly over to where she stood rooted. "If it isn't the Princess, in the flesh. You're looking beautiful." He said this last sentence quietly as if to himself, or perhaps he did not wish to be overheard, not even by Jennie.

"Jason, what are you doing down here?" She was too much taken off guard for subtlety.

"Well for one thing your father sent me down here to keep an eye on you. For another, I have business here — the clubs, the gambling casinos, you know — " She didn't know what to believe. She searched his eyes for a moment, for a glint of sarcasm, but they were unreadable.

"Jason, what are you talking about — keeping an eye on me — for God's sake." She felt as if her head would break open. She had dreamed of meeting him again as a woman, and now he made her feel like a defensive child. People kept coming and going, milling around the desk; he lowered his voice intimately and said with a cool anxiety, "I don't know. That's what I'm here to find out." It seemed to her that he was making an effort to keep his eyes averted from her face — her body — but she could not resist staring at him, searching his face, his eyes, for clues, and when her eyes momentarily locked with his dark liquid gaze, she felt the sudden warm rush of color in her cheeks — for remembered pleasures —

"And here are some papers your father wants you to sign, I was just leaving them at the desk for you." Businesslike, impersonal as ever. As her Aunt Leah frequently said, "Ice water runs in his veins." *No, she knew differently.* He must be mad, she thought — *Just a little crazy, like everyone connected with my father.*

Impeccably dressed in spite of the five-hour-long plane trip, he appeared awkward here, unbending, among the loosely garbed, relaxed vacationers. "Okay, Jenna," he said as if signaling the end of an interview. "Just sign there," he indicated the place with his finger, "and leave them in my box. It's number 623, okay? I've got to go up with the boy now, take a shower, change clothes, and go to work. Have fun, and listen," he said gently, drawing her close for a moment, "behave yourself."

"Then you're staying here — " she said confused.

"That's what your dad wanted, and who am I to argue with the boss . . . ? Besides, what's wrong with this place? It's gorgeous," he said, looking around appreciatively, "except that I don't expect to have much time to enjoy it. I've got a lot to do here." She felt let down, once again squeezed out of his life.

"Well then it looks like you won't have much time to — what was that — keep an eye on me."

"I'll have a week," he said, "that should be enough." He was smiling as he walked toward the elevator with the bellboy.

Jennie walked slowly out of the lobby to the outside veranda where it was usually cool and quiet, neglected by the ardent sunworshippers because it did not get the blaze of the sun, only its slight residual odor of ultraviolet and the raw green of palm fronds — she had a brief flash in her mind of the Palm Plaza Hotel — that night — during the war . . .

She sat on the bench and put her head back against the cool cement of the wall and tried to think, but she could not. She could only feel. She felt sweet with sensation, weak and moist all over. Her body was set for loving him.

She knew almost from the first moment she had seen him what she would do. She had known this man all her life, intimately now, and yet she felt the chill of strangeness.

*

She knocked on the door to his room. He opened it quickly, seeming to think it was a bellhop or housekeeper, someone he'd expected in connection with the check-in.

She entered a room that was much larger than her own, with an alcove dressing room that gave it the effect of a suite, and a glorious view of the ocean.

"I brought the papers," she cut in immediately, clearing the path with her excuse. "I wasn't sure if — if — it was safe to leave them with the desk. I see that once again I'm secretary of some phony corporation or other."

"Yeah, so am I," He laughed, "Looks like we're partners — in crime."

"Again?" It was the first reference either had made to that day in September. But she felt childish in his presence, too clumsily *young* to be ironic.

There was a long silence while they stood there locked in indecision. And then he said to her softly, already vanquished, "You know, Jen, you shouldn't be here, I ought to send you away — "

"Why should you? What better way to keep an eye on me."

Opening his tie, rolling up his shirtsleeves, moving around the room efficiently — away from where she stood — he said, "I should never have come down here, to this town, to this hotel."

"But you did, Jason, you did — why?"

"Oh, Jennie, Jennie," he said, shaking his head, once again the indulgent smile. "You are used to your own way. You must have everything you *think* you want, only to find out once you have it, you don't really want it in the first place." He seemed to be waiting for her to object.

"You don't even *know* me, Jason, you've never given me a chance, you just decided from way back when I was a little kid that because I was *his* daughter, the only daughter — "

"I'll *tell* you what I decided," he cut in. "I decided that you are a luxury I can't afford." There was silence and then Jennie began walking slowly toward the door. He came over to her swiftly and held her wrists tightly, binding her so that she could not move. "God, how I don't want to love you," he said against her hair. "Loving you is one crazy luxury." In that moment she slid her arms around his waist. He pulled her to him roughly and they kissed.

"Jace, Jace," she murmured his name, just being able to say it to him a blessed relief.

"You're all I thought about in these months," he said.

"Then why, why didn't you call me?"

"What was there to say?" He kissed her again, there was a knock on the door. The housekeeper with extra soap and they didn't hear the rest — they ignored it. She tried her own key, but the door was bolted.

Her body felt young beneath his, tender —

*

Lying now in his arms while he slept, she took inventory of this man, as if he already belonged to her. This man . . . He was about thirty-seven or thirty-eight years old, and he looked his age. There was a permanently etched tiredness to his fleshy face. The slight discoloration beneath his eyes looked to her as if he had lived too much, but she knew that his life was cut out to the pattern of her father's, and that he had never really lived at all . . . His body, strong but smooth, was pallid from the constant indoor life he led. He lay on his side, holding her close to him, her own body limp and aching from the long languorous encounter. She had watched him sleeping for some thirty minutes perhaps, the gentle whir of the air conditioning lulling her into a trance. But her mind was fighting, warding off bravely images of her mother at the clinic, her dull, disappointed acceptance if she knew, her brothers' laughter, teasing with their disapproval — images of her father, his revulsion. He would look at her as if she were permanently an unclean thing. But what did she care for them now. Everything in her rushed toward this stranger in her arms; she could not think seriously of anything else.

He stirred and woke. He drew her head back down to the warm hollow of his neck. She kissed the beat in his throat, the brown velvet mole close to his mouth. "Feels like I'm nuzzling a kitten," he said dreamily. His lips slid down her breasts to her firm, flat navel. He told her how beautiful and smooth her body was, how almost childlike still, its every secret part so small and dainty, and opening for him now like waking flowers. He moved his mouth to her thighs, brushing his lips gently across them, then his mouth slipped to the soft mound of her body, but she reached down and pulled his head away gently — "Please, darling," she said, "I'm — I'm still filled with you — from before — I . . ." Those words, their suggestion, seemed to entice him further, to drive him to a frenzy . . . She felt herself go hot with shame . . . She felt herself slowly disintegrating. He took her again — her body warm and milky with the wildness he knew he had created.

*

Jennie in her half trance saw reality return in blotches — his still unopened suitcase, their clothes scattered along the floor near the bed — and began to wonder if either of them would ever be able to claw their way out of this alive, or be whole again, apart.

For a few minutes he lay on his back with that perfect tranquility she had come to associate with him alone, so different from her own nature, her family's. He lit a cigarette, inhaled it deeply, eyes open, regarding the pastel ceiling as if asking for some divine guidance. He felt for her hand and held it. Still looking upwards, he said, "Jennie, you're the first lovely thing I've ever really had in my life. I've been going crazy without you these months, but I tried so hard not to call you, and since you stopped coming down to the office I almost figured I would make it — "

"Then why did you come here to me now?"

In his beautifully modulated voice he tried to explain.

"When your father asked me to come down here for him, to the concessions at Green Acres, the Colonial Inn, those places, he told me that he was worried about you, he had heard things, crazy things on the grapevine, I don't know — I didn't want to know, and yet, I did desperately. I couldn't fight it anymore, I had to see you again, see for myself."

"What," she said, "see what?" She had been growing cold with hurt while he spoke.

"Well, he was worried, became suspicious of your prolonged stay. He said you might have gotten mixed up with some bad characters — "

"By mixed up, he means — you mean — in bed, isn't that what you mean, Jason?"

"No, no, Jen, but in a way I hoped so, I hoped that maybe there was someone in particular. You know, rich girls usually have a gangster hidden somewhere in the folds of their lives — or their skirts," he was smiling now.

"I know," she said, "and now I have one too. Isn't that what my mother always called *you?*"

"Yeah," he murmured, "to my face a couple of dozen times."

"You, all of you who work for Dad . . . I know what you think of me, that I'm just a wild spoiled kid."

"What's the difference *what* I thought," he said in a tired voice. "I don't think that now."

She could not let the subject rest. She felt obliged to pull it out like taffy. "Go on," she said, "you thought that I was a tramp like all women. That's the general "party line," I believe, down in the checkroom, isn't it?"

"I don't know what I thought. I didn't think about you, Jennie, only when I saw you — then — then I couldn't *stop* thinking about you. And I felt foolish, an older man making a fool of himself over a young girl, and the least likely girl in the world — *the boss's twenty-year-old daughter.*" He said this as if he couldn't comprehend it.

"Jason, there's only been *one* other man in my life so far, and then I've only been to bed with him twice — I'm *practically* a virgin!"

"I'm surprised your old man let you get away with *that* much," he said drily as he got up and took a terry cloth robe from his suitcase. "What happened to him, by the way — to — to — Peter Schore?"

"Has this family no secrets from you? So you knew."

"I knew that you were *supposed* to be getting engaged a couple of years ago and that there was some problem about school but — What did happen?"

"Oh I don't know, he came along too soon, I was bedazzled by being eighteen, I suppose, maybe I just wasn't ready." She wondered, how many times in her life would she be expected to make excuses for this?

Jason said nothing. He sat down again on the bed, obviously tired, and touched by the depression that often follows in the wake of fulfilled desire.

"No matter who, or what he is, your old man will never let it happen; he doesn't want to lose you, Jennie — to anybody." He spoke as if he were sharing a grave confidence that was difficult for him.

"My brothers and I are three wholly owned subsidiaries," she said with an edge of bitterness, "And Aaron is the parent company — is that the sort of thing you're driving at?"

"Well for one thing you are making a home for him in a way, you and your brothers, and he needs that." *So much so, that he's already preparing for our departure, already feathering a new nest — but she could not say these things to Jason, not to him —* and she thought wistfully that in these last few years with Aaron she had the first real home she'd ever enjoyed. "So in that benevolent way he'll make you see that 'the guy's a bum,' and he will compare him to himself, compete with him ferociously and the poor kid hasn't a chance in hell — and finally *you'll* feel guilty, like you're cheating on your father." Then he said softly, looking downward, "With me it's different, I *am* your father in a way."

There was a fragile silence while Jennie struggled to understand

— and then understanding, rejected his meaning. "Oh, Jace, are you still going on about our age difference? Are you going to let sixteen or seventeen years get between us?"

"Actually I wasn't thinking about that, but you know it *is* kind of funny when you think of it — it's like the age difference between Martha and your father, except ours is still greater."

"Jason, that was cruel."

"No, listen to me," he said urgently pulling her down beside him on the bed. "I only want you to love me with your eyes wide open, to understand — "

She touched his face with her fingertips. He took her hands gently away, as if not to be deflected from his narrative.

"I can't forget, I was there through all the years of your mother's bitter complaints against your father, to everyone, to *you* especially. In her way she made you feel that it was *forbidden* to love him. Now you feel the same way loving me — and perhaps that's what intrigues — "

There was silence while Jason's long, handsome fingers toyed nervously with the pack of cigarettes on the night table.

"If you think I'm here with you, Jason, because of some distorted love for *him*, then why are *you* here? Tell me that — I must know — Can it be the other side of the coin? Have you *hated* him so much through all these years, years that he's held you back, refused you an interest in the business — kept you down, shoved you under, when all the time you could have walked off with the whole thing? Before the war, before they were getting these enormous sums for concessions, you could have done it, Jason. Why didn't you?"

"Because I love the guy," he said, an honest, straightforward statement without inflection — Jason, the knight errant, with a medieval respect for honor.

Jennie did not wish to ask why, to argue it. She sensed the reasons. They went back before her time — Jews so tied backward in time. "Love *and* hate, what's the difference, they keep jockeying for position and it all comes out resentment, with everyone connected with him, and so there is no peace in the lives of those around him," Jennie said.

"Jennie, you don't really know him. He's a good man, he loves you very much. I wish it weren't true, then I wouldn't feel so rotten! I feel sorry for that man," he said with genuine feeling. "Your mother threw him out all of a sudden, right in the middle of everything, when he was just getting to the best part. She spoiled it for him."

"Jason, you are a hopeless misogynist." She knew his allegiances — like Aaron an orthodox man in an unorthodox business.

He got up, stretched languidly, and crossed the room toward his still-packed suitcase. "Look, darling," he said, "for some crazy reason we have this week — one lousy, beautiful week out of a lifetime, let's make it wonderful, let's not ask any more questions."

She went to him and they embraced, and he said gently, "For whatever it's worth, I do love you — Jen, so much. Please, darling, be here when I get back. It might be late, but please be here," he said urgently. He gave her the extra key. "I have to get going, honey, believe it or not I'm here to work." He walked quickly to the bathroom, she heard the soft rush of the shower, and closed her eyes, thinking of that other time. It was four P.M. The rest of the afternoon and most of the night stretched out before her like a wasteland, without him. She thought of her mother with renewed sympathy for her loneliness, for her life — it's gradual coming apart.

*

After he left, she went downstairs to her own room. Beneath the door it was choked with telephone messages. The room looked cold and lonely now with its tightly made bed. She tore one bed apart and rumpled the pillow, for the maid to see. She glanced at one or two of the messages. "Your father called — your father called." If only her father would phone now, how wonderful — everything normal, natural, the way it should be.

She soaked in her bath, letting the water sluice over her. In a haze of lovely drunkenness she took stock of her growing obsession for this man. She groped for its meaning, for the one word that she could fasten on to explain it — *compassionate,* she thought, yes, that was the quality that she sensed in him, found sexy, more irresistible because it ran beneath the surface of the man like a rich vein of gold. She lay back in the tub and tried to make the acquaintance of this new wild creature, Jennie Abel. But experience made her sad and she longed for the innocence of yesterday . . . She knew that nothing would ever be the same again. New sensations had left their mark on her mind, like the bruises on her body. They were burned into her essence and she did not even know if she wished to be cleansed of them.

She put on fresh clothes, packed a small overnight bag, and returned to Jason's room. She turned on the radio, one of those lilting Cuban love songs. She hung up her clothes slowly. She smoothed her fragrant lingerie carefully into the drawers. Then she began unpacking Jason's things. She wondered, floating, detached, if Dolly had packed them so precisely for him. No, she would not think about that now. She placed his personal items and toiletries next to hers on the counter in the dressing room. She hung up Jason's suits, so beautifully tailored, hanging gracefully even without him in them, counted his silky shirts a dozen times —buried her face in them —

THE NEXT MORNING, a partly cloudy Tuesday, they woke late and then spent it leisurely, staying in bed for breakfast, which Jason received while Jennie hid in the bathroom. It was not a large hotel and any guest staying as long as she had was known by most of the help in the hotel. They gossiped avidly about the guests.

They remained in bed most of that day, making love, drinking coffee, just luxuriating in being together. Jason, not a man much given to indulging himself, appeared surprised by his own capacity for pleasure.

The telephone began ringing after twelve noon, the time when night people usually began their day. Jason was generally short and businesslike with them, but Jennie had the distinct impression that they were being handled. He was a great handler of people, particularly with the half dozen or so girls who called within the hour, to get set up for the night or the coming weekend.

Around four-thirty in the afternoon, he began to prepare for an appointment he had at six. After that there would be a series of appointments that usually culminated in going to the four or five places at their prime times, anywhere from nine until two in the morning, and staying around for a while at each one. Jennie knew the routine well — by heart — but today was already drawing to a close, the end of the second day — time was running out.

While he dressed, she sat at the dressing table brushing her hair thoughtfully — and the telephone rang again —

Jason answered quickly. They had been dreading Aaron's inevitable call. After a moment she knew that it was his wife. He was warm, friendly, but strangely impersonal, speaking mostly in monosyllables. Impersonal to a wife, how was that possible . . . ? She was doing most of the talking. She seemed to be reporting something or other about his mother. If it isn't children that force a marriage together, Jennie thought wryly, it's aging parents. But always the wife ends up as keeper of the flame, bearing up some substitute tie with which to bind when the self is no longer binding. Jennie arose and walked discreetly into the bathroom. She wondered if that was all that life would hold for her in the final analysis — to be a supplicant at the other end of a long-distance wire, the blackened, ugly cord of a burnt-out marriage.

When Jason finally hung up (it seemed to Jennie an eternity) she was stung by his manner. He offered no explanation. She had hoped he would confide in her about their conversation. There was a long, tight silence. He did not come into the dressing room where she was for a while.

When finally he came into the room, foraging around for cuff-links, she pretended to be brushing her hair, but she was watching him carefully in the mirror. When she could not catch his eye she threw down the brush and went over to him. Wrapping her arms around his neck, her head on his chest, she said, "Jace, how come you never had a child?"

Jason put her gently out of the way. "I've never had much respect for the parent-child relationship and anyway, there was the *religious* thing with Dolly."

"Are you sorry now?"

"About what?" Jason asked, coolly buttoning his shirt front.

"About both, marrying Dolly, and *not* having a child."

He looked at her straight, and without his usual cynicism, he said, "The answer is no — on both counts."

"Do you love her, Jason?" she asked in a small, choked voice.

He was silent while he seemed to be struggling with an answer. "Oh, I don't know — we had something once, I suppose, a long time ago."

"So you're living off the residuals, is that it?"

"No it's more than that, Jenna — Twelve or more years, if you count those years before — "

"Jason, that's no answer. I asked you a question. You must answer it," she said urgently.

"Jennie," he said softly to her now, "if you were older you'd understand that that was an *honest* answer — "

"Please stop patronizing me."

"Jennie, what you're really asking me is, do I still make love to my wife, isn't that it?"

"No, no, Jason, I don't *want* to know, I don't want to hear it. Please — " She put her hands over her ears . . . But she knew, they both knew it was not Dolly who was between them in that room, but only Aaron.

He came close to her, took her hands away from her ears. He kissed her earlobe and whispered to her, "Darling, darling, I haven't made love to my wife in more than a year and I can't even tell you why — or that there was any particular reason that I was conscious of. After a while we just ran out, that's all. But it feels so great to be alive again," he said softly.

"But Dolly, how does *she* feel about it? Dolores, that is," she said with an edge of sarcasm.

There was a pause in which his eyes begged for a change of subject.

"Jen, I thought we decided that we weren't going to probe, to ask any questions during the time we have left." She wondered if tearing at him like this was a natural prelude for women in love, new love — and then she thought sadly that love was already old for them, almost from the same moment it had been new.

"Jace," she said dreamily, as if she had not heard, "what kind of parents do you think we'd make?"

"Jennie, stop," he said sharply. "Don't get any crazy ideas." He pulled away from her now, and finished tying his tie before the mirror. "Anyway the answer is 'lousy.' You're just a kid yourself and a spoiled one at that — and I'd make a lousy father. That's why I'm not one," he said, with a final tug at his tie.

"Nonsense, that's just sour grapes," she had to have the last word. He shook his head, smiling a little, in spite of his irritation.

"Jason," she said, "you really don't think very much of us, do you?" She thought how he looked upon her family indulgently, as if they were all his children, the way ordinary people so often regarded the very rich.

He seemed not to hear. For an answer he only shrugged into his jacket and checked his pockets for wallet and cigarettes. She had a brief flash of a young Jason, checking his gun, emptying it of bullets . . . a child's imagination —

She thought with a pull in her stomach that he looked very hand-some — what a handsome couple they made. She wanted to be seen with him, to walk proudly by his side in a slick proprietary manner. She had a sudden urge to cry out, "Jason, take me with you —," but she thought that it was useless. As if reading her mind, he said, "Aren't there any friends you could phone up or go to a movie with or have a drink with downstairs? I know this must be awfully lonely and dreary for you."

"Jace, I don't want to go anywhere unless it's with you." She said this with such emotion that he pulled her close to him and kissed her with a desperation that was alien to him. "Take me with you, please, darling," she whispered. "We can have dinner together like *real* people." When he spoke, his voice was husky with wanting her, "Well that's got to be the best way to keep an eye on you. Tomorrow night I'll arrange something for us, we'll do the town. I don't want to waste any more precious evenings either."

Before he left he reminded her not to answer the telephone — "But if your dad calls, tell him I'm out."

"Very funny," she said. Now the rest of the evening would not seem so long, and it would be much more bearable. She almost looked forward to being alone, planning for tomorrow, an uninterrupted day and night with him. She thought of what she would wear, how she should fix her hair —

God. She suddenly thought of her friends, Babe and his group of happy hedonists, and how they'd be going crazy looking for her. She had this shred of an idea — of calling them up — running around with them tonight. She might even run into Jason somewhere, or come back just a little after him so that he would worry and be hurt. But she knew she could not; there would be no pleasure in it, in anything for her anymore, unless he was in it.

He returned around two-thirty in the morning, exhausted, pale, limp, with cigarette and liquor odors clinging to his clothes, his hair. She saw clearly, as if for the first time, what her father's life had been like in all of those glory years.

*

At ten the next morning Jennie woke to the sound of Jason's shower and the telephone ringing crazily. She was about to reach for it when she realized where she was. She ran to call Jason. He emerged soaking and grabbed a towel to put around his waist.

It was Aaron, she almost knew it by the restless urgency of the ringing.

"I see her here or there in the lobby, almost every day. You must just be missing her. I don't know, Aaron, but I'll check it out . . . Oh yeah?" he said curiously. "Sure — but you think she'll want to go with an old man like me?" Jason seemed in high spirits today, she thought, bantering gaily with her father on the telephone. And then it was business as usual. They talked about the Miami concessions at the Latin Quarter, at the gambling clubs like Green Acres and the Colonial Inn. She knew that gambling was unofficial here at the Beach, but the town was making a fortune as a result of it, and most of the politicians were looking the other way — generously paid off by the Mob. Her father's voice was loud and strident over the phone. Jason had to hold the receiver a little away from his ear.

"If those bastards are in there again, I don't know if it pays, Miller."

"Aaron, it pays," Jason said, "it pays big."

"But look, what the hell, there are no coats 'n hats and —"

"Who needs them. If they win at the tables they tip big for everything, anything. And then there *are* the ladies' wraps — they're not going to stand around a crap table holding onto a mink jacket, are they? And the rest of our stuff sells for three times the usual price." They talked some more. Her father sounded agitated, Jason was calm.

He hung up, it had been a long call. They looked at each other for a minute, wordlessly, and then began to laugh.

"For chrissakes, get up, you sleepy head, or I'll tell your old man what a lazy little broad you are." They were still laughing as he lay back on the bed, still damp from the interrupted shower, and took her in his arms. "He's worried about you, honey, can't find you anywhere. He told me I should *try* to take you out some night, find out where you've been hiding, what you're doing, and when you're coming home. So-o-o-o — tonight's the night," he said, kissing her lips lightly, playfully.

"Tonight and every night, for the few we have left, Jace, please — "

"Well I guess I can always say that I was keeping you out of trouble." He was amused.

Jennie, suddenly serious, sat up and said, "Does it matter so much *what* you say? Is your job such a good one that you are terrified of losing it?"

Jason freed his arm from around her and reached for a cigarette. He lit it thoughtfully and said, "No, not really. It's true that I probably could have made a helluva lot more money on my own if I had wanted to, but it wouldn't have been the same," he said, in a distant voice.

"Does it have to be?"

"Yes, in a way it does, in a way that you probably wouldn't understand, Jennie. I came to your father at the onset of the depression. I was a pretty hungry kid. To be a part of our thing now has meaning for me, it's grown into something wild, it's been one glorious adventure. A few little concessions here and there to call my own would mean nothing to me, a little more security, perhaps, but it would be second rate — and sleazy."

Glorious adventure, she thought, like a child at play. "It wouldn't have had to stop there, you could have gone on, you could have gotten more. They love you on Broadway, you *know* that."

"To begin with, it takes money, the kind of money I just haven't got."

"*Why*, Jason? Why haven't you got it?"

"Why?" He laughed. "For one thing I never really wanted it very much; your father was proof positive that there wasn't any great affinity between money and happiness. I've always had what I needed, for another — I spend it. And for a third, there never was that much to begin with. You know, your old man, he doesn't exactly believe in letting those around him wax fat. And maybe he's right. Who knows? If I'd have had the money I might have left him and done exactly what you — you little troublemaker," he said, kissing the tip of her nose — "have been steaming me up about.

Anyway, I've made a few investments of my own on Broadway, shows, revues — Lou Walters' new show for one thing. Some have paid off, some haven't."

"But you're still young, darling. Why do you sound already resigned, defeated? My father is much older than you and *he* isn't — "

"Listen, there are two kinds of people in this world, the victors and the vanquished. Your father is a victor — a survivor. It is rare that one ever crosses over into the other's territory."

"Who made that rule?" she asked, her voice harsh.

"Ah-h-h, now you *are* his daughter." He laughed.

Jennie felt satisfied, as she had all the times throughout the years that her mother leveled the same accusation at her.

"He should have given you a couple of 'the places' as a gift, or bonus, or at least in partnership — "

"Jennie, baby," he said, looking into her eyes, "nobody *gives* anybody anything in this life. You've been so sheltered. If I've done one thing that's been good for you, it's to bring you out into this world a little — Well let's look at it this way," he said, oddly detached, "I might have just blown it all at the track, and I'd be right back where I am now."

"That's right. I almost forgot — You *love* the horses." She said teasingly, "I'll bet you're dying to go to the track."

"I'm here to work, remember," he said, crushing out his cigarette and taking her in his arms. "But we can go tomorrow if you like. It's already noon now and if we're going, I'd like to get there in time for the double."

"Oh, Jace, that would be fun. I don't think I've ever been to the races."

He was satisfied. He seemed to feel redeemed, being able to initiate her once again, no matter how slightly.

"Jace, let's go to the beach, the public beach, and get a beautiful tan for tonight. You look so pale — you have that nightclub pallor."

He smiled and reminded her that they had an early dinner reservation at the Colonial Inn.

"Oh, darling," she said and urged him down to the pillow beside her.

They fell back on the bed laughing, silly, Jason's laughter fading as her body came in contact with his. "Baby," he said softly, "I may be too old for *you* but I'm not ready to go just yet — You want to put me in an early grave?"

(59)

S HE WAS SHOCKED by her own abandon, living with a man in the most intimate of circumstances — and a man who belonged to another woman — in a relationship that she had never before deemed possible outside of marriage, and yet it seemed almost natural now. A scarlet woman, she thought, not without satisfaction. She imagined a flaming *A* branded between her breasts.

As they dressed to go out for dinner and the evening, Jennie felt euphoric. They had spent most of the afternoon on the beach, lying close together in the warm sand, conspiratorial, like wayward children, drinking thick piña coladas, eating raw coconut from the shell sold by a Cuban vendor. She had a fresh burn, turning her skin lightly bronze. Jason's olive skin was already deeply tanned.

She dressed carefully in a pale green chiffon dress that accented her startling green eyes, the lovely myopic sea-foam eyes of her mother's family. She was not pleased with the new styles from Paris, long skirts that trailed well past the calf. She was proud of her good legs. Jason was in navy blue sharkskin, the white of his shirt sharp against his suntan, his dark good looks. She was right, they made a handsome pair.

Walking through the lobby she held her head high. She prayed that she would not run into anyone she knew, like Babe, for instance, and then she prayed that she would. She could just hear Babe's jazzy comment — "Such love," he would say succulently — she knew it was there in her eyes. Everyone turned to stare as they passed, staff and guests alike. Jason had warned her that they would probably be running the gauntlet all night, he knew a million people in town, at "the places." They swung uptown and sped over the Seventy-ninth Street causeway.

During the long drive out to Hollywood they didn't talk much. Jason smoked a lot. He told her how lovely she looked. She kissed the hand that gripped the wheel; it smelled faintly of suntan lotion and aftershave cologne. Only twenty, and she thought that the best part of her life had already come and gone. She thought how other girls she knew were busy building their lives now, their futures — while she was intent on the destruction of hers, and unwilling to relinquish one moment of it.

The lights glittered dazzlingly around the large, beautiful, once-private estate that had been converted into a gambling club some years ago. The Colonial Inn sprawled majestically among acres of palm and palmetto, here and there the quick scent of flowering bougainvillea or honeysuckle. The night air was balmy, whispering with the sounds of trees and ocean.

"Good evening, Mr. Miller," the doorman said amiably. "Is it business or pleasure this evening?"

"Oh a little bit of both, Duke," he said, smiling and walking briskly, guiding Jennie by the arm. It was almost eight o'clock and gorgeous pale convertibles of varied pastel hues were choking the driveway for the dinner rush.

Their table was, for them, a good one, in an intimate corner of the large circular room with its handsome curving staircase that wound its way up studded with crystal chandeliers.

After they were seated, Jason leaned forward and explained to her, "I'll have to jump up and down a lot, honey, so order a drink, and I'll get back to you as soon as I can. After dinner we'll go on to some of the other places. Okay?"

"Jace," she said, "does my father have the concessions here, or are you working on getting them now?"

"Well he has this one; it's a question as to whether he wants to take the rest of the gambling. They're run largely by one big syndicate and the more places we go into, the heavier our involvement — " He looked uncomfortable. "I'm not sure yet just what we should do — " He seemed to want to change the subject. He called the captain over by name. Jennie, not knowing really what to drink, asked Jason to order for her. He ordered scotch and water for both of them — "Always the best and the cleanest drink. Anyway if I'm going to start you off on the stuff, I might as well break you in at the top."

"I never see *you* drink."

"Tell you the truth, I can't bear the stuff. Anyway I need to have my wits about me at night." At that moment a tall, distinguished man of about fifty-five approached their table. He had a shock of white hair that stood out like neon lights around his sun-tanned face and he was dressed in formal attire.

Jason sprang from his seat and said, "Hello, Mike, how've you been, long time no see. Mike, I'd like you to meet Jennie Abel. Mike Dinardo. Mike's the guiding genius here."

"Abel," he said, "Abel — related to Aaron?"

"She's his daughter," Jason said, not without a trace of pride. He was still standing. Mike seemed taken off guard but regained his cool instantly. She wondered if Dolly had been here with Jason, other times. If Mike had met her too . . . men confused her — "C'mon sit down, Mike, have a drink with us," Jason said.

He declined, pleading the necessity of complete sobriety during the season, "when it's so crazy here." "You know how it is, kid, I don't have to tell *you*." They wisecracked a little. While he spoke, he gave Jennie an appraising glance and said, "Hey, how'd you get so lucky, Miller?" "Guess I just know the right people," Jason said, sitting down again, laughing easily. How could he be so casual about — everything? She felt momentarily estranged from him. A squeeze on Jason's shoulder signaled good-bye and Mike slid over to another table, his shoulders high under his collar

—a certain studied posture that she found irritating, though it was evidently enormously popular among the more affluent males around this town.

They looked at each other for a moment and then they began to laugh. "I'll be the envy of everybody in the business and they don't even know how lucky I *am*," he said. She reached across the table for his hand and he said, "Uh, uh," in a low voice, as if chiding a naughty child, "none of that. That's just plain crazy."

Chastened, she fell silent for a moment. "Is there a show here tonight?"

"Not until midnight, I think, and we'll be gone well before that time." She was relieved. She wouldn't have the patience for one of those roisterous revues, and she wasn't anxious to share Jason's attention with a stageful of half-naked girls.

The drinks came. She took a sip. "Ugh, it's medicine," she said. He teased her about the terrible face she made, pushed his chair back, and said, "I'll have to move around awhile. We're getting busy. Will you be all right here, Jen?" Then, as if answering his own question, he said, "Well you know what it is, I suppose; I don't really have to tell you. You've done this with your father sometimes, haven't you — " Sometimes, she thought, he must be teasing — she had been dragged up on these places. All those "visitation days" of her life — she had been left at more checkrooms than a café society top hat. But she only answered, "But it's different now, here with you."

"I should hope so," he laughed, and was gone in one long streak of movement.

She was glad that the table was out of the way in a corner. She felt a little strange and uncomfortable. The room throbbed with people, everyone in large, laughing groups — belonging. She noted with surprise that she had finished her drink in spite of her distaste. Maybe it was the unfamiliar reaction to the alcohol, but she felt a sudden surge of enlightenment. It was strangely stimulating. She had been inundated with a thousand new sensations in these last few days, but this was of a distinctly different sort.

She thought to herself how all of her life she had wished devoutly to belong, to fit in, how she had prayed that her parents would bend just a little, and although they had struggled to comform, they were never able to make it. Now it suddenly occurred to her that they were not *like* everyone else and could never be. She wasn't really sure that *she* wanted to be either. She was beginning to realize that happiness came haphazardly where and when you found it, in rare and juicy chunks, but that you paid for what you took in life. [the price consummate to the prize. What remained for her to solve were the ethical questions — one grew dizzy from the ceaseless convolutions of the merry-go-round. Enlightenment was painful. She wanted Jason, needed his serenity. Everything would be all right when Jason came back. She felt overwhelmed by the knowledge that in a few days there would be no Jason to turn to.

As the room continued filling up, it began to sway a little before her eyes — it was madness, with its cumbrous crowd of glittering people, the women's jewels crying out harshly in the glaring overhead light. She wondered dizzily if and when they would dim the lights here. She saw Jason walking rapidly toward the cigarette girl, who was wandering around forlornly, obviously a novice; her long legs in their net stockings and high heels looked seductive. Jason propelled her firmly but wordlessly toward the checkroom.

After dinner they drifted into the gambling rooms at the back. Here the lights were dimmer, but above each green felt table a white-hot lamp swayed dizzily, illuminating the faces that were moist with perspiration, melting make-up — and greed. The room seemed to have a physical life of its own, a heart beat. It pulsated and throbbed and breathed heavily like an asthmatic matron. She had been to a gambling casino a few times before in Havana with Aaron, but she had not been permitted to play. She wondered what it would feel like to win — to lose. Money itself had never seemed important to her, but she could understand the thrill of *chance.*

"Let's go over to the crap table," Jason said. "Now *that* table is for the really high rollers," he whispered.

"Do you gamble, Jace?" she said, an excitement beginning in her loins.

He looked at her for a moment and then said laughing, "Only the horses, baby," and steered her out of the room.

Outside, the lovely rush of tropical night air made her feel better. There were some twenty people waiting ahead of them for their cars, but Jason called the boy over and handed him the ticket and some money.

Jason appeared restless, cracking his knuckles nervously. The gesture seemed out of place for him. She took his arm possessively, inclining her body toward him intimately. He moved away as if he had been touched by fire. She felt hurt, but not surprised.

Jack Taglitz climbed out of a black Rolls Royce, accompanied by his beautiful young wife and a party of lavishly dressed people.

"When the hell did you get into town?" he said, enveloping Jason with a noisy salutation. "Staying at my joint?"

"Yes, where else, Jack?"

"So where have you been keeping yourself? I haven't seen you around anywhere."

"Well here I am."

Just then Jason's car pulled up and Jennie, still without formal introduction, signaled Jason.

"Jeeze, is this gorgeous kid with you, Miller, you lucky dog? She looks awfully familiar. Aren't you gonna introduce me?"

"This is Jenna Abel — "

Jennie smiled wryly. They had met.

"Oh — sure," he said, playing out his little charade. "Well — just keeping an eye on the boss's daughter, eh?"

"How about that?" Jason said. "See, there *are* fringe benefits in this work." He waved and ran down the stairs loose-kneed to his waiting car. Jack looked momentarily confused — and pleased. Living and working for twenty years in this honky-tonk resort, this garish midway of a city, had sharpened his nose for scandal, and he ferreted it out the way a hog digs for truffles.

((60))

THE PATTERN OF THEIR REMAINING DAYS together continued in much the same way — the nights a long embrace.

Each evening they went out together, she waiting quietly at a
small round table at the back of the club somewhere, usually near
the checkroom, so that they could keep one another within view,
and he running over to her every few minutes like a bridegroom,
warm color seeping into his suntanned cheeks, unmindful even of
the aura of intimacy they were undoubtedly creating. In a kind of
foggy bemusement she wondered if this could be the same im-
passive man she had glimpsed throughout a lifetime, almost chilling
in his indifference.

In the last few days there had been calls from Dolly and calls
from Aaron, as if firmly nudging them back to reality. Twice
Jennie had called her father at Jason's insistence, assuring him that
everything was all right. Yes, she had seen Jason a few times, yes
he had "very kindly" taken her with him on his business rounds.
Yes, she saw the Latin Quarter show, it was gorgeous! Yes, they
had gone over to the Five O'clock Club, Martha Raye singing and
clowning around there. Her mother — yes, she had called the
hospital once or twice; Mother wanted to leave the clinic; it was a
miracle that she had stayed this long. Why hadn't he been able
to reach her? Well, she couldn't be expected to sit in her room all
day and night, could she? No, no, she didn't want him to come
down there and stay with her. *God no!* She wanted to go home —
desperately. She was anxious to enroll in school, she said — perhaps
Hunter, her mother's alma mater, yes. Her conscience was beginning to batter at her psyche.

Sunday morning she woke in his arms and arched herself closer
into his warm, half-sleeping body, her naked flesh warmed by his,

and then she was struck with the bitterness of what this day meant. He stirred and woke. She watched, enthralled. His long black lashes opening slowly to consciousness, and then as if he too sensed the dread, closing again, unwilling to accept this day. He pulled her closer. His eyes still closed, his hands caressed her body, lingered on her breasts. He drew her tightly to him, buried his lips in her hair. They made love wordlessly, too much absorbed for words.

Jennie had sworn to herself that she would not beg, but in the end she did — begged him to stay for one more night. He could leave early on Monday morning and still have a full business day, she said. "Just one more night, what harm if it is to be our last?"

"Jenna," he said, teasing, and indulgent, "you have a keen sense of drama. If I'd had *you* in a couple of those plays I've invested in I might have been a rich man today, and then think of the delightful possibilities," he said, feigning mystery, laughing. How could he tease her now, acting so casual. She thought he was already preparing his mind for surgery — to detach himself from her — to gingerly cut through the flesh and blood and sinew that had so magically coalesced.

But in the end, reluctantly, he stayed the extra night. It was a Sunday, no rounds to make. They had a quiet dinner in the room.

Jennie had wanted to fly home with him — four more uninterrupted hours together — but he was adamant. That would be folly, and he needed those hours alone to adjust his thinking, to accustom his body to doing without her.

Early mornings to her were melancholy, with the vestiges of dreams still clinging sweet, like cotton candy. On this day Jennie awoke tired. She had slept fitfully, hardly at all during the night.

Foggily she saw Jason moving about the dim room, quietly, without lights, as if not to wake her — could he have meant not to wake her? She sat up quickly. "Jace," she said. He came over to her, held her young morning face in his hand, and tousled her hair. "Go back to sleep, baby," he said quietly. "I'm leaving now." She was furious with herself — all night while he slept she lay awake, restless. When he was ready to get up she fell asleep.

He stood by the edge of the bed and dialed the bell captain. She could only see his long legs. She laid her cheek against the smooth trousers, already clothed for New York and business. He sat down heavily on the bed. They looked at each other for a moment, the tension of love between them. She could not speak.

"Well, I waited for you for a long time, Princess, a lifetime really. You took such a long time to grow up." He looked away from her, into some secret of his own. "But it was worth waiting for." He stood up and walked a little away to light a cigarette. She jumped up from the bed, threw on a wrapper, and ran over to him, her negligee flapping open. He tried to keep his eyes from her body, so sweetly familiar now.

"I know now that I have loved you all of my life — that's why there could be no one before you," she said.

He shook his head slowly. "No, no, Jennie, don't say that, it's not — " he was agitated, choking with words. "You can't, you don't even know what love is. You — you need a young husband, children, a life of your own, all the things loving me can't give you — "

"Jason," she said, putting her arms around him, "I don't care about all that, it doesn't matter. *You* are the life of my own — I only know that I love you."

"No, no," he began to shake her hard. "Stop saying that . . . You can't say that, you don't love me, do you hear — you don't know — " He held her by both arms, shaking her wildly, her head rocking on the slim stalk of her neck. "You can't — " and then reflexively he gathered her to him and cradled her head against his chest and kissed her face with small kisses and whispered her name over and over.

The bellboy knocked. With trembling fingers she pulled her wrapper together, the tears still wet on her face. She walked slowly to the bathroom and closed the door.

She heard the brisk, bright sounds of all hotel departures, the heavy door slamming shut, and she knew he was gone.

This room alone — she must leave it — she must leave there. Now her own room seemed a sanctuary. She would not look around.

But odors — light — evasive . . . so sweet with recollection that they flood the senses . . . moments already beginning to dissolve into the feathery water colors of memory . . . Love ballads of the day become painful to the ear . . . the rude shock of departure, separation always a little like dying for her — since childhood . . . now seem like the numbness preceeding death.

Jason, she whispered, and her being closed around the name, the last of him that she could physically hold on to. She began to tidy the bed, smoothing the bedclothes over and over again, as if to smooth out the rumpled fabric of their lives . . .

*

Three days later on the plane alone, feeling her aloneness like a solid object pressing on her body, she picked up the Miami Herald and leafed through it listlessly. Behind her, suntanned men, loud with martinis, talked of women and write-offs. Scanning Leonard Lyon's column, her eye was caught by a brief one-liner sandwiched in between a dozen other Broadway tinglers.

"Hatcheck king's beautiful blonde daughter seen doing the town with his prime minister." That was all.

IT WAS MORE THAN THREE YEARS since the war had ended and the lights had gone on again all over the world. But nowhere had they appeared brighter or more welcome than on the Great White Way, New York, U.S.A.

Aaron hadn't been able to rake it in fast enough; business was at an all-time high. He was breathless with gold dust, it was choking him, he was buried in it.

He knew this was the peak and that soon there would be a steady downslide. The Big Bands were already on the wane, there was talk of television, of the great exodus to the suburbs, the people tired of running, of displacement. They wanted to settle down in split-level harmony, with a nine-to-five job, a Frigidaire, and a new De Soto.

But in the meantime it was good investing. Who could turn it down? It was just there for the taking. So he went to Atlantic City to buy the Steel Pier — in partnership with Hamid, from the pier across the boardwalk. He went to Chicago to buy the ball park and stadium concessions, he ran to Boston to help finance the Coconut Grove Club, and back to New York for the other palm-decked palace, the Copacabana — for eighty thousand dollars — cash up front (the highest he'd ever paid for one concession). People were going crazy, he said. Didn't anyone ever stay home at nights anymore? He ran propelled by his own steam, not knowing why exactly, just running blind, out of habit, like a stampeding elephant. He could not be everywhere at once, could not tear himself in half — besides he didn't care much for traveling, he was exhausted. He had a good-sized organization now, "good people" working for him (to admit that took plenty), but *training* he didn't have the patience for it, and *honesty* he didn't have the time for testing — so he was limited in his personnel: Jason in general charge, and four or five others in strategic positions. He wasn't complaining, he could do worse, and of course there were some fifteen hundred or so employees to oversee now, between the checkroom, novelty, cigarettes, camera, and restroom personnel.

*

The telephone never stopped, it raged day and night whether Aaron was home or not. Calls for deals for financing — everyone from Billy Rose to Michael Todd, who wanted money for a film version of Jules Vernes' *Around the World in Eighty Days*. Everyone on "the street," and plenty off, knew he was sitting on a barrel of cash and everyone had a proposition.

Home was not a very peaceful place nowadays and when Jenna returned from Florida she was sorry that she had.

The constant jangle of the telephone assailed her nerves. Like a reflex she wanted to rush to answer it, but she knew she must not. She thought her father must have spoken to *him* a dozen times since she'd been home these two weeks, but she did not dare to ask. Sleep, sleep, she wanted only to sleep.

Evenings she closed herself in her room, close beside her private telephone. While swooning music came from the radio, she lay on her bed, encouraging the flow of memory, enhancing the torment. She stared stonily at the telephone, but it stared her down mutely. Her girlfriends called from time to time. Pete even called one evening to tell her he was getting engaged. She wondered confusedly why she rated a personal announcement — was she expected to give or withhold approval? Gladys would tell her all about the girl; Jennie knew they had gone to college together for a while. But she never got around to asking Gladys. It slipped her mind, like everything lately, but him. She felt ashamed — like a schoolgirl. Well, she really was just a schoolgirl after all. It was hard to be a woman, she thought, too easy to feel ill-used. But then she saw, made herself see, the unfairness in that.

She had barely been back two weeks when Jason telephoned. It was past midnight, he was calling from one of the clubs, she could hear a piano in the background and the soft din of those places. Her body liquified. He spoke to her gently in his deep, reassuring voice. He wanted to know if she was all right, to tell her that no matter what happened, he really loved her and missed her, how sorry he was about everything. There was a breathy silence and she began to cry softly.

"Please, Jennie, don't," he commanded, and she stopped.

"Can I see you somewhere, somehow?"

"It seems inevitable," he said.

"What does *that* mean?"

"Jennie, what's the *use?*"

"So don't fight it," she said with a desperate levity.

"You know that's *not* what I meant."

"Don't be coy, Jace," flirting with him a little, like old times. "Has my dad said anything to you out of the ordinary?"

"Funny thing is, he hasn't talked to me much lately, about anything."

"Not about business?"

"Not even much of that. Of course we've been busy as hell!"

"Come to think of it, he seems to be avoiding me too."

There was a silence — "Did you see that line in the column?"

"Yeah, doesn't mean a thing." For some reason she was hurt by
his answer.

"You would rather lose me, than lose *him*, wouldn't you?"
Another silence.

"I will lose both," he said without inflection.

"It doesn't have to be like that, Jason."

"I won't sneak around with you — degrade you — myself. And
we both know that anything else is — impossible — " He was
speaking so low now, she had to grind the phone hard against her
ear to hear him.

"I don't think I can face my life without you in it — "

"Jennie, you think that now, but you are young, your whole life
is ahead of you, it will pass — For me, it's different. My whole life
came and went in a week."

*

Aaron hunched over his steaming Cream of Wheat, wholly absorbed, first salt, then butter, then cream, no — a dab more butter
(weight was never a problem), a shake more of salt. Mamie walked
quickly back and forth, bustling and officious. Everything was
permeated by the smell of burning toast — Aaron's favorite.

Twelve o'clock of a grey, slushy February day. The kind of a
day that is made for love, or dreaming about it — Like a shadowy
extension of those very dreams, she saw him then, in the foyer, leaning up against the front door as if seeking added support. Hungrily
her eyes digested the tableau. Aaron, seated, eating, Jason standing
a distance away. Herself dressed in black and wearing the new
fashionable longer length skirt. She walked through into the foyer,
then stopped and wavered a little on her high heels.

At first she said nothing. They looked at each other for a split second. Then she said, "Oh hello, Jason, how've you been?" It was barely audible. He straightened up a little and said, "Good afternoon, Miss Abel," still a touch of the old teasing manner in his greeting. "I almost didn't recognize you between the suntan and all those grown-up clothes."

She reddened through the remains of her tan. Aaron kept his head down intently, buttering his toast.

Jennie fell into the nearest chair. Her legs seemed unfit for their small task of sustaining her weight. Aaron and Jason talked on about *averages* and *stealing*.

"It's very important to stay on top of them over there at the Copa, because that joint costs such a fortune." *And all the while she is reveling in the intimacy of their shared secret, their conspiracy of two.* On and on they buzzed, tallying the lunch hour. "Is it in our contract?" she heard Aaron ask. Jason seemed more lackadaisical than usual, answering in monosyllables.

Brazenly, she looked at Jason now — directly. He tried pretending that he didn't notice, averting his eyes, but he couldn't. The green grasp of her eyes caught and locked with his dark, brooding gaze.

He fumbled for a cigarette, and lit one with a trembling hand. She noted this with some satisfaction. He leaned his head against the door and blew the smoke out of his nostrils.

She has an overpowering urge to go to him, to touch him, to inhale his familiar fragrance, to lay her head against his chest, if only for a moment, and listen for the wild beating of his heart — to lie once again in the coil of his arms.

"You'll have to get Meyer and Grissman over there in time for the cocktail rush, Miller."

To show ownership, to say to her father you will never guess this secret, never believe this, but this man standing here before you is mine, he belongs to me — or to some dark inner me.

Her father was absently thumbing through the jumble of papers beside him, flecks of cereal stuck to his lips.

"I can't find the goddam affidavit, shoulda let the lawyer keep it — just a minute, Jason, I'll look in the bedroom." He jumped up and went to the back of the apartment. They could hear him fumbling around with keys and papers.

Jason continued to stand there, his back against the entrance door. He looked elongated, dramatic, in the shadows of the entry hall.

They stared at one another wordlessly, then Jason breathed her name, an explosion of pain —

She went to him then, put her arms around his waist, her head on his chest, and his tightness seemed to collapse around her and he bent to put his lips on her hair.

"Oh baby," he said " — in another time and another place it could have been so beautiful for us."

"It's beautiful for us now, right here." She felt him tense and pull away. "Are you mad?" he whispered. "You must be crazy, your father's in the next room, he's coming back at any moment — what, what are you doing?"

But it was already too late. Aaron, with his quick, nervous stride was already in the room as they pulled apart. His shoulders slumped in a barely perceptible gesture of disappointment, he looked from one to the other sheepishly, so that at first it seemed that he would beg their pardon and retreat to the bedroom.

Suddenly he rushed at Jason against the door, flinging Jennie out of his path, as if she were weightless as fluff. He pushed him hard against the wall, held him by his shirt and collar, she saw Jason's dark head jerk up spastically. Aaron, with his eyes dilating crazily, cried, "I didn't believe them, I didn't believe the bullshit I read — who'd believe it — Now — " he gasped, "now I still don't believe it, when I see it with my own eyes — they're not mine," he said, "they're someone else's eyes I'm seeing with." Jason, white and silent, closed his eyes, the sublime martyr. Aaron continued to shake him, to bang his head against the door. Between clenched teeth he said:

"After twenty-five years, after all I've done for you, this, this is how you repay me!"

"No," Jason said loudly and clearly, throwing Aaron's hands from his collar in a broad gesture of release, heaving the slighter, smaller man from him with ease. "I have already repaid you, standing on my feet every night for twenty-five years — with my life's blood I've repaid you."

"*That* you throw up to me! Where the hell would you have been if I hadn't given you a chance," he spat the words into Jason's face. "What the hell are *you* gonna do *now*? What the hell else are you cut out for, a godamned croupier, a pit boss maybe if you're lucky (that and a dancing teacher were to Aaron about the lowest depths to which a man could sink). And then he pinned him to the door again and began slapping his face, first one side, then the other, like a punch-drunk fighter — "Look," he screamed in a voice thick with the phlegm of tears, "out of a thousand girls you could have picked from, why did you have to pick *my* daughter to fuck, huh? Why her? All the tramps in the checkroom weren't good enough for you? Why her — you're almost old enough to be her father. You, you bastard," he said. His voice was shredded with pain.

She felt suddenly inundated by all of the checkroom backwash, like stale vomit — she was drowning in it. "It's just you — your checkroom mind — You smell everyone's rottenness but your own" she screamed, and her mother's words bounced back at her.

Aaron kept on slapping his face — but gently now, first one side and then the other, as if bringing him back to life. He clung to his neck, he held him in a stranglehold — the years of street fighting on Division Street, of Big Bennie's lessons, of sparring with the punks at Stillman's — he was in shape. He appeared now to be holding Jason around the waist as if dancing, a terrible waltz of love and hate and hurt — She felt left out, unimportant — excluded, really — two men embracing in the embers of a dying friendship. She saw now with a coruscating clarity that life could not be based solely on emotion. She had always lived for relationships, allegiances, old dependencies — passions that fluctuated, people who let you down. Her senses were keenly developed; now she knew she must develop a whole self. Symbiosis was a luxury, independence a necessity — but her father resented independence, fostered helpless people he could manipulate.

She ran over to them and pulled her father from Jason. He felt light, light as a feather, he did not resist, it seemed to her that, trancelike, he just floated away.

At the small dining table Aaron sat down woodenly, and began to cry — those early tears of middle age. He put his head in his hands and sobbed, his broad athletic shoulders shook with his sobs.

Jason was straightening his tie, his hair, shrugging his jacket on right. A civilized man, he had cultivated an unhealthy self-detachment. "I love her," he said obliquely to Aaron.

Aaron looked up quickly and said, "Christ, get the hell outa here. I don't ever want to see your face anywhere I am ever again. You're dead to me, do you understand? And I'll see that you never work in this business again — ever. You're lucky I didn't kill you altogether — or have you killed," he shouted as Jason slowly let himself out the front door.

She felt helpless, as if she had been watching a dream in slow motion or one of those grainy, misshot family movies her father was so fond of taking. There was a fragmentary silence.

Then, in a choked voice, as if out of the dust of ashes, "God, how you must have hated me — All of us — the checkroom — like your mother did," he said in a terrible whisper.

She wanted to cry out, No, you're wrong, I loved you all, I was proud of you, of everything you did that made my life singular, eccentric, wonderful. You — even Mother — Jason — I wanted to belong — just that — . But she thought that he would not understand.

Women are frightened people really, overprotected, insulated from life, first by their mothers, and then by men, she told herself. My mother was one of them. She dared to make it alone — and fell apart trying.

Sitting like this in defeated silence, both enveloped in their secret thoughts, she wondered if it was possible to live without love . . . It is possible, she thought — you keep on living.

Unraveled Kingdom

FIFTY YEARS OLD, he thought. He'd lived a half century already. 1951 — the century was moving into the second half and he was moving into the second half of his life right along with it — but it was strangely reminiscent of the first. He was dizzy with a sense of déjà vu.

He found himself once again in Prospect Park, sitting on a bench while Jill, his four-year-old daughter, played in the sandbox or whooped up and down the slide. Sundays in the park . . . he recalled bittersweet visiting days with his older children or sweeter days without the bitterness, when they were toddlers like Jill, before the separation.

He had just been to visit his brother Max. Max was ailing, "his ticker again." Aaron seldom got to Brooklyn anymore nowadays, he was living in Jersey, working in Manhattan. He had to live in Jersey, out of state. (He had gotten only a Mexican divorce before remarrying.) He had decided to take Jill along for the day. He must cultivate this little girl, get to know her, like he had never had enough time to do before with the others, with Jennie and Evan and Reid.

The park, a sentimental place, looked the same. Nature, at least, was dependable, changing only its outer dress for the seasons, but retaining its solid credibility. Aaron did not like to be reminded of the passage of time, yet he enjoyed remembering.

So he sat amidst the weighty, weeping trees of oak and birch, the birds pecking at the fallen leaves, the children — his child — playing in the sand again, and he thought what a joke life really was. He was tired, really did not have the patience to start afresh, but here he was starting a new season like the autumn all around him, a new family — and Martha pregnant again (what the hell was she trying to prove anyway, he wondered, irritated), and a new aspect of his business, real estate. The concession business was dwindling, he hated to see it go, succumbing to the power of the television tube. It had had bravura, it was something he had created out of the seething morass of his life. It had his indelible stamp on it, like the broad black initials *A.A.* clearly marked on his checkroom stubs.

He got up to go to the swing and whistled something that came unbidden to his lips. All week long that tune had haunted him. God only knows why, it was archaic. Even before *his* time. "Memories, memories, days of joy and love," he sang softly and did a tentative little shuffle to make the child laugh as he waited at the foot of the slide for Jill, round and blonde, to come down the chute, like a large yellow gumball. "Childhood days, wildwood days, days of joy and love — tum-de-dum-de-dum — I'll build you a home, dear, I'll make you my own, in my land of memories . . ." Yes, that was it, he was flooded by memories lately, inundated by yesterdays. He used to croon that song to Eve when they were courting. He thought of her innocent rosy face, its elegiac sweetness — No, the park was a poor choice for him in his present mood. He went back to the bench and sat down heavily. Eve . . . he was thinking of her more and more lately. He thought how she had been deprived even of a wedding. She to whom the amenities of life were so important — No, he would not let his mind dwell on it, lest he recall hidden doubts, lost options, guilts, no, he would not wander empty rooms alone — Anyway *she* had chosen, it was she who had made the decision, the lifetime choice; he was absolved. Yes, he really felt absolved, relieved, since she had come out of the clinic. Didn't seem to have done her much good, though, as far as he could tell. Ah, those shrinks — four-flushers, screwballs all of them. Well she did seem quieter, less scorchingly angry, but on the other hand she didn't seem much happier, even with the beautiful big apartment he'd passed on to her, and up until this fall she'd had Reid for company. But he too had left for college. Even now she was traveling in Europe with Jennie. He'd have to find her a smaller place when she returned — if she returned. She had often threatened to move to London permanently, but he doubted that she would leave the children. Capricious, he thought. The convolutions of that old merry-go-round — She ended up back at the Centennial and he was out again — in a hotel suite — a little like being back at the Y, except that he really had no choice now. In the midst of all this flux, Jill pops into the picture, secretly. Why had he been so secretive about it, why hadn't he let the children in on it — what was the shame? Coward, he thought bleakly. But he knew Eve would have torn him to shreds legally — or certainly verbally, to the children. After all, they still were not divorced. But it had only turned out worse this way, had driven an even greater wedge between them. Why? Who knows why, he thought. Many reasons. For one, he would not spend what it would cost him to get a bona fide divorce from Eve, who didn't want it herself now. Anyway, for some perverse reasons of his own he didn't really want it either. He never had, even when she had begged for it in the beginning. The courts, the scandal — the children might suffer. They had just let it ride. Martha didn't even seem to care anymore; she considered her child her security, and she was probably right. Nothing seemed to matter so much anymore — the old passions were worn down by attrition.

It had all fallen apart when the children left. Evan for Yale. Jennie to Cornell this time. They seemed to be making it now. He must have done something right, he thought with satisfaction. Jennie had just graduated from the School of Journalism, was planning a career after all . . . That reminded him: Maybe when Jennie returned he would get her a job on a big paper, like the *Times* or something, pull some strings — yeah, maybe he could swing it. Well she was probably right — changing times — a woman needs an education, a career nowadays, if only so that she doesn't become simply a plaything for a man. Not *his* daughter anyway, look

what it had brought her only a few years ago. So young for — for
that sort of mess — no, he would not dwell on that either, it was
too painful. But he kept on thinking of the last thing Jennie had
said to him in those tense, unhappy months before she had gone
back to college. He had only asked her one question about — about
the affair (even now he could not particularize it). "Why?" he
had asked with a tremor, "just tell me why."

"I don't know exactly, I only know I was happy," she said
simply, "for a week, I was happy. I'd never been happy before."
He was stunned, he had failed. All of his money, his efforts to build
a life — for whom — for what if not the children, only to find he
had made no one happy. He stared at his hands as if they were
strangers. Some sixty million dollars must have passed through his
hands in these last fifteen years and what was there to show for it,
he thought angrily. The furious money making, the crazy success,
hadn't changed anything . . .

He had never really gotten out of the ghetto after all. Never
really had a home, never really had a woman he thoroughly enjoyed, never had a friend who wasn't Jewish, in fact never really
had a friend — except maybe Jason — and — well, he didn't want
to think about that now. But so much of the past was tied up with
Jason that it haunted him, especially since he had run into him last
month at Bill Miller's Rivieria in Jersey when he was doing some
rounds. An after-theater party was being given by some big
theatrical agent, a close friend of Jason's. He'd heard Jason was investing in the theater, Broadway shows. Damn fool — without
the security of a steady salary. He had been making fifty thousand
dollars a year and more when he was *fired* (but his mind couldn't
quite form that word — it just wasn't that kind of relationship).
He knew that Jason had a few concessions down in the Village.
Oh the irony, he thought, that's where I started, but Jesus, I was
twenty then . . . half his age.

They didn't speak. Jason was sitting at a large table with a lot of
people. Aaron thought Dolly was there. He wasn't really sure because he had looked away so fast. But he knew that Jason saw him.
He felt suddenly ineffectual, he had an urge to go to him, do some-

thing, say something that would set it all right, but he felt a fresh anger rising and turned away. That night at the Riviera, Bill, the owner, had told him a funny thing. He said, "You know I like the kid" (they persisted in calling him a kid, Aaron thought irritably — he had to be over forty by now, but everyone remembered him nineteen for some reason — even Aaron), "and frankly, Abel, I offered him the concession here once. I woulda made him easy terms, I wasn't strapped for dough. But he just looks at me funny like and says 'no-o-o-o,' a long, drawn-out 'no' like a sigh and says, 'I'm satisfied with my few places in the Village, I don't come up-town or go over the bridge into Abel's territory.'" For a moment Aaron had stared hard at the gorgeous galaxy of bridges that glit-tered at him from the huge surrounding windows. He had felt curiously assailed — he hadn't known whether to laugh or cry. Predictable, though, he thought. He'd never accused Jason of vaulting ambition. He knew instinctively that anyone with ambi-tion could not have worked for him for twenty years — going headlong up a dead-end street — any more than he would have tolerated it. No, he didn't depend on anyone, it had always been a one-man show — that's the way he wanted it. Jason had been start-ing to think of himself as indispensable, so in the end his daughter had solved the problem for him. Yes, every coin had a reverse side . . . But only lately he had begun wondering if maybe she was, well, unhappy over that damn thing with Jason Miller.

But now his mind wandered back to Atlantic City again, that bawdy carnival with its rotting boardwalk lined with junk shops. And that picture of Jesus, omniscient, in the window of one of them — the crowds it attracted, patiently waiting for Him to slowly close and open His eyes. Jennie used to stand transfixed, fascinated by the illusion. And the Fralinger's Salt Water Taffy stands every few blocks, the rhythmic throb of those machines, pulling the candy, stretching it out taut, twisting slightly — like the sinews of his life. The kids swore they could taste the salt water in every bite, kind of tangy and fragrant. He kept seeing the decaying old hotels with their scallops of white rocking chairs, and the rolling chairs of beautiful caramel cane . . . made him feel guilty, sitting in one of those things that seemed designed for the old and infirm when he was still in his prime, and his children were small and strong, and his wife young and beautiful, and plenty of "that ole green stuff" in his pocket — that's what he'd say to the laughing Negro men who rolled them along their merry way. He wondered how many toothless old colored men had rolled them along those splintering boards through the years into the intensely rose sunsets slipping into mauve dusks behind the boardwalk. At *this* moment he thought it had been merry. He couldn't recover the emotions of the past, only the objects around them.

Grudgingly he asked himself, what he, "Mr. Ice Water," would have to say about his Steel Pier deal with *them*. It wasn't as if he had gone in with foreknowledge of whom he was dealing with. In good faith he had bought the Pier (one hundred thousand dollars for his half of that salt-sogged old pleasure palace) in partnership with Hamid, the Turk — then thought it had been a mistake. Atlantic City was going down.

He wondered, with a strange fear of the future, why seaside resorts went first to the aged, then rotted away into obsolescence. It was as if the damp corroded, moldered, and finally called them back into the sea.

One day he gets a phone call from Joe Adonis, he wants to see him, he says, "to discuss the Pier." A few days later Joe — the patriarch himself, he thought now with some misplaced pride — was sitting in his office at Thirty-fourth Street with his legs crossed nattily. (Not quite what his name suggested, an Adonis, although there *were* traces.) He wore a gray vested suit and spats — 1945 and spats? Aaron, though still dapper, thought wistfully of his earlier fastidious tastes. Smoothly, gently, politely (Aaron was familiar with this comedy of manners), with only a faint residue of street dialect, he told him of his friendship with the last partners at the Pier, a certain vending company, and of his even warmer friendship with Atlantic City's boss, Senator Farley. More he wouldn't say, only a promise to send Stumpy around to see him during the week. He would explain everything. Aaron knew

Stumpy, and he felt no fear. He had seen him around Broadway for years, a powerfully built dwarf with crafty eyes set off by a baroque frame of curly black hair, he was bagman for the Boys. Stumpy explained how, since Aaron would naturally be taking over all of the concessions, the vending company would stand to lose a fortune every year. It would be smart business he said, to stay on good terms with Farley, who "sort of ran things around there" and was in fact legal counsel for the vending company. When the dwarf left the office after their brief and "friendly" meeting, Aaron had agreed to put Farley on the payroll for ten thousand a year as his "legal counsel." It rankled. He had come this far without those bastards; now he was taking their orders. All his life he had lived by his concessions, now he was making concessions in order to live — In his lifetime he had made very few. But in return they promised him Las Vegas. They had just begun to infiltrate that resort town; Bugsy Siegel had just completed the Flamingo. Aaron didn't say anything, but he knew he didn't want any part of Vegas, he couldn't handle that sort of thing — not anymore.

Sixty million dollars — where was it? What had he personally to show for that crazy kind of money making? A three-room suite in his hotel in Newark. He'd never traveled anywhere more am-bitious than Florida. He felt excluded. His wife and daughter were doing the Grand Tour now, courtesy of A.A. (or "yours truly," as he always referred to himself). He felt beneficent — neglected.

Of course it wasn't all his fault. Plenty went to the government, and a healthy chunk into real estate investments — and then, oh Christ, there was that thieving bastard, Vic Chase, his former chauf-feur. He could've written the book *How to Steal a Million*, except he had helped himself to four times that much. All cash. Who knew what there was there? Even he himself didn't know exactly. But what killed him was, How did that clever *mumser* ever find it? It was hidden beneath the floorboards, an aging green salad . . . pickling there beneath the floor in an intricate, tricky safe he'd con-cocted. But not safe *enough*. So Vic Chase was luxuriating some-where in South America with his hard-earned millions, and he was powerless to prosecute. The wonderful irony made him smile. The money didn't really matter much in the overall scheme of things; he was a very rich man.

"Daddy, Daddy, push me on the swing. C'mon, c'mon." Jill was tugging at his sleeve insistently. Aaron didn't look up at first, abstracted as he was by his thoughts, a thousand years away. He had forgotten the childish dependency of the call of "Daddy, Daddy." He was growing more fond of the past than the present, or even the future — the sign of an unhealthy psyche. He was not so old, his natural exuberance made him seem ageless — Why did he live with one foot so firmly planted in the past? Judaic oversentimentality? Fifty years only, that is a life, he thought? That is only half a life. He saw it this way: To be young and hopeful was to be alive. But to grow old with all the goals richly realized was to be dead. He felt like an ingrate, ungrateful for his still enormous health and vitality. How lucky he was compared to his parents, who had lived and died within a joyless framework of soup bones and pullets, of weak tea (to save the tea bag) and the *Jewish Daily Forward*, his father's tenuous connection with the outside world. Papa . . . he thought of Friday night candles and the benediction — but Friday night candles had long ago burned out.

He thought of his mother, dead now these five years. How she had stayed on in the old house in Williamsburg until the end. Aaron had begged her to leave, to live with him and the children at the apartment or take a small apartment somewhere with Rachel, but she would not budge. Bennie had wanted to sell "the old dump" a thousand times. The neighborhood was changing; well, the neighbors anyway. No, she wanted to be near Joseph, she said. Here where he had died she would die. So Bennie stayed too. "What the hell," he said, "if they were stuck with the goddam place, why pay rent elsewhere?" But he was seething with anger at his mother (he'd lose a big "profit on the house if they waited much longer, it would be worth less," he said), furious with Aaron, too, for "going along with the old lady." "Always had been a mama's boy," he said. Aaron felt the old resentments rising. He'd always felt uncomfortable about Ben. He worked with him through the years, even invested with him, but he never trusted him — or his ignorance. But he envied him his marriage, a lifetime with the same woman, like all of his brothers. It seemed to him a luxury to be able to reach out for the hand of the woman who had grown with him through all the years, had been welded to him through incident and error and pain. But for Aaron there was no such woman. He who travels alone, travels fastest.

The little girl, unable to gain her father's attention, wandered away forlornly in the direction of the sandbox, approaching the strange children as if testing for friendly natives. It could have all been so different, if only he had known what to do then. Eve had been just the kind of woman he had wanted, he had chosen well. It was just that he could not understand tears, searing oceans of tears. Tears on the telephone, in the locked bathroom, in bed — his marriage was an ocean of tears. He used to feel he was drowning in it and suffocating in hillocks of words. He hadn't known what to do, he had been so young, so preoccupied . . .

Words foamed on his lips out of the world of his youth — dark, ignorant, deprived — a childish song learned at Cheder. How was he expected to suddenly bring forth a life that was shimmering, ideal, modulated, unselfish, inflicting no pain, accepting with equanimity? He hummed fragments of a song in forgotten Hebrew . . . eight years old . . . He remembered selling newspapers. In the freezing cold he stood on the corner of Rivington Street, shrunk into his older brother's voluminous coat, and, with his imagination, carved out the insides of that magic building called school.

Funny how he could recall with ease the name of any of the streets of his boyhood, but lately he was having difficulty remembering street names in his present. Just as he could summon up easily names of boyhood friends, but could rarely remember the names or faces of the canny young promoters who were infiltrating Broadway and the whole entertainment field. He remembered reading somewhere that "growing old was like finding yourself on unremembered corners, surrounded by a flood of forgotten association." How true, he thought sagely. Aaron had noticed with some alarm that he was spending more time at the bathroom sink lately, his toilette took longer, there were more rituals—more potions and lotions — more pills to swallow. Ah, life was a round trip, he thought — the philosopher now: In the beginning you can't wait to get to the end and toward the end you find yourself yearning for the beginning. It starts with the innocence of youth, then all the wise years drift back into the innocence of old age . . .

He had a sudden yearning for the old vaudeville at the Palace, to walk down the popcorn-strewn aisle at Minsky's, to see Joan Crawford at a sixteen-cent Saturday matinee, to wear his cake-eater duds — to start all over — to have none of it — to have all of it back again — he didn't know what. No one had yet discovered culture shock. Maybe he was just tired. He'd been overworked, over-pressured since Jason had gone.

Dusk was descending gently, and he realized that the park was almost emptied of people. He shivered a little and wished this once he had worn an overcoat. He was surprised to find Jill scrunched beside him on the bench sound asleep, worn out from her solitary play.

He thought he'd better be heading home, it was a long trip — he had to cross many bridges. Martha would be worried. He thought about her not without a tingle of pleasure — that woman *thought* with her flesh. But lately Martha spent most of her days entertaining various members of the Catholic clergy, drinking her way to divine redemption, or at the very least into the good graces of the Catholic church. He looked sadly at the sleeping child beside him and thought that now, now that he had more free time, time for philosophy, there was no one left to talk to.

Well, perhaps he had missed out a little on the poetry of life, the music, the poetry — but it was not too late. Maybe he could still find it. There was longevity in his family. He did not think the word *recapture*, but rather *find* — anew. He would be honest with himself now.